"Born in Oklahoma Novemb[...]T0112801[...]ade known as the 'Dirty Thirties.' A time w...... .....]ke up far too much prairie sod and planted wheat to cash in on the government's price support program. This led to soil erosion and the most difficult times captured in the compelling novel *A Cup of Dust*. The author does a great job of giving the reader a feel for those dark days in our nation's history. Very intriguing reading!"

—Virgil Dwain McNeil, a Dust Bowl survivor

"I have just finished reading Susie Finkbeiner's *A Cup of Dust*. The story is excellent and an accurate story of the dust storms. I lived thru it in southeastern Nebraska and it would get so dark, the chickens would go to roost at 3 pm. My Dad had to go to Iowa to get hay to feed our cows. There was none available to buy in Nebraska."

—Phyllis M. Wagner, Lincoln, Nebraska

"Riveting. An achingly beautiful tale told with a singularly fresh and original voice. This sepia-toned story swept me into the Dust Bowl and brought me face-to-face with both haunting trials and the resilient people who overcame them. Absolutely mesmerizing. Susie Finkbeiner is an author to watch!"

—Jocelyn Green, award-winning author of the Heroines Behind the Lines Civil War series

"Without a doubt Finkbeiner's best work to date, *A Cup of Dust* is simultaneously intimate and epic. The compelling voice of young Pearl describes a world of biblical-proportion plagues unleashed on the Oklahoma Panhandle in a way that is both grounding and disturbing—with the plague of frogs replaced by jackrabbits, boils by pneumonia, locusts by unyielding walls of sky-blackening dust, and the growing sense that there may not be a God who hears their cries for deliverance very much unaltered.

"At every turn gritty and historically accurate, *A Cup of Dust* allows us to weather the dust storm of a few months in the hope-and-rain-deprived Great Plains of the 1930s. As I tore through the often sobering text, I found the back of the storm to bring insight, deep empathy, and an enduring sense of redemptive hope."

—Zachary Bartels, author of *The Last Con* and *Playing Saint*

*A Cup of Dust: A Novel of the Dust Bowl*
*A Trail of Crumbs: A Novel of the Great Depression*
*A Song of Home: A Novel of the Swing Era*

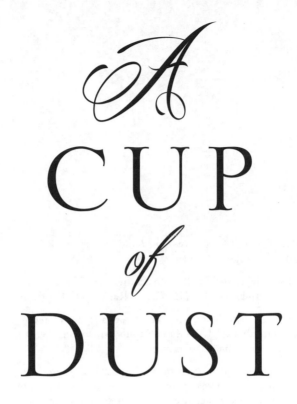

# A CUP *of* DUST

*A Novel of the Dust Bowl*

## SUSIE FINKBEINER

Kregel
Publications

*A Cup of Dust: A Novel of the Dust Bowl*
© 2015 by Susie Finkbeiner

Published by Kregel Publications, a division of Kregel, Inc., 2450 Oak Industrial Dr. NE, Grand Rapids, MI 49505.

Published in association with the literary agency of Credo Communications, LLC, Grand Rapids, Michigan www.Credocommunications.net.

Scripture quotations are from the King James Version of the Bible.

Poem by John Blase on page 10 used by permission.

The persons and events portrayed in this work are the creations of the author, and any resemblance to persons living or dead is purely coincidental.

ISBN 978-0-8254-4388-6

Printed in the United States of America
21 22 23 24 / 5 4

*For Jeff.*
*I love you.*
*Thank you for loving me.*

❈

# ACKNOWLEDGMENTS

I could never live the life of a reclusive author. I'm far too flighty and neurotic. In order to be the best writer I can be, I need people. I just so happen to have some pretty amazing people who prop me up, challenge me, and encourage me. I'd like to tell you about a few of these folks.

Ann Byle is the best agent a girl like me could hope for. She believes in me when I don't know if I've got what it takes. She doesn't let me whine too much and she tells it like it is. I'd trust her with my life. More than that, I'd trust her with my kids. That's saying a lot.

Jocelyn Green, Tracy Groot, and Julie Cantrell are authors who have influenced my writing of *A Cup of Dust*. I learned how to write historical fiction by reading their novels and learned about life by being around them. They are good mentors and even better friends.

Amelia Rhodes became my friend just before we both plunged head-first into the publishing world. She answers her phone when I call, knowing full well that I might be a hot mess with a brain full of doubts about teeter-tottering self-confidence. She talks me off the ledge, gives me a pep talk, and reminds me of how far God has brought both of us in our five-year-old friendship.

Pam Strickland is the giver of hugs and smiles and overflowing encouragement. She's quick to listen and even faster to pray. She knows how she helped this novel come to be and she wouldn't like me bragging about it. Just know she's part of the reason you have it in your hands.

The team at Kregel has made me feel welcome from the very moment

I signed my name on the contract. They have taken my small efforts and collaborated to make Pearl's story come to life.

A good portion of this book was written at a table at my local Starbucks. That place has become my own personal *Cheers* because of how great the baristas are. They kept me caffeinated and smiling during the rougher days of writing. Marcia, Catrina, Hananiah, Jaimee, Jeff, Kasey, Lydia, Melissa, Sam, Shawn, Stephanie, and Travis aren't just great at making a cup of coffee, they've become sweet friends and I'm thankful for them.

I wouldn't be who I am without the love of my Father, the Author of all life. He is the same yesterday, today, and forever, and in that sameness is His unfailing love for His children. He sees us in our weakness, in our vulnerability, in our failings. He doesn't reject us. Instead, He scoops us up and brings us into His family. I can think of nothing more powerful, more beautiful. Pearl's story is mine. Yours. Ours. It is the story of God's great love for His people. He is the one who saves.

# AUTHOR'S NOTE

Part of the writer's task is to find and utilize the exactly right word. For the writer of historical fiction, the job is to match word choice to the commonly used vocabulary of the era. In all honesty, some words that were often used in the 1930s are now considered hurtful, abrasive, and racist.

When writing this novel I had to make difficult choices when it came to terms used as identifiers for people of various races. Writing words such as *Negro*, *Injun*, and *colored* made me uncomfortable. However, in keeping with the times, I felt they were consistent.

Since the founding of our nation, race has been a sensitive issue. We look back at the horrors of slavery, civil rights abuses, and the unjust way in which the American Indians were driven from the land. As we experience the racial tensions of our own time, we do well to remember the consequences of dehumanizing others based on the color of their skin. And as we hope for a peaceful future, we can grapple with our various backgrounds and appearances and find that we have a shared heritage that no title can fracture.

"He picked you out,
He picked you up,
He brought you home."
—Jeff Manion

❧

YOU'RE MY GIRL by John Blase

In that second I first held you
I sensed you as fragile.
Not like a demitasse that if
dropped would break
but like the peach that will
bruise if not carefully kept.
So that is what I've tried to do,
to permit only the irritants necessary
for you to shine.
You must know, my girl, that this
has been and is my happiness.
For you are the best thing that has
ever come into my life.

# CHAPTER PAST

*Red River, Oklahoma*
*September 1934*

As soon as I was off the porch and out of Mama's sight, I pushed the scuffed-up, hole-in-the-soles Mary Janes off my feet. They hurt like the dickens, bending and cramping my toes and rubbing blisters on my heels. Half the dirt in Oklahoma sifted in when I wore those shoes, tickling my skin through thin socks before shaking back out. When I was nine they had fit just fine, those shoes. But once I turned ten they'd gotten tight all the sudden. I hadn't told Mama, though. She would have dipped into the pennies and nickels she kept in an old canning jar on the bottom of her china cabinet. She would have counted just enough to buy a new pair of shoes from Mr. Smalley's grocery store.

I didn't want her taking from that money. That was for a rainy day, and we hadn't had anything even close to a rainy day in about forever.

Red River was on the wrong side of No Man's Land in the Panhandle. The skinny part of Oklahoma, I liked to say. If I spit in just the right direction, I could hit New Mexico. If I turned just a little, I'd get Colorado. And if I spit to the south, I'd hit Texas. But ladies didn't spit. Not ever. That's what Mama always said.

I leaned my hip against the lattice on the bottom of our porch. Rolling off my socks, I kept one eye on the front door just in case Mama stepped out. She was never one for whupping like some mothers were, but she had a look that could turn my blood cold. And that look usually had a come-to-Jesus meeting that followed close behind it.

She didn't come out of the house, though, so I shoved the socks into my shoes and pushed them under the porch.

Bare feet slapping against hard-as-rock ground felt like freedom. Careless, rebellious freedom. The way I imagined an Indian girl would feel racing around tepees in the days before Red River got piled up with houses and ranches and wheat. The way things were before people with white faces and bright eyes moved on the land.

I was about as white faced and bright eyed as it got. My hair was the kind of blond that looked more white than yellow. Still, I pretended my pale braids were ink black and that my skin was dark as a berry, darkened by the sun.

Pretending to be an Indian princess, I ran, feeling the open country's welcome.

If Mama had been watching, she would have told me to slow down and put my shoes back on. She surely would have gasped and shook her head if she knew I was playing Indian. Sheriff's daughters were to be ladylike, not running wild as a savage.

Mama didn't understand make-believe, I reckoned. As far as I knew she thought imagination was only for girls smaller than me. "I would've thought you'd be grown out of it by now," she'd say.

I hadn't grown out of my daydreams, and I didn't reckon I would. So I just kept right on galloping, pretending I rode bareback on a painted pony like the one I'd seen in one of Daddy's books.

Meemaw asked me many-a-time why I didn't play like I was some girl from the Bible like Esther or Ruth. If they'd had a bundle of arrows and a strong bow I would have been more inclined to put on Mama's old robe and play Bible times.

I slowed my trot a bit when I got to the main street. A couple ladies stood on the sidewalk, talking about something or another and waving their hands around. I thought they looked like a couple birds, chirping at each other. The two of them noticed me and smiled, nodding their heads.

"How do, Pearl?" one of them asked.

"Hello, ma'am," I answered and moved right along.

Across the street, I spied Millard Young sitting on the courthouse steps, his pipe hanging out of his mouth. He'd been the mayor of Red River since before Daddy was born. I didn't know his age, exactly, but he must have been real old, as many wrinkles as he had all over his face and the white hair on his head. He waved me over and smiled, that pipe still between his lips. I galloped to him, knowing that if I said hello he'd give me a candy.

Even Indian princesses could enjoy a little something sweet every now and again.

With times as hard as they were for folks, Millard always made sure he had something to give the kids in town. Mama had told me he didn't have any grandchildren of his own, which I thought was sad. He would have made a real good grandpa. I would have asked him to be mine but didn't know if that would make him feel put upon. Mama was always getting after me for putting upon folks.

"Out for a trot?" he asked as soon as I got closer to the bottom of the stairs.

"Yes, sir." I climbed up a couple of the steps to get the candy he offered. It was one of those small pink ones that tasted a little like mint-flavored medicine. I popped it in my mouth and let it sit there, melting little by little. "Thank you."

He winked and took the pipe back out of his lips. It wasn't lit. I wondered why he had it if he wasn't puffing tobacco in and out of it.

"Looking for your sister?" His lips hardly moved when he talked. It made me wonder what his teeth looked like. I'd known him my whole life and couldn't think of one time that I'd seen his teeth. "Seen her about half hour ago, headed that-a-way." He nodded out toward the sharecroppers' cabins.

"Thank you," I said with a smile.

"Hope you catch her soon," he said, wrinkling his forehead even more. "Her wandering off like that makes me real nervous."

"I'll find her. I always do," I called over my shoulder, picking up my gallop. "Thanks for the candy."

"That's all right." He nodded at me. "Watch where you're going."

I turned and headed toward the cabins, hoping to find my sister there but figuring she'd wandered farther out than that.

My sister was born Violet Jean Spence, but nobody called her that. We all just called her Beanie and nobody could remember why exactly. Daddy had told me that Beanie was born blue and not able to catch a breath. He'd said he had never prayed so hard for a baby to start crying. Finally, when she did cry and catch a breath, she turned from blue to bright pink. Violet Jean. The baby born blue as her name. Just thinking on it gave me the heebie-jeebies.

When I needed to find Beanie, I knew to check the old ranch not too far outside town. My sister loved going out there, being under the wide-open sky. I was sure that if a duster hit, God would know to look for her at that ranch, too. Meemaw had told me that God could see us no matter where we went, even through all the dust. I really hoped that was true for Beanie's sake.

Meemaw had told me more than once that God saved us from the dust. So I figured He was sure to see me even if Pastor said the dust was God being mad at us all.

In the flat pasture, cattle lowed, pushing their noses into the dust, searching out the green they weren't like to find. I expected I'd find Beanie standing at the fence-line, hands behind her back so as to remember not to touch the wire. Usually she'd be there looking off over the field, eyes glazed over, not putting her focus on anything in particular.

Daddy said she acted so odd because of the way she was born. She could see and hear everything around her. But when it came to under-standing, that was a different thing altogether.

I found Beanie at the ranch, all right. But instead of looking out at the pasture, she was sitting in the dirt, her dress pulled all the way up to her waist, showing off her underthings in a way Mama would never have approved of. Mama would have rushed over and told Beanie to put her knees together, keep her skirt down, and sit like a lady. I didn't think my sister knew what any of that meant.

Being a lady was just one item on the laundry list of things my sister couldn't figure out. I wondered how much that grieved Mama.

Mama had told me Beanie was slow. Daddy called her simple. Folks around town said she was an idiot. I'd gotten in more than one fight over a kid calling my sister a name like that. Meemaw had said those folks didn't understand and that people sometimes got mean over what they didn't understand.

"It ain't no use fighting them," she had told me. "One of these days they'll figure out that we've got a miracle walking around among us."

Our own miracle, sitting on the ground grunting and groaning and playing in dirt.

"Beanie." I bent at the waist once I got up next to her. My braids swung over my shoulders. "We gotta go home."

The tip of Beanie's nose stayed pointed at the space between her spread out legs. Somehow she'd gotten herself a tin cup. Its white-and-blue enamel was chipped all the way around, and I figured it was old. She found things like that in the empty houses around town. Goodness knew there were plenty of abandoned places for her to explore around Red River. Half the houses in Oklahoma stood empty. Everybody had took up and moved west, leaving busted-up treasures for Beanie to find.

She'd hide them from Mama under our bed or in our closet. Old, tattered scraps of cloth, a busted up hat, a bent spoon. Everything she found was a treasure to her. To the rest of us, it was nothing but more junk she'd hide away.

"You hear me?" I asked, tapping her shoulder. "We gotta go."

She kept on digging in the dirt with that old cup like it was a shovel. Once she got it to overflowing, she held it in front of her face and tipped it, pouring it out. The grains of sand caught in the air, blowing into her face. I stood upright, pulling the collar of my dress over my face to block out the dust. She just didn't care—she let it get in her mouth and nose and eyes.

"That's not good for you," I said. "Don't do that anymore."

Little noises came out her mouth from deep inside her. Nothing anybody would have understood, though. Mostly it was nothing more than short grunts and groans. Meemaw liked to think the angels in heaven spoke that same, hard tongue just for Beanie. Far as I knew it was nothing but nonsense. Beanie was sixteen years old and making noises like a two-year-old. She could talk as well as anybody else, she just didn't want to most of the time.

"Get up. Mama's waiting on us." I grabbed hold of her arm and pulled. "Put that old cup down, and let's go."

Scooping a cup of dust, she finally looked at me. Not in my eyes, though, she wouldn't have done that. Instead, she looked at my chin and smiled before dumping the whole cupful on my foot.

Some days I just hated my sister so hard.

"I seen a horny toad," Beanie said, pushing against the ground to stand herself up. She stopped and leaned over, her behind in the air, to refill the cup. "It had blood coming out its eyes, that horny toad did."

"So what." I took her hand. Scratchy palmed, she left her hand limp in mine, not making the effort to hold me back. "Mama's gonna be sore if we don't get home."

"Must've been scared of me. That toad squirted blood outta its eye right at me. Didn't get none on me though." She looked down at her dress to make sure as she shuffled her feet, kicking up dust. Her shoes were still on, tied up tight on her feet so she wouldn't lose them.

Mama moaned many-a-day about how neither of her girls liked to keep shoes on.

"That toad wasn't scared of you," I said. "Those critters just do that."

We took a few steps, only making it a couple yards before Beanie stopped.

"Duster's coming." Dark-as-night hair frizzed out of control on her head, falling to her shoulders as she looked straight up. Her big old beak of a nose pointed at the sky. "You feel it?"

"Nah. I don't feel anything."

Her long tongue pushed between thin lips making her look like a lizard. Her stink stung my nose when she raised both of her arms straight up over her head. She would have stayed like that the rest of the day if I hadn't pulled her hand back down and tugged her to follow behind me.

After a minute or two she stopped again. "You feel that poke?" she asked.

"Just come on." Hard as I yanked on her arm, I couldn't get her to budge.

Goose pimples bumped up on her arms. Then I felt them rise on mine. A buzzing, fuzzing, sharp feeling on my skin caught the breath in my lungs.

The same feeling we always got before a dust storm rolled through.

"We gotta get home." Finally, my pulling got her to move, to run, even.

Flapping of wings and twittering of voice, a flock of birds flew over us, going the opposite way. They always knew when a roller was coming, all the birds and critters did. Beanie did, too. I wondered if she was part animal for the way she knew things like that.

We stopped and watched the birds. Beanie's coal black eyes and my clear blue, watching the frantic flying. Beanie squeezed my hand, like we really were sisters and not just one girl watching over the other. For a quick minute, I felt kin to her.

Most of the time I just felt the yoke of her pushing me low, weighing about as much as all the dust in Oklahoma.

❖

The winds whipped around us, and a mountain of black dirt rolled along, chasing behind us. Making our way in a straight path was near impossible, so we followed the lines of wire fence, watching the electric air pop blue sparks above the barbs. We got home and up the porch steps just in time. Mama was watching for us, waving for us to get up the steps. Reaching out, she pulled me in by the hand, our skin catching static, jolting all the way through me and into Beanie.

Just as soon as we were inside, Mama closed and bolted the door. "It's a big one," she said, shoving a towel into the space between the door and the floor.

"Praise the Lord you girls didn't get yourselves lost," Meemaw said, stepping up close and examining our faces. "You got any blisters? Last week I seen one of the sharecropper kids with blisters all over his body from the dust, even where his clothes covered his skin. And we didn't have nothing to soothe them, did we, Mary?"

"We did not." Mama moved around the room, busying herself preparing for the storm.

The nearest doctor was in Boise City, a good two-hour drive from Red River, three if the dust was thick. When folks couldn't get to the city or didn't have money to pay, they'd come to Meemaw and Mama. I thought it was mostly because they had a cabinet full of medicines in our house. Meemaw'd said, though, that it was on account of Mama had taken a year of nurses' training before she met Daddy.

"That poor boy. We had to clean out them sores with lye soap. I do believe it stung him something awful." Meemaw shook her head. "Mary, did we put in a order for some of that cream?"

"I did." Mama plunged a sheet into the sink and pulled it out, letting it drip on the floor. "Pearl, would you please help me? This is the last one to hang."

We hung the sheet over the big window in the living room. Mama's shoes clomped as she moved back from the window. My naked feet patted. I remembered my shoes, still under the porch. I crisscrossed my feet, one on top of the other, hoping she wouldn't notice.

"You can dig them out in the morning," Mama said, lifting an eyebrow at me.

Mama never did miss a blessed thing.

Rumbling wind pelted the house with specks of dirt and small stones. Mama pulled me close into her soft body.

"Don't be scared," she said, her voice gentle. "It'll be over soon."

Then the dust darkened the whole world.

Wind roared, shaking the windows and rattling doors. It pushed against the house from all sides like it wanted to blow us into the next county. I believed one day it would.

The dust got in no matter how hard we tried to keep it out. It worked its way into a crack here or a loose floorboard there. A hole in the roof or a gap in a windowsill. It always found a way in. Always won.

Dust and dark married, creating a pillow to smother hard on our faces.

Pastor had always said that God sent the dust to fall on the righteous and unrighteous alike because of His great goodness. I didn't know if there were any righteous folk anymore. Seemed everybody had given over to surviving the best they knew how. They had put all the holy church talk outside with the dust.

Still, I couldn't help but imagine that the dust was one big old whupping from the very hand of God.

I wondered how good we'd all have to be to get God to stop being so angry at us.

Pastor'd also said it was a bad thing to question God. If it was a sin, sure as lying or stealing busted-up cups or tarnished spoons, I didn't want any part of it. I didn't want to be the reason the dust storms kept on coming.

I decided to fold myself into my imagination instead of falling into sin. I pretended the wind was nothing more than the breath of the Big Bad Wolf, come to blow our brick house down. Problem was, no amount of hairs on our chiny chin chins could refuse to let it in. Prayers and hollering didn't do a whole lot either, as far as I could tell.

The daydream didn't work to push off my fear. Mama's arm around me tightened, and I turned my face toward her, pushing into the warmth of her body. She smelled like talcum powder and lye soap.

I stayed just like that, pressed safely against her, until the rolling drumbeat of the dust wall slowed and stopped and the witches' scream of wind quieted. The Lord had sent the dust, but He'd also sent my mama. I wondered what Pastor would have to say about that. I wasn't like to ask though. That man scared me more than a rattlesnake. And he was just as full of poison.

Mama loosened her arms and rubbed my back. "It's done now," she said. "We made it."

"Praise the Lord God Almighty," Meemaw sang out.

Sitting up, I felt the grit the storm left behind on my skin and in my hair and under my eyelids.

"You think Daddy's okay?" I asked, blinking against the haze hanging in the air.

"I have faith he is." Mama stood and shook the dirt from her skirt. "I would bet he's worrying about us as much as we're worrying about him."

A flickering flame rose as Meemaw lit a lantern. It barely cut through the thick air. Still, the light eased my fear.

# CHAPTER TWO

Beanie couldn't sleep after dusters rolled through. They got her too wound up to relax. Since we shared a bed, when Beanie didn't sleep, I didn't either. Both of us tossed and turned, flipped and flopped all night. She about kicked me out of bed a dozen times.

If I could have gotten three wishes somehow, I would have used every one of them on getting a bed all to myself. But since I had yet to find a genie-in-a-bottle buried in all the sand, I didn't like my chances for that one to come true.

Meemaw had come to our room early, before the sun was halfway in the sky. She put a cool washrag on Beanie's forehead and shushed her.

"Now, calm yourself, child," Meemaw said. "Be at peace, Beanie Jean."

Beanie stilled, and I wished Meemaw could have come in hours before.

"Our God is the God of salvation." Meemaw pushed Beanie's hair off her forehead. Then she closed her eyes tight, praying. "'For thou hast been a strength to the poor, a strength to the needy in his distress, a refuge from the storm, a shadow from the heat, when the blast of the terrible ones is as a storm against the wall.'"

Soon as Beanie heard Meemaw's voice, she quieted her grunting and let her body ease a bit. I thought Meemaw must have been part fairy to work that kind of magic.

As for me, I wasn't about to fall asleep. Too many ideas passed around in my head for me to find rest.

I got out of bed and pushed aside the curtains. Outside my bedroom window I would see three things, four if the air wasn't thick with earth.

One was Mama's mostly-dried-up and buried-in-dust vegetable garden. The only thing that seemed to grow in that soil anymore was potatoes. They were the saddest looking potatoes in the history of our great state, at least that was what Daddy had said.

The next thing I could see was our chicken coop. We only had three or four scrawny laying hens left. The rest had suffocated or become dinner at some point to go alongside those sad-looking potatoes.

Third was an old windmill that stood a few yards behind the coop. Daddy had told me that it was older than our house. He had often said the first settlers in Red River had put it in. The way it creaked whenever the wind blew, I believed it.

Last, and only on clear days, I could see straight out to the sharecroppers' cabins. The folks that lived in those little shacks had to pay the rent with the crop they harvested. Seeing as nobody had a crop to speak of for years, most of them had been forced out by the banks. A few had managed to hold on, though nobody could figure out how.

The first in the line of cabins belonged to Ray Jones. At least, it was his parents' and he lived there with them and his little sister, Baby Rosie.

Ray was about the only friend I had. He was a full year older than me, but he didn't seem to mind being around me too much.

Watching out my window, I hoped to see Ray himself, sitting outside his family's old dugout. It turned out to be one of the days when I could barely see the windmill, though.

Still in my nightie, I slapped my bare feet on the floor and went out of my bedroom and down the gritty steps. From below, I heard the scratching of Mama's broom on the linoleum. I knew she would put me to work right away if she knew I was up and at 'em, so I turned to go right back to my room.

I'd forgotten about the creak in the middle of the third step from the bottom. Just my luck, the step hadn't forgotten and sung out under my weight.

The broom stopped scratching. Mama's shoes clicked on the floor. She'd caught me.

I used a bad word. But only in my head so Mama wouldn't know. I didn't want to get my mouth washed out with soap first thing in the morning.

"That you, Mother?" Mama always called Meemaw Mother even though she was Daddy's mama.

"It's me," I answered, taking the last few steps, slumping in my defeat.

As soon as she saw me, Mama handed me a wet towel and went about scrubbing down the windows and walls and anything that could stand the punishment of her washrag.

"Wave that in the air, Pearl. It'll knock the dust down so we can sweep." Her behind moved right along with her scrubbing hand. "We have got to get all that dirt out of here. I swear, this grit is going to be the end of my sanity."

"Where's Daddy?" I asked, swinging the towel around my head.

"Out making rounds," Mama told me. "Now, don't whip that thing. Be gentle."

"When will he be home?" I tried to make the towel billow, but could only manage to wave it up and down. "Will he be home for dinner?"

"I don't know." Mama sighed. "He's got a lot of stops to make before he can take a break."

I knew that meant he was checking on everybody in Red River, making sure they'd made it through the storm. That was what good sheriffs did. And Daddy was the best there ever was. I was sure of it.

"He'll be home soon enough." Mama's washcloth streaked black, oily dirt on the windows. "I do believe all the dirt in Kansas is here in my kitchen. Can't hardly think of eating with all this grime."

The ache in my belly didn't care if the house was half full of spiders. I never told Mama that, though. She'd have told me I would care plenty enough if I had spiders crawling in my oatmeal.

She would've been right about that.

We worked for a good long time, all the while my hunger distracting me more and more. She turned toward me when my stomach rumbled and shook her head.

"Why don't you go on and get dressed. Then I'll get you something to eat," she said, taking the towel from me. "Don't wake your sister, though."

I did my very best to be quiet as I made my way up the stairs and into my bedroom. Meemaw was awake and smiling at me, so big I saw the five or six gaps where she was missing teeth. I wondered how she could chew anything at all.

Beanie had finally fallen asleep, and she snored with her mouth wide open. Meemaw put a finger to her lips to let me know I should be quiet. Then she winked at me, making me smile. Meemaw's eyes were deep brown like Daddy's and Beanie's. What I liked most about them were the wrinkles that collected at the corners. Even when she wasn't smiling, the crinkles were there in her skin. Years of smiling and laughing had made those lines. She complained about them, calling them her crow's feet. I thought they were pretty, though. They made her look as kind as she was.

I smiled back at her extra hard so when I got old I'd have wrinkles in the corners of my eyes, too.

Remembering my empty belly, I turned to get dressed, hoping Meemaw wouldn't watch me. I'd gotten private about things like that.

My closet only had a couple dresses in it, but they were clean and they fit me just fine. All but one of them were made out of old sacks. Most all the girls and ladies in town wore dresses made of bags. Flour or sugar or feed bags. Almost nobody had money to pay for new fabric, so they used what they had. And what we all had were empty sacks made of cotton and the know-how to sew them into little dresses.

Touching my few frocks, I remembered the day Mr. Smalley got a shipment of sugar for the store. Mama and I went to get a couple groceries, and he showed us the bags of sugar. They each had flowers printed all over them. So many different colors I couldn't help but smile to see them.

"They're putting flowers on the bags now," Mr. Smalley had said, his eyes bright as a little boy's at Christmas. "Guess they wanted the little girls to have something fine to wear."

Mama had turned away from him and started crying. All I could think of to do was smile at Mr. Smalley until he gave me a stick of candy to suck on.

That was when I learned that kindness could break a heart just as sure as meanness. The difference was the kindness made that broken heart softer. Meanness just made the heart want to be hard.

Running my fingers across the hung-up dresses, I picked the one with red flowers and stepped into it. The buttons matched as well as they could. They were all plain white, even if a couple were smaller than the rest. Mama and Meemaw had collected buttons over the years, keeping them in an old coffee can.

My top buttonhole had a loose string. I wrapped it around my finger, popping it free.

"Oh, don't do that, darlin'." Meemaw stood from her seat next to Beanie, teetering before she righted herself, grabbing the bed frame. Once steady, she whispered, "Praise Jesus."

The few steps she took toward me seemed to hurt her every joint, she walked so stiff. Still, those smile wrinkles lined the place by her eyes.

"You don't wanna pull your dress to shreds, do you?" She patted me with her crooked fingers. She straightened my collar. "Such a pretty girl. God bless you, darlin'."

Meemaw and I looked eye to eye. She'd shrunk, and I'd grown, and we were about the same height even though she didn't like to admit it. I tried to mirror her smiling eyes. When she kissed my cheek it made my heart feel all kinds of warm.

Meemaw sat back down in her chair and took Beanie's hand again. She hummed a little bit of a song and rocked her head, closing her eyes. That was how she prayed. Humming and rocking and smiling with her eyes shut.

I wondered if, under her eyelids, she could see what Jesus looked like. The way she smiled, I had to believe He was grinning right back at her.

My grumbling tummy reminded me of Mama's promise of breakfast, so I got back downstairs.

Mama stood at the bottom of the steps, waiting for me with two bis-cuits, one in each hand. She handed them to me and nodded to the front porch. "Go on outside. Make sure you share one of these, hear?"

Through the window I saw that Ray Jones stood on the porch, hands tucked into the front pockets of his overalls. Even from the other side of the still-streaked glass I could see the gold-tan of his skin.

I didn't wait a second longer than I had to. I got out the door with Mama calling behind me, "Dig out your shoes."

Soon as I was outside, Ray took a leap off the porch. He'd even done it with his hands still shoved in the pockets. When he landed, he went down into a low squat the way all the men did and wiggled his bare toes in the dirt. Those toes were stained from a couple years of not wearing shoes. I wondered if his mother ever scolded him for being so filthy. Mama would never have stood for that in her home. If Ray was her boy, she would have tossed him in the tub for a good scrubbing.

Then again, Mama kissed me all over my face and held me close. Ray's mother didn't so much as look at him twice in a week. That didn't make sense to me whatsoever. I thought Ray Jones was the nicest thing to look at in all Cimarron County, dirty toes and all.

I joined him, but I went down the steps knowing Mama would holler if I'd jumped.

"Mama said to give this to you," I said, handing over one of the biscuits.

The year before, he would have gotten mad about me giving him something like a biscuit. Would've slumped off and not come back around for a couple days. Things had gotten harder for his family, though. All the families in Red River had it rough. Folks were less likely than before to refuse a biscuit or a can of beans. They'd take the food but didn't like meeting the eyes of the giver after.

I wondered why they held onto shame like that.

Ray ate eagerly, without dropping so much as a crumb. I figured he was even more hungry than I was. Still, as much as I wanted to shove it in like Ray did, I knew Mama was watching, so I ate real dainty, just like she'd taught me. I didn't even try to spit the grit out from my mouth. I just let it crunch between my teeth.

Wasting food in front of Ray would have been a sin.

Ray's family didn't always have enough to eat. I knew that because Daddy had told me. But he'd also said I wasn't to ever say a word about it to Ray or any of the Joneses. It shamed them enough to take the relief the government sent. Daddy said they didn't need a little girl dumping more embarrassment on top of them. Having the government truck stop in front of their old dugout once a month did plenty of that.

I hadn't gotten to see what was on that truck. Daddy got paid at the end of every month so we always had more than enough. One hundred and twenty-five dollars could buy all the groceries we needed. Mama had told me never to tell Ray or anybody else about how much Daddy made. I also wasn't to tell that Mama sometimes dropped off loads of food to neighbors when they weren't home or that she often paid off a family's bill at Mr. Smalley's store. She liked to surprise them.

Meemaw had told me they would have refused the food or money if they knew where it had come from.

"Wanna go out to the old cabins?" Ray asked me, wiping the sweat off his upper lip before popping the last bite of biscuit into his mouth. "I hear one of them got its roof caved in."

"Doesn't matter to me." I shrugged my shoulders. "I guess so."

"Let's go, then." Shoving hands back into his pockets, Ray started walking. He checked over his shoulder to make sure I followed.

I sped up. The last thing I wanted was for him to think I was a slowpoke.

"My pa seen a picture show last week," Ray said. "He was over to Boise City for work or something."

I knew Ray's father hadn't been working. It was more likely that he was gone doing the "something." Whatever that meant. But when Mama and Daddy talked about Mr. Jones, they both stopped short of saying what was wrong with him and raised their eyebrows. When I'd asked, they'd just said he was thirsty.

Why he had to go off to Boise City to relieve his thirst when Red River had drinking water, I couldn't figure out.

"My pa said there was this newsreel before the movie." Ray coughed and spit. "Said they done a story on a man who got hung for sticking up a bank. They said his head popped clean off."

"Did not." I knew Ray liked to tease me.

"It's the God's honest truth," he said. "Pa said the hangman forgot to put the bag over the fella's head. All the folks that watched got sick to their stomachs."

"That isn't true."

Ray laughed and gave me a sideways grin. When he made that face, I couldn't tell if he was saying the truth or not. "He said the man's head turned purple before it busted open."

The picture that created in my head was enough to keep me full of nightmares for a good month.

We passed by the house where Pastor Ezra Anderson lived with his crazy old wife, Mabel. She was the kind of crazy that would get up in the middle of the night, screaming about seeing demons floating above her head. And she was the kind of crazy that thought a jar of old brine was a good birthday present.

Most people stayed clear of her, and Pastor kept her inside almost all the time. But if a scary story needed telling, it usually had something to do with a thing Mad Mabel had done throughout the years.

Meemaw had said she wasn't always crazy. She said Mrs. Anderson used to be a real nice lady, after she took Jesus into her heart. Meemaw'd also told me that Mrs. Anderson made the best goulash this side of Berlin.

Something had just snapped in her mind, Meemaw had told me. One day she was all right and the next she was the town loony. Nobody could make heads or tails of it.

But Pastor wouldn't leave her no matter what, and Meemaw had said that was the mark of a good man.

"Would ya look at that," Ray said, nudging me. "Look what Mad Mabel's done now."

All along Pastor's fence were hung dead snakes, belly up, drying in the sun. The mouths hung wide, and the eyes were open but dull. I wondered how she'd found so many of them and how she'd killed them without getting bit. Thinking on it made a chill travel up my backbone.

"Why'd she do that?" I whispered.

"Probably thinks it'll make it rain or something." Ray cleared his throat. "Come on. Them things give me the willies."

Not twenty paces from us, the sharecropper cabins lined the road, half buried in the land. Dugouts, they were called. Mama said she'd sooner live in Daddy's truck than in one of those dugouts. She told me the centipedes skittered on the walls and fell in people's hair when they were sleeping.

It made my scalp itch to imagine it.

Ray's family lived in the first dugout on the right. When I'd asked him once about the centipedes, he told me he ate them alive. He'd catch them in his mouth when they dropped from the ceiling. Said he liked the way they tickled on the way down. Then he'd given me that sideways grin and raised his eyebrows.

I never could tell when he was joshing me.

Mrs. Jones stood to the side of their front door, shaking a rug, dust falling off it. When she looked our way, she nodded, not smiling like Mama would have.

When I dreamed of ghosts, they looked like Mrs. Jones with empty eyes, see-through as glass. I didn't think I had ever seen her smile. If she'd ever had so much as a happy thought, I wouldn't have known it to look at her. She was about as blank as an empty sheet of paper.

We kept on walking. Past a pile of things folks had left when they took off, leaving Red River forever. A bed frame and a rusted-out basin, a half-buried hand plow, and a couple old tires. We climbed over a broke-down tractor, Ray turning the steering wheel this way and that before jumping back to the ground. I couldn't hardly remember when all the cabins had people living in them. It had been such a long time since things were good.

Ray led me farther down the line of shacks and stopped right in front of the very last one. It was all the way above ground and had a cellar, even. The porch sloped so badly I wondered if somebody could stand on it without sliding right off. The one window had a half-broken-out pane of glass and a dingy piece of cloth hanging across it, shredded and bleached by years of scorching from the sun. A big skull of some animal hung on the outside wall right next to the door.

Of all the haunted places in No Man's Land, that one made me feel the loneliest.

The family that had lived there left a year or so before, off to find work out West. Nothing but orange trees that needed picked, they had said. Work for everybody who'd want it.

When I'd asked Daddy why we didn't pack up and leave, he'd said that everything we had in the world was right there in Red River. I'd told him I would work picking oranges in California if he'd let us move. All he'd said was that it wasn't as easy as it sounded.

"It don't look like that roof caved all the way in," Ray said, cocking his head to one side. He climbed up on the porch to look in the window. "Nah. Just half of it. I'm going in for a look-see."

I crossed my arms and watched him.

"Come on," he said.

"I can't go in there." I shook my head.

"Come on, Pearl. Just for a minute."

"My mama would tan my hide if I went in there."

Ray stepped around a pulled-up nail in the porch. "Nobody's in there. They ain't lived here for more than a year."

"I don't care. I don't want a whupping." Mama wouldn't have whupped me, and I knew it. Still, I didn't want to get in trouble for breaking her rules.

Neither of us said a word about why Mama had such a rule, but we both knew. The folks who had last lived in that cabin were Negro. Mama wasn't a hateful woman or one to prejudice. She just thought people should stick to their own kind.

Somehow, though, it had been okay for Negroes to wash our clothes and clean our house. When I'd asked Mama about that, she didn't have an answer other than, "They're just different than us."

"If you're gonna be a little girl about it, I'll go in by myself." Ray stepped closer to the door. "You can go on home. I don't need you tagging around."

I couldn't have Ray thinking I was being a little girl. I scrambled up on that porch, making sure to miss stepping on shards of broken glass and dodging the pulled-up, rusty nails. I ducked through the door ahead of him.

It was brighter inside than I expected. The half-caved-in roof let in plenty of light. With all the dirt mounded up on one side of the floor, it was hard to imagine that anybody had ever lived there, let alone a whole family with kids and everything.

They'd left nothing but a box of trash. Or at least somebody had come along and took what had remained. It was just four walls, a window, a door, and a pile of dirt that stacked all the way up to where the ceiling had been.

Ray had walked in behind me. He elbowed me, "What's that?"

He took a few steps before squatting next to the box. It was nothing special. Just an old crate with a blue stamp smudged on the wood. He reached in and grabbed a yellowed newspaper. Mouse droppings rolled off it. He held it up, squinting to look at the date, but it had been rubbed off long before. Torn edges at the bottom told me that something had been important enough to get ripped out. An article or a picture, maybe.

Ray took the insides of the paper and flipped through them, leaving me the front page. I ran my fingers along the tear, the soft edge tickling my skin. What could have been so important that somebody kept just one part of the paper, I wondered.

"There's funnies still in here," Ray said, drawing my attention away from the missing article. He turned the paper toward me, showing me the treasure he'd uncovered. I hadn't seen his happy, little-boy smile in too long.

Ray and I eased onto the dust pile in the corner of the room. We made divots in the dirt with our backsides. The dirt was soft as flour. The firm part of Ray's shoulder supported my back. Metal from his overall strap dug into my skin and his warm breath smelled sour. I didn't tell him to move, though.

"Read 'em out loud," he whispered. Ray couldn't read more than a couple words. He'd told me so one time, making sure I promised to never tell anybody else. He said the letters do-si-doed across the pages when he tried putting them in order. He'd quit coming to school after he learned to write his name. As far as he cared, that was all the school knowledge he needed.

"Which one first?" I asked.

"Start with Dick Tracy."

We read through all the comics, every single one of them. A couple times Ray leaned forward and let his chin rest on my shoulder, our cheeks almost brushing together.

For somebody who couldn't read, he sure liked stories. He'd get pulled right into the middle of them. I wished I knew how to fix his eyes so he could read the words for himself whenever he wanted.

Once we'd finished with the funnies, Ray pointed at the paper on my lap. I'd almost forgotten it was even there.

"What's that say?" he asked, hitting the headline with the knuckle of his middle finger.

I shook the paper a little to work out the wrinkles and rested it on my knees.

"'Jimmy DuPre struck down in Red River,'" I dragged my finger under the words as I read them. Just saying that name, Jimmy DuPre, made goose pimples stand up on my arms.

When I dreamed of monsters, I saw Jimmy DuPre's rat face.

I'd heard tales about Jimmy DuPre most of my life. All the kids in Red River had. He'd become something of a myth and a caution for children to make good choices and do the right thing.

Better obey your parents or you might end up like Jimmy DuPre. Don't sass the teacher—you don't want to go the way of Jimmy DuPre. Go to church, do your chores, say a prayer before meals so you avoid the epic fate of Jimmy DuPre, who ended up dead in the street, a bullet stuck in his chest.

"Read it." Ray knocked me forward with his shoulder.

"Quit it, would ya?" I said. "You know what it says."

As much as I didn't want to, I read it to Ray, even though we both knew the story. Jimmy DuPre, a boy from Kentucky or somewhere, had come to Oklahoma. He stuck up a bunch of banks and killed a couple people along the way. He was hiding in Red River when the urge to rob somebody else got to him. Problem was, he stuck up Mr. Smalley's grocery store while Daddy was picking up a bag of flour for Mama.

Jimmy ended up dead. Daddy was the one who shot him. That was it. End of story. Jimmy was the bad guy and Daddy the hero.

Clean your plate and mind your manners so you'll end up like the good sheriff Tom Spence.

Ray studied the picture of Jimmy DuPre and cocked his head, squinting. "He never should have come to Red River."

I handed the paper to him so he could look at it closer.

"I would've thought he'd have sense enough not to hide out in a small town. Boise City would have been a better place." Ray shook his head. "Why anybody would pick to live here is beyond me."

"You think you'll ever leave?" I asked.

"I'm fixing to." He crumpled the article about Jimmy DuPre into a ball. "I won't go taking from anybody else to do it, though. Not like he done."

"Would you come back?"

"Nah. I wouldn't think about this place again." He dropped the paper ball on the floor and kicked it. It scuttled across the dirt to the other side of the room.

If Daddy had given me bruises like the ones I sometimes saw on Ray, I'd want to leave, too.

"Ain't nothing here. Nothing but dirt," he said.

"And rabbits." I smiled at him, but he didn't look at me.

"I'm about sick of all the rabbits." He shook his head. "I hate them."

"There's a drive tomorrow. I saw a sign at the store."

Daddy'd told me the jackrabbits had come looking for water, but there wasn't much to find. They'd take over a field, blending in with the dirt. When they moved all at once, it looked like the land was moving and shaking.

Just about every other Sunday that year, the men had gotten together to catch as many of the jackrabbits as they could. The varmints had nibbled up every green thing the dust storms didn't bury. Daddy had never let me go to one of the drives. He made me stay home with Mama and Meemaw and Beanie. He'd told me that it wasn't good for a woman to be out in the fields on the Sabbath.

How it was fine for the men to un-holy the Sabbath Day, I didn't know. But I didn't dare ask him. Daddy hardly ever said anything about one of the commandments, so I knew he was serious about that one.

"You coming to the drive?" Ray asked.

"Girls aren't allowed at those," I answered.

"Sure they are. Plenty of girls come."

"Mama needs me at home."

Ray fell back, sprawling out on the dirt. He lifted one of his hands, putting it behind his head. I saw that he'd started sprouting a little hair under his arm, just a couple wiry ones. I figured he was awful proud of the few he had, the way he smiled when I looked at them.

"Rabbit drives is men's work, anyhow," he said.

"I could do it."

"Couldn't neither. It would make you cry." He stood up and grabbed my hand, pulling me to my feet. "A girl like you ain't made for man's work."

I had never won an argument with Ray Jones, and I didn't figure I was like to. So I let him pull me out of the cabin and onto the porch and didn't snap back at him, much as I would have liked to.

"The other day I seen a jackrabbit get caught in a piece of barbed wire." Ray squinted, looking across the wide land. "The air was all full of static like it does. That dumb rabbit got zapped so hard it cooked it all the way through."

"You're lying." I let go of his hand.

"Am not. It singed all the fur off and everything." Ray hopped off the porch. "Just needed a little salt and pepper's all. Tasted just fine."

"You never ate that." I stepped off the porch and shoved him. "I don't believe you."

"You don't?" He grinned sideways. "Ask my ma. She'll tell you. Said it was the best thing she'd ever ate."

I rolled my eyes, trying to pretend I wasn't even a little tickled by his story.

Under our feet, the ground rumbled. We looked at each other and smiled. Without thinking twice we both took off running toward the sound of the train whistle. The tracks weren't far off from the sharecroppers' cabins. We got to them long before the train reached the old, boarded-up depot. I crossed my arms over my chest, waiting. Ray held one hand like a visor, shielding his eyes from the sun-glare.

"How many cars you think this one's got?" Ray watched the engine chug toward us. "You think there's any hobos?"

Roaring and blowing at my skirt so I had to hold it down, the train rushed by. My hair raised up and waved all around my head, and my heart thudded. Ray and I turned, watching as it went.

"One, two, three . . ." Ray counted the cars.

A handful of men jumped off the last box cars. They shifted knapsacks on shoulders or pushed hats on top of their heads. Once the train was past, most all of them crossed the tracks and went off to one of the old, dried-up fields.

One of them didn't follow the rest. He stood right where he'd landed and stared at me. He was a small man, short and skinny. And even though it was a hot day, he wore a black coat. His eyes never left me as he walked toward us, taking his sweet time.

I could tell from the smirk on his face that he was the kind of man looking for trouble. It wasn't that he was ugly or mean looking, exactly. The way he stared me down made me all kinds of uncomfortable. That man was up to no good. I was sure Daddy would have thought the same thing.

Ray and I stood still, like our feet had sunk in the ground, held fast by the dirt. The up-to-no-good hobo stopped in front of us. His smirk curled into a smile that didn't look one bit sincere. Mama would have asked what he was selling.

"Pearl?" he asked, peering down at me with his blue eyes. "Pearl Spence, right?"

I didn't answer. I doubted I would have found my voice even if I'd tried.

"You the welcome wagon round these parts?"

I shrugged, not knowing if I was supposed to answer that question.

"Well, I guess I'll be seeing you around," he said.

He winked at me before turning to walk away, slow and like he owned the place.

"Who's that?" Ray asked.

"I don't know," I answered, watching the man, afraid to take my eyes off him.

The day was hot enough, but my blood felt icy cold.

## CHAPTER THREE

I had one dress that wasn't made out of a sack. Mama had paid good money at Mr. Smalley's grocery store for the fabric. She'd even spent a little extra for brand-new buttons that all matched. Mr. Smalley'd had to order them and, when we picked them up, he'd stood behind the counter and smiled at me, telling me what a lucky girl I was.

That dress was my birthday present and I'd done my very best to keep it from getting stained or ripped. That was why I only wore it on Sundays. On Sundays I went to church, then sat around the house all day, reading books. It hardly had a chance to get dirty.

Besides, I felt bad wearing my best dress all around town. Most of the girls in Red River had ratty dresses, dingy and falling apart. It didn't seem right that I had one as yellow and crisp as sunshine with buttons that shimmered. I wondered if my dress didn't make them all feel poorer.

I smoothed the dress over my legs when I sat on the davenport after church, my fairy-tale book next to me. Pulling my long braid over my shoulder, I felt of its thickness and tried to pretend I was Rapunzel.

Flipping through the pages, I fingered half-a-dozen birthday cards I'd used as bookmarks for as long as I could remember. One of the cards had a prairie girl on the front. Another had Raggedy Ann. One was Mickey Mouse, and the last one had a bird in a top hat.

Daddy had delivered all of those cards on my birthday over the years with a warning to keep them a secret from Mama. Not a single one of the cards had been signed. When I'd asked Daddy who had sent them, he just lifted his eyebrows. I imagined I had a fairy godmother somewhere. It made about as much sense to me as anything else.

I turned to the story of Rapunzel and examined the watercolor picture on the first page. Rapunzel's parents handed her over to the ugly, big-nosed witch. Rapunzel was nothing more than a little bundle of a baby in the picture. I'd read that story so many times I didn't even have to look at the words to know what happened to her.

She never knew her true parents. Not even after she escaped the tower. She never learned that the witch wasn't her mother.

I took my hands off my braid and put one finger on the picture of the baby, the one who would never be with the folks who really loved her. I wondered if she ever feared that she'd become as ugly and big-nosed as the witch who raised her.

The only reason I was even close to good was because I'd gotten it from Mama and Daddy. Everything good inside of me was from them.

The clunking of Mama's heels on the steps pulled my attention. She rushed into the living room, her eyebrows bunched together in the middle. "Pearl, have you seen Beanie?" she asked.

"No, ma'am," I answered, closing my book.

She leaned forward, looking out the big front window. "Where could she have got off to?"

Mama shook her head and climbed back up the stairs, calling my sister's name.

I left my book next to my seat and stepped out the front door. More likely than not, Beanie was wandering in some dust-buried field or rummaging through an abandoned cabin.

Nobody could hunt down Beanie like I could. I was fixing to find her and have her home before Mama knew I'd left. I even left my shoes on, I'd be back so quick.

The streets were empty of people except for me. All the men and boys were at the rabbit drive and everybody else was home. In Red River, most folks kept the Sabbath Day holy by tending to the land and their homes, not that it ever made much difference.

Daddy had told me once that he met God more in getting dirt under his fingernails and sweat on his brow than sitting in church getting hollered at.

I wanted to meet God like Daddy did, but Mama said it was just his way of getting out of holding down a pew most Sundays.

I walked across the bone-dry dust, remembering how Meemaw had told me once that the place where Jesus lived was just as dry and dirty and hot as Oklahoma. Meemaw said a lot of things about Bible times and some of them seemed a little strange to me. But the part about Jesus living in a drought sounded right.

When I thought on it, Jesus did work on the Sabbath. Plenty of it, as a matter of fact. I decided I would have to talk that over with Mama.

As I went along, I pretended I was Mary Magdalene, following behind in the dust of Jesus's sandals, rubbing wheat heads between my fingers, humming a hymn or two. I wondered if they would have sung "Onward Christian Soldiers." It seemed a good walking-around-the-desert song to me.

I quit humming, though, when I saw That Woman walking toward me on the same side of the street. I had never learned her name, but I reckoned she did have one. Mama just called her That Woman and said that I wasn't to speak to her. Not ever. Mama's rule was that if I met her on the street I was to cross over to the other side.

I took one step off the sidewalk to act in obedience but remembered that Pastor had talked about the Good Samaritan in church that morning. The only ones crossing to the other side of the street ended up being the bad guys. Besides, I didn't know what was so wrong about living in a cat house like I'd heard That Woman did.

Mama wasn't watching that day—only God was—so I decided to be the Good Samaritan and stay on the same side of the road as That Woman. If I'd had a donkey, I would have let her take a ride on it, even.

The closer I got to her, the lower she held her head and the farther to the edge of the sidewalk she stepped. I wondered if she would cross over to the other side of the street so she wouldn't get too close to me.

She never did, though.

"Hi," I said as soon as I got close enough.

She stopped and glanced at me, her head still hung low. I figured I'd surprised her by the way her eyes got wide. We stood like that for longer than felt comfortable, and I wished I hadn't said "hi" to her at all. I knew I needed to say something else to make it less strange. I thought about telling her that she was pretty. Or that I'd never seen a woman wear as much color on her face as she did. It was as if she was painted. But I thought twice about that.

Instead, I settled for what I'd learned the first day of school. I smiled wide and looked her right in the eyes, and stuck out my hand.

"What's your name?" I asked.

She didn't say a word, just breathed in and out, her chest moving up and down. The way she looked at my face was odd, like she was trying to find something there. I couldn't figure out what it was she thought she would see.

"I best be going," she said, rushing past me with her arms crossed over her stomach like she was going to get sick.

She looked over her shoulder for one last glimpse of me. She was sad, her whole face frowned. I guessed that if most of the town hated me as bad as they hated her, I would have been sad, too.

My heart feeling unsettled, I went on my way, trying to imagine how it felt to be That Woman. But I couldn't think on it too much. It would have been plain awful to be her.

The closer I got to the sharecroppers' cabins, the harder the ground became. Hard as cement. Dry and flakey and cracked. If ever it did rain, the drops wouldn't know how to break through that scab of earth. Nothing was like to grow there again.

Ray's mother stood outside their dugout, hunched over a big old basin, scrubbing clothes on the washboard. She always had something to scrub. I never saw her sitting idle. I wasn't sure she knew how to be still.

Baby Rosie sat up all by herself like a big girl at her mother's feet. She owned Ray's heart, that baby did. I rushed over to the porch and made silly faces for Rosie to get a good old baby smile on her face. She didn't giggle, though. She was too busy slobbering away on an old toy truck that used to belong to Ray.

"She's working on getting a tooth," Mrs. Jones said, not turning to me or taking a break in her scrubbing. "What are you doing out?"

"Looking for Beanie." I reached for Baby Rosie's foot. "You seen her?"

Mrs. Jones looked up and out over the fields but didn't stop working. Steam gathered around her arms as she worked the lye against the fabric.

"I ain't." Tilting her head in my direction, she raised one thin eyebrow. "You think she would have gone down to that rabbit drive?"

I shrugged and tickled Rosie's knee.

"You ain't fixing to go down there, are you?" Turning her face back to the work, she lifted the clothing, wringing it so hard my throat felt the strangle. "That ain't no place for a girl like you. Beanie neither."

"Yes, ma'am."

"I know you think you're half boy, but you ain't."

She pulled a dress from the basket on the ground next to her. Powder blue with purple flowers and a thick, white collar. It had a baked bean stain on the front. I'd worn that dress just two days before and spilled on myself at dinner. Mama had puckered her lips and shook her head, fretting that I'd never be able to eat like a lady.

That dress in Ray's mother's hand was mine. She caught me looking and plunged it into the water, sloshing and scrubbing again. The place between my heart and my stomach swelled.

Baby Rosie dropped the toy truck and it landed just out of her reach. She whimpered until I grabbed it and, wiping off the dirt, handed it back to her. Into her mouth it went.

"If I see your sister, I'll make sure she gets home," Mrs. Jones said, the hard edge of her voice softened.

"Thanks, Mrs. Jones."

"All right, then." She worked at the stain with her thumb nail.

"Bye, Rosie," I whispered.

I walked away from the centipede-infested dugout and Mrs. Jones's empty eyes and Baby Rosie's too-skinny-body and my stained dress.

❀

Beanie had me stumped. I couldn't find her any place, and I'd searched about everywhere. The old homestead where she could hide in the empty silo. The alley behind the post office and Mr. Smalley's grocery store. I checked every one of the empty cabins.

The last place I could think to look was at the Watsons' ranch, where the men were herding the rabbits. I headed that way, knowing Daddy would be there—he could help me. And I wished so hard that I'd get the chance to watch a little of the drive.

Back when I was younger and the ranches were full of fat cattle, Daddy would take me to watch the cowboys drive the herd from one stubbled pasture to the next. Not much grass grew even then, but the ranchers fed them the Russian thistles that would otherwise blow all about the streets.

Those days of cowboys and cattle were like magic to me. Watching the dogs dart around, nipping at the heels of the cows, I'd listen to the ranchers holler back and forth, letting hard words shoot from their mouths. Words Mama would have washed my mouth out for. Sometimes, in alone moments, I'd try letting those same words come from my lips. It felt like power when the tough sounds spilled out in my whispered voice.

I couldn't imagine a rabbit drive being much different, apart from the stock being moved was much smaller. But the same cussing and spitting and chewing tobacco, the nipping and barking dogs. I didn't know why Daddy had wanted me to stay away.

The closer I got to the ranch, the more I could hear of the men and boys and their rough, wild voices full of rocks and gravel and sharp edges. The sound of them excited me, made me run faster. Pulled on me to come see, hear, smell, and touch.

Oh, how I wanted to touch a rabbit.

Slowing to a walk when I'd about reached the drive, I watched the men corral the rabbits into a circle-shaped pen made out of chicken wire. They hooted and hollered at the animals, waving their arms and trying to get the zigzagging creatures to turn toward the pen. The closer they got to the wire, the tighter the line of men became. Frenzied rabbits tried to jump up and over the chicken wire. They tried to break their way through.

I forced my eyes off the rabbits to see if I couldn't find Beanie's face among the ladies and girls standing or sitting in the shade of an old barn. It made me sore that all those girls got to watch the drive and I wasn't supposed to.

A couple girls, close to Beanie's age, sat at the base of a naked tree, pointing at the men and giggling. It made me feel bad, watching them, knowing that my sister would never have them for friends. She never had any friends at all, except for me. Those girls only would have made fun of Beanie, and that gave me a sad feeling. One of the girls caught me looking and rolled her eyes at me. I about stuck my tongue out at her, but she turned away before I had the chance.

I decided I needed to get higher up to try and see Beanie or Daddy, so I climbed the old wood fence. Standing as tall as I could and keeping my balance, I still didn't see either of them. So I sat on the top rung to rest my legs a minute. Mama would have gotten after me for sure, risking my Sunday dress like that, but she wasn't there to holler at me. I promised myself I'd be extra careful not to get a snag. I kicked off my shoes and pushed off the socks. Stretching out my toes, I wiggled them in the air.

As soon as I got settled on my perch I noticed that the men carried hammers and wagon spokes and baseball bats. The wind caught the bits of my hair that had gotten loose from my braid. Still watching the men, I let go of the fence and smoothed the wispy hair, but it didn't help. It just kept right on moving with the wind.

"All right, fellas," a man hollered over all the other noise. "Let 'em have it."

The men lifted their clubs in the air, hovering over the rabbits. The looks on their faces made me have to grab hold of the fence again. Sneers and curled lips and flared noses, the mob of men rushed at the animals.

Rabbits jerked, their ears tugged up in the hands of the men. Blunt thuds fell down on them, crushing them. The sound of thwapping beat in my chest. The brown bodies swung from their ears after getting knocked with such force.

Frozen by fear, I couldn't do so much as blink.

The rabbits screamed shrill. They sounded like babies being hurt. No matter how hard the men hit them, the rabbits wouldn't die right away. The men had to hit them once. Twice. More. Then they tossed them on the ground, the bodies still jerking and twitching and hopping. Boys went through the pile, stilling them with smashing clubs and stomping feet.

Ray went around the edges of the pile with a plank of wood. He didn't look my way, and I was glad for it. I hated for him to see me cry.

The heap of rabbits grew, widened. A plague on the hard dirt.

Pastor had told us over and over that the jackrabbits were a curse for our stubborn ways. Sure as the frogs and the bloody river were to the Pharaoh of Egypt, the dust was punishment for our black sin. We'd gotten the locust and darkness already. Punishment upon punishment. Plague stacked on top of itself.

One rabbit got loose from the chicken wire. It bolted right toward me, stopping under my feet. Its ears were so tall they could have touched my toes, but I pulled my knees up, pushing them into my shoulders.

For all the wishing to touch a rabbit, I couldn't bring myself to pick that one up.

It screamed, the jackrabbit did. I imagined it begged me to save it. Loud and rough and savage, it called right to me.

All I could do was sit and stare and let the scared eyes of the animal work their way into haunting me.

A man from the line turned toward me. When he smirked right at me, I knew it was the same man who had jumped off the train and said my name. He strutted, making his way to me, and nodded in the direction of the rabbit. He didn't hurry. He took his time, keeping his eyes fixed on mine.

His eyes were blue as the brightest, clear-day sky. Blue as a cornflower.

Eyes that I thought could have been kind if he wanted to make them so. Instead, they cut through me, making me think that kindness wasn't his way.

He sauntered so close to me I could smell the sharp stink of his skin. I breathed in and out real shallow, and my head ached.

Reaching down, he yanked the rabbit up by the ears like all the other men were doing. But he didn't hit it. The animal kicked in the air, inches from my face. The man held it so tight, though, that all its fighting was worth nothing.

I could have grabbed hold of it. Could have taken it and run away with it. But it looked so big, and I didn't think I had the strength to move my arms. Every muscle in my body had grown heavy.

The man moved the rabbit closer to me and right when I found the power to raise my hand to touch it, the man jerked it back away from me. The man laughed as the animal screamed louder.

Thud of wagon spoke struck the jackrabbit. Just enough to stun it. The screams stopped. So did the kicking. The man smirked, dark shadowing over the light of his eyes. He hit it again, bloodying its face. The rabbit screamed once again past broken teeth.

The man swung and hit, swung and hit. Again and again. Warm splatter of blood speckled my face. My eyes stayed on the blue eyes that stayed on mine.

I couldn't tell if the rabbit was still alive. I couldn't stomach the knowing. After a minute or so, the man flipped his wrist, swinging the rabbit. A crackling of neck bones and the man finished off the animal. Stinging bile in the back of my mouth made me want to get sick.

He dropped the jackrabbit so it landed on top of my shoes.

The smirking man snarled, showing his teeth. Tobacco-juice-stained teeth. The blood of the rabbit dotted his face. He got even closer to me, cupping my cheek with his rough hand. Rotted-out-tooth smell made my sick stomach worse.

I tried to pull away from him and wondered why nobody was coming to help me. He laughed, red tobacco spit moving up the inside of his lip.

"I knew who you was soon as I seen you. I seen a picture of you. You're sure prettier in person, ain't ya?" He spit on the rabbit. Dribble trickled down his chin. "You'll be seeing more of me. I think we'll be good friends."

He let go of me. Before he turned to walk away, he kicked the dead rabbit.

I couldn't have run faster if my feet had wings on the heels. Chasing behind me were the screaming rabbits. The hollering men. The stink of rust-red teeth.

❊

Kicked-up dust stuck to the lines of wet on my face. Mud and tears and blood streaked on my skin. I couldn't seem to remember which way I had to go to get home. I ran one way, then switched back the other way. A couple times I got close to running into a tangle of barbed wire hidden under mounds of dust. Every tan-colored field looked the same as the next. All the pushed-over barns and sunk-in roofs, empty silos, crumbling fences.

The ruins of Red River.

Wind picked up. A swirl of dust spun in front of me like a ballerina. I ran through it, hands first, pushing past it with my eyes closed. Still, sharp grains of dust pushed in under my lids.

Far enough from the field that I couldn't hear the rabbits anymore, I stopped. I threw up my lunch in the dirt.

Crouching, head hanging over my own sick, I remembered that I hadn't found Beanie. Empty of strength and courage, I didn't know how I could go on. I didn't think I would ever find her.

All that was left to do was go home. Turning around and around, I still couldn't figure out which way I needed to go. Fear blinded me as sure as the dust did.

Shuffling and struggling forward, I cried all the way from my empty stomach. Heaving, gulping, crying. When the winds started pushing me around, anger joined the fear, and I about growled along with the sobs.

Then the church bells clanked. It was a soft noise, but enough to give me some hope.

"Whenever you get lost, listen for the church bells," Meemaw had told me no less than a dozen times. "When you hear them, you'll know you're close to home."

Stopping, I listened for them again. I turned to my left and followed the gentle sounding.

"Keep ringing," I said. It felt like a prayer.

Never before had those old church bells sounded more like music. I ran toward them until I saw the steeple topped with a dingy-looking cross. Long before, it had been painted gold. The dust had licked all the glow right off it, showing that it was nothing but wood underneath.

I made it all the way to the church steps. We lived in the house right next door, but I couldn't get myself to move one more inch. Sitting on the steps, I waited for a moment, trying to catch my breath.

One of my toes was stubbed and bleeding under the nail. Dust had jammed it, though, stopping the red from oozing out. I wrapped my hand around the toe, hoping to stop the throbbing ache. It didn't work.

"Pearl?"

I heard my name.

"Pearl Louise!"

It was Mama calling for me.

"I'm here," I tried to yell, but the dust had my voice clogged. "Right here."

All the windows of our house were open wide and through them I heard Mama moving about.

"Mama," I called out, trying, for all my strength, to be heard.

The front door of our house opened, and Mama stepped out on the porch. She shielded her eyes against the blazing sun. I knew her body would be soft and warm and smell of flour. As much as I wanted to run to her, I couldn't get up off those steps.

"Darlin'?" She looked down at me and touched her lips.

"I can't move," I whispered. "I'm too tired."

Mama took careful steps down the porch, holding on to the rail. Once on the ground, she forgot herself. She rushed to me. It was only a few yards, but she rushed. Ran for me. I had never seen her run before.

Ladies didn't run. That's what she had always told me. But that day she did. Her face told me enough. Ladies could run when they were scared.

"What happened? Where were you?" Her whispered gasps pushed out when she reached me. Her knees hit the ground next to the steps and she touched me all over. "Where are you hurt?"

Thick and dry, my tongue wouldn't allow any sound to come out. I'd about cried out all my tears, too. Mama looked from my eyes to my feet, her hands holding my shoulders.

"I never found her," I said, my voice cracking and throat sore.

"Who, darlin'?" She touched my cheek, the very same spot the smirking man had. But her hand was soft and gentle. She didn't mean me any harm.

"Beanie," I answered.

"I don't understand."

"I went looking for her."

"Pearl, she was here the whole time. She was hiding under the bed." Her dark eyes looked straight into mine. "I was so scared, darlin'. I didn't know where you got off to. You can't go running off like that."

"I'm sorry." I swallowed. My dry throat burned. "I thought I was helping."

"Where did you go?"

"The rabbit drive." I wanted to be sick again, but I had nothing left inside me. "I should have listened. I thought I'd see Daddy there."

"Are you hurt?"

"No." I pinched my eyes closed and my last few tears squeezed out, dropping on my spoiled dress. "I ruined it. My dress is ruined. And I lost my shoes."

I blinked hard, trying not to imagine the rabbit bleeding on my Mary Janes.

"Don't you worry about a thing." She scooped me up in her soft arms and let out a deep breath when she picked me up, carrying me to the house.

I hadn't known she possessed the strength to lift me.

Keeping my eyes closed, I prayed that God would let me forget the screaming rabbit and the cornflower-blue eyes.

❧

I leaned against the bathroom wall while Mama filled the tub for me with water she'd pumped out back and boiled on the stove. She made sure the water steamed. Mama believed a person didn't get truly clean unless the water stung the skin.

Stepping into the tub and lowering myself down little by little, I let the water singe my skin. It hurt, but I was eager to wash the rabbit blood off my body. I wished I could scrub away the memory, too.

Mama knelt next to the tub and released my hair from its messy braid. "I always wanted blond hair," she said.

I pulled my knees up to my chest, covering myself from her. I couldn't remember when I'd become embarrassed by my own body, but I thought I understood how Adam and Eve had felt.

"Blond and straight." She smiled, still working on my hair. "Not dark and curly like I got."

I thought Mama had pretty hair, and I told her so.

"I don't know. It's more trouble than smooth hair."

Mama was the prettiest woman I'd ever seen. Her cheekbones curved high on her face and stood out strong under her dark eyes. She had a pointed nose, like Beanie had. Her skin didn't have a single freckle on it.

I didn't look a thing like her. Freckled skin, blue eyes, light hair, button nose.

"Mama, who do I take after?" I asked, taking the soapy washrag from her.

"My pa had blond hair," she answered, standing. "So did my sister."

I nodded.

"Now," Mama said, opening the bathroom door. "You soak until the water gets cold."

"Yes, ma'am."

"Everything's okay now."

She closed the door behind her.

After I'd soaked and scrubbed and put on a fresh nightie, I slid into my bed and slept through the rest of the day.

❧

In my dream that night, I chased Beanie through a field. Loose dirt sunk under my feet, making me fall. My sister, though, kept right on running, her big feet slapping the dust. As soon as I caught up to her, she turned and looked right into my eyes.

Then she screamed. Jolting and frantic screams. Something from behind her had pulled her hair, sending her falling backwards onto the ground.

"You wanna pet it, Pearl?" The smirking man stood over Beanie, club in his hand.

I jerked awake before he brought the club down on her face.

❧

Daddy was in his chair in the living room. He'd fallen asleep there, a newspaper spread across his lap.

"Daddy?" I called from the bottom of the steps.

He woke right away. He'd always been a light sleeper. Being sheriff meant his sleep got interrupted quite often.

"Come on over, baby," he said, knocking the paper off his lap. His voice was thick with exhaustion. "You have a bad dream?"

I nodded and crawled onto his lap and curled into his arms. My lanky legs jutted out to the side.

"It was a bad one," I said.

"I don't doubt that for a minute. Rabbit drives ain't easy to see." He pushed the hair off my face. "I don't much like them myself."

"I went there to find you." My head on his shoulder, I studied his profile, the way his nose bumped at the top and how his mustache covered the top part of his lip. He turned his head to face me.

"Why weren't you there?" I asked.

"I was out looking for you." His mustache tickled when he kissed my forehead.

"You were?"

"Sure was." He smiled. "I was at the courthouse doing some of my paperwork. Your mama came to get me. She was scared."

I tucked my head under his chin and felt his Adam's apple bob up and down against the side of my face.

"I was scared, too," he said.

His deep in-and-out breaths calmed me and eased me back to sleep. He held me like that all the way to morning.

# CHAPTER FOUR

When Mama called us for supper, it meant we best have clean fingernails and a fresh dress on. Our hair should be brushed and pulled away from our faces. Of course, Beanie wasn't one for cleaning up so well, but she did her best. Mama wanted her family to be presentable at the supper table.

Mama's last stand against the invading filth.

But between Mama setting the table and all of us arriving at it, scrubbed pink, a fine layer of dust had covered over everything. It was why Mama had put the dishes and cups upside down.

"Now, come on, y'all," Mama called, rushing between the kitchen and the table. "The food's not getting any warmer."

Mama believed that letting food get cold was as much a sin as dancing and playing cards.

We gathered around in our usual seats. Beanie between Meemaw and Mama. My parents together. I was between Daddy and Meemaw. We never changed seats, and I liked that a good deal.

I could hardly resist running my finger across the tabletop, tracing a flower into the dust. I would have gladly made a whole field of them if Mama hadn't hollered at me.

"You're just making more of a mess, Pearl." She swatted at my hand with her washrag. "You stinker."

"Well, I had an interesting day." Daddy took the washrag from Mama and got to wiping the bottoms of each plate before putting them right-side-up. "We got some folks who set up a Hooverville out to the other side of the tracks."

Ray had told me about Hoovervilles. Camps full of people who didn't have any other place to rest their heads. Most of them were on their way west and needed somewhere to stop at for a day or so to get off the road. I'd heard that sometimes the folks held a square dance at the camps. And every night the kids got to sleep out under the stars.

I bet old Herbert Hoover liked having camps named after him.

"Can I go see it?" I asked, hoping Daddy would say I could. Seemed to me it would be the most exciting place on earth.

"Don't even think about it, Pearl," Mama said from the kitchen. "They don't need you going down there to stare at them. It might make them feel bad."

"Did you go out there with Millard?" I asked, handing Daddy my plate.

"Pearl Louise, mind your manners," Mama scolded. "You're to call him Mayor Young."

"But he told me to call him Millard."

"I know what he told you." Mama shook her head. "But I'll have none of it."

"Yup," Daddy said. "Mayor Millard E. Young, esquire, went along with me to check out the Hooverville."

"I seen a man eatin' a jackrabbit." Beanie rocked in her chair. "It smelled good."

"Now, Beanie Jean." Mama pursed her lips. "You haven't been down to that camp, have you?"

Beanie nodded, her eyes full of wonder. "They all eat jackrabbits."

I wished she would stop saying that word. Thinking back on the rabbit drive killed my appetite.

"I want you staying away from that camp. You hear me?" Mama carried a couple water glasses to the table. "Nothing good can come from you being down there. You've got no business bothering those folks."

"The man was drying out the rabbit skins. Said he was making himself a hat. He let me pet the fur." Beanie smiled, showing her crooked teeth. "It wasn't soft as it looked, though."

A picture of the rabbit bleeding out of its mouth flashed in my mind.

"You washed your hands didn't you?" Mama asked, making a sour look on her face. "Those rabbits have got mites."

"Yes, ma'am," Beanie answered. "Can we eat a jackrabbit?"

"Not so long as I'm alive you won't." Mama looked to Daddy. "They aren't really eating the rabbits are they?"

"Some are." Daddy crossed his arms. "They don't have anything else."

"They shouldn't be eating them." Mama put the baking dish on the table. "You've got to stop them."

"Now, I'm sure them rabbits are just fine if they get cooked through." Meemaw spooned goulash onto Beanie's plate. "Worse thing is they're probably real tough and gamey."

"Tom, you can't let people eat those things." Mama pulled out her chair.

"I told a couple of them the rabbits weren't good for eating." Daddy spread the cotton napkin over his thigh. "A couple kids over to Boise City got rabbit fever a week or two ago from eating the meat. Problem is, a man can't hear things like that when he's got hungry kids. He's gonna take a chance just to see his family fed."

Mama made a noise that was part sigh and part grunt.

"Mary," Daddy said, leaning forward. "They're starving. Folks in the Hooverville will die if they don't eat. Those rabbits are the first thing they've had in a long time that's stuck to them."

Mama didn't say a word for a couple minutes. She busied herself with making sure Beanie held her fork right before she sat in her chair and put her napkin on her lap.

"I'll take a couple loaves of bread out to them tomorrow," Mama said, looking at her own plate.

"It'll take more than a couple loaves. A couple dozen wouldn't even stretch." Daddy took my hand for grace. "There's a lot of people living down there."

"The Good Lord ain't never been held back on account of too little bread." Meemaw bowed her head. "Jesus Almighty fed the multitude on just a couple loaves and some fish."

Daddy said grace, and I imagined Jesus in His bleached white robes and blue sash, His soft hair dancing in the wind. He stood on top of a dust mound and handed out loaves of bread to hobos and drifters living out in the Hooverville. He never called them "Okies" or "trash." He just did a lot of smiling and hugging of necks. Then He asked all the little children to come to Him and held them on His lap, telling stories about lilies of the field and sparrows of the air. The kids looked up at Him and smiled, their bellies fuller than they'd been in a year or two.

Full of bread from a crop that couldn't be buried under dust no matter how hard it rolled in.

As Daddy blessed the food for our family, I prayed that Jesus would come to Red River to make Mama's bread be enough for all the folks. I prayed extra hard but still held a crumb of doubt.

For all I knew, bread miracles didn't work on cursed people.

❧

Daddy and I sat on the front porch after dinner. He busied his hands, rolling a cigarette. I cooled my toes in the late evening air.

Curling his fingers to block the wind from scattering the loose tobacco, he pinched and folded the paper, rolling it snug as a bug. He licked the edge, smoothing it down. Then tap, tap, tap against the heel of his hand he packed it. Once he put one end in his mouth and lit the other, he relaxed his shoulders, letting down the weight of the world he'd carried all day. After a few puffs, he kicked off his boots.

"Did I ever tell you about Jed Bozell's traveling show?" he asked, pulling on his cigarette again.

He'd told me about that show a hundred times or more, but each time with a different attraction. A big fat pig that wore a top hat or a man with tattoos he'd make dance by flexing his muscles. Even a bull named Misfit that could jump over a house.

I didn't believe a single one of those stories was true. In fact, I never could find anybody else who had ever heard of Jed Bozell. But I liked the make-believe of it just fine.

"Well, one time when Jed Bozell's traveling show rolled through town, he had this lady with him. A lady like none of us had ever seen before. She had on a beautiful dress, and she wore her hair all piled up on top of her head."

"What did her face look like?" I asked.

"That's the thing nobody knew. She had this mask she wore all the time. I imagine she even slept with it on. It looked like the face of a porcelain doll, all painted and shiny." He knocked a bit of ash off into the dust. "All the young fellas in town fell all over themselves to meet her and get a peek under that mask. They were just sure she was the world's most beautiful woman."

"What did she do in the show?"

"That's another thing nobody knew. Not until they went into her tent and paid her their nickel." He leaned in close and half whispered. "Turns out she was the Incredible Cussing Woman."

I giggled, covering my mouth with a hand to catch it. Daddy laughed out his nose and smoke puffed out behind it.

"A fella would pay, and then she'd say all kinds of cuss words. Enough to make even a cowboy blush." He finished off his cigarette and tossed the still-burning end into the yard. "Now, I was too young and curious for my own good. I got myself a nickel. Told Meemaw that I wanted to see the stinky pig or something like that. Then I waited for my turn in the tent."

"Did Meemaw ever find out?"

"No. And she isn't going to, right?"

I nodded, and Daddy winked.

"Before that woman started cussing," Daddy continued, "I asked if she wouldn't mind taking off the mask. She said if I could hear all her cussing without blushing or getting mad or crying, she'd let me see her real face. We shook on it and she started in on the most foul words I had ever heard."

"What did she say?"

"Well, darlin', if I repeated any of those words, Meemaw would wash my mouth with soap. Even now."

I tried my hardest to keep my giggle from turning into a big old laugh.

"Anyhow, she kept cussing, and I breathed in deep and didn't let one of them words get me worked up. Turns out I've got myself a good poker face." Daddy made his face blank and blinked twice. "When she was finished, she was stuttering, trying to think of more dirty words to say."

"Then what happened?

"I'm getting there, darlin'." Daddy grinned at me. "She agreed to make good on her end of the handshake promise and reached behind her head to unfasten the mask. She pulled it off, and I about fell out of my chair."

"What did she look like?"

"Under that mask and all the golden hair piled on top of her head was the face of a goat. She even worked her jaw around, chewing the cud."

"What did you do?"

"The only thing I could do. I ran fast as I could." He made a face like he was terrified. "She was the second scariest person I had ever seen."

"Who was the first?"

"What's that?"

"Who was the first scariest?"

"Oh, I don't know, darlin'." His smile fell, and his face turned serious, the way it did when something bothered him. He started to roll another cigarette. "It was just an old story."

"Was it Jimmy DuPre?"

Daddy didn't answer. He focused on rolling.

"I saw a newspaper with Jimmy DuPre in it." I rubbed my eye, working out a grain of dirt. "It was the story about him and you."

"That so?"

"Was he the scariest person?" I asked, knowing that if I asked enough Daddy would tell me eventually.

"I reckon so." His deep voice was just above a whisper. "Don't mind if I never meet another man like him."

"You shot him, though," I said. "You won."

"I had to shoot him, Pearl. Hated to do it. He was real young. Maybe all of twenty years old. That's still a boy, really." Daddy tipped his hat to the back of his head and rubbed at his forehead. "He was just a boy who never worked out how to be a man. Never got a chance, either."

Daddy lit his cigarette and smoked for a bit without saying anything else. A baby cried somewhere from the direction of the Hooverville. Daddy looked over that way but didn't seem worried about it.

"I tell you, the way that boy Jimmy looked at me, like I wasn't even there, I knew he'd kill me without thinking twice about it. It wouldn't have bothered him one bit." The calluses on the palm of his hand scratched against his stubbly face. "Killing him brought me no satisfaction. It wasn't justice. It never feels good to shoot a boy in the chest."

"You had to, Daddy."

"Maybe. But killing Jimmy didn't make things right. It didn't fix what he'd done." Daddy smoked that second cigarette down to a stub. "He had his pistol pointed right at my head. If I'd waited, he would have ended my life. That wasn't my day to die."

"I'm glad you did it. I'm glad it's him that's dead and not you."

He turned toward me, his eyelids closing and a long, deep sigh pushing out his mouth. He reached his arm around my shoulders, pulling me close. "I shouldn't be filling your head with nightmares. Your mama would holler at me if she knew I was telling you about that man."

"Can I tell you something?" I whispered from the safety of tight-in-his-arms. "There was a man who scared me, too."

"Who was it?"

"A man who jumped off the train."

"Fella got here just the other day? Blue eyes and shorter than me? Little guy?"

I nodded. "He killed a jackrabbit."

The words to describe what had happened were out of my reach, and I stumbled over the sounds in my mouth.

"At the rabbit drive?" Daddy asked. "You seen him there?"

"Yes, sir." Swallowing, I closed my eyes, remembering how bad it felt when he touched my face. "He hit it so hard."

"Darlin', all the folks there were doing that. Killing jackrabbits is what those drives are for."

"But, Daddy—"

"Don't you worry about him," he said. "I've already talked to him. He's just here looking for a little make-work so he can move along to California. He's all right, if you ask me."

"But—"

"Nah, darlin'. Don't give him a second thought." He let go of me. "He won't bother you."

I opened my mouth to tell him that the man had known my name and that he'd looked at me in a strange way. But no sound came out.

"Now, don't you tell your mama we've been talking about old Jimmy. She'd be sore at me for a week."

I nodded.

"I hope you never have to be so scared of a man like that in your life." He helped me to my feet. "I'd give my life to make sure of it."

Daddy scooped me up and carried me inside, all the way up to my room.

He left his boots on the front steps.

❉

Jimmy DuPre visited my dreams that night.

He pointed his gun right at my head and said every cuss word he knew. His rat face was held in a tight grimace, and he worked his jaw around, chewing on something.

Blood gushed from a hole in his chest. Still, he aimed the pistol right at me.

"You don't know how close I got to you, Pearl," he growled. "You nearly were mine."

His cornflower-blue eyes pierced right through me.

# CHAPTER FIVE

Mama made good on her promise to take food to the Hooverville. She packed up loaves of bread and lots of gold-brown biscuits and jars of baked beans in every basket and box she could find around the house. We helped her load the flatbed of Daddy's work truck.

"It won't be enough," she worried to Meemaw. "I wish I had more to take."

"Mary, you can't starve your own kids to feed them folks." Meemaw patted her hand. "It's more than they've got now."

Mama took one more trip around the kitchen to see what else she could pack while Meemaw and Daddy waited in the truck. She collected a few extra linens and blankets we didn't use.

"Just in case," she said.

She tapped her fingers against her chin, making sure she wasn't forgetting anything. Her hands were bare. So was her head.

Mama always wore her gloves and hat when she went calling. She wore them to church, too. It seemed funny to me that she would have forgotten them that day.

"Do you want me to get your gloves and hat?" I asked.

"No thank you, darlin'," she said. "I'll go without today."

Then I noticed she was still wearing her flour-sack dress with a faded apron over top, and her everyday shoes. Those shoes of hers were so worn they couldn't come to a shine no matter how hard she rubbed at them.

Mama was dressed in her normal, work-around-the-house clothes like the women she was going to meet.

I thought Mama was about the best lady in all of Cimarron County.

"Can I go with you?" I asked, following her all the way to the front door. "I'll help."

"No, darlin'. Not this time. I need you here with Beanie." She smoothed my hair, messy from the morning of working in the kitchen with her. "You know we can't leave her alone. She's like to go off wandering."

"We could make her go with us."

"Well, it's best that she stays in bed." Mama leaned near me and whispered. "It's her time."

"What's that?"

"Oh, you'll understand one of these days." Mama kissed my cheek before standing straight. "Soon enough you'll get your time, too."

I decided that I needed to figure out what my time would be and when it would come so I could do whatever it took to avoid it. If Beanie had it, I sure as heck didn't want it.

Ray would know. He knew about all the things adults liked to keep secret. I decided to ask him next chance I got.

"Mrs. Jones should be stopping by soon to pick up the laundry." She turned the knob on the front door. "You make sure she takes the lye on the kitchen counter, hear?"

"Yes, ma'am."

"Tell her that I'll be by later to pay." She smiled before walking out the door and closing it behind her.

I listened to Mama's heavy shoes on the porch steps and watched out the window as she climbed in the truck and Daddy drove away. Meemaw waved at me. I raised my hand to her, but they were gone before she saw me.

Shuffling around the living-room floor in my bare feet, I looked at all the pictures on the wall. One of me and Beanie from a few years before, our faces close together. Somehow whoever had taken the picture had got her to look right into the camera. If I hadn't known better, to look at the photo I wouldn't have thought anything was wrong with her at all.

Next I stood in front of the old, wooden cross that Mama had hanging in the middle of the wall. It had been there ever since I could remember. Millard kept a cross on the wall in his office too, but his had Jesus still on it with a white cloth around His middle and His head tipped to one side and a red gash across His belly. I asked Mama why we didn't have one like that. She said it was on account we were Baptists.

I was glad we were Baptists. I couldn't stand looking at Jesus hanging like that. It would have broke my heart every single day.

Right next to the cross, Mama had put a picture of President Roosevelt. I studied that portrait of good old FDR and told God a thank-you prayer for letting him be our president. Then I asked if He couldn't make the man hurry up with fixing Oklahoma.

*In Jesus's precious name, amen.*

On the table next to the radio sat a black telephone. I picked up what Mama had told me was the receiver and held it against my face. It didn't make a sound, and I knew it wasn't connected to anything.

All the telephone poles in our county had been broken in half over the years by dust storms.

Useless as it was, Mama liked to keep it out. She said it was pretty. I thought it was just one more thing to gather dust.

Even though Mama had told me not to play with that telephone at least a dozen times, I still put my finger in the hole of the dial and moved it all the way around. It clicked as it turned and then sped back to place when I pulled my finger out.

Jutting out my hip, I put my hand at my waist like Mama had done when the calls did go through.

"Yes, hello," I said into the silent receiver, making believe there was a person on the other end. "This is Ms. Spence calling for—"

Hard knocking on the back door made me jump and hold the receiver to my chest. Whoever was back there rapped against the glass over and over, shaking the door in its frame. I hung up the telephone, my hand shaking.

I knew Mrs. Jones would have gone to the back door, I just hadn't expected her to knock so hard.

The pounding grew louder, more impatient.

"Anybody home?"

The voice was low. A man's voice thick with insistence.

"Hello?" he called.

I couldn't place that voice, but something about it made my stomach sour with dread.

The knocking went on and on, only getting louder and louder.

"Anybody in there?"

Curiosity always did get the better of me and I made my way to the back door. The closer I got, the more my heart thudded along with the knocking. I stood flat against the wall, hoping not to be seen. More and more fear set in where my stomach wobbled. Still, I couldn't stop myself from looking.

Mama had a lacy curtain that covered the top part of the glass in the back door. Through it I saw the outline of the man, fedora on his head. Lifting his hand, he knocked yet again. I thought he looked shorter than Daddy and a good deal slimmer, too.

The man lowered his face and peeked into the window through the small gap under the lacy curtain. His eyes met mine, freezing my feet where they stood.

Those eyes were the blue that haunted me in my sleep.

"Pearl? That you in there?" His voice dropped the insisting. He talked like we were good pals. "Remember me?"

Fear pulsed through me so thick, and I couldn't even nod my head. In the days after I'd last seen him, I had pictured him as one of the savages in Daddy's book about the Old West. The picture in my mind was of an Indian holding up the scalp of a white man, just the way the smirking man had held the rabbit.

I couldn't make out his whole face through the glass, just his eyes with the dark thickness of brows over the bright blue. Still, I was sure he had a wicked grin pulling up one side of his mouth, a wad of chaw stuck in his lip, and a shirt in his pack splattered with rabbit blood.

"Aw, come on, Pearl. Don't be like this. I ain't fixing to hurt you." He winked at me. "I'm just hungry. Out looking for a little grub. You wouldn't send away a hungry man, would you?"

Rubbing sweaty palms against the sides of my dress, I wondered if Mama would send him away if she was home. Then I remembered the goats and the sheep and how Jesus had scolded those who didn't feed the hungry. The smirking man on the back porch was hungry, and if I didn't give him something to eat, I'd be denying Jesus.

Besides, he looked so different from the way I'd imagined him. His wink had been kind. Daddy had said he was okay, that he wouldn't bother me.

I took a step toward the door.

"That's it, Pearl. I ain't a bad man. Come on and open the door for your old chum."

My shaking hand turned the lock. I reminded myself that I was only doing it for Jesus. The lock made a grinding sound of gears before the door creaked open.

The man stood upright, grinning down at me. He turned and spit out a wad of chaw before smiling with his full mouth.

"Well, howdy there, little missy." He looked over my head. "Say, you here by yourself?"

"No, sir."

"That's good. Never know when a strange man's liable to knock on the door." His tongue moved across his lips, reminding me of a wolf licking its chops. "Who's here with you?"

"My big sister."

"Big sister, eh?" He stepped past me into the house. "She pretty as you?"

"I don't know," I answered. "I guess so."

"With two good-looking girls in a house, I'd think a man would take better care." He touched the lye soap on the counter. "He's the sheriff. Ain't that right?"

"Yes, sir."

He turned to me and got real close to my face. Sour milk and tobacco breath hung in the air between us, making me want to cough. "Ain't he never told you that it's dangerous to open the door for strangers?"

A thin line of spit trickled out of the corner of his mouth. He wiped it off on the back of his hand.

"Yes, sir," I answered.

"You don't mind so good, do you?" Pulling back from me, he scratched himself in a way I'd been told wasn't polite. "It's all right. We ain't strangers, are we? You and me's thick as thieves. Pearl and Eddie. Eddie and Pearl. Gonna take over the world, you and me."

It made no sense to me, what he said, and I half wondered if he was loony as Mad Mabel. But at least I'd learned his name.

"Where is that sheriff?" He took a few steps through the kitchen, running his fingertips over the counter. "Out shooting bad guys?"

He turned to see my reaction. I didn't give him one.

"He does shoot bad guys. Right?" He tilted his head. "The sheriff's the same one that shot down that DuPre boy, ain't he? What's his name?"

"Tom Spence," I answered.

"No. I mean that DuPre boy."

"Jimmy DuPre." The rat face sneered in my mind.

"That's the one." Shaking his head, he crossed his arms and leaned against Mama's counter. "Know what I heard? I heard little Jimmy DuPre never had no gun. Just put his hand in his pocket. Like this."

Eddie shoved his hand in his own pocket and pushed it up against the fabric, making it look like a pistol.

"See what I'm saying? That's all the DuPre boy done, and the sheriff shot him. Cold blood." Eddie pulled his hand out and crossed his arms again. "What do you think about that?"

"My daddy's a good man." My voice shook. "He never would have done that."

"You really believe that? How cute." Eddie pushed off the counter and made his way to the living room, looking at all the things that made it a home. "Y'all don't seem to be hurting none. Y'all got a nice place here, don't you? A radio and everything. Well, I'll be. I bet you really like living here."

"Yes, sir. We like it fine." I followed him only with my eyes. I didn't want to get too close to him but didn't want him stealing anything, either.

"Lord, but would I ever like me a house like this." Eddie took in the air through his nose. "Nice and clean. I bet y'all got somebody that cleans for you. Some colored woman to scrub the floors."

"No, sir. We do the cleaning ourselves." Out of the corner of my eye I saw the laundry basket. "We do have a lady who does our laundry. A white woman. She'll be here any minute, if you want to meet her."

"You're trying to get rid of me, ain't you?" He stuck out his bottom lip. "You're about to hurt my feelings, Pearl."

"How do you know my name?" I asked, narrowing my eyes at him and crossing my arms so he would know I meant business.

"Well." He wagged his finger at me. "You're not about to get all my secrets all at once. I'm fixing to keep the best ones to myself for a little bit. I got a list of stuff to do first."

Turning toward the back door, I saw Mrs. Jones was making her way up to the porch. She tapped on the open door and looked in at me.

"Your mama leave some washing for me?" she asked.

By the time I glanced back to where Eddie had been, he was already gone out the front door. He hadn't even bothered to shut it behind himself.

"You hear me, Pearl?" Mrs. Jones called to me. "Your mama said she had laundry for me."

"Yes, ma'am." I fumbled, trying to walk toward her and look out for Eddie, too. A chair wobbled after I knocked into it.

"Are you feeling okay?" She squinted her eyes at me from where she stood. "You upset?"

"I'm all right." Steadying the chair, I tried hard as I could to keep myself from shaking.

"This the load right here?" She stepped inside and lifted the basket of dirty clothes.

"Yes, ma'am." Then I remembered. "Mama left the soap there on the counter."

She took it and put it on the clothes. Her empty, white-blue eyes didn't leave my face. I wondered if, when she was younger, she was pretty. Ray got his looks from her, I bet.

"Mama said she'd bring money by later," I told her. "She's out running errands."

"That's just fine." Her eyebrows came together, thin as they were. It made her face look stern. "You sure you're all right?"

A sob threatened to bust its way up out of my chest, I'd been so scared. I didn't allow myself to show how I felt, though. I forced it down and nodded, thanking her for being so kind.

After she was gone, I locked the back door and rushed to the front. It was still open from when Eddie left. I pushed it 'till it latched and then turned the bolt.

When I looked out the front window, I saw Eddie standing across the street, leaning against a boarded-up house.

He tipped his hat at me before I pulled Mama's thick curtains closed.

CHAPTER SIX

Out of the twelve kids still going to school, I'd have bet every one of them wished a duster would come and flatten our one-room schoolhouse. The only person who wanted to be there was the teacher, Miss Camp.

She stood in front of the class, her behind toward us, pointing her yardstick at the map pinned to the wall.

"Mississippi . . . Arkansas . . . ," we called as she tapped the syllables of each state against the map. "Georgia . . . Florida . . ."

I tried extra hard to pay attention. I'd pinch myself to keep from daydreaming and open my eyes as big as they could get. And when Miss Camp asked a question, I worked at finding the right answer.

Mama was in a prayer group with Miss Camp at church. I never knew what snitching on me had to do with praying that the rain would come, though. I did know that if Miss Camp told Mama I wasn't paying attention, I was in for a stern talking-to and a day full of Mama's sighing.

"Now the Midwest," Miss Camp called.

"Michigan . . . Ohio . . . Indiana . . ."

"Psst." Johnny Smalley tapped me on the shoulder from behind.

Johnny spent all his time outside school at the store his father owned. That meant he got all the candy he could eat, which made him the only kid in Red River whose britches weren't falling down.

"Hey," he whispered at me, poking me in the back. He sat in the desk behind me, much to my annoyance.

I turned around, making my eyes big and round and mean so he'd know

I wasn't fond of being bothered at school. Getting in trouble on account of Buck-Toothed Johnny didn't rank high on my list of things to do.

"Ray coming after school?" he asked, not even bothering to whisper anymore.

I shrugged and turned back to Miss Camp and her big old yellowed map.

"Wisconsin . . . Illinois . . ."

"Pearl." Johnny poked me again. "I seen a hobo."

"So what?" I hissed back at him.

"I heard a man got stuck out in a duster." When he swallowed his whole head moved like he was a lizard. "Ray told me about it. Said he got blew all the way to New Mexico."

"Would you shut up, Johnny?" I didn't exactly whisper that. It was more of a half yell.

"Miss Spence?" The teacher's voice turned me around in my seat. "May I please have your attention for the last few moments of class?"

"Yes, ma'am." I knew enough not to argue that it was Johnny's fault I wasn't listening. And I knew enough that I shouldn't stand up and smack the boy across the face. I would have just gotten in a bunch more trouble for that.

Miss Camp turned back to the map.

"Iowa . . ."

The minutes clicked away on the old clock hanging on the wall. I wondered how it worked with all the dust that had collected and piled under the glass. It took all my will to keep from looking out the window to see if Ray had come, since Johnny put the thought in my head. Most days, Ray met me in the school yard to walk me home or lead me on some kind of foolish adventure. But that week he hadn't come at all.

It was Thursday, and I missed him something awful.

"Great Plains," Miss Camp called.

"North Dakota . . . South Dakota . . . Nebraska . . ."

I gave in, looking out the window. Ray wasn't there. I squinted, hoping to see some trace of him. Nothing.

"Pearl Spence," Miss Camp called. "I'd like you to stay behind. Everyone else is dismissed."

She hadn't even gotten to Oklahoma.

The handful of kids rushed out of the schoolhouse. All but Johnny. He stood next to me with his round belly leaning on my desk.

"What did you do?" he asked.

"None of your beeswax." I was so angry at him, I could have kicked him in the shins. I didn't though, for fear he would kick me back. He wore cowboy boots that had a sharp point to them.

I stayed in my seat until Miss Camp waved me over to her desk. The woman didn't have a single pretty or graceful way about her. She was straight as a board, and her frown was the cause of many deep wrinkles around her mouth. Besides, she had billy-goat whiskers coming from her chin.

When I dreamed of Daddy's Incredible Cussing Goat Woman, I saw Miss Camp rapping a yardstick against the palm of her hand and chewing the cud.

Miss Camp talked on and on in a sharp tone that was meant to remind me that she was the boss. Her words were heavy with threats to talk to both Mama and Daddy. She said she would move me to a separate corner of the room from the other students. Then she said that she would have to mark me down in my grades.

"You're too smart a girl to be wasting your schooling," she said. "Playing make-believe is for little children. You are no longer a little child, do you understand that?"

"Yes, ma'am," I mumbled, not really understanding that I was no longer a little child. I sure seemed little next to her and all the other adults I knew.

Feeling ashamed, I looked down at my shoes. I'd had to borrow that pair from Mama until the ones she ordered for me came in. The borrowed pair were enough too big that I couldn't hardly run without them falling off. I kept tripping over the toes of them when I walked.

But at least I had shoes.

"You're a lucky girl. Not all the kids around here are smart," Miss Camp said. "You hear me? You are smart."

I nodded.

"You owe it to your parents to do your best." She raised an eyebrow and stared at me, not blinking, until I thought her eyeballs would dry out. "What do you have to say for yourself?"

"I'll try harder, ma'am." It was the only thing I could think to say.

"Very well." She lowered her eyes to the paper in front of her. "You may go."

All the way home I tried not to daydream. I decided instead to name all forty-eight states.

"Washington . . . Oregon . . . California . . . ," I said under my breath.

I could only remember about ten of them.

Miss Camp had been wrong about me.

❧

Our front door was pulled to, but not latched. That wasn't too out of the ordinary for when I came home from school. I pushed it open, hoping to be welcomed by the smell of bread baking and a kiss on my forehead from Meemaw.

Mama's shoes had worn a blister on one of my heels and rubbed a raw spot on the side of the other foot. I squatted down to take them off. The buckle gave me fits and I couldn't get them loose.

I kept working on them until I noticed Beanie sitting in Meemaw's rocking chair. She held a dry washcloth in her hand, wringing it one way and then the other. She breathed in and out through her clamped-shut teeth.

"The baby's sick," she said. Her eyes were wide and fearful.

"What baby?" I asked.

The most terrible coughing I'd ever heard came from the kitchen. It sounded like whoever was doing the hacking had a lung full of something heavy that didn't want to come out. A weak crying took the place of coughing. Not too much later the coughing started up again.

Beanie winced at the sounds, wringing that washcloth even harder.

I walked on my toes to the dining-room table, careful not to let the hard heels of Mama's shoes clomp on the floor. Mrs. Jones sat sideways in the chair so she faced away from the table. Baby Rosie lay on her back across her mother's lap. The little girl's cheeks were red as could be. They about glowed. Her face was wet with tears, and her wispy hair stuck to her forehead with sweat.

Mama put her hands on the baby's cheeks. "She's burning up."

"I can't keep a mask on her. It don't matter what I do, she just keeps pulling it off soon's I turn my back." Mrs. Jones didn't lift her eyes off Rosie. "She keeps breathing in all that dust. I don't know how to make her keep her mask on."

"Ain't no use blaming yourself," Meemaw said, patting Mrs. Jones on the shoulder. "The Good Lord's got this little one in His hands."

"Luella, we need to get her to a doctor." Mama kneeled beside them and dabbed a washrag against Rosie's forehead. "There isn't much I can do for her."

Just then, little Rosie coughed so hard I thought her body was like to fall apart. It broke me up. I didn't want to cry, but I just couldn't help it. I held a hand over my mouth to keep myself quiet.

When she finally quit hacking, she wheezed in and her face pinched up from what I thought must have been pain.

"This'll pass." Mrs. Jones wiped a finger under her eye, catching a tear. "This ain't the pneumonia, is it?"

"I'm afraid it is." Mama handed Mrs. Jones the washcloth and stood. "We need to get her help."

"We don't got the money." Mrs. Jones shook her head.

"Didn't Si have work a couple weeks ago?" Meemaw asked. "He must've got paid something for it."

"It's all gone." Mrs. Jones's forehead was full of worried wrinkles. "All's I got is what I make from taking in laundry. That's only enough for a couple groceries. Si took all the rest of our money with him."

"He ain't home?" Meemaw pursed up her lips.

"No, ma'am."

Mama sighed but didn't say anything.

I wondered where Mr. Jones had gone and what he needed money for. Whatever the reason, nobody in that room liked what he was up to.

"Besides, how am I gonna get her up to Boise City?" Mrs. Jones asked. "We don't got money for gas. Our old jalopy ain't running, neither."

"Tom would drive you." Mama knelt by Mrs. Jones. "And we could pay for the doctor."

"I couldn't ever pay you back."

"We don't need you to." Mama touched Mrs. Jones's knee. "First thing tomorrow, we'll go."

"For now, let's get a little something in her." Meemaw stepped forward and patted the baby's head. "Broth might feel good on that throat, huh?"

"Pearl, go on over to the store." Mama turned her face up to me. "Tell Mr. Smalley we need a couple cubes of beef bouillon. Have him put it on my charge."

"Mary, you know I don't like taking charity . . ." Mrs. Jones closed her eyes.

"Luella, I won't have you arguing with me now." Mama bent to get a pot from under the sink. "Pearl, hurry on now, hear?"

❀

I waited at the counter for Mr. Smalley to finish up with a customer that was there before me. Tapping my fingers on the countertop, I worried I'd get back too late and that Baby Rosie would be all out of strength and not be able to swallow.

Finally Mr. Smalley noticed me and wiped his hands on his apron while he stepped my way. He wore a big, wide smile on his face. Always did.

"You seem like you're in a hurry," he said, winking at me. "What can I get for you today?"

"Baby Rosie's real sick." At first the words came slow, then they bubbled up out of me. "She's got to have some beef bouillon or else she'll never have the strength to cough all the dust out of her lungs."

"This the Jones baby?" he asked, his smile lowering. "She got the dust pneumonia? Lord have mercy."

I nodded and swallowed. "My mother said to put the bouillon on our bill. We need a couple cubes."

"Yes. Of course."

Mr. Smalley moved around the store collecting bags of dry beans and flour. He stacked my arms full of things like oil and molasses and a can of evaporated milk. Last of all, he placed the bouillon cubes in my hand.

"Tell her no charge," he said, the smile returning to his face, but it didn't reach his eyes. They stayed sad.

The whole world was full of hardship. Always was. Always would be. I thought that was the sad in his eyes.

"You all right, Mr. Smalley?" I asked.

"I'm trying to be."

"I wish you weren't sad."

"Can't much be helped, can it?" he asked.

He patted the counter twice with the palm of his hand before turning back to the wall of dry goods to fuss with a few things there.

❖

I rushed down the sidewalk toward home, my arms loaded with the gifts for Mrs. Jones and Baby Rosie. I hoped so hard that she wouldn't be ashamed to take them. If she was, I figured I would tell her they were all for Rosie anyhow. She couldn't refuse them in that case.

Trying to get home fast as I could, I forgot to watch my footing. I caught the tip of Mama's shoe in a bumped-up corner of sidewalk. I about fell flat on my face with no way to catch myself, but I kept my arms tight around the bundle of food for Baby Rosie.

Out of nowhere a pair of hands reached out and caught me, steadying me back on my feet.

"Easy," the man said, still holding my arms.

My eyes followed the dirty nails up past fingers and wrists to rolled-up sleeves. Then I looked up to his chin and the plug of chaw that bumped up his stubble-covered lip and up to his blue eyes.

Eddie's eyes were fixed on my face, soft and with his eyebrows raised.

Knowing it was him that caught me caused me to gasp.

"I didn't hurt you none, did I?" he asked, taking his hands off me.

I told him he hadn't. But where he had caught my arms was red from his grip.

"You sure was racing by with all them groceries." He stepped toward me and touched the bouillon cubes I clutched in my fingers. "You need help carrying all this?"

"Why are you here?" I asked, stepping back from him. "Why do you keep bothering me? Daddy said you wouldn't bother me."

He didn't answer, and I could tell he wouldn't, the way he turned his head and spit.

"Didn't nobody ever teach you to respect your betters?" The kindness melted from his face, and he glared at me like I was nothing more than a mound of dirt on the ground. "My ma would've whupped me good if I ever talked to somebody like that."

"I've got to go," I said, making sure to step over the bumped-up sidewalk.

"You ain't even gonna thank me for catching you?" Eddie cleared his throat. "I suppose you'd rather've fell down and skinned up your knees."

I thought of Baby Rosie's weak cough and didn't stand there a moment longer. Walking away and leaving Eddie standing there was the right thing.

I didn't have a doubt in my mind.

❖

In the middle of the night, my eyes jolted open to the black-dark of my room. Hard knocking on one of the doors had broken my sleep.

Just a dream about Eddie, I thought to myself.

I climbed over Beanie, who was snoring like she didn't have a care. Feet on the floor, I stretched, letting go of a good, long yawn. More knocking. Grabbing a pinch of my skin, I clamped down to make sure I wasn't dreaming.

Then the screaming started.

I stumbled my way to the window and pushed aside the curtains. Silver moonlight thinned the outside darkness. Ray stood on the back porch, holding his face with both his hands, and he screamed like the world was about to end.

Down the steps I rushed, to the kitchen, and grabbed the door knob. Daddy pushed me aside and opened the door himself.

"Ray, son, simmer down." He put a hand on Ray's shoulder and pulled him inside. "I can't understand a word you're saying."

Ray gulped in air, his mouth gaping and his hands working at rubbing tears off his face.

"Son, what's this all about?"

"It's Baby Rosie." Ray's voice fizzled into a barely there whisper. "She's gone."

"No." Daddy sighed the word.

"She got to coughing, and she couldn't stop," Ray went on. "She couldn't catch another breath."

"Your father isn't to home, is he?"

Ray covered his eyes and shook his head to say no. He barked out his sobs. Daddy grabbed hold of him and pulled him close, circling around him with strong arms. He held him until Ray's crying quieted. Loosening his hold, he put his hands on Ray's shoulders.

"Son, listen here. Look at me. Listen. You go on home. Your mama's needing you to be strong. Hear?" Daddy lowered his face to Ray's. "She can't see you like this. Get together before you go home. Then—do you hear me, son? Then you got to put your arms around her and let her cry for a bit. Like I done with you."

Ray nodded, shaking loose a couple tears. His jaw jutted out, and his lips pulled thin.

"You about ready?" Daddy asked.

"I don't want to go alone," Ray said.

"I'll go with you then." Daddy stood up. "Just let me get dressed."

Ray's whole body shook, but his face stayed strong. He looked more like a man than I ever saw a boy look.

"When your father gets home, you come over here, and I'll let you sit in my root cellar and cry it out," Daddy said, turning to go to his bedroom.

Mama stepped toward him. I hadn't realized she was there. She hadn't even taken the time to swing a robe over her shoulders. The dark of the room and the moonlight made her nightgown seem wispy as fairy wings.

"Tom . . ." She touched Daddy's back when he passed her.

"We need a board. Something to put the baby on." Daddy turned his head toward the table.

Mama nodded and the two of them pulled on either end. Daddy lifted one of the wooden leaves out. They pushed, clunking the table back together.

"I'll get Hank Eliot," Mama whispered.

It was then I realized that when Ray said Baby Rosie was gone he meant she'd died. Nobody ever sent for Hank Eliot unless they needed an undertaker. I let myself slide down the wall to the floor.

Without another word between them, Mama put the day's leftover coffee on the stove top while Daddy went about getting dressed. He buttoned his shirt and strapped on his holster. Mama poured the coffee into a thermos and handed it to him as he made for the door, the table leaf tucked under his arm.

"You lock up behind me," he whispered. "I'll be back later on."

Mama locked the door like he'd said. Her fingers lifted one side of the lacy curtain so she could watch him and Ray out the window. After just a few breaths, she backed herself into a chair, the same one Mrs. Jones had sat in with Baby Rosie on her lap. Mama's shoulders curled forward, and her body shook with crying. After a moment of silent sobs, Mama moaned and coughed out her sadness.

I had never seen Mama cry before that moment, and it shocked me, stealing my breath. I'd never realized before that mamas could weep.

Whenever I cried, Mama would rub little circles on my back with the meat of her hand and whisper "hush" into my ear. She shushed my whimpering many-a-time with that warm, gentle voice of hers.

That night, I wanted to do that same thing for her.

I pushed myself up off the floor and shuffled my feet toward her, fine grains of dust pushing into the soles of my bare feet.

When I touched Mama's back, she turned and, without even looking at me, wrapped her arms all the way around me, pulling me onto her lap. She cried into my hair and held me tighter than I ever remembered her doing before.

❖

Meemaw knew what had happened without Mama or me having to tell her. She came in, her body slouched over and her steps stiff, and fried us up a couple eggs from the few laying chickens we still had. She started the percolator to gurgle new coffee.

The sun hadn't even started to rise, but we were up.

Mama waited until the coffee was ready and slung back a cup of it before getting dressed. She told Meemaw she was going for Hank.

I waited until Mama'd left and I had forced down half an egg before I asked Meemaw if she'd tell me something.

"What'd you like to know?" she asked, busying herself with scrubbing the fry pan.

"Daddy said he needed a board for Baby Rosie," I said.

"Uh-huh."

"He took a leaf of the table."

She turned and tilted her head at the table. "Oh. So he did."

"Why did he need to take it?"

"To lay her out on."

I didn't ask her to explain what that meant, and she didn't go on. I figured it was something that would've only made me even more sad than I already was.

I ate the rest of my egg, even though I didn't feel hungry. I didn't feel much of anything except for the loss of Rosie. Loss so large I forgot about everything else in the world.

❧

They couldn't bury Baby Rosie in Red River. The cemetery was in a grave of its own under mounds of dust. So the Jones family piled into Daddy's truck, Ray and his father in the back with the tiny coffin, and Mrs. Jones and Mama up front with Daddy. They drove east, a few counties over where they could give her a proper burial.

I couldn't go, and I understood why not. Still, it made my heart hurt to stay home on that day.

I expected the ache in me was about half of what it was in Ray.

# CHAPTER SEVEN

Mama had invited Millard and Mrs. Jones over to listen to the president's fireside chat. She set out a few straight-backed chairs in the living room, making a semicircle around the radio, and perked a fresh pot of coffee, the smell of it filling the house with richness.

Once they'd arrived, we took seats, and Daddy switched on the radio. Millard passed out candy to Beanie and me, and we were already sucking on the sweets, letting them melt on our tongues. Ray hadn't come. Mrs. Jones said he didn't feel all too well.

I asked if he had a cough, and she shook her head. Just a stomachache, she told me.

The president's voice warbled, singing over the pop and crackle of the radio. I pretended that it was the noise of his fireplace. Half of his words sounded like a foreign language to me, but it seemed that all the grown-ups understood him just fine. Their heads nodded, and sometimes one of them would make a *hm-mm* sound in the back of their throat.

"Why's he talking like that?" I asked Mama.

She shushed me.

"He's from New York," she whispered in my ear. "That's how they talk there."

I guessed folks from New York didn't use the letter *r* as much as Oklahomans did. I tried a few of his words under my breath.

"Owe-nahs" and "tray-dahs."

I only got to try a few before Mama whispered my name and shook her head.

All I had left to do was listen, and I just didn't follow too well. He used so many big words I didn't understand. A lot of his ideas were beyond my knowledge. But he had Daddy and Millard's interest.

As for me, it didn't make monkey sense.

He did say something I understood well enough. "My friends," the president said. He said it so many times I decided to believe him, that we really were his friends and that he was ours.

Friends came to visit, and I imagined how it would be when he would come. He would drive into Red River in a long car. The sun would glint off the automobile, but not in a way that would hurt anybody's eyes. The president would have a big map spread out on the seat next to him with a circle drawn around all the places he'd stop on his trip. Red River would be ringed in bright blue. All the town would come out of their houses and dugouts and line the streets, waving at him as he drove past.

A regular old parade like folks around Cimarron County had never seen before.

He would make sure to go slow so that he wouldn't kick up too big a cloud of dust behind him.

Once he reached our house, he'd cut the engine and get out of his car. He stood at least a head taller than all the other men from Red River.

"Sorry Mrs. Roosevelt couldn't come along this time," he would tell us, shaking hands with Daddy and winking at Beanie. He would tell us how she was busy sewing dresses for orphans and canning jelly for widows. "Next time I'll bring her along for the ride."

He would come in for a cup of coffee and a thick slice of Mama's johnnycake. He'd let her drizzle molasses all over top of it, even if he was from New York. He'd hum as he ate it because it tasted so good. He'd make sure to ask for her recipe so Mrs. Roosevelt could make it for him at home.

After he'd had his bite to eat and his cup of coffee, I would take his hand and march him right over to the Jones's dugout. He'd let our hands swing between us as we walked.

Once we made it to the sharecroppers' cabins, I'd point at the Jones's place and say, "You see that wall caving in there? And if we go inside, you'll see the centipedes."

He would shake his head. "Oh my. Oh my."

Last, I would hold his hand tighter so that we'd both have courage when we looked at Baby Rosie's empty cradle. We'd stand together, gazing down at it and making no noise at all because we would want to respect her memory. I would pretend not to see the tear that hung on his eyelashes.

President Roosevelt would see with his own eyes what the dust had done to us. He couldn't help but let his heart get broken.

"I want to help," he would say, setting his jaw.

He would walk right up to Mrs. Jones and shake her hand.

"He-yah's a little something to help you, my friends," he'd say, reaching into his own pocket for a wad of folding money. "I'll have Mrs. Roosevelt send ov-ah some fresh socks she's been knitting. My good friends, everything is going to get bett-ah for you."

Mrs. Jones would wipe her eyes, taking the money into her hands. She would thank me for bringing the president over so he could help them. Mr. Jones would be there, too. Maybe he'd even get a job out of the whole thing. He'd make enough money to build a new home above ground.

Then the president would walk me home, lifting me high on his shoulders. Even though I was far too big for that kind of thing, I'd let him carry me. A man that kind had to have been mighty strong.

The click of the radio turning off broke through my daydream.

"Well," Daddy said, standing.

He and Millard walked Mrs. Jones home, and Meemaw put away the mending she'd been working during the talk.

"Mary, let me get them dishes washed up." Meemaw sighed when she got up, her face wrinkling with the effort. "Pearl, I'll ask you to do the drying."

In the kitchen, Meemaw let the water rise up over her blue-veined, thin-skinned hands and well up past her wrists. She sighed and smiled. "That feels mighty good on my old fingers."

After a minute or two of soaking, she started washing up the dishes and handed them to me to wipe with the towel. It only took us a minute or two to get them all washed up and put away.

"Now," Meemaw said, her dishrag dripping. "Go on and give your mama a kiss. Tell her good night."

Mama hadn't moved from her seat since Daddy had turned off the radio. Her eyes were rimmed red with purple crescents under them.

"Good night, Mama," I said.

"Is it time for bed already?" she asked.

Nodding, I stepped toward her and leaned over to kiss her cheek.

"That was nice, darlin'." She smiled, but not the kind that would have showed her teeth.

"Are you okay, Mama?"

"I will be," she answered. "I've just been thinking about Rosie a lot."

Mama's fingers fumbled with a bit of hair that had gotten loose from my braid. She pushed it behind my ear.

"I'm sorry about Baby Rosie," I whispered.

"Me too, darlin'."

❧

Beanie and I lay next to each other in our bed. The springs under our mattress creaked as she flipped and flopped, trying to get comfortable.

"Quit it," I said.

She didn't.

Before I even gave it a second thought, I jabbed her with my elbow. "Lay still," I grumped.

That time, she did what I said. Except she cried out, too.

Hurting her made me feel all kinds of mean and terrible.

"I'm sorry," I said.

Her hollering cry turned into a whimper, which turned into her staring at me with her out-of-focus eyes.

Beanie was born good as dead. That was what Mama had told me.

Something or another was wrapped around her neck, cutting off the air she needed. She was blue and not breathing. Somehow they got her untangled, and she got enough air in her lungs to come to life.

Baby Rosie was born just fine. Mama had told me that, too. She was pink and screaming her entrance into the world. Then her air ran out.

Jesus didn't call her forth or take her hand and ask her to wake up.

Boy, did I ever wish He would have woken her up.

❀

I dreamed of Baby Rosie. She lay on a leaf from our kitchen table, her arms crossed over her chest and her eyes closed. The whole town of Red River stood outside the Jones's dugout, crying and carrying on.

Jesus came along and walked right up to the dugout, ducking His head to go inside. He knelt next to Rosie and picked up her hand.

He called her "My friend."

I did believe He meant it.

# CHAPTER EIGHT

Mama stood out in the back yard, beating her curtains, knocking the dust out of them. She wore a mask over her mouth and nose, so I couldn't see much of her face, but I was sure she wore a snarl under the cotton. The way she attacked those curtains with her rug beater, I was glad not to be on the receiving end of her wrath.

Shoulders slumped and chest heaving, she tucked the rug beater under one arm and smoothed her hair.

Mama fought the dust every day and lost each time. Even so, she wouldn't give up. Problem was, her never-ending battle meant we had to fight alongside her.

"Pearl," she called to me when she caught me watching her. "Did you girls get all the clothes that need washed out of your room?"

Without waiting for my answer, she turned back to the curtains, pulling them from the line.

"Go on and get everything. Mrs. Jones is coming soon."

"Yes, ma'am."

Beyond Mama, on the road from the sharecroppers' cabins, Mrs. Jones shuffled in the dirt toward our house. I tried to hide the disappointment that Ray wasn't coming alongside her.

"And tell Beanie to bring her laundry, too," Mama hollered.

When I got to our room, Beanie had her few dresses crumpled up on our bed. She still had on her nightgown, even though it was the middle of the afternoon. That nightie of hers was stained with sweat around the neck and under the arms, and I could tell just by looking at her that it smelled.

"You need to change so Mrs. Jones can wash your nightie," I said, collecting a pile of clothes from the floor. "And get your dirty stuff together."

"It's all dirty." She sniffled. "I don't remember when nothing was clean."

"That's why Mrs. Jones is coming."

"She can't get it clean. It don't matter how hard she scrubs it, she can't get the dust out."

"Girls," Mama called from the bottom of the steps. "Come on."

I grabbed Beanie's pile and shoved it into her arms before taking up my own. We carried them down the steps, me in front. Beanie had to stop a couple times to pick up a sock she dropped or a dress that had almost gotten tangled in her legs. She slipped, her foot kicking the back of my calf.

She would have pushed me all the way down the steps if I hadn't rushed down the last few stairs.

Mrs. Jones stood just inside the back door. Way down in my stomach felt sore when I looked at her. Even though she kept her face pointed at the floor, I could see that something was wrong with her eye.

"Well, Luella, what in heaven's name happened to you?" Mama's voice went up in tone, like she was singing. "Come in here. Let me see what I can do for that."

"It's fine," Mrs. Jones said, waving her off. "It's nothing."

Beanie about knocked me over, but I didn't take my eyes off Mrs. Jones. Her cheek was red and purple, and her eye was swelled shut.

Meemaw caught a gasp in her hands, and she shook her head. "Oh, darlin', you can't let him do you this way."

"Mother," Mama warned. "Luella, you go on and sit down there at the table. You hungry?"

"I ain't never hungry no more." Mrs. Jones sat at the table. "Mary, I'm fine. I am."

Mama soaked a washcloth in clean water, wringing out the extra drops. "Well, that eye doesn't look fine. It looks sore."

"That ain't why I come here."

"I know why you came, and we've got it all ready for you." Mama looked over her shoulder at us. "Right girls? You go on and put the clothes in the basket over there."

When Mrs. Jones took notice of us, she covered the side of her face with one of her hands.

"What happened, Mrs. Jones?" I asked, dumping my load into the basket.

"Pearl Louise, mind your manners." Mama shot me her hush-up look. "I'm sorry, Luella. She knows better than that."

"It's all right." Mrs. Jones lowered her hand, letting it rest in her lap. She opened her hurt eye as much as she could, wincing at the pain. Under the thick lid was her eye, red and just a sliver of gray.

"Does it ache?" I asked, stepping toward her.

She nodded. "Something awful."

"Who hit you?" I stepped closer yet.

"Pearl Louise," Mama scolded.

"No, Mary. It don't do no good to get after her. She's got to learn about the ways of men sometime, I reckon." Mrs. Jones let a tear roll out from her good eye. "I wish somebody would've warned me about how they can be."

"How who can be?"

"Men. Husbands." She let the sore eye close again. "Mr. Jones ain't been doing so good since Rosie . . ."

She didn't say the word, but I knew what she meant. I was glad she didn't say it. We all would have broken if she had.

"I said something wrong. I told him he should've been here when Rosie took sick," she went on. "He took all his sadness out on me. He don't know what else to do with himself. I can't hardly blame him, I guess."

"Luella, you're scaring the girls." Mama nodded at me to go upstairs.

"I'm sorry." Mrs. Jones shifted in her seat and looked at me with her one eye. "Girls, I'm sorry."

"He shouldn't hurt you." Beanie still had the dirty clothes in her arms. "Nobody should hurt nobody else. It ain't right."

Mrs. Jones turned toward Beanie, her mouth wide open. "Sometimes men just get mad. He blames me for Rosie." She licked her lips, but they still looked dry. "I suppose I could've done more for her. I tried my best."

"It don't matter." Beanie held her dirty clothes tighter against her filthy, stinking nightie. "He shouldn't hurt you."

"He's not in his right mind." Mrs. Jones's voice cracked. "He's been drinking a lot."

"Ain't you hearing me?" Beanie stomped her foot. "Ain't nobody got a right to hurt nobody else!"

She dropped the clothes on the floor and ran out the back door.

"Pearl," Mama called to me. "Catch her."

I ran out after my sister, leaving Mama and Meemaw to see to Mrs. Jones. I hoped they'd give her something to make that eye stop hurting.

Beanie wasn't too far ahead of me and I could have caught her easy, but I reckoned she needed a minute or two all to herself. I slowed down to a walk, keeping my eye on her. Never had I seen her upset like that. She cried so loud I could hear her from ten paces behind. She stumbled a couple times, and I wondered if her eyes were tear-blurred.

She made it all the way to the courthouse and up the steps. Still in her dingy nightie, she pulled on the doors with all the muscle she had. The doors wouldn't budge. She slapped them with both of her hands and called for Daddy.

"He's not there," I called to her. "He's out with Millard."

Crossing her legs, she collapsed on the old marble porch, rocking the way she always did, the fabric of her nightgown pulled up too far on her thighs. When I got closer, I could hear her grunting noises.

If the sounds Beanie made really was the language of angels, like Meemaw said, I hoped they were listening up. And I hoped she talked to them about Ray, too. I wondered if he had an eye that matched his mother's.

Taking the steps on tiptoe, I watched my sister. She pinched her eyes shut, clamping them for all she was worth, grimacing like she was in pain. I plopped down next to her and about yelped when the cold steps slapped against my legs.

She didn't move or even show that she knew I was next to her.

"It's okay, Beanie," I said, trying to break her trance.

It didn't work.

So, I wrapped both my arms around her shoulders and rocked and swayed right along with her. My body close to hers didn't make her slow down or quiet her voice. I wondered if she could feel me, even.

"It's bad and bad and bad," Beanie said, still rocking.

"What is?" I asked.

"All of it." She opened her eyes for a second before pinching them together again. "All."

"I know." I thought I knew what she meant.

I closed my eyes against the sun that beat down on us, feeling the dust-thick air as I breathed it in. We'd had green fields once. And blue skies, too. A long time before, everyone had plenty. More than they needed, in fact.

With the sun soaking through my eyelids, making behind the lids red, I remembered the days of plenty. It was a hard-to-hold memory, I'd been so little then. Still, I remembered enough to make me long for those easier times.

When I opened my eyes, all I saw was a land drowning in dust.

But then I saw something else. Eddie walking down the street, smoking a cigarette. He got to the end of the road and walked off into a field of nothing.

❖

We were all at supper when Daddy heard about Mrs. Jones's black eye. He breathed out of his nose and shook his head but kept on eating.

"Si's gonna feel real bad about it once he sobers up," Daddy said, pushing a piece of bread across his plate to sop up the gravy.

"I don't believe that man ever is sober," Meemaw said, pinching her lips tight together.

Daddy shrugged. "You might be right about that."

"Aren't you going to do something?" Mama asked, her own dinner just picked at. "She can't live like that. Ray neither."

"Not much I can do, Mary. Luella would just say she fell."

"She never did fall," Beanie whispered. "That man hit her hard as he could."

We finished eating, just the sound of silverware on plates filling the space between the five of us. Daddy leaned back in his chair and crossed his arms, his eyelids blinking heavy.

"I don't like it either," he said. "Not one bit. It's just the way of things."

❈

Daddy peeked in our room late into the night. Another night of not being able to sleep for both of us, I guessed.

"Daddy?" I whispered, trying not to wake Beanie.

"That's me." He stepped in from the hallway. "Why aren't you asleep? Bad dream again?"

I didn't say a thing, but I did sit up and crawl to the foot of my bed. Beanie kicked at us in her sleep before curling up in a ball.

"I don't know that I could sleep with her kicking me, either." He smiled at me—I could just barely see it in the dark room. He pulled me close to him and kissed the top of my head.

"Why do men hit women?" I asked, trying to remember to be quiet for Beanie's sake.

"Well, I don't reckon I've got a good answer to that." He cleared his throat. "You seen Mrs. Jones's face, didn't you?"

I nodded.

"Was it bad?"

"Yes. She couldn't hardly open her eye."

"She'll be just fine once the swelling goes down. I've had a few shiners like that myself," he said. "Not all men hit their women, you know."

"Yes, I know."

"I've never hit your mama. Never would." He pushed me forward, turning me so I could see right into his face. The in-between place of his eyebrows scooped up toward his forehead. "You never let a man hit you, hear?"

I nodded and licked my lips. "What if a man does?"

"Fight back."

Daddy held me close, his scent of cigarettes and coffee and sweat wrapping around me. On anybody else, the smell would have made me cover my nose. But on Daddy, it smelled like being safe.

"I ever tell you about the time I broke up the still over to the other end of town?" His voice changed, dipped lower in tone. His storytelling voice.

"Yes, but tell me again, please."

I hoped the story would get the picture of swelled-shut eyes out of my mind.

"Well, there was a bunch of bootleggers that came to Red River to make hooch. That's what they called liquor, you know. Of course, this was when booze was against the law."

"Why was it against the law?"

"Now, that's a whole other story, ain't it?" His mouth opened wide in a yawn. "Anyhow, these bootleggers come from Arkansas and set up a still. That's what they made the booze in. Well, the old federal marshal followed them here and carted them all to jail. Folks here in Red River were pretty sore about that."

"But they were outlaws, weren't they?"

"Criminals making moonshine for a bunch of dry men." He laughed. "Well I was the one had to go out to the place and break up that still so nobody'd get a mind to make their own booze. I didn't want some dumb kid killing a bunch of folks with bad liquor. So I took the whole thing apart. You know what I found in there?"

I shook my head, even though I did know.

"Pounds of sugar. So much of it, I needed to use a wheelbarrow to move it." My head bounced on his chest when he laughed. "I took that sugar and gave a little to all the folks around. Kids were following me all through town. It was like a parade. I never did feel more like a hero."

He helped me get back to my place in bed, moving Beanie's foot so I had enough room. The clean sheet pulled under my chin, he kissed my cheek.

"I do love you, Pearlie Lou."

Sleep came fast and with it, dreams. Dreams of my daddy.

# CHAPTER NINE

The whole summer had passed by without revival coming to Red River. That was fine by me. I never much cared for them anyhow. All the strangers setting up in town and the big tent pitched in one of the old fields. The preachers hollering about the wrath of God and how we all deserved the fires of hell. Then they'd collect the money and move on to the next county.

It seemed that year all the traveling preachers had forgotten about us, and most of the town didn't miss the to-do.

Meemaw, though, she'd gone on and on all summer about it. She determined that a week of revival would come to our small town even if she had to bring it herself.

When Meemaw made up her mind on something, it was near impossible to convince her otherwise.

She'd even invited Pastor Ezra Anderson and Mad Mabel to dinner to talk it over with him.

"This town needs getting brought forth to life," she'd told him, spooning a second helping of peas on his plate. "We need ourselves a great awakening."

"That's true, sister. It is." Pastor paused to push his peas into a line on his knife. He stuck his tongue out the side of his mouth in concentration. "Trouble is, we don't got the money to pay anybody to come out here to preach."

Mad Mabel stabbed her peas with a fork, stacking them one on top of another.

"Then you do the preaching." Meemaw refilled Pastor's coffee cup. "You want a little sugar in that?"

"No thank you," he said, lifting the knife of peas to his mouth and letting them tumble to his tongue. He chewed a minute and then sipped his coffee. "I guess I could do the preaching. Problem is, we don't got a tent to meet in."

"Yes we do." Meemaw's whole face wrinkled with her smile. "Rather, you do."

"Sister . . ." Pastor shook his head and then glanced at his wife. "I know what you're thinking, and I don't like it all that much."

Mrs. Anderson's eyes switched back and forth, back and forth like she was seeing something swing in front of her face.

"Brother. Pastor. I got plenty of thread. I don't mind patching that old thing up." Meemaw spread a little soft butter on a slice of bread and put it on Pastor's plate. Then she sat next to him, leaning close toward him. "Pastor, we got all kinds of folks coming through town these days. They ain't staying but a night or two, maybe a week. But they're all hungry. Hungry for bread of flour and yeast and for Bread of Life. Mary and me will make plenty of the rising kind, you got to provide the life-saving one."

Pastor folded his bread in half before taking a bite.

❖

Meemaw's prayer circle planned a revival like our town hadn't seen in twenty years. Not that I would have known the difference, but that was what they told everybody. They had arranged for Mama to play the piano and lead the hymn sings. Each night, all the folks that came would take home a loaf or two of bread.

They had it all figured out. The last part was the tent.

Less than a week before the revival was to start, Meemaw had Millard and Daddy drag an ancient, shredded tent into our living room.

"Now, you boys spread it across the floor," she instructed, a large grin spreading on her face.

"Yes, ma'am," Millard said, bundling the edges so they would fit within the walls. "This old thing's as dusty as—"

"I won't hear no complaining. I ain't asking you to do the mending, am I?"

"Where's this from?" I asked, stooping so I could touch the edge of the tent. It was thick canvas, worn soft by use.

"Oh, Pastor's had this old thing up in the church steeple since, heavens, I don't know how long." Meemaw made her way to the rocking chair and stuck her needle between her lips when she steadied herself to sit. "Hand me that edge, would you?"

I lifted the canvas, draping it on her lap like a blanket.

"Thank you, darlin'," she said. Then she made her fingers busy, threading the needle. "I reckon he put this up there right before he went off to fight in the war."

"Tell her how he got it," Millard said, crossing his arms and grinning. "Pearl, you'll never believe it."

"I'll tell her soon's she starts patching this up with me."

I crawled closer to the tent and took a needle and some thread from Meemaw's sewing basket.

"Back before the war, he traveled around with a circus." Meemaw's eyes twinkled.

"He did?" I was sure my eyes would pop out of my skull and my mouth would get stuck open.

"Yes indeed," Millard said. "And I'll leave you ladies to cluck about it."

Millard nodded for Daddy to follow and they left the house. I pushed my needle through the canvas, feeling the thickness of the fabric.

"Back when we were all much younger, Pastor was the ringmaster of a circus that went all over the country. Never did see such a good show." She stuck out her tongue, working a difficult spot. "He had a couple clowns and an acrobat and a bearded lady."

"Was her beard real?" I asked.

"Mind your stitches, Pearl." She nodded at my idle hands. "Yup, her beard was real, all right. It grew right out of her face like a man's. Always had somebody pull on it to check. She didn't mind knocking them out when they done that."

"What is going on in here?" Mama asked, standing in the front door.

"It's Pastor's revival tent."

"It looks like a circus tent." Mama knelt on the floor beside me, checking my stitches.

"I was telling Pearl about Pastor's circus. And the bearded lady." Meemaw pulled on the tent. "A few of the fellas asked her to prove she wasn't a man. I do believe she broke a couple noses for that."

"Mother," Mama scolded.

"There was even a two-headed cat for a while. Never knew if that thing was real or not." She closed her eyes and chuckled. "I guess one of them heads was real, at least."

While I pushed my needle up and down through the old tent, I thought about how much more folks would enjoy church if Pastor had his bearded lady there and the two-headed cat.

"Mrs. Anderson used to read tea leaves," Meemaw whispered. "You know what that means?"

"Now, don't fill her head—"

"She'd tell people's fortunes," Meemaw interrupted.

An awed gasp pulled into my lungs.

"She believed in witchcraft in those days. Not no more, I reckon."

I thought of the snakes turned belly up on her fence and wondered if that wasn't witchcraft, I didn't know what was.

"Pastor married her before he found Jesus." Meemaw went back to her quick stitching. "Both of them turned from their ways. But then Mabel lost her mind."

"Is she a witch?" I asked.

"Pearl, that isn't something for a girl to say," Mama said. "Mrs. Anderson isn't a witch. She's touched."

"You ever have her potato salad?" Meemaw asked. "Takes witchcraft to cook like that."

"How did Pastor find Jesus?" I asked.

"Well I don't know exactly. But it happened after the war," Meemaw said.

"He find Jesus in all that fighting?" I asked.

"Nah. I don't reckon he seen God in any trenches." She shook her head. "I suspect he found a place God wasn't."

"God's everywhere," Mama said.

"Well, I guess there's some places He's harder to see." Meemaw clucked her tongue. "We never do find a need for Jesus until we're some place where we can't find Him so easy."

The three of us sewed for a good time, none of us finding a word to say. The sounds of people walking past our house caught my attention. I tried to see them out the window, but they'd already passed.

What I did see outside was Red River. Streets lined by boarded-up buildings and dead dreams. Ruined fields and falling-apart lives.

"Meemaw?" I asked, easing back down, the tent weighing heavy on my lap.

She responded with a humming sound.

"Is God in Oklahoma?" I half feared she'd get upset at me for the question, but I had to know. "Or did He leave?"

She lowered her sewing and her hands to rest on her thighs. Then she smiled at me so that I could feel the warmth of it.

"He didn't go nowhere, Pearl. He's here. All's I got to do is look at you to know it's so."

"But He's real mad at us, isn't He?"

"Well, that's a question, ain't it." She licked her lips. "What makes you think God's mad?"

"The dust." I shrugged and pushed my pin into the canvas. "Pastor says God sent it to punish us."

"Darlin', the dust just came. It's a thing that happened, that's sure. But it ain't judgment, honey." Clearing her throat, she winced and touched the spot on her neck below her chin. "Pastor says all kinds of things, don't he? He ain't right about all of them. He means well. It's just . . ."

I waited for her to finish, not wanting to break the idea she had in her mind.

"It's just when a man's done as much wrong as Pastor did in the old days, he wants to make sure he's right with God. I think he's so scared of being wrong, he's got to be loud and holler to convince himself he ain't going back to his old ways."

Mama tsked and didn't look up from her stitches. I wondered what that could mean.

"We all done wrong, Pearlie. It's the way of people," Meemaw said. "But the gospel good news is that Jesus come and took the load of what we done."

"I wish Jesus could come and take all this dust from us," I said, feeling the sting of tears in my eyes.

"He will, darlin'. One of these days, He'll save us."

Meemaw went right back to patching up the tent.

❖

With only a few days until the revival, Meemaw sent me around, knocking on doors, to invite folks to come hear the Word of the Lord.

"In case any of them haven't heard about it," she'd said.

She said this as we stood on the porch, looking out at the big, newly mended tent sitting in the middle of a field. I thought if anybody didn't know about the revival, they were most likely blind. The green-and-orange-and-red panels of the tent broke up the tan landscape so you couldn't have missed it if you wanted to.

Daddy and Millard had set it up the day before with a crowd of kids gathered around their heels, thinking the circus was coming to town. They were more than a little disappointed when they found out it was just a revival.

"Go on and tell them that meetings start at six on Sunday evening, hear?" Meemaw said, pushing me down the steps. "And don't forget to tell them about the bread."

Most folks met me on their porches and nodded when I told them all about the revival and the bread. They thanked me and watched to make sure I made it to the next place okay.

I was tired and hungry and thirsty by the time I got to the sharecropper cabins. But not too many of them still had people living there, so I got from house to house real quick.

I saved the Jones's house for last, hoping Ray would be there.

I'd hardly seen him since Rosie died. When I did, all he wanted to do was walk. It was on one of those walks that he told me his father wasn't right in his mind for all the moonshine he drank. He said that was why he'd get so mean.

Knocking on the door of the Jones's dugout, I got a nervous stomach, worrying that Ray's father would answer and that he'd be mean to me. Stepping back, I waited. No one came to the door, so I knocked again.

I heard coughing from out back behind the dugout, so I followed the sound.

Mr. Jones sat on an overturned bucket, his hands holding the weight of his head. The whole of his body shook and jerked. He moved so strangely I wondered if he was having some kind of a fit.

I didn't know what I could do for him or if I should. He looked so much smaller than I'd ever seen him look before. That man who had swelled his wife's eye with a strike of his fist. The man who poured all the money they had down his throat in the form of whiskey. That man sat behind his broken-down house and cried like a little boy.

He sure seemed weak to me.

The stronger part of me wanted to kick a toe-full of dust at him and tell him he had no right to cry. To tell him that misery was what he deserved because it was what he'd dealt to his family for years.

But a weaker side of me felt soft toward him. I hated that side of me and wanted to shut it up. I just couldn't, though.

I gathered up my breath and took a step toward him.

"Mr. Jones?" I said.

He tucked his head tighter to his body.

"You okay?" I took another step.

He waved me off with one of his floppy hands.

"Go on," he said. "Get."

When I didn't move, he lifted his head. Crooked lines of red cut through eyes stained yellow where they should have been white, and his face looked like it could use a good shave. All of him was filthy. I could smell him from where I stood.

"Please," he hissed at me through broken and tobacco-stained teeth. "Get."

I never did invite Mr. Jones to the revival. Instead, I ran all the way home, more angry than sad.

❖

It took Daddy and Millard plus a couple other men from town to move the piano from the church to the revival tent and put it on the makeshift stage. Then they set up benches and hung a couple lights from the ceiling.

Meemaw had her table of bread all set up, and Mama put hymnals on each seat. Beanie and I had paper fans to hand to everyone who came in, and Pastor stood at the door of the tent to greet the arrivals.

I watched his face as the folks came in. He started with a big smile and bright eyes that fell into half a grin and droopy eyes as only a few people came. Most of those who took seats on the benches were of gray hair and wrinkled faces. Not a one of them was from the Hooverville.

"Well," he said, slapping his hands on his thighs. "I guess we'll get more tomorrow night."

Mama started off pounding out the songs on the piano. She didn't have to look at the music in front of her—she'd played those hymns all her life. When she'd get to a part of the song that touched her, she'd close her eyes. I liked to think that was because she felt the music all the way down to her toes.

The last hymn on the list for the night was "Amazing Grace." All the voices around me shook out the words. Meemaw hugged the hymnal to her chest and closed her own eyes, swaying a bit from side to side.

Daddy had told me once that Meemaw had been a Holy Roller back in the old days—that was why she rocked when she sang. Mama just said it was how the Spirit moved her.

Whatever it was, I always got a bit choked up when Meemaw did it. It seemed she understood God in a way I never would. I figured if Meemaw loved Him, He must be somebody worth paying attention to.

Mama got to the last verse, the part that said, "The earth shall soon dissolve like snow," and she stopped playing. The few around me kept on singing even without the piano. She closed the cover over the piano keys and stood up from the bench.

I didn't think she wanted everybody seeing her cry.

When I looked around, I saw that she wasn't the only one.

❖

The third night of the revival, a family from the Hooverville showed up. I figured it was for the bread, but they sang all the words to the songs without having to look at the hymnal. And they even closed their eyes during the prayer time.

Mama put her hand on my leg to let me know I should stop staring and pay attention.

Pastor went on about the parable Jesus told about the man who stored everything up in his barn. He had so much, he built another barn so it would all fit. Pastor hollered about how the man had done all that saving and packing away just to have his life required of him.

I didn't have one idea why Pastor was hitting so hard on his Bible as he told us that story. There wasn't a single person in Red River or even all of Oklahoma who had built a second barn to hold all their extra food. The barns they did have were full of nothing but dust, and I knew for sure they wanted to get rid of that soon as they could.

I snuck a few extra peeks at the Hooverville people. A man, woman, and three boys. All five of them with eyes half closed with tired. Those ten eyes stayed stuck on Pastor as he went on preaching.

Then, one of the boys, the smallest of the three, caught me watching them. He watched me back.

When I smiled, he lowered his eyes, but I could see the corners of his mouth turn up and his cheeks grow red.

I figured if my barn was stuffed to overflowing with crops, I would share with the shy, smiling boy.

CHAPTER TEN

More and more people from the Hooverville showed up each night of the revival, filling the benches under Pastor's patchwork sideshow tent. On the last night, a spark caught fire in his soul, and he let loose a fury of God's Word like Red River had never heard before.

The power behind his words shook me so that I pushed my hands under my thighs to stop them from shaking and kept my eyes on the ground. Whether it was Pastor's yelling or the power of the Holy Spirit, I didn't know for sure. Whatever it was, I couldn't decide how I felt about it.

"Y'all, the Lord God Almighty wants your hearts," he yelled from his spot on the stage. "You come under this tent to hear the Word of the Lord. I'm fixing on bringing it to you. Can I get a *amen*?"

He got a few. But those couple *amen*s were loud.

"You look outside. Go on. Take a look. You see all the dust crushing the roofs and killing the livestock. You know what that is?" He waited. I turned my head up to see his wild eyes surveying the crowd. "It's the wrath of God Almighty pouring down on us. Blowing round our heads all day and all night. And we're too blind and stupid to see it's all our own doing."

Narrowing his eyes, he made a face like he drank milk that had gone blinky.

"You know what we all best get doing? We best get on our knees and beg God to take us back. Beg Him to forgive our sins and to take us back."

Jabbing his finger in the air in front of him, he pointed amongst the crowd.

"We all best be asking ourselves what's our share of the dust wrath."

I prayed that what Meemaw'd said about Jesus taking our load of sin was true. When I looked down the row at her, she nodded, winking her eye at me as if she knew what I was thinking.

Pastor pushed the steel-gray hair off his forehead and closed his eyes, sighing like he was about to give up. For a moment I thought he was near to falling over, his face paled. But he didn't faint like I feared he would. Instead, he stepped off the stage and right into the aisle between the rows of benches.

As he walked past me, a drip of sweat dropped off the end of his nose and fell to the dirt floor beneath his feet. His hands shook at his sides.

"Brothers and sisters," he said, his voice just a little over a rasp. "All this week I been breaking my back trying to get y'all to hear me. To get y'all to finally let go of them black and dirty sins. All's I wanted so bad was for you to turn and repent. To get baptized for the forgiveness of sins and the gift of the Holy Spirit."

His steps were slow. One after another. And his eyes were fixed. But the crowd of folks in the tent was so thick with strange faces that I couldn't see who he was staring at.

"What are you doing here?" he growled at someone toward the back. "You here to work your seduction on these men? You come to talk them into your bed and out of their money?"

He stopped in the middle of the aisle and spit right on the floor.

"How many among us have fallen for her tricks?" He thrust his hips one way and then the other in a way that made me real uncomfortable. "Her wiggling and waggling her sinful way, offering us to come and taste of her sweet damnation."

Mama turned, lifting up off the bench. When she relaxed back on her seat, she sighed and whispered in Meemaw's ear.

"Who among us has rebuked her snares?" Pastor went on. "Who among us has declared that he will no more give in to his lust for her soft, smooth flesh? She the whore of Red River."

Mama's arm draped over my shoulder and pulled me close, putting her lips to my ear.

"You gotta go," she whispered. "Take Beanie and go on home."

I nodded, not understanding. Mama had never sent us out of service before. Then again, Pastor'd never used the word *whore* in a sermon before. "Meemaw and I will be home as soon as this is finished."

Standing, I grabbed hold of Beanie's hand. For once, she didn't struggle against me. As I ducked under the sideshow tent flap, I turned to see Pastor with his finger pointing right into the face of That Woman. For about half a minute, I watched, expecting her to run off, red-faced from the shame. But she did not. She crossed her arms and stood, staring him down.

❖

Beanie shuffled her feet all the way home. She yawned loud with her mouth hanging as wide as it would go. She could have laid down right in the field and gone to sleep for all I cared. It was just nice to be out from under the stuffy air that hovered, thick as mud, inside that tent.

I did wonder, though, what I would have done if Pastor had yelled at me right in the face like he did to That Woman. I couldn't see myself being as strong as her to stay quiet and not fight back. And I certainly would have let out a little bit of a cry, too.

Our house was dark when we finally got to it.

"No lights," Beanie said.

"Daddy must not be home." I rubbed the back of my neck. The muscles felt tight and sore.

"Where is he?"

"Probably playing cards with Millard or something." I prayed God wouldn't be too mad at Daddy for that. Millard, too. They were real good men even if they did play cards and skip church every once in a while.

I let go of Beanie's hand and climbed up to sit on the top step of our front porch. "We better wait for Mama out here."

Truth was, I hated going into a dark house without Mama or Daddy. My imagination created too many monsters and ghosts with no light to wash them away.

"I'm hungry." Beanie stood at the bottom of the steps. "Mama said I could eat something."

"Nah, she never did. I would've heard her." I reached out and grabbed hold of her hand, trying to pull her up on the porch. "Sit with me. It's nice out here."

She pulled her hand right out of mine and crossed her skinny arms over her chest. The way she stood reminded me of That Woman, the stubborn look in her eyes, too.

"You can pout all you want." I smoothed my skirt across my knees. "I'm not fixing anything for you."

"I wanna eat." She stomped her foot, making a poof of dust around her.

"You can do that all you want, too," I said, trying to make my voice stern like Mama's could be. "I'm not letting you eat until somebody comes home."

The slap stung my cheek before I knew she'd struck me. I cupped my hand on my face. It smarted so bad, I was sure it would turn red quick. On her face was no expression at all. No anger and no more of her pout. She stared at me, her face blank. Before I could get up on my feet, she had run up the steps and into the house, slamming the door and locking it behind her, leaving me on the porch with a sore cheek and a raging temper.

I could have spit I was so mad.

Mama would have had a snit fit over me spitting. She had a set of rules that included no spitting, no cussing, no yelling or running in the house. I didn't obey the one about cussing that night. And I didn't whisper it, either.

I wondered how much dust wrath Pastor would have thought that was worth.

"Mama's going to tan your hide," I hollered, feeling the heat from my face. "You're in for it this time."

Even though I knew she'd locked it, I twisted the knob just the same and pushed against the door. It wouldn't budge, and I said the bad word again.

I jumped off the porch and tore around the side yard, fixing to get to the back door before Beanie thought to lock that one, too.

Just when I got to the other side of the house I ran into something firm and fell back on my behind. All I could make out was the shadowed outline of a man.

"Whoa there. What's the rush, Pearl?" Eddie's voice. I knew it was his because that voice had played over and over in my mind. "I heard that curse word. What's a girl like you yelling cusses for? You sure got a mouth on you, don't ya, girl?"

He stepped closer and out of the shadow, reaching his hand to help me up. I swatted at it and got up all on my own.

"Well, ain't you a spitfire?" He laughed. "Shouldn't you be at the revival still? Last night of it, ain't it? Don't wanna miss none of the hooting and hollering. Might go to hell if you ain't there."

"Mama sent me home with my sister." I tried to get around him with no success. Everywhere I moved, he stepped in front of me.

"I seen her." He turned his head and spit. "You told me she was pretty as you. My opinion? She ain't even close."

His fingers curled around my shoulder and pulled me close to him. It smelled like he hadn't had a good scrubbing in a long time. The reek from his mouth told me his teeth weren't cleaned enough, either. I tried to hold my breath.

"She favors her mother, don't she?" He smirked. "A bit plain, ain't they?"

"Mama isn't plain." I jerked from him, trying to loose myself, but Eddie had a real tight hold on me. "I got to get inside and see to my sister."

He let go, but then caught me again, putting his arm around my waist. I was sure his musty skin would rub its stink off on my dress.

"Gotta see to her, huh?" he asked. "I hear y'all gotta take care of her most all the time. I hear she's a idiot."

The mad rose up from my gut all the way to my head, heating my cheeks so I was sure they were blazing. I was half scared I'd break a tooth in half, the way I clenched them together. My hands on his side, I shoved him away from me with all my strength.

"What's that? Why'd you do that? You mad?" He stumbled a bit before settling down on his haunches. "I wasn't fixing to make you mad. Just telling you what folks around town was saying."

"She isn't an idiot." My teeth didn't stop grinding together when I spoke. "She's a miracle."

Eddie's face went blank, and he seemed to be thinking of something. He pushed up with his hands on his knees.

"Settle down, would ya," he said, tipping his hat back on his head. "Lord, do you ever have a temper on you. I thought you was about to punch my lights out."

He pulled out a tin of chewing tobacco, pinching some of it and working it into the space between his teeth and lip.

"Does it ever feel like you're somewhere you don't belong?" he asked.

"I don't know what you're talking about."

"What's not to understand?" An edge sharpened his voice. "Lord Almighty, I thought that other girl was the idiot, not you."

I shot him a look full of sass. All it did was make him laugh at me.

"I mean, you ever feel like you're supposed to be somewhere else?" He spit. "Like maybe you ain't meant to be in this house, with this goody-goody family. Maybe you're supposed to be somewhere else, but you got pulled out of where you belong and put here instead."

"You're not making sense," I said.

"Do you ever get the feeling that you ain't who you always thought you were?" He touched the side of his head with his pointer finger. "You think on that, Pearl. Think on that."

"You're scaring me."

Our back door sometimes stuck in its frame, catching and rubbing when it was opened. I heard the rough sound and turned. Mama stepped out on the stoop, a rolling pin in one hand. She gripped it so hard the veins stuck out on the back of her hand.

"Who are you?" she asked, glaring at Eddie.

Meemaw poked her head out behind Mama and waved for me to come up on the porch. I obeyed and let her wrap her arms around me.

"You okay?" she whispered.

Mama lifted the rolling pin, like it was a sword she meant to use on Eddie. "I asked you who you are."

"Evening, ma'am." He leered at Mama, up and down in a way that made me feel small. He fanned himself with one hand and smiled. "Sure is hot tonight, ain't it?"

"What are you doing bothering my girl? Isn't it a bit late to be standing in folks' back yards?" Mama's voice was hard as rock. She rested the rolling pin on her shoulder.

"Just looking for a bite to eat, ma'am. Maybe a little make-work." He winked at me. "Ain't that right, little lady?"

I tried crossing my arms and standing firm, but it just made me feel smaller yet.

"I've got nothing to give you. Best move on now." Mama cleared her throat. "Don't let me find you around my house again."

"Yes, ma'am." Eddie tipped his hat at Mama. "You have yourself a good evening, ma'am."

Mama rushed us inside and shut the door, locking it. She watched out that back window until she was sure Eddie was gone. Only then did she let her arm drop with the weight of the rolling pin. Meemaw pulled me even closer to her, burying my face into her soft chest. I didn't cry, even though I wanted to. All my shaking made her think I was, though.

She hushed me until I could stand still.

"He didn't touch you, did he, darlin'?" Meemaw asked.

I told her he hadn't, which wasn't true. I didn't tell her he'd put his arm around me. Something told me that wasn't the kind of touch she meant.

❀

The minute Daddy got home and before he could step foot inside, Mama went after him to drive all the hobos out of Red River. She shook and waved her arms around her head. As strong as her voice had been with Eddie, it was weak and quivery with Daddy.

"I don't like it, Tom," she said. "Not one bit. Strange men coming around, asking little girls for food. It's not fitting."

"I'm sure he didn't mean any harm," Daddy said, stepping into the house and closing the door behind him.

"Go on up and ask your mother. She saw him, too." Mama reached around Daddy and locked the door.

"Mary, don't worry." Daddy took hold of Mama's hands and kissed them both. "I've been down to the Hooverville half-a-dozen times this week with Millard. All that's down there is families and a couple men tramping around. They're harmless."

"You didn't see that man, Tom." Mama's voice trembled. "The way he was talking to Pearl, it was just—I don't know. It made me so uncomfortable."

Daddy turned toward me where I sat on the davenport. "He scare you, darlin'?"

I nodded. "It was that same man from before."

"From before?" Mama asked.

"He was at the rabbit drive," I answered.

"That man's not going to do any harm." Daddy puffed up his cheeks. "If he comes around again—"

"He's not going to. I told him to stay away. And I told Pearl she isn't to talk to him again. Not ever." Mama brought her fist down on the table, making a pounding sound. "I just wish you'd send all them out. Hobos or whatever. I don't want people near my house like that."

"Mary, sugar."

I loved it when Daddy called Mama "sugar." I didn't believe she liked it so much. But when he said it, his eyes would get all wrinkled up in the corners. "I don't have it in me to kick them all out. They're just down on their luck."

"Thomas, I can't see how you don't."

I sure didn't like it when Mama called Daddy his given name. It meant she was sore at him. Her eyes would get real narrow when she said it.

"How do we know that man didn't mean harm?" she asked. "He had evil written all over his face."

The smell of Daddy's fresh-lit cigarette wafted over to me. "Them folks have been kicked out of every place from here to the other side of the country. They've got more nothing than anybody I've ever seen. From all I hear, California isn't gonna be much better. The least I can do is let them find a little rest here for a day or two."

"My lord, Tom. It's one thing to stay over at a place. It's another to come around, begging for food from little girls." Mama rubbed her eyes. "I swear, if I see that man here again, I'll crack open his head."

"I'll see to him." Daddy looked over at me again. "Did he hurt you?"

"No, sir," I said.

"He just scared you?"

I nodded.

"Strange men'll do that sometimes." Daddy walked to me and kneeled next to my seat so his face was right next to mine. "I'll make sure he doesn't come around here again. Okay?"

My eyes filled with tears, and I didn't know why.

"His name's Eddie," I whispered.

Daddy pulled on his cigarette, letting his eyes squint.

"That's real good, darlin'," he said. "You catch his last name, too?"

"No, sir."

He blew the smoke out toward the ceiling. "Eddie should do just fine. I'll catch up with him."

Daddy got up on the davenport next to me and patted his thigh. I climbed onto his lap, wondering how much longer I'd fit there.

"Now," he said, holding his cigarette away from me. "That revival's done, ain't it?"

"I don't mind Pastor's preaching, but I'll be glad not to sit in service for a good while." Mama leaned against the wall. "I don't remember a revival ever wearing me out so."

"One day until Sunday and you'll be right back in church," Daddy said. "Were it up to me, I'd give y'all a week off from it. Pastor, too."

"Just what would we do instead?"

"We'd all go to the theater to see a movie. Seems like forever since we seen a movie." Daddy gave me a peck on the cheek. "Anything exciting happen at the revival? Any clowns show up? I mean, other than Pastor Ezra Anderson and Mad Mabel."

"Tom," Mama scolded but smiled anyway.

"You know That Woman? The one who lives at the cat house?" I asked. "She came and stood in the back."

"Winnie did?" Daddy turned to see Mama's nod that agreed with me. "What was she doing there?"

"Don't know." Mama shrugged. "But she sure did get an earful from Pastor."

"I'd have thought she'd know better than to show up at a revival."

"He called her bad names," I said.

"That so?" Daddy drew in the last of his cigarette and pushed out the lit end in a dish Mama brought him. "He go on about the lust of the flesh?"

"Tom," Mama said, shaking her head. "She's heard enough for tonight."

"Well, did he?"

I nodded.

"Pearl," Mama said. "You go on up to bed now."

"Yes, Mama." I hopped off Daddy's lap and made my way up the steps. I didn't go all the way into my room. I stayed outside the door and listened.

"You best be careful who you say such things to," Mama said. I thought she meant to whisper, but I could hear her just fine. "You'll turn everybody away from Pastor talking like that."

"That man knows more of Winnie than most men in town." Daddy cleared his throat. "I reckon half the tithe money ends up on her bedside table."

"You don't know that for a fact."

"Don't I?" Daddy coughed. "Even if he weren't a customer of Winnie, I don't like what that man's spouting. It's just ugly what he preaches."

"Your mother seems to think he's bringing hope to the people."

"He never gave up the ringmaster act, Mary. He's playing this town for fools." Daddy's voice got lower in tone. "I'd trust Si Jones before I'd ever go to Ezra Anderson for anything."

"Si's a drunk."

"Still, he ain't standing with a Bible in his hand and playing at something he's not, is he?"

❖

"You ain't who you think you are." The shaking voice in my flimsy dream echoed. "Think on that."

The dark figure in front of me tap, tap, tapped on the side of his head. "Think on that."

Another person stood next to him, holding a mirror. "Look into the mirror of scripture," he hollered. "What do you see?"

I looked. All I saw was me, my long yellow hair soaking wet and my dress soiled with blood and dirt.

"I'll tell ya what I see." The man's voice rose so loud, it hammered in my ears. "The whore of Red River. Seducer of the flesh. Pulling that flesh down and down and down until it's nothing but dust. The dust of God's hate for you."

"Think on that, Pearl." The dark figure stepped into the light. Eddie's eyes glowed from his face. "You ain't who you think you are."

When I woke, I shivered for all the sweat cooling on my skin.

# CHAPTER ELEVEN

Daddy never did force all the hobos out of Red River. He didn't take down the Hooverville, either. What he did, though, was talk to all the men and tell them to steer clear of the kids in town.

When Mama asked him about Eddie, Daddy said he didn't find him around. Folks that knew of him said he must have moved on.

Still, Mama decided that I wasn't allowed to wander around by myself until Daddy had found Eddie and sent him to California with a swift kick to the rear.

"Take your sister with you," Mama said to me, keeping her focus on the socks she was mending.

I glanced out the big front window. Ray was still standing on the porch, waiting to hear what Mama would say about me going for a walk with him.

"I'd be with Ray," I said. "He would never let anything happen to me."

Mama raised one eyebrow and pulled her stitch through, tying it off at the end.

"Take your sister." The tone in her voice told me I'd better mind or else. "She could use a little walk, anyhow."

"Yes, ma'am." I tried not to sound too disappointed.

When I stepped out on the porch with Beanie behind me, Ray scowled.

"Mama said we have to take her with us." I shrugged.

"I guess that's all right just so she don't do nothing to cause trouble." Ray looked at Beanie. "You gotta stick with us, got it? No running off."

Beanie's nod seemed to satisfy Ray.

I knew why Ray wanted to get away from town. It was the day the relief truck came, and he never wanted to be around to see it.

I couldn't hardly blame him.

President Roosevelt sent his men with flatbeds full of food to Red River every so often. Daddy had told me those trucks went to just about every town in the U.S. of A. I didn't care if it went to Egypt. I was just glad it came to our town.

I'd heard from Meemaw that the bundles on the truck were of flour and beans and cooking lard. Sometimes the men would bring a little meat for all the folks. She said there was never sugar, though. I had half a mind to write to good old President Roosevelt about that.

I just had to believe he would write back, attaching the note to a crate full of sugar—enough to last a good year. The note would say, "Enjoy the shug-ah."

Ray hated to be home when the relief trucks came. He said it made his mother cry and his father mean. Daddy told me that most of the men in town were shamed to death to take the charity. And the women were embarrassed for the sake of their husbands. Daddy had said that, if it had just been grown-ups, most of the people in our town would have let themselves starve. But they took the relief to keep their kids fed.

A man could make himself die of hunger to save his pride, Daddy had said. He was less like to do so when it was his kids with the empty bellies.

When the three of us—Beanie, Ray, and I—stepped off the porch, I noticed the old bucket on the ground. Ray picked it up by the handle and carried it as he walked.

It was already half full of dried-out, sun-bleached cow patties.

Ray walked in the direction of the old, empty pastures. I rolled my eyes, knowing that he wanted me to help him fill his bucket to the brim with crumbling cow turds.

Mrs. Jones used them to heat their dugout. Sometimes she even cooked over them. It seemed a dirty thing to have to do, and I hated that anybody found a need for it.

I decided I'd write about that in my letter to the president.

We made it all the way to one of the old pastures, and Ray hopped over the fence. I put one foot on the old wood and pushed myself up, hoping it wouldn't crumble under my weight. Turning to see if Beanie was behind me, I squinted against the dust in the air. She was a few yards back.

"Come on, Beanie," I called, looping my leg around the top rung of the fence.

She shook her head, wild hair brushing against her shoulders.

"Mama said you had to stick with Ray and me." I put my hands on my hips, swaying in order to balance myself. "Now, come on."

On a normal day, I would have moved along and let her find her own way home. She might have had it in her mind to stay put in that one spot all day long, to dig in the dirt and watch the clouds sail over. I didn't need Mama getting mad at me, though.

"Come on," I hollered a little more angry than I should have. I didn't like the way my voice sounded so mean.

Ray's bucket clanked on the hard ground. "What's wrong with her?"

"Don't know." I turned from my sister for no more than a second so I could climb down. When I turned back, she had started running the opposite way from us. The way she took off, I wasn't sure she'd thought ahead to where she was going.

My sister might not have been the smartest person I knew, but she sure was fast.

I used the kind of words ranch hands would have said. Ray didn't hear me, so I repeated them for his benefit.

"She's going for the Hooverville," Ray yelled, running right past me, leaving his bucket behind.

Ray and I ran after Beanie along the shore of what had once been the Red River. Now it was nothing more than a scar in the earth. Once, long before I was born, a wide line of water rushed through. They'd put the railroad tracks running right alongside it. When the rain stopped wetting the land, the river dried up. That was when a lot of the troubles began.

Dusters had blown a dune up against a barbed-wire fence, and Beanie stumbled her way up the mound with Ray not too far behind.

With my shoes on, I couldn't work my toes into the dirt to gain a hold. All I could do was slide back down once I got a foot or so up. Over and over this happened, draining my energy.

"Ray," I hollered only to get a mouthful of dirt. "I can't get over."

He'd already hopped down on the other side. I wished he would have waited just a few seconds for me. I thought about all the names I could call him. Names Meemaw would have blushed at and Mama would have washed my mouth out with soap for. I didn't say any of them, though, because I remembered that his baby sister had died. I figured I should be more charitable than that.

Scrambling and digging into the dirt with the toe of my shoes, I finally got up to the top and jumped down right next to Ray. He nudged me with his elbow. I let him know it hurt and rubbed it with my hand, deciding not to push him back for the same reason I didn't call him a name.

"Look," he whispered.

Dingy canvases made roofs that hung over old pallets and mattresses. Folks I'd never seen before sat in the shade of their makeshift tents. One woman held a baby against her breast, her blouse pulled up just so. I couldn't see much of her skin, and I was thankful for that. A couple kids stared at Ray and me, their eyes tired and faces filthy.

As dirty as Ray was, he was nothing close to as grimy as some of the kids in the Hooverville.

Ray dug at the dust with his bare toes and looked off to where the tents made zigzagging rows. A kid tossed a handful of dirt in the air and let it fall atop his head.

"I don't see her." Ray narrowed his eyes. The sun had gotten so bright it cast a glare on just about everything.

It wouldn't have done a bit of good to cry, and I knew it, even though I wanted to. I choked the urge back. Especially when Ray touched my hand.

"Don't worry," he said. "We'll find her."

"What's that smell?" I whispered, hoping nobody but Ray could hear my question.

Ray just shrugged his shoulders.

It smelled like they'd been using the whole camp as an outhouse. Nobody had gotten around to putting one up, probably because they only fixed on staying a few nights before leaving again.

Goodness, but did they need to do something about that smell. A body couldn't live among that too long without getting downright sick. I wondered what Mama thought about it. It wasn't like her to not throw a fit about something like that.

I was sure she'd think of some way to clean it up. I knew she didn't want all of Red River smelling like a barnyard.

As for me, I was glad I'd worn my shoes that day.

Ray and I wove our way around tents and rusted-out cars until we found Beanie. She sat on the ground, playing with a toddling child. I couldn't tell if it was a boy or a girl. All it had on was a filth-stained diaper and nothing else.

Whatever it may have been, it was laughing at the faces Beanie made. Big and wide smiles and air-filled cheeks. Crossed eyes and stuck-out tongue. I couldn't remember seeing her act like that before.

A man sat on a pallet under the tent nearby, watching the two, his stubbly face droopy and sun-burned. He nodded at Ray and me.

"Howdy," he muttered.

Ray greeted him back.

"Beanie." I marched right up to her. Mad as I was, I pulled on her arm and didn't hide my temper. "You can't run away like that."

She didn't take her eyes off the baby, but she yanked her arm away from me.

"I found her," she said, reaching for the child who didn't come to her. "I seen her and knowed it was her."

"Who?" I squinted at the baby, trying to recognize its face.

"Baby Rosie." Beanie beamed. "She went away, and now I found her."

Ray made a sound behind us, one that was almost like choking or coughing or both.

"That isn't Baby Rosie," I said. Then I made my voice a lot quieter so only she'd hear me. "You remember? Baby Rosie died."

"No." She shook her head hard. "No. No. No. I found her. She's right there."

"Something wrong with that girl?" the man asked from his pallet. He pushed the greasy hair off his forehead and stood, unsteady.

"She's all right. Just a little slow is all." I touched Beanie's shoulder. "Come on. We best get home."

Beanie snatched the baby, holding it close to herself. I knew she hadn't hurt it, just startled it. The baby wailed and struggled, afraid of Beanie.

"Put him down, hear?" the man said from where he stood. "Let him go."

"She ain't sick no more," Beanie said, still holding on tight.

"You let go of him." The man rushed over, putting his hands on Beanie, pulling on her arms. "Leave him be."

"She's got to go home to her mama. Her mama misses her." Beanie fought against the man, trying to move away from his grabbing hands. "You ain't got a right to keep her away from her mama."

Ray dropped to his knees next to Beanie.

"Let me try," he said to the man.

The man took a step back but still within reach, his face still bothered.

Ray put his hands on Beanie's shoulders and got his face close up to hers.

"Beanie, simmer down a little, okay?" He blinked a tear from his eyelashes. "Can you look at me?"

Beanie didn't loosen her grip on the baby, but she stopped jostling him.

"That ain't Baby Rosie." Ray swallowed hard. "That's a baby boy you got. Do you remember? Baby Rosie was a girl."

"This ain't a boy," Beanie said.

"This baby is. His daddy over there said so." Ray kept his voice calm. "See him standing over there?"

Beanie looked at the man and then back at the baby.

"And Rosie had red hair." Ray touched the baby's blond curls. "See, it ain't Rosie."

"But I thought . . ." She trailed off.

"I know. You tried to do good." Ray moved his hands under the baby's armpits. "Can I get this boy back to his daddy? His daddy loves him just as much as we all loved Rosie. Do you understand? We gotta give this baby back."

Beanie released the boy to Ray.

"I'm sorry." She didn't look at the man, but I knew she was talking to him. "I just thought . . ."

"No hurt done." The man took the boy and patted his back. "He'll be fine."

Ray walked off a bit by himself. Every few steps he'd wipe at his face with the back of his hand. He was headed for the spot where we had climbed over to chase Beanie.

"Come on," I said to my sister. "We'd better catch up to Ray."

"Wouldn't if I were you," the man said, lowering the boy back to the ground. "Man needs time. 'Specially when he's got that look in his eyes. I don't know what that boy's going through, but he needs him a little time to be alone."

Beanie touched the dust, scooping it up in her hands and letting it sift through her fingers. She had little tears dropping fast from her eyes to the dirt, making beads of mud.

"She gonna be all right?" The man nodded at Beanie.

"Sure she is." I touched my sister's head, smoothing the frizzy hair.

The baby wobbled over and stood in front of Beanie. He stuffed most of his hand into his mouth and stared at her. She didn't wipe off her face but looked at him and pulled her lips into a funny line. He gave a big, from-the-belly baby laugh.

"Seems Joshua's forgave her." The man squatted. "I don't mind letting them play a spell."

"Thank you, mister." I kneeled in the dirt. "It'll do her some good."

❖

After a little while, Joshua finished with their play and needed a rest. The day wasn't too hot, being October, still I could tell it was nearing time for us to go home for the middle-of-the-day meal. We said our good-byes, and Beanie kissed the baby on his forehead and hands.

The man didn't act too nervous about it.

Neither of us talked while we headed out of the camp and over the dune. It was easier to climb it from that side, and I was glad for it.

Once we climbed over, Beanie grabbed for my hand.

She held it all the way back home.

My sister didn't eat any dinner. She went to bed and slept all the way through the day and night until the next morning. It worried Meemaw something terrible.

I never told Mama or Daddy about Little Joshua or Beanie's fit. It was her story to tell, and she did hold onto it.

We never talked about it again.

A lot that happened that year and into the next never earned a discussion.

Mostly, it was because we found it all too hard to speak of.

# CHAPTER TWELVE

Mama moved about the kitchen in an awful rush, packing glass jars into a wicker basket, baking biscuits, and checking on the coffee she had perking on the stove.

"How's the porridge coming?" she asked, looking over my shoulder.

"Okay," I said, stirring the watery oats. They were so soupy I could have sucked them up through a straw.

"They need a little thickening." She bumped me with her hip to fix the mess I'd made of breakfast. "Go on and get the bowls from the cupboard, please, darlin'."

She spooned the oats into the bowls and helped me carry them to the table. I put one in front of Daddy. He drizzled a little molasses on his and winked at me.

"Tom, are you still going down to the Jones's?" Mama asked.

"Sure am." He shoved a spoonful of oatmeal into his mouth.

"I'm worried I've got too much in this basket. It's heavy." She tested it, lifting it from the handle. "I don't want these jars breaking out the bottom. This is my good basket."

"It's fine." Daddy scraped his bowl.

"Don't you think it'll be too heavy for you to carry?" She poured him a cup of coffee. "Maybe you should drive it over."

"Mary, I'll manage. No use burning fuel when I can walk." He took the cup from her. "Thank you."

"I'm just worried you won't be able to carry it."

"I've got plenty of muscles." He held up one arm, flexing for her.

"Oh, Tom." She giggled and swatted at him with her hand.

"Pearl, you want to walk over with me?" He blew steam off his coffee. "I thought you might want to see Ray for a spell."

I never answered him. But I did gobble the last of my porridge.

"Don't slurp," Mama warned. "You'll give yourself an upset stomach."

"We're in no hurry." Daddy stood from the table. "They don't even know we're coming. Your mama has planned a nice surprise for them."

He kissed Mama's forehead.

"You, Mary Spence, are a good woman." His eyes sparkled when he said that.

❖

Daddy carried the basket of canned goods and I had a plate of still-warm biscuits. He took long strides, and I had to move my feet double time to keep up. I didn't mind, though. Hardly thought of it, as a matter of fact. All that I cared about was that I got to be with Daddy.

"You coming along all right?" he asked.

"Yes, sir," I answered, trying to hide my breathlessness.

I wished I had thought to wear a sweater. Early November wasn't cold, exactly, but my skin wasn't used to the chilled air.

"I'm glad you come with me. I don't believe I could have carried that plate along with this basket." He smiled. "Mighty glad for the help."

We reached the road that led to the sharecropper cabins. Daddy switched the basket to his other hand before we started up again.

"You ain't seen that Eddie character around lately, have you?" he asked.

"No, sir," I answered.

"That's fine."

"Do you think he's gone for good?" I asked, keeping my eye on the road.

"Can't know for sure." He stepped off the road and along where there had once been a path to the cabins. "We'll just have to see."

We got in sight of the Jones's dugout, and Daddy put the basket down again, rubbing his hands.

"That thing was heavier than I thought it'd be." He chuckled. "Your mama was right. It's about to break out the bottom. Good thing we're here."

Linens hung on the long laundry lines to dry. The way the sun shone through them and the wind made them sway, it looked like they were dancing. I would have been happy to stay and watch the movement all day long.

I remembered over the summer being in that same place. Ray and I chased each other between the hanging clothes and sheets. Mrs. Jones had hollered at us to be careful not to knock anything off the lines. She held a basket on one hip and Baby Rosie on the other while she watched to make sure we didn't kick up too much dust.

She put Baby Rosie on the ground to play for a bit at her feet as she pulled the dry linens off the lines. Somehow she got everything folded, even with Rosie tugging at her. The baby had babbled and giggled so that Ray and I couldn't help but stop our running to go play with her.

But Baby Rosie wouldn't be among the dancing clothes that day or ever again. A burning ache spread up from the middle of my chest. I used the back of my hand to take care of the tears and hoped Daddy didn't see them.

"Well, I'll be," Daddy said, a smile in his voice. "Si's out in that old jalopy of his."

Squinting against the sun, I looked at the ancient, rusted-out car. It had been in that same spot for as long as I could remember, and in all that time Mr. Jones hadn't so much as turned over the engine. Ray had told me that he didn't know if the hunk of metal was broke down or just out of gas. Most nobody in Red River had any money for gas.

"Wonder if he'd mind a little help," Daddy said, walking toward the car with a quicker step, not waiting for me to catch up.

I let my eyes wander back to the graceful flutter of sheets on the line, the rippling shadow moving under them on the dust.

Then I heard the jars knock together, clattering and clinking. Daddy had dropped the basket, his hand still open, hovering over it.

"Go on. Get in the house," he said to me. "And don't look out the window."

I hesitated, nervous at the hard sound in Daddy's voice. The plate of biscuits slipped out of my hand and hit the hard ground. I didn't look to see if the plate had broken.

"Run," he told me.

I obeyed.

Inside the house, Mrs. Jones sat on the floor, hands over her ears. She hummed. Not a song, just one note, drawn out until she ran out of breath. She took a long gulp of air and then hummed again. Her eyelids wrinkled and bunched, she held them shut so tight.

Ray stood by the window. He glanced at me when I walked in, but turned his eyes back out to watch what would happen in the car.

Daddy had said not to look out the window. As much as I wanted to obey, I couldn't. If I didn't watch, my imagination would have created all kinds of terror and all of them ending bad for Daddy.

Standing next to Ray, I tried to watch what was happening outside. Lifting up on tiptoes, I could just barely see, but it was enough. Ray's hand was sweaty, but I didn't pull mine away when he grabbed it.

Even with our hands held tight together, we both trembled. I didn't know why I should be afraid, but Daddy's voice and Mrs. Jones on the floor and Ray holding my hand made it so.

Outside, Daddy took steps so slowly, he hadn't even made it to the car yet. Mr. Jones's voice growled, and his head shook back and forth.

"Leave me be," he yelled.

Daddy didn't stop his slow steps. Both men kept their eyes on each other. Daddy reached and opened the passenger door of the jalopy.

That was when I saw the rifle resting between Mr. Jones's knees, the barrel digging right into the soft place under his chin.

Daddy climbed in. The slamming of the door made my whole body tense.

"He done it yet?" Mrs. Jones's voice shook. "Ray, has he done it yet? Was that it?"

Ray grunted but didn't turn to his mother. I looked over my shoulder, wondering if she'd understood Ray's answer. Her ghost-gray eyes stared at the floor.

"Wish he'd just get it done with if he's gonna do it," she muttered.

I let go of Ray's hand. It slapped against the side of his overalls. On my knees, I inched closer to Mrs. Jones.

She held her hands in front of her, watching them tremor. The cracked skin around the thick and split nails looked sore. She had the thinnest wrists I'd ever seen. The more she held her hands like that, the more they shook.

"He said all he's got is just one bullet left." She started rocking again. "Said a man can't even afford to blow his own head off no more."

I knelt right next to Mrs. Jones, not knowing if I should say something back to her. It was such an ugly idea, what she'd said, and too much for my mind to take in. I wondered if I shouldn't just wrap my arms around her neck to give her a little comfort.

Since I was little, Meemaw had told me that I ought to do unto others as I'd like them to do unto me. So, I pulled Mrs. Jones into a hug. She didn't lift her arms to hold me back and that was just fine by me. She did sink into me, though. It was like she was melting from blazing hot sadness. I held her limp body so she wouldn't fall to the floor.

Then Ray cried out. Both Mrs. Jones and I tensed.

"What?" I asked.

Ray just clamped his teeth shut and leaned on the wall by the window.

The gun blast sounded like something had crashed. My heart jerked up into my throat and then down to my gut, making me feel dizzy. I fell backward, my arms losing their grip on Mrs. Jones's neck. She supported herself, gasping in air, her eyes open wide.

"He done it," she whispered. "He really done it."

I couldn't find the strength to move so much as my little toe, and I had the hardest time catching a breath. In my mind, I saw Daddy as the one with the blown-off head, not Mr. Jones.

That was when I started to pray. I begged God not to let it be my father who was dead. Then I felt all kinds of selfish for praying it.

Mrs. Jones crawled to Ray. He helped her to her feet, and she stood facing the outside.

"Lord God," she sobbed and groaned and scrunched her face all up on itself. "Oh, Lord."

Ray reached an arm around his mother and pulled her to himself.

Too stunned to cry, I stayed on the floor, unable to move. All I could do was feel the thudding in my chest.

"Pearl."

Daddy. It was Daddy who called for me.

"Pearl," he called again. "Let's go home."

My numb body made it hard to get up, but somehow I managed. The air around me felt thick, slowing down every move I made. I got to the door without knowing how. Holding onto the doorjamb was the only way I could be sure not to fall down.

"Tell your pa," Mrs. Jones said, not turning from the window. "Tell him thanks for what he done."

Daddy stood in front of the house, Mr. Jones's rifle in his hand. He pushed the basket of canned goods by the door with the plate of biscuits resting on top.

He reached for me with his free hand.

"Come on, darlin'," he said, still reaching.

I was too afraid to move, even to take his hand. Scared that I'd catch a glimpse of the old jalopy with Mr. Jones inside, his head blown off. So I held tighter to the doorjamb.

"Pearl, come on." Daddy's voice was deep and smooth, but his hand shook. "Trust me, honey."

I let go and shuffled forward, my feet too heavy to pick up. Daddy stepped up and took my hand, tugging me toward him.

"Is he . . ." My throat clamped on the word *dead*. "Mr. Jones?"

"He's okay," Daddy whispered. "I fired the shot into the dust so he couldn't use it."

Turning, I saw Mr. Jones still in the car behind the steering wheel. He held that wheel with both his hands, like it was what kept him from falling off the face of the earth. From where I stood, I could see he was crying, his whole face wrenched up and his mouth open as if he wanted to roar all the hurt out.

As far as I could tell, he wasn't making any noise at all.

❈

My hand throbbed, Daddy held it so tight. And my feet rubbed inside my stiff-soled shoes. We never stopped or slowed down. I was sure I'd get blisters by the time we reached home.

Daddy turned on the main road, pulling me along with him. A few men, old farmers with nothing to do but wait around, watching folks, stood with their backs against the empty building across from the court-house. The overhang shaded their faces.

"Hey, Sheriff," one of them called out.

Daddy didn't even notice them. He kept on moving, pulling me along.

We walked up the steps to the courthouse, and he used a key to unlock the door. Both of us wiped our palms against our sides, they were so sweaty from holding together so hard.

He locked Mr. Jones's rifle in an old gun safe, slipping the key into his shirt pocked. He let a cuss word slip from his mouth and slammed his fist into the safe.

I'd never seen Daddy like that, and it scared me so I took a few steps back from him.

"I'm sorry," Daddy said, not turning toward me. "Sorry if I scared you just then."

He said another cuss and rubbed his hand on the back of his neck.

Men couldn't just cry like women did. I didn't know why not, but that was the way of things. Sometimes they used a cuss word and an angry fist as their way of pushing out the scared or hurt that was inside them.

Cussing was a man's way of crying.

"You go on home." He still didn't turn to face me. "Tell your mama she best not expect me for dinner. I'll be home before long, though."

"Yes, sir," I said.

I went to leave, trying to figure out if I wanted to run all the way home or take my sweet time getting there. On one hand, I wanted to be with Mama right away, smelling the food cooking in her kitchen and out of the chilly air. On the other hand, I didn't figure I could talk to Mama or Meemaw at all without crying my eyes out.

I still didn't know what had happened or what any of it meant.

So I just walked like I would have any other day. Not too fast and not too slow.

I even howdied back at the men standing with their backs against the building, watching folks go by.

# CHAPTER THIRTEEN

I'd asked Meemaw to put my hair into two braids on either side of my head. She told me she would be happy to do just that. Pulling on my hair, she crisscrossed it, making it tight as she could. Crooked as her fingers were, somebody might have thought she couldn't do that kind of work anymore. But she did and never with a word of complaint.

"Ain't your hair long?" She secured the braids with a couple ribbons. "Most girls I seen got their hair cut all the way up to their chins."

"I like mine long." I felt of the braids, making sure she'd made them even.

"That's my girl." She leaned on my shoulder and pushed herself up. "I best get downstairs and help your mama."

"Thank you, Meemaw," I said. "You did a nice job on my hair."

"That's all right, darlin'." She smiled. "You ought to come see if she wants your help, too."

"Yes, ma'am."

She left me to myself. I sat on the bare wood of my bedroom floor and folded my legs like I thought an Indian girl would have done.

Daddy had let me read an old book about Sacajawea and Hiawatha. In those books, the girls had skin lighter than what I would have expected an Indian girl to have. All the Indians I'd ever seen were brown, not creamy-white colored. The girls in the book were almost as fair as me, but with black-as-midnight hair.

Dropping my braids over the front side of my shoulders, I pretended they were shiny and dark.

When I closed my eyes, I wondered what it had been like for them the first time they saw a man with skin so white they could almost look right through it. Would they have thought red hair was made of fire? For some reason I thought they must have been afraid when they met face-to-face with a blue-eyed man.

With my eyes closed, all I could see was Eddie's face. His blue eyes.

Just thinking of him gave me the willies, even after a month of him being gone. I tried to shake off the thought of him, but he'd become like a tick under my skin.

All the sudden, I didn't want to be alone in my room anymore, so I got up and hustled down the steps.

❀

Mama wouldn't let Daddy keep the radio on while we ate our Thanksgiving dinner. Not that we had anything special to eat. Just a chicken, some stuffing, and a bowl of mashed potatoes. Still, Meemaw and Mama insisted that we have a nice meal. After all, Millard had come to eat with us.

I caught Meemaw making eyes at the old mayor more than a few times. Millard made them right back.

Beanie had found herself a feather somewhere. Pure black and oily. Mama had told her it was dirty and that she was not to have something so full of sickness at the Thanksgiving table. Beanie had screamed and thrown a regular old snit fit until Mama gave up. I didn't figure Mama had seen the way my sister grinned when she won.

Beanie sure did know how to get her way.

Daddy said grace, and we all sat still and quiet. He never did believe in long prayers. He was more for saying his few words and being done with it. I knew Meemaw would have liked him to go on a bit more. But Mama was glad, I believed, because he never prayed so long the food got cold.

Daddy's was a simple faith. He lived it with easy words and the sweat of his brow. I believed God liked that well enough.

After Daddy said "amen," Mama smiled at him in her way, soft and long. I liked it when she looked at him like that and the way he returned it. That was the way I wanted to look at my husband when I got one.

Daddy carved the small chicken, and Mama started passing around the potatoes. Clinking of serving spoons on Mama's good dishes and smells of rich food put a pit of happiness in the center of my body.

I thought a simple prayer of my own. One of thanksgiving for my family.

Even Beanie.

❋

Millard and Daddy had pulled two straight-backed chairs into the living room right by the little radio. They sat knee-to-knee, leaning close to hear the football game, and sipped the cups of coffee Mama had carried over for them.

"Who ever thought of making these boys play on Thanksgiving?" Meemaw shook her head. "Don't they think their mamas would want them home?"

"I don't know that they mind too much," Daddy said. "Football players make decent money. I'm sure their mamas are just glad they've got a job."

"Well, I don't mind so much." Millard slurped his coffee. "Hearing this game gets my mind off matters for a spell."

"Who do you like to win?" Daddy balanced the cup on his thigh.

"Chicago." Millard scratched his chin. "Now, I know full well Detroit's had a good season. I still say Chicago's the better team."

"Well, then." Daddy smiled and picked up his coffee cup. "Guess that leaves me with Detroit."

"I hope you boys aren't placing bets." Mama sat on the davenport next to Beanie. "We've got nothing to wager but a yard full of dust. You're welcome to it if you want it."

"No thanks," Millard said, chuckling. Then he winked at me. "How about you, Goldie Locks? You got a favorite team?"

"I don't know." I flipped the page in the Sears and Roebuck catalogue on my lap. "I guess I like whoever Daddy does."

"That's my girl." Daddy patted his knee. "Come on over here."

"Ain't she too big to sit on your lap?" Meemaw watched me walk to Daddy. "She's almost a lady now."

"Nah, she ain't too big." Daddy pulled me up on his lap with one hand. The other held his cup to one side. "Beanie Jean, how about you come over, too?" He handed Millard his coffee before extending his arm toward Beanie. "God gave me a knee for each of my girls."

I shifted to make room for my sister and tried not to get upset that he wanted to hold her, too. Some days, I just wanted Daddy all to myself.

Beanie stayed on the davenport and shook her head, making that oily feather loose, almost tumbling out of her frizzy curls. "I wanna stay here."

Daddy sighed out his nose and raised his eyebrows at me. "Guess you get me all to your lonesome, then."

I leaned back against his chest and rested my head on his shoulder.

Some kind of action was happening in the game. The announcer's voice traveled up in pitch, and he talked faster. Both Daddy and Millard moved their heads closer to the radio for just a second. The excitement ended with Daddy smiling and Millard shaking his head. Whatever the words the man on the radio said, I couldn't make any sense of.

"It's looking good for my team," Daddy said, sitting back in his chair and pulling me against his chest.

"It don't matter," Beanie said.

"You don't have a favorite, darlin'?" Daddy asked. "Lions or Bears?"

Beanie shook her head again, the feather finally falling all the way out of her hair and onto her lap. "Wolves always win anyway."

"I never heard of a wolf playing football," Millard said. "I reckon that would be one heck of a team."

Millard laughed and looked over my head at Daddy, winking at him. One thing I liked about Millard was that he never said a mean thing about my sister, even when she said something that made no sense at all.

"You know, I been up to Michigan once," Daddy said.

"When did you go there?" I asked.

"Before your mama and I got married. A real long time ago."

"You got family up there, don't you?" Millard finished off his coffee and put his cup and Daddy's on the floor.

"Sure do. A cousin of mine has a farm up there," Daddy answered. "Good old Gus."

"I thought he was a blast fool for moving north." Meemaw clucked her tongue. "Now who's the fool? Last letter we got from him, he said he's got more crop than he knows what to do with. And look what we got."

"Was it cold there, Daddy?" I asked, hoping he'd go ahead and tell one of his stories.

"Cold enough. I didn't see no snow, though. It was fall when I was up there. But it was colder than I've ever felt it here."

"Did you see an Eskimo?"

"Nah. But I seen an Indian or two."

"What did they look like?" I glanced over and saw Beanie playing with the feather, twisting it between her thumb and pointer finger.

"Like the ones we've got here. Just those ones had more clothes on."

"Tom," Mama scolded. "Don't go filling her mind with more of those stories."

"All right." Daddy kissed my cheek and pretended to whisper. "Your mama doesn't want me talking about savages on Thanksgiving. But I think it's fitting, ain't it?"

"You can tell me about them later." I liked being in on jokes with Daddy. He winked at me.

We all listened to the end of the game, me still on Daddy's lap. I never did figure out who won. Didn't much care, either. All I wanted was to be held by Daddy, imagining the Indians tromping around in their loincloths with feathers sticking up tall out of their hair.

In my daydream, every single one of them looked like Beanie.

❦

After dark, Millard said his *thank-you*s and *good-bye*s. He even kissed Meemaw's hand, making her cheeks turn red as apples. Daddy insisted on walking him back to his room at the courthouse. It seemed that men always found something important to talk about that the women weren't allowed to hear.

Meemaw chattered about what a nice man Millard was while she and Mama cleaned up the coffee things. Mama answered with "uh-huhs."

"Did you see how he ate?" Meemaw asked, a smile lifting her face. "Like he's not had a good meal in ages. That man needs a woman to cook for him."

"A woman like you?" Mama asked, grinning.

"Now, what do you mean by that?"

"I mean it's clear you're in love with that man." Mama hung her damp rag to let it dry. "And the way he looked back at you, I'd say he feels the same."

"Now, I don't know what you're talking about." But the way Meemaw looked out the corner of her eye at Mama with a smile playing on her lips, I knew she wasn't too upset at the thought. "I'm too old for falling in love, anyhow."

"How old is too old to fall in love?" I asked.

"Never you mind," Meemaw answered, giggling.

"Now, who is that?" Mama asked, tilting her head to look out the window over the sink.

Meemaw stood next to Mama and squinted. "I can't see anybody."

"It's . . ." Mama turned and, seeing me, left off. "Pearl, how about you go on up to bed now."

I nodded.

"Make sure your sister cleaned her teeth. And do your own, too." Mama reached for me, touching my cheek. "I'll be up in a bit."

On my way to the steps, I snuck a peek out the window. That Woman was standing on the back porch, lifting her fist to knock on the door.

"Darlin'?" Mama said, making the I-mean-business look. "Go on."

That Woman knocked on the door, and I went running up the stairs.

Halfway up, I stumbled, knocking my shin. I didn't dare cry out, not with the way Mama had glared at me. I just sat on the step and grabbed my leg, letting the tears drop on my knees. Where I hit my shin was bleeding, and already a bump was raising. I didn't figure I'd broken my leg. That would have made me faint like the ladies in the movies. Still, it hurt like the dickens.

Downstairs, the door opened, and I heard Mama say, "What are you doing here?"

"I want to talk to her," That Woman answered. I could just barely see her from where I sat on the steps.

"You're drunk." Mama's voice was full of disgust. "I can smell it on you. Why would you come over here smelling of booze?"

"You don't know what it's like—"

"Nope. I don't imagine I do."

"Days like this," That Woman said, then paused. "I'm lonely. See? I don't got nobody."

"That's none of my doing."

"Isn't it?" That Woman scrunched her eyebrows when she said that.

Meemaw stepped forward, the hem of her skirt swinging in and out of my view. "Listen here, you're the one who—"

"Mother," Mama said. "Leave it alone. She knows what she did."

"All I want is to see her. That's all." That Woman hugged her arms all the way around her front.

"You can't come here." Mama almost whispered. "You know that."

"But he said I got a right," That Woman said. "He told me she needs to know who I am."

"Who said that?" Mama asked.

"I think he's right." That Woman licked her lips. "She needs me."

"Who is telling you this?" Mama waited. Then she yelled it. "Who is telling you that you've got the right?"

"Eddie," That Woman answered.

I took both hands off my bleeding leg and covered my mouth to hold in any noise that might want to break out. The metal taste of my blood stung my tongue, but I didn't care. All I could think about was breathing in and out and not letting myself get scared.

For all I knew, it was a different man. Eddie of the blue eyes and the smirk hadn't been around in a long time.

"Eddie who?" Mama asked. "Do you mean that hobo?"

"He ain't a hobo."

"Fine. The man that hopped off the train and begged around for food, then." Mama sighed. "What does he know about this?"

"He knows plenty," That Woman said, her voice strong if slurring. "And he says I've got a right to see her all I want."

"He doesn't know anything about it." Mama grabbed the door. "Now go on. I'm closing this door, and I don't want to have to toss you out first."

That Woman took a step back, and Mama pushed the door closed, clicking the lock into place.

Mama cried after That Woman was gone.

"I don't want her to find out like that," Mama said. "I'm not ready for her to know."

"We've gotta tell her some time, Mary." Meemaw's voice was a gentle song. "We can't keep secrets forever."

"Just not yet." Mama cleared her throat. "How does that hobo know anything about us?"

All kinds of wonderings clattered around my mind. I went to my bed, shin still bleeding, and tried to make sense of That Woman's words and Mama's tears.

# CHAPTER FOURTEEN

U sed to be, before the dust drove most of the people out of Red River, that an old Negro woman would clean the courthouse once a week for Daddy and Millard. She would sweep off the steps and mop the one jail cell. She bleached the linens and even tidied up Daddy's desk when the papers got piled too high. All without saying so much as one word or lifting her eyes off her hands.

I remembered her quiet way and simple brown dress and the kerchief she wore on her head, but for the life of me, I couldn't think of her name.

It didn't much matter, anyhow. She and her family had been gone for a while, and Mrs. Jones had taken her place as the courthouse maid. I wasn't to tell Ray or Mrs. Jones that the city wasn't who paid her. The money came right out of Daddy's check.

Sometimes I worried we'd run out of money the way Mama and Daddy gave so much away.

On cleaning days, I'd come straight to the courthouse after school. Ray and I would sit and play with Millard's old checker set. I wasn't any good. Ray was, though. I liked letting him win just fine. It was nice to sit across from him inside for a change. The only sound between us was the tapping of round, wood pieces on the board.

Ray and I sat on an old church pew Daddy had put in the long entrance of the courthouse. We usually played on the marble floor, but Mrs. Jones had just mopped it. I didn't give her so much as a glimpse, all I wanted to do was pay attention to Ray.

"Y'all don't even look at that floor until it dries," she instructed. "I don't wanna see no footprints. Hear?"

"Yes, ma'am," Ray and I both said, not taking our eyes off the game.

Ray reached across the board as his mother left the room. He moved his piece, skipping half a dozen of mine, all the way to my side. The sleeve of his shirt pulled part way up his arm, showing purple-and-yellow marks all over his skin.

My stomach flipped one way, then the other, and my chest got tight.

"You gonna king me or what?" he asked, not realizing that I'd seen his bruises.

"What happened?" I touched his hand with my fingertips, so soft I wasn't sure he'd even feel it. "Did you fall?"

He flinched back, knocking a round checker to the floor. When he bent down to pick it up, I could see him blinking and jerking his eyebrows up and down like he always did when he was upset.

I didn't know why I'd asked him. I knew full well that his father had done it.

I'd known other kids who got split lips and black eyes from their fathers. Sometimes they even had marks from their mothers. But this was Ray. My Ray. It hurt harder that he was the one getting beat up at home.

Ray scowled at the game board and waited, pulling at his sleeves to hide the wounds.

"It's nothin'," he mumbled.

"Does it hurt?" I stared at the top of his head, wishing he'd look up at me.

"I said it was nothing." He scratched his scalp. "You gonna play or not?"

"Sure I'm gonna." I grabbed an extra checker and stacked it on his piece.

We didn't talk anymore. We just finished our game and checked the floor before putting our feet down. Then we tiptoed to Millard's office to put the set away.

Millard stayed in a room that was built as an office. Bookshelves lined the walls, and there was no closet to hang up his shirts. He made do, though.

I wandered around the room. He'd told me he didn't mind so long as I didn't get into anything, which took all my strength to obey. He had plenty of small boxes and drawers that begged me to explore them. I put my hands behind my back to keep the temptation away.

Millard had a dozen or so pictures hanging on the walls that I liked to look at. One of him and his wife, who had died long before I was born. She wasn't the prettiest woman, but they looked happy. Another picture was of Main Street in Red River before everything shut down. Folks walked up and down the sidewalks in fine clothes, and cars were parked on either side of the clean street. It must have been something to see.

Last, I looked at the picture he had of Beanie and me. In the photo, we were on the porch. Beanie looked off to the side and held her hands in her lap. I was next to her, my chubby feet dangling from the steps. It made me feel special that he kept that picture where he would see it every day.

Millard was the closest thing to a grandfather I had.

Ray reached up to the top shelf and slid the box of checkers next to a couple old notebooks. A book on the shelf below caught my eye.

"What's that book?" I asked, pointing.

Ray touched the spine. "This one?" he asked.

I nodded, and he took it off the shelf, handing it to me. He went to the window and looked out, his hands stuffed in his pockets.

The book was old—I could tell by how brownish yellow the edges of the pages were. I wondered if it was even older than Millard.

On the brown cover was stamped a picture of a gold-colored cow. Like the cow the Israelites made for themselves to worship. Boy, I wished I had been there to see Moses pitch his snit fit over that idol. Closing my eyes, I imagined him throwing down the tablets of God's law on the ground, breaking them into a million little pieces.

The golden cow under my fingertips bumped and grooved on the cover. The words beneath it were stamped in the same gold, but most of the sparkle had been worn off, leaving just the valley of the words on the brown.

*How to Get Rich on the Plains*, it read.

Careful not to flip too hard, I opened the front cover. On the inside was

141

swirling, penciled handwriting. It recorded rainfall and crops and how much wheat had sold for.

The years from 1930 through 1933 had been labeled as "bumper crop" years. The old timers in town still talked about those times and the mountains of wheat they'd harvested. I remembered how everybody had money then. They bought new cars and had suits made and put a fresh coat of paint on their houses.

I closed the book, looking at the golden cow, knowing that wheat had been what we had danced around, the dust of the busted commandments under our fingernails.

"What was it?" Ray asked, still looking out the window.

"Just an old book," I told him before putting it back on the shelf.

Mrs. Jones was waiting for us to come back from Millard's office. She stood next to the pew we had been sitting on. She didn't say anything to either of us, just waited.

One of her eyes was black, and her cheek was bruised. Her bottom lip was swollen, and I reckoned it must have hurt to talk.

She pulled the neck of the sweater together, turning her face toward the door of the courthouse. That sweater was the color of butter, creamy and yellow. Little rose shapes had been knitted around the collar that she held onto so tight. It had been one of Mama's favorites until Beanie splattered bleach all along the bottom of it. Mrs. Jones didn't seem to mind the white spots so much.

"Come on," Mrs. Jones finally said to Ray. "Say good-bye to Pearl."

Ray nodded at me, not meeting my eyes. "Bye."

The two of them walked out the big courthouse doors. Ray turned and gave me a quick, slight smile.

It was the kind of smile that said everything was going to be okay.

❖

Daddy and Millard sat on either side of Daddy's big desk. Daddy reclined all the way back in his chair, with his boots resting on a pile of old newspapers that Mrs. Jones had stacked for him. Millard sat straight with his arms crossed and a toothpick moving up and down between his lips.

Neither of them spoke, which was a normal occurrence between them. Mama had told me once that two men could sit in a room for days without saying so much as a single word to one another.

That was the closest thing to crazy I could think of.

"You finished with the checkers?" Millard asked, keeping the toothpick between his teeth.

"Yes, sir," I answered, studying that toothpick, hoping to figure out how he talked without it falling.

"Who won?"

"Ray did."

"Well, you don't gotta be modest. I know you let him win." Millard gave me a wink. "You put the set away?"

I nodded.

"Good girl."

"Ray and Mrs. Jones leave already?" Daddy lowered his feet and yawned into his hand.

"Yes, sir."

"That's fine."

"Daddy?"

"Yes, darlin'?" He smiled at me with his eyes half open.

"Can't you do anything about Mr. Jones?" I leaned my hip into the desk, right by where his feet had been on the newspapers.

"What do you mean?"

"He hurts his family," I whispered.

"Yes." Daddy leaned forward, resting his elbows on his thighs. "We've talked about this before, darlin'."

"Can't you make him stop it?"

"I wish I could." Daddy turned to Millard and shrugged. He licked his lips and smoothed his mustache with his fingers.

Finally, he sat back in his chair and let out a long breath, reaching for his tobacco and rolling papers. I let him put together a cigarette and light it up.

"You don't hurt us like that," I said.

"You're right. I don't." He breathed in through his cigarette. "A man shouldn't hurt his family."

"Mr. Jones hurts Mrs. Jones." I leaned toward him. "Did you see her face? Her lip was swelled up."

"I seen it."

"And he hurt Ray, too."

Daddy leaned forward again and grabbed my hand, pulling me closer to him.

"Darlin'," he said, "there ain't a single thing I can do."

Millard's chair complained as he got up from it. "I best go." He nodded at Daddy. "Good luck, Tom."

I waited to be alone with Daddy before going on.

"Daddy, I don't want Ray getting hurt."

"I know it." He sighed and stubbed out his cigarette, even though it was only about half burned down. "But a man's got a right to privacy in his own home. It ain't none of our concern, Pearl."

"Couldn't you go talk to him? Tell him to stop?"

He rubbed over his whole face with his hand, pulling the skin of his cheeks down to make jowls at his jaw. "I wish with all my might I could do that."

"Isn't it the right thing to do?"

"It ain't that simple."

"It's right to protect kids, isn't it?" I felt my insides get warm and soft as the sadness flooded all the way up and out of my eyes.

"It is."

"You always do the right thing, Daddy." My voice shook. "Always."

He rubbed the back of my hand with his thumb and didn't meet my eyes. "Nah. I don't. I don't always do the right thing."

Something heavy and hard as a rock dropped from my heart all the way to my feet, threatening to knock me right over. But Daddy had a good hold of my hand.

"I don't understand," I sputtered.

"Pearl, your mama and me, well, we haven't done everything right." He let his eyes flick up to mine for only a moment before he looked back at my hand. "I'm the one who done the wrong. It's on me. I should have been more honest with you. But I was scared for me and for you."

"What do you mean, Daddy?" I asked, my head feeling light and swimmy.

"See, when you were born . . ." He hesitated and really concentrated on our hands. "I've got to tell you something—"

The door of the courthouse opened, banging into the wall so hard I was sure it would leave a hole. Daddy's head snapped up toward the man who'd rushed in. Standing, he turned toward the courthouse doors.

Daddy dropped my hand and pushed me behind him as he stepped around the desk, hand on his holster.

"What is it?" he asked.

Peeking out from behind Daddy, I recognized the man as one who lived in a sharecropper cabin. He swallowed hard, his face whiter than any sheet I'd ever seen. He got up close to Daddy and pulled on his arm.

"Now, hold on here," Daddy said, stopping the man. "What's this about?"

"We got a emergency." The man clenched his jaw, sinewy neck muscles stuck out under his skin. Looking at me out of the corner of his eye, he nodded. "Don't wanna say more'n that in front of the girl."

Millard had come out of his office by then, his hat already on his head. "Tell us on the way."

"Darlin', I'll be back soon as I can," Daddy said, turning to me on his way out. "Don't you worry. Everything's all right. Hear?"

I nodded because I believed him. Some kid had gotten tangled in barbed wire or bit by a snake, I figured. Maybe even a roof collapsed on one of the cabins with somebody inside. Things like that happened about every day in Red River.

I ran to the window, wiping away a smear of grime on the glass that Mrs. Jones had missed, and watched the men walk away. They talked to each other as they went.

After just a few words, Daddy took off running.

❖

The courthouse had more creaking and clunking and bumping sounds when I was alone in it. I tried to pay attention to the clock keeping time, trying not to think about the ghosts that must have haunted that place.

Not that I really believed in ghosts. It was just that Ray had told me that they used to kill the murderers and thieves in a locked room at the end of the long hallway. He'd said that if I listened close enough I'd hear them screaming from the pain of being jolted with electricity.

I tried to remind myself that what I heard was just wind or the building settling.

"Daddy'll be back soon," I whispered to myself. "Don't be scared."

The big wood doors opened, and I expected Daddy and Millard to come through, talking about what had happened. The emergency would be over, and they'd both want to smoke a cigarette before calling it a day.

I hoped Millard had one of his pink candies for me.

It wasn't Daddy or Millard that walked in, though. It was That Woman. She hadn't seen me yet, on account she had pointed her eyes right at the freshly mopped floor and pushed the door closed behind her.

She wore a pink dress, one that had to have been store bought a long time before. I could see where she'd mended it, and not too well, either. It puckered with the black thread she'd used. I wondered why her mama hadn't taught her how to sew better than that. Her hair was silky straight. A tired attempt at a curl curved the bottoms. Really, it looked like she'd slept a good long time on her hair.

"Hi," I whispered, not sure if she would hear me.

She took in a sharp gasp, finally noticing me. She raised her shoulders and touched the middle of her chest with one of her small hands. She stared at me almost a whole minute before she blinked.

"I didn't mean to scare you," I said. "I'm sorry."

"Is the sheriff here?" she asked, looking right at me. It wasn't that I minded so much, her staring at me. It was the way she did it that made me feel funny, like she knew something I didn't.

Adults always looked at children that way.

I swallowed hard, trying not to be nervous about the way she eyeballed me. "Pardon?" I asked, even though I'd heard her question just fine.

"I asked if the sheriff's here."

"No, ma'am." I paused, repeating the words to myself in a whisper.

"You know where he's at? I come to see him."

"Oh, he's down at the sharecropper cabins. He said he'd be back real quick." Not knowing what to do with my hands, I clasped them behind me. "Something happened down there. I don't know what, though."

"Maybe I'll just wait here." She looked at the pew but stayed standing. "If that's all right."

"Sure is."

"You care if I sit down?"

I shook my head.

That Woman lowered herself into the pew, smoothing the skirt over her thighs and crossing her ankles.

"Would you like to see some pictures?" I asked.

She shrugged her shoulders.

I carried over a shuffle of pictures I'd drawn over the last few weeks. Putting them on the pew next to her, I wished so hard she'd pick them up and give them a good study. I wanted her to admire them the way Mama never seemed to have the time to do. If she had, I would have offered to let her take them all home.

But That Woman didn't hardly glance at them. Instead, she folded her hands in her lap.

"I drew those pictures." I took a step back from the pew. "I like to draw sometimes. Miss Camp—she's my teacher—she says I'm pretty good at it."

"Uh-huh."

"Did you know the sheriff is my daddy?" I shifted on my feet.

She nodded and turned toward the door.

"I wasn't sure you knew," I said.

For a good minute or two, she sat without hardly moving except to breathe and blink. I wondered if I'd said something wrong or if she was just the kind who didn't like talking all that much.

"I know he's your father," she said. Then she turned and blinked her eyes. "Is he good to you? I always wondered if he was."

"Yes, ma'am." I tilted my head. "Why did you wonder that?"

"Because not all fathers are good."

"I know." I thought of Mr. Jones. "My daddy is, though. He's real good to us. He never hits my mama."

She pushed her lips together and dipped her head. "I'm glad."

"Is your father good to you?" I asked.

"He's dead," she answered, not changing the way her voice sounded. "He's been dead a long time."

"That's sad." I felt sorry for asking the question.

"I ain't sad about it." She fingered a place on her neck under her jaw. "Some people ain't worth our sadness."

"Was he mean to you?"

Mama would have grabbed me by the ear and tugged me into another room, where she would have scolded me for having asked too much. She would have told me to hush up and stop being so rude and to let That Woman be.

She would have been sore that I'd said a word to That Woman in the first place.

But Mama wasn't there right then to stop me.

"My pa drank," That Woman answered, blinking hard so that her whole face moved with it. "He treated everybody ugly. That was just how things were with him. I don't think he knew another way."

"That's too bad." Again, I thought of Mr. Jones and wondered if he didn't know another way.

She lifted both her shoulders then let them slump. "I guess it don't matter no more, does it?"

"Guess not." I took a seat, just the stack of drawings between us. "My name's Pearl."

"I know your name." She cocked her head when she looked at me. Something about her eyes was soft like Mama's even though they were blue instead of dark brown. "I always did love that name."

"Thank you." I flashed a smile. "What's your name?"

"Winnie." She smiled small, like she was shy. "My ma called me Winifred. Guess that's my Christian name. I never took to it, though. It sounded too much like a man's name."

"I like Winnie just fine."

"Thanks kindly." She turned her face to her hands and went to work on a piece of loose skin by her fingernail.

"How do you know Eddie?" I asked.

She turned her head away from her hands and looked at the doors. "It's getting late."

"I heard you talking about Eddie to my mama." I leaned forward. "You came to my house on Thanksgiving. Do you remember that?"

"Sure. I remember." Winnie sighed and faced me, her eyes had grown large. "Yeah. I know him."

"Is he your friend?"

"No." Her chest rose with a deep breath. "He's a bad man."

"Then why do you talk to him?"

"Because he's the only one who can help me."

"We would help you," I said. "We help lots of folks."

"Your mother don't want nothing to do with me."

"I'm sorry she was so cross with you when you came over."

"She had a right to be." Winnie uncrossed her ankles and smoothed her skirt again. "I best go."

She stood quick, her hands still touching her skirt.

"It's okay." I stood, too. "Daddy'll be back soon."

"This was a mistake. I don't know why I thought this was a good idea." She shook her head. The way she talked at the floor made me think she was saying the words more to herself than me. "Eddie was wrong."

"No, stay. Please."

"I gotta get home." She reached for the door.

"To the cat house?"

She whipped around toward me again, her cheeks red and her hands clenched. I was afraid she would hit me. She didn't look into my face, but at my shoulder. Releasing her hands, she slouched.

"I don't know where you heard a thing like that," she said. "But it ain't such a nice thing to say."

"Why not?'

"It just ain't." She stammered. "It's just that . . . it's not nice."

"I'm sorry." Tears about flooded out of my eyes. "I didn't mean to say anything unkind. I don't know what's wrong with living at a cat house."

She blew out air and reached into her purse, grabbing a cigarette and lighting it. "Listen here, Pearl," she said, not angry exactly. "I wanna tell you something important, all right?"

I nodded.

"I know Eddie's talked to you. I just don't know what all he's told you." She pulled on her cigarette again. "But you need to know, it's all been for you."

"He's bad."

"No. Not all the way." The cigarette shook in her hand, breaking loose a flutter of ashes to the clean floor. "I've done a lot of wrong, you know. More wrong than good. And I hate all I done. But I'm trying to make some things right."

"Do you hate the cat house?"

"Closest place to hell I can think of." She reached both hands toward me, but before she touched me she pulled back. "I been foolish and wicked. And I done terrible things. But you're okay."

She turned and pulled open the door just enough to slip through.

❋

Daddy didn't come back and the evening was turning darker. Night made the courthouse sounds worse, so I decided to go home.

I left a note for Daddy on his desk.

Walking along the dirt-covered sidewalks from the courthouse to my front porch, I knew I needed to tell Mama that I'd talked to Winnie. That Woman. Bracing myself for Mama to be sore at me, I took one step at a time up the porch and opened the front door.

"Mama?" I called, breathing in the smell of potatoes. My grumbling stomach called out, too.

"Darlin'," Meemaw answered. "I'm in the kitchen. Come on in here."

Meemaw stood at the stove, pushing a pile of food around in a black skillet. She cracked a few eggs, mixing them in. I raised up on my toes to see if she had any sausage in there, too. No such luck.

"Where's Mama?"

Meemaw looked over her shoulder at me. Moist and red, her eyes were swollen from crying.

Something bad had happened.

"What's wrong?" Dread squeezed the air out of me.

She flicked the burner off under the food and turned all the way toward me. Her mouth worked around words she didn't say. I wished she would just tell me what had happened, but something held her back from it.

"You hungry?" she asked, reaching for a plate in the cupboard. "Go get your sister, hear?"

I did as she asked, and the three of us ate our eggs and potatoes in quiet. We stacked our plates in the sink, and Meemaw walked Beanie and me up to our room.

"I'll just leave the dishes for tomorrow," she said. "I'm so tired."

She tucked us in our bed without making us change our clothes or clean our teeth and turned down the lights. Beanie rustled around for a while before drifting into a snoring sleep.

I tried my hardest to stay awake, determined not to fall asleep until Mama and Daddy got home.

❀

I couldn't stay in bed a moment longer. Beanie groaned and rolled in her sleep, pushing me near the edge of the bed. When she moved back to her side, she took the covers with her.

Climbing over her, I got out of bed. The chilly floor sent a shiver from my bare feet all the way to my shoulders. As quiet as I could, I took my sweater from its hanger and pushed my hands through the sleeves.

The downstairs of our house was quiet except for the ticking of our clock. I sat, rocking in Meemaw's chair until I saw Mama and Daddy walk up the front porch. Daddy held the door for Mama.

"I sure could use a drink," Daddy said.

"Quiet, Tom," Mama whispered. "They're all asleep."

"Not everybody." Daddy nodded at me.

He didn't wear his usual smile.

"What are you doing up?" Mama asked, keeping her voice low. "You should be in bed. It's real late, darlin'."

"I was worried," I answered.

"About what?" Mama unbuttoned her sweater.

"I don't know."

"There's nothing to be worried about." The way Mama's voice shook, I knew she wasn't telling the truth.

"We have to tell her some time," Daddy said, facing Mama. Then he shrugged and shook his head. "We have to."

It felt as if my heart stopped beating.

Mama sat on the davenport, and Daddy came to me, kneeling on the floor. It wasn't until his face was close that I noticed the bags under his eyes and the droop of his mouth. He licked his lips, and his chin quivered. He cried. I'd never seen Daddy cry.

"Honey, something happened," he said, touching my knee. "Something real bad."

"What was it?" My mind passed through all the faces of people something bad could happen to. I knew it was no one in our house. At least that was a relief.

"Darlin', I'm fixing to tell you something that's hard. You might have questions, but I don't know if I got any answers." He blinked a few times. "I don't have answers for any of the questions I've got myself."

"What happened?" I whispered.

"Well, it's hard to say exactly." He sniffled, and his nose sounded full.

"But when Mrs. Jones and Ray went back home this afternoon, they found Mr. Jones."

He paused and swallowed a good couple times. He didn't blink, but I didn't figure his eyes would dry out for all the tears.

"He'd hung himself," he said. "He's dead."

"Did Ray see it?" I asked. I remembered the story Ray'd told me months before about the man who got hung. I wondered if Mr. Jones had gotten the idea to do that from the newsreel. "Did he see his father?"

Daddy nodded.

"Is he okay?"

"Mr. Jones is dead, darlin'."

"I mean Ray."

Daddy shook his head. "Nobody should have to see what he seen today."

"Did you see him?"

Daddy nodded.

"Was it really bad?"

"Yes." Daddy's voice cracked, but he didn't lose himself. Instead, he cleared his throat.

"You shouldn't have had to see it, either."

His whole forehead wrinkled. "We're gonna do everything we can to get Ray and Mrs. Jones out of that dugout. I don't know how we'll do it, but there's got to be a way."

"Luella won't leave, Tom," Mama said. "That dugout's all she has."

"That man spoiled everything for her, didn't he?" Daddy locked his jaw and closed his eyes.

Mr. Jones had taken so much from that family. I wondered if he thought taking himself from them was the best thing he could have done.

## CHAPTER FIFTEEN

Beanie didn't understand a whole lot of things. One of the things that plain didn't make sense to her was death. She couldn't figure out how a body could have breath and a heartbeat one moment and the next be still and without life.

I wasn't sure I had a good handle on it, either, for that matter.

Mama tried to explain Mr. Jones's death anyway. The fact that he'd killed himself confused Beanie even more. We sat at the table, Mama trying to get it through my sister's head.

"He's not coming back?" Beanie asked. "Like Baby Rosie?"

"That's right," Mama answered.

"Did he get full of dust?"

"No. Remember, I told you he died a different way." Mama reached across the table and patted Beanie's hand. "He did it to himself."

"Baby Rosie's in heaven." Beanie pushed her eyebrows together the way she always did when she tried real hard to figure out something. "So Mr. Jones is in heaven, too."

Mama let out a big sigh and pinched the very top of her nose.

"They're together in heaven." Beanie nodded and smiled.

"Rosie sure is," I said.

"Mr. Jones can take care of her now."

"He never took care of her when he was alive," I snapped, surprised by how good it felt to be angry at that man.

"Pearl Louise," Mama gasped.

"It's true," I said. "If he's in heaven, I hope he's not allowed anywhere near her."

Mama didn't say anything against that because she knew how mean Mr. Jones was.

"You think he's in heaven?" Beanie asked, looking at me.

"I don't know where he's at," I answered. "All I care about is that he can't hurt anybody anymore."

Beanie sat for a long time, her eyebrows pushed together. All at once, she got up and stormed up the stairs and to our room, slamming the door behind her.

"Leave her be," Mama said.

She didn't have to tell me twice.

❖

Beanie never came downstairs for dinner, so we ate without her, as much as it bothered Meemaw to do it.

"She's going to get hungry," Meemaw argued.

"Mother, she's near grown," Daddy said. "She's got to learn. Life's hard, but we can't go into a temper tantrum every time something goes wrong."

"She just don't understand, is all." Meemaw crisscrossed her fork and knife across her empty plate. "You should know better than to tell her things she can't understand."

"Mother," Daddy said, his voice smooth and calm. "Beanie is going to be all right."

"I wish I knew that was the truth."

"Would it make you feel better if I went up and checked on her?" Daddy sipped the last of his coffee.

"It would, and I thank you." Meemaw dusted a crumb off her chest.

"Excuse me," Mama whispered, getting up from the table, her shoulders tense as she moved. She carried her plate to the counter.

"It don't make no sense to me, Mary," Meemaw said.

"What don't?"

"Why you would tell Beanie a thing like that. You knew it would just get her all in a bunch."

"She had to know." Mama poured water into a pot and put it on the stove to boil. "We can't keep these girls from knowing what goes on in this world. I don't keep secrets from my children."

Meemaw huffed out air and shook her head. "Since when? Seems to me you've got a whopper of a secret under your hat."

"Mother," Daddy said, glancing at me. "Don't. That's not the way."

Mama turned, her cheeks red. "I'm doing the best I can."

"Well, Beanie ain't never gonna understand things." Meemaw folded her hands in her lap. "I'd have thought you'd know that by now."

Mama grabbed her plate and threw it to the floor, smashing it. Meemaw yelped and lifted her hands to her chest, and Daddy stood. My heart beat so hard, it shook my whole body. Mama lifted her hands to her head and gathered bunches of her hair in her fingers.

"You think I don't know that?" she yelled. "She is my daughter. I know her. I know she isn't right. I do. And I wish to high heaven I could fix that for her, but I can't."

Daddy stepped toward Mama with his hands out as if he was cornering a steer.

"No." Mama shook her head, eyes huge. "Don't you—"

"Mary, I need you to calm down." Daddy took another step.

"I just want you to leave me alone." She turned her head this way and that, as if she was searching the kitchen for something. "All I want is to get out of this county. Out of this godforsaken state. Everything's dying here. It's all falling apart. And I think I'm coming to pieces along with it."

She touched the counter, running her hand across it, pushing off a layer of dust.

"It doesn't matter what I do. This house is always dirty. It's filthy. All I do is scrub and sweep, and it doesn't make one lick of a difference." Mama's voice weakened. "Tom, if you want me to stay married to you, you best find a way to move this family. We can't live here no more."

"Mary—"

"Thomas, I'm not just talking." She gritted her teeth. "If I have to stay here another day I very well may end up like Si Jones."

"Don't you dare say something like that." Daddy smoothed his voice like he was calming a child. "You know you wouldn't. We need you too much."

"You hear me? The girls and I can't live like this anymore. We can't take it." She pointed right at him, jabbing her finger into his chest. "I'll take the girls, and I will leave you behind."

"I ain't never thought I'd let a woman talk to me like that." Daddy shook his head and pushed his lips together.

"What are you going to do about it?" Mama trembled. "You gonna beat me?"

"I wouldn't—"

"Well, you didn't stop Si from beating Luella." She crossed her arms. "Maybe you think it's not a half-bad idea."

"You don't know what you're saying." Daddy stepped away from her. "You best calm yourself."

Daddy turned from her and made his way to the steps. "Mary, I love you dearly. You know that."

He took the stairs two at a time. I followed him.

"Daddy?" I said.

He didn't respond, not even to let me know he'd heard me.

"I don't want to leave." I touched his back. "I wouldn't ever go anywhere without you."

"I know." He glanced over his shoulder. "Neither would your mama."

He turned the knob of my bedroom door and pushed, but it didn't budge. He pushed harder.

"Beanie Jean, you come on and open this door," he said, his voice raised. She didn't answer him.

"I'm gonna have to break this door down if you don't open it."

Still, she didn't answer.

Daddy put his shoulder into the door, grunting as he shoved it. A skidding of furniture across the floor and the door opened. Beanie had shoved the bed in front of the door. How she'd had the strength, I didn't know.

Daddy and I stepped into the room.

The curtains moved in the wind that blew through the window.

"Beanie?" Daddy called, looking in the closet and under the bed. "Violet Jean?"

Her shoes were set on her pillow, the laces tangled and frayed.

She was gone.

❊

Mama paced the living room, her shoes tap-tap-tapping as she walked. For all the carrying on with Meemaw before, Mama was quiet and pale as she could be. Her breaths came in short gasps.

"She's going to be cold," she said, holding Beanie's one sweater in a lump against her chest.

Water made a tinkling song as Meemaw filled the tea kettle and put it on to boil. We didn't have any tea, I knew that much. Mama had put it off for months, saying she didn't need it. Still, Meemaw boiled water and Mama drank it just like it was, sipping it dutifully before she went back to pacing.

The clock struck eleven times. Outside, the sky was black as tar, and the air was just as thick. Mama had finally sat down on the davenport.

After the clock chimed twelve, Mama got up and went out to the porch. I followed her, so tired, but too scared to sleep. My sister had never taken off into the night before.

Standing next to Mama, I wrapped my arm around her waist, but she didn't act like she even knew I was there. She just stood still, glaring into the black.

"I should go help them look," she said. "I wish Tom would've let me help."

Daddy had gotten Millard and a few other men to form a search party after an hour of looking on his own for Beanie. He'd taken his truck so he could cover more land. Most of the other men had lanterns with them. Every once in a while, I'd see a bright dot of flame or headlight off in the distance. Like fireflies.

Meemaw was inside the house, praying. Her quivery voice called out to God, loud as it could get. She begged God so much I was embarrassed for her. I didn't think I had the stomach to listen to her much longer. Her praying made me even more afraid for my sister.

Leaning back against the porch, I said a little prayer of my own. Mine was inside my head or my heart, I couldn't decide which. If God heard it, I couldn't tell. Not right away, at least. All I could do right then was hope He was listening. I wondered if that was what faith felt like.

My prayer was just two words that I thought over and over. "Help Beanie." That was all I could think of. I'd closed my eyes, hoping it would work even better.

Then Mama spoke.

"It's him," she said. Then she said it again, louder, and just about jumped off the porch. She ran down the path to the street.

Daddy's truck rumbled along the road toward our house. The headlights were so bright against the dark I couldn't see much else. As it got closer, I could see a man driving and two men riding in the back.

I could tell that the men in the back were Millard and Daddy. They leaned over something.

"Pearl, the door," Mama shouted. "Hold the door."

I pulled it wide and held it, afraid I wasn't doing enough to help.

The truck pulled as close to the porch steps as it could before stopping. Daddy and Millard jumped off the back and helped Beanie out. Daddy steadied my sister as she stumbled up the steps. She held tight to his arm and kept her face blank. She didn't look at me as she passed by.

Mama followed close behind.

I still held the door even after they were all inside, waiting for Millard and the other man to come in, too.

"We'll wait out here, Pearl," Millard said. "Go on in."

I went inside like he said and closed the door.

"Have her sit there," Mama said, pointing at the davenport. "Mother, my basket of bandages. Please."

Daddy moved slowly with Beanie, helping her to sit. He was so careful with her, so gentle. And she didn't want to let go of him, not even with her backside resting on the soft couch. She kept her arms tight around him and moaned when he tried to release her hands.

He didn't force her and didn't fight her. Daddy just knelt down next to her and let her cling to him. He wrapped his arms around her and let her head rest against his chest.

"She's in a bad way." Daddy turned his head as much as he could manage. "Real beat up."

"Good Lord," Mama said, covering her mouth. "What happened? She get caught up in the barbed wire?"

Daddy and Mama met eyes, and neither of them said a thing. The quiet was only stirred by Beanie's groaning.

"Somebody did this to her. Whoever it was . . ." He stopped talking, smoothing Beanie's hair and pressed lightly over where her ear was. "Whoever done this meant to kill her, I think."

He pushed her hair aside and showed the marks on her neck.

"What is that?" Mama asked.

"Marks from the hands of whoever did this to her. He tried to strangle her."

Mama's knees bent and then straightened again, as if her body couldn't decided what it needed to do. She reached one hand out and held it on top of Beanie's head.

❧

Beanie was in our bed, resting. Meemaw had insisted that she needed to be with her. The way my big sister sobbed when Mama cleaned her wounds broke all of our hearts. I wanted so bad to be with her and to hold her hand. But Mama said I'd need to sleep on the davenport for a few nights.

"Grab the end," Mama said, holding up a sheet.

We lifted the sheet in the space above the davenport and it domed up before landing lightly.

"Go on and lie down." She nodded. "I'll put the covers over you."

"Where's Daddy?" I asked, curling up on the fresh sheet.

"Out on the porch." She pulled another sheet over top of me. "He'll be back in right soon."

"Is Beanie going to be okay?" I nestled into the pillow Mama handed me. Mama sat on the edge of the davenport, her hands folded in her lap.

"It's late," she whispered. "You need to get some rest."

I closed my eyes, even though I didn't think I'd ever fall asleep that night. Pretending to drift off, I breathed slower and rolled so my face would be toward the back of the davenport. Mama fixed the blanket, pulling so it would cover my feet.

The front door opened with a creaking and clicking sound. I didn't stir, hoping Mama would still believe I was sleeping. The adults were looser with their lips when they thought I was asleep.

"How is she?" Daddy's voice. "Has she woken up at all?"

I knew he meant Beanie. I didn't figure they'd be talking about me for a good long time.

"No." Mama shifted, pushing her rear against my legs. "I hope she sleeps through the night."

"Pearl fell asleep fast."

"Sure did." Mama sighed. "She was real scared. It wears a girl out."

"I bet."

"You got any idea who did this to Beanie?" Mama asked.

"Not yet."

"I can't imagine anybody doing such a thing."

"The fella who found her is still out on the porch with Mill," Daddy said. "I told them they should go on home. The other fella's all shook up. Says he doesn't want to leave until he knows she's going to be okay."

"They don't have to stay outside," Mama said. "Tell them to come in. I'll make some coffee. I've got some potatoes I could fry up too."

Mama got up and went to the kitchen. I heard her shuffling around and filling the percolator.

"Come on in here," Daddy called out the door. "My wife's perking some coffee. You drink coffee, do you?"

"I do believe we could both use a little coffee." It was Millard's voice.

As slow as I could, I rolled over to my other side and opened one eye, the one closest to my pillow. All I could see were three sets of booted feet. Daddy's and Millard's I recognized. But the other pair were scuffed up and dusty.

"Mary," Daddy called. "Come on in here, darlin'. This here man found Beanie."

"Oh," Mama said. "It's you. You're the one?"

"This is my wife, Mary," Daddy said. "Mary, I believe you've seen this man before."

"I believe so," Mama answered. "You're the one found Beanie?"

Mama had the edge to her voice she held for folks she didn't care for.

"Just doing my good turn for the day," the man answered.

At the sound of his voice all the breath in my lungs got sucked out. I didn't dare open my eyes any more than they were. Instead, I shut them tight as I could. So tight, orange burst across my vision.

"Eddie here was just telling me he got back to town just tonight," Daddy said.

"That so?" Mama asked. "Seems convenient."

"I had work out to Boise City for a couple weeks is all," Eddie answered. "Found your daughter on the way into town."

"Well, Eddie, you're welcome here any time." Daddy's voice sounded like it was smiling. "A regular old part of the family now. We do appreciate you helping our girl."

"I'm just glad I heard her," Eddie said. "She was crying and carrying on so, I thought it weren't nothing more'n a hurt jackrabbit."

I couldn't help myself, I opened my eyes all the way. Eddie stood looking right at me with those cornflower-blue eyes and a smirk on his face.

The big bad wolf had found his way into the brick house, and there was nothing I could do about it.

❖

"He's the one who was here begging for food, Tom," Mama said. "I don't trust him."

Millard and Eddie had been gone from our house for only a minute or two before Mama and Daddy whispered to each other about him.

"Mary, he's not a bad man," Daddy said. "He's just tramping around the country. That's all."

"I get a bad feeling from him."

"He found Beanie. A bad man would've just left her there."

"Maybe he wants some kind of a reward." Mama yawned. "Folks like him don't do anything for nothing."

"Well, I can keep an eye on him if you want. But I don't think we've got to worry about him none."

They were quiet a minute or two, and I almost opened my eyes to see if they were still in the room with me. But then Mama sighed.

"You really believe he's all right, Tom?" she asked.

"I do."

It was the first time I doubted Daddy's wisdom.

CHAPTER SIXTEEN

As soon as news spread around Red River about Eddie rescuing Beanie, he became the town hero. Men slapped him on the back to congratulate him. Women apologized that they didn't have sugar enough to make him a cake.

Eddie didn't have any problem telling and retelling his story of finding my sister, her carrying on in the ditch, tangled in the rusty barbed wire. How he did his best to calm her as he pulled the barbs away from her flesh. How she'd held on tight when he lifted her. That out of the corner of his eye he saw a man running west down the railroad tracks.

A Negro man, he claimed. Though I didn't know how he could have been able to tell that, what with how dark that night had been.

Each time he told the story, it got fatter, thick with added details to make it more of a drama. He heard a rattler down in that ditch and feared it would bite him. A coyote howled in the distance. How he had stumbled as he carried her, but pulled together all his strength to keep from dropping her.

Wherever he went, a group of men and boys stood around to hear him tell the story. I was about sick of hearing his voice.

Meemaw told me that a hopeless people are always in the market for a hero. "Just remember King Saul," she'd said.

All I could remember of King Saul from the Bible was that he was a head taller than everybody else. Eddie, though, was a head shorter.

Nobody in Red River seemed to care so much about that.

"I just wish the newspaper was still running," Millard had said. "Eddie deserves a front page for what he done."

Best they could do was have a picture of Eddie made to hang in the courthouse right next to the newspaper clipping of the shooting of Jimmy DuPre.

Folks in town wanted Daddy to find the maniac who had attacked Beanie. He went around, door-to-door, tent-to-tent, asking after anybody who had seen anything the night of the attack. No one had.

He'd even asked my sister to go over what had happened. She never did come up with the words to explain it. All she kept saying was that she couldn't see anything that night. She repeated that it was too dark, and there were no stars. The one thing she did remember was that someone or something had hit her real hard on the back of the head.

Then she'd end up crying until she dropped off into a deep sleep. She wouldn't wake up again for hours.

"Eddie says he saw a Negro running away," Mama said after another day of wondering and Beanie's crying.

"Eddie isn't exactly the ideal witness." Daddy stood. "I like the guy, but I can't go and arrest the first black man I see just cause Eddie said so."

"But Eddie saved her," Mama said. "Why would he lie?"

"The way I see it, God's the one who saved her, Mary," Daddy answered back. "I know I'm not a church-going man, but I believe it. Eddie just happened to be in the area at the moment. And I ain't saying he lied. Just saying he might not have seen what he says he did."

But the good folks of Red River wanted a man to pay for what had happened to Beanie. Daddy could barely step off our porch without somebody talking to him about a colored man they'd seen in the Hooverville or walking through the town. I even heard one man talk about a "good, old-fashioned lynching."

"It's our right to keep this town safe," the man had said.

"Leave it to me," Daddy had told him. "Don't go hanging anybody on account of my family. I won't have it."

Two weeks until Christmas and no peace on earth to be found.

❧

On weekdays, either Daddy or Millard would walk me to and from the schoolhouse, holding my hand. "Just in case" was what they said. Whenever I asked to walk to Ray's house, Mama said I shouldn't. Even sitting on the porch by myself sent Mama and Meemaw into a tizzy.

Things were too dangerous, they believed. They were thinking of how to best protect me from whoever might hurt me.

Most of the time, I just sat on the davenport, reading my fairy-tale book over and again, wishing Ray would come to visit. I even would have been happy if Beanie sat with me.

It was a lonely time.

At night, Mama set up a bed on the davenport for me. She said she wasn't sure when I'd be up in my room again. Beanie had nightmares most nights, kicking and hitting in her sleep. I didn't mind sleeping in the living room all that much, really.

One night I woke up when it was still dark out. I sat up, forgetting where I was. The book I'd fallen asleep reading fell to the floor with a bang. Peeking at the clock, I could just barely see that it was too early in the morning to be awake. I nestled back down on my pillow and pulled the blanket up to my chin.

Yawning, I closed my eyes, trying to put all extra thoughts out of my head so I could fall off to sleep.

The scratching of a match strike made me open my eyes. Flame touched the end of a cigarette and it turned orange then faded.

"Daddy?" I whispered.

"Nope," the man answered from across the room.

I knew that voice too well.

I sat up, scrambling to the end of the couch farthest from him and pulled the blanket up over myself again.

Eddie sat in Daddy's chair, smoke puffing out of his mouth.

"Did I wake you up?" he asked.

"What are you doing here?" I asked, trying to cover up the fear in my voice. "You shouldn't be here."

"Says who?" He puffed on his cigarette again. "I would've thought you'd be happy to see me."

"It's the middle of the night. You shouldn't be here."

"You're afraid of me." He stood up and walked around the room. "You don't gotta be afraid of me."

"Am not." I pretended to be brave even though I was scared down to my toes.

"Nah, I know you are." He smirked at me. "I can see it in your eyes."

He turned and looked at the picture of President Roosevelt.

"You probably should be afraid of me. You don't know nothing about me." He thumped a knuckle on the portrait. "Dangerous men are everywhere."

Reaching down, I felt for Mama's mending basket. She hadn't touched it since Beanie got hurt, but it still sat under the davenport. While Eddie's back was turned, I grabbed the long bladed shears. I sat up, hiding them under the blanket.

"Winnie told me she and you talked," he said, glancing over his shoulder at me. If he noticed that I flinched, he didn't let on. "I don't expect she got to tell you everything she had on her mind."

"That's none of your business," I said, slipping my fingers into the handle of the shears.

Eddie pushed his hands into the back pockets of his pants and turned toward me.

"You sure got a mouth on you, you know that?" He winked. "I do believe Mary would smack you silly if she heard you talking to an adult like that."

"You ought to call her Mrs. Spence."

"See what I mean? Mouthy."

I glared at him, hoping he'd see how much I hated him.

"I never said I didn't like a sassy girl, did I?" he asked.

He stepped closer to me, so close I could have swung the shears at him or jabbed them into his side. He would have screamed, I just knew it. Would have cussed so loud everybody in the house would wake up and come out to help me.

But he turned and walked past me to Meemaw's rocking chair. The wood crackled under his weight, even though he couldn't have been any heavier than Meemaw.

"Winnie told me she's fixing to change a few things. She said she don't wanna live in the cat house no more." He leaned forward, the chair rocking with him. "She said you shamed her."

"I don't know what you mean."

"I think you do."

"I didn't do anything to her," I said.

"She told me she wants you to be proud of her." He rocked back and let out a quiet chuckle. "A thing like that."

"I don't know why she cares. I hardly know her."

"Oh, but she sure knows you. She's been watching you grow up all these years." He stubbed out his cigarette in Daddy's ash tray. "She never dared talk to you before, though. Too scared about what would happen to her if she did. Besides, she didn't want any bad to come to you."

"Why would something happen to me?"

"Isn't that the question of the hour." He leaned back and crossed his arms. Opening his mouth, he smacked his tongue against his lips. "You know, I sure am thirsty. I'd like me a glass of water. Or hooch, if you got that sort of thing around."

He sat, rocking his chair back and forth and smirking at me, waiting.

"We don't keep booze in this house," I said.

"Water's just fine." He laced his fingers together over top of his flat belly.

"I'm not getting you anything," I said, lifting the side of my lip into a snarl.

"Well, that ain't so neighborly of you."

"You aren't my neighbor."

"Ah, I would've thought you knew your Bible better than that." He tsked at me. "Didn't Jesus say everybody's your neighbor?"

I couldn't think of a single thing Pastor had ever preached about how to protect myself against an evil man in my living room demanding water or liquor. So I didn't say anything at all about it.

"What's her name?" he asked after a long time of quiet.

"Who? Winnie?"

"No. I know her. Believe me, I know her. Winnie was darn near my sister-in-law." He shook his head. "Nah, I mean the idiot girl. The one I rescued."

"She isn't an idiot."

"Right. You said that before." He sighed. "But you know who I'm talking about."

"Her name is Violet Jean," I said, my sister's real name feeling weird coming out of my mouth. He didn't deserve to know the name we all called her.

No matter what he thought, he wasn't one of us.

"Yeah, Violet Jean. You know, old Violet Jean was crying like a pig in that ditch. Just rolling around in the dirt, making all kinds of weird noises." He shook his head. "She ain't right. Probably would've been better for her if I'd left her there."

"Why did you help her?" I made sure I had a good hold on those shears. "Why didn't you just walk on by?"

"Now, that's a question I would've expected the sheriff to ask." He scratched his scalp. "The right answer is that I helped her because it's the decent thing for a man to do."

"What's the real answer?" I asked.

The rocking chair didn't make a sound as he got up. Before I had time to think, he was face-to-face with me, his thumb and finger lifting my chin. I was so scared, I couldn't find the strength to push the shears into him.

"You and me, we're alike, you know." His whispered words stunk of rot. "You ain't such a goody-goody, are you? You've got dark thoughts and bad dreams. Just like me."

He pressed his lips hard against my forehead. They left a moist spot there that I thought for sure I'd never be able to wash off.

"I never did help that idiot girl." He lowered his face so we were eye to eye. "Fact is, I just happened to be in the area at just the right time."

"What do you mean?"

"What do you think that means?"

I didn't know but was too afraid to say another word.

"You tell anybody I was here, and I'll tell them you're lying," he said, his face still too close to mine. "This was nothing more than a dream."

Then he was gone.

❖

Somehow I managed to fall asleep after Eddie left. It was a fast and shallow sleep. One that didn't give dreams or even rest.

I woke more exhausted than the night before.

Bubbling coffee sounds and the warm aroma of oatmeal floated out of the kitchen, along with Mama's humming of Christmas carols.

"Mama?" I called out, weak and quiet. I didn't reckon she would hear me, so I took in a good breath and called out again.

"You up?" she asked from the kitchen. "Was I making too much noise? I didn't mean to wake you."

I shook my head no.

Mama set the table with bowls and water glasses. Smiling at me, she stood up straight.

"Your hair needs a good brushing," she said. "I can braid it for you if you like. Later, though. Maybe after breakfast."

She turned back to the kitchen and took a stack of cotton napkins from the drawer.

"Mama." That time my voice came through loud enough that she turned.

"Yes, darlin'?" Her forehead wrinkled, and one of her eyebrows raised.

"I've got to tell you something," I said. "And I don't want you to be mad at me."

"Why would I be mad?" She put a fist on her hip. "Did you do something?"

"No." I swallowed hard, but nothing went down but dry. "Eddie was here last night."

"What was that?" She tilted her head.

I told her what I'd said.

"He never was here yesterday." She turned to the table and put the napkins beside the bowls.

"Everybody was asleep. I woke up and he was sitting right in Daddy's chair." I cleared my throat. "He was smoking."

"You were just dreaming, Pearl."

"I wasn't. It was real."

"Don't you think Daddy and I would have known he was here?" She walked to the drawer for some spoons. "We would have heard him."

I wondered why they hadn't heard him. A flicker of doubt lit in my mind. Maybe it had just been a dream. I touched the place where he'd pressed his lips, wishing it hadn't been real.

"Eddie scares me, Mama." My eyelids fluttered, tears coming quicker than I could blink them away. "I don't think he's good."

"Pearl, darlin', he's not bad. He saved Beanie, remember?" She turned back to the kitchen, and I heard her moving a pot around on top of the stove. "If he wasn't good, he wouldn't have helped her."

"Mama, he knew my name."

"Because we told it to him," she said.

"No, Mama. He knew it right when he got off the train." I wiped my nose.

"When he got off the train? He said he walked here."

"He lied."

"Pearl Louise," she scolded. "It's not nice to make accusations."

"Remember the rabbit drive? The one I went to? When I went to find Beanie?"

She nodded. "I remember."

"He smashed a rabbit right in my face." My voice shook and I couldn't help it. "Remember the blood on me?"

"Pearl."

"He's everywhere, Mama."

"You must have dreamed it all. He hasn't been around for months. He even said so." She carried the pot of oatmeal to the table, balancing it on the edge as she ladled runny spoonfuls into the bowls. "You have got to stop reading so much. It's spoiling your mind."

"Mama, he's bad."

"He is not," she said, her voice raised and hard. "He saved your sister."

"He told me she was crying like a pig."

"Why in the world would you say something like that?" She frowned at me. "What a terrible thing to say about your sister."

"Winnie told me that Eddie was a bad man!" I yelled the words. Yelled them as loud as I could.

Mama jolted, losing her hold on the pot. It toppled and she jumped back just in time for the slop of hot oats to miss her feet and splatter on the floor.

She looked at the mess and then at me. She sobbed.

"How many times have I told you to stay away from That Woman?" Her body jerked with the crying. "Don't you understand? I want to protect you. How can I protect you if you won't do as I say?"

"I'm sorry," I whispered, still under the blanket. "I should have listened to you."

She turned her eyes back to the oatmeal.

"You're right," I said. "It was all a dream. I imagined all of it. Everything was make-believe."

Pulling on the edge of her apron, she brought it to her eyes and wiped under them.

"I never wanted you to get hurt," she whimpered.

"I'm not hurt, Mama." I pushed the blanket off my lap. "Dreams don't hurt me. It was all just a dream."

I stood up. The shears fell to the floor with a clatter.

❈

Mama and I never did talk about Eddie or Winnie or jackrabbits again.

We cleaned up the oatmeal without a sound between us. She did keep an eye on me the whole time. From then on, she watched me. Her lips weren't as ready to smile at my wonderings anymore. Her gaze seemed heavy on me, like she was trying to hold me down.

I knew she meant to protect me, but from what I didn't know.

She made me sleep in bed with Beanie again, even if I did get kicked all night long.

I stopped telling Daddy about my nightmares, even though I'd never had so many. And never before had they been so dark.

It was truly a very lonely time.

# Chapter Seventeen

Pastor stood still at the front of the sanctuary. He held a Bible at his side with one finger holding his place. With his free hand, he hiked up his trousers.

I noticed that both the knees of his slacks had been patched. His shirt was worn and faded. Even the tie around his neck looked tired.

More people had come to church that day than normal. Daddy and Millard had both put a tie on and warmed pews as a Christmas gift to Meemaw. Mama had told me that folks felt like hearing about God around holidays.

Even Pastor's wife, Mad Mabel, sat in the congregation. I wondered if she planned on behaving herself.

It seemed the only two people in town that weren't in church that day were Winnie and Eddie. That was just fine by me.

"Jesus didn't come to earth as a babe raised in a castle," Pastor said. "He come to a humble family."

When he used the word *humble*, I knew what he meant was poor. Poor like Ray and Mrs. Jones and the folks living a couple days at a time in the Hooverville. Poor like the people moving along with no place to go.

"Jesus understands hungry. And He knows being without a roof overhead, and He knows what it's like to wander." Pastor pulled a hanky from his worn-out slacks and wiped at his eyes. Eyes that were a little less wild than usual. "Church, we've got a lot wrong. We've been getting it wrong for a long while, I expect. How long did we bow down before the idol of wheat? Cattle? A good many years."

Somebody cleared their throat. It sounded like they about choked.

"I know, it ain't a popular thing to say. But I'm gonna say it. You don't like it, go on over to the whorehouse and get your fill of something else. I'm preaching here."

Daddy sighed, and Mama cleared her throat.

"Go on," a woman called from the back.

"I remember the mountains of wheat we'd have come harvest. I know you remember it, too." Pastor shifted his weight. "That wheat gold bought y'all cars and new suits and good shoes for the kids. Y'all remember?"

A few people "uh-huhed" him.

"We'd grown that wheat. It was of our doing. Our sweat and tears and blood and guts." He thumped himself on the chest. "It was of us. And we was proud of it."

Daddy moved in his seat. Beanie yawned so the whole church could hear.

"I'm boring y'all, ain't I?" Pastor said with a smile. When he smiled, he looked nearly handsome. I could see the circus ringmaster in his eyes. I sure wished he would smile more. "I ain't got the Spirit moving me this morning. It's just I'm plum wore out."

"You ain't boring no one," Meemaw hollered. "Go on."

"Thank you, sister." Pastor smiled again. Then he turned to the rest of the congregation. "Anybody here still got any of that wheat money? Even a penny of it?"

No one said a word or made a sound or so much as moved a finger.

"It's all gone, ain't it?" He sighed. "It's all spent. Gone. Ain't it?"

"That's right," Millard said.

"And to that," Pastor said, "I say, amen. Praise God. And hallelujah."

He got that old wild look in his eye. But that morning it wasn't angry. It was something altogether different. It was more akin to mischief than anything. It was the look I imagined him wearing under his circus tent back in the old days.

"Jesus comes to the poor," he said. "He comes when we got nothing left to bow down to. Far as I know, none of us is fixing to worship our fields of dust."

"You got that right," someone said.

Pastor laughed and looked down.

"Thank you, brother." He kept the smile on his face. "Church, Jesus Himself said it, 'Blessed be ye poor: for yours is the kingdom of God.'"

Mama crossed her ankles and smoothed her skirt.

Pastor went on about the promises God made to the poor, but I was only halfway listening. My eyes were on Mama's mending-scarred hose. And I was thinking that if I had all the money in the world, I would get Mama a whole dresser drawer full of fresh hose. So many that, if one got a tear, she could throw it out and go get herself another pair. If I had the money, Mama would never have to mend another thing for the rest of her life.

I worried, though that if Mama had all those hose, she'd miss out on being blessed for being poor like Jesus's mother was. I still hadn't worked out how having nothing made a body blessed, but the Mary in the Bible was blessed, and so was Mama.

I imagined that Jesus chose to come to the poor because He knew they'd be the ones to take the best care of Him. Poor little Virgin Mary would hold Him close to herself. She wouldn't have the money to hire a nanny to raise Him. And Joseph, not even being His real daddy, would love Him like his own. Mama held me and Beanie tight to her, and Daddy sure loved us. If that was the blessing of being poor, it seemed worth the bother to me.

The way I figured it, Jesus had the poor close to His heart because they were the ones who had nothing else to hold onto.

❖

Right when we got home from church, Meemaw went to her bed.

"I'm feeling a bit off," she said. "I think all I need is a little rest."

She slept until supper but didn't feel like eating. Mama sent me up to Meemaw's room with a mug of bouillon and a slice of bread.

"Thank you, darlin'," Meemaw said. "Just put them on the bedside table, would you?"

I did as she asked.

"Will you read to me a little bit?" she asked. "My Bible's on my dresser."

I sat on the edge of her bed, reading out loud from her heavy Bible. I could barely hold it, even when it rested on my lap. A few of the words stumbled out of my mouth, but Meemaw didn't mind. She watched my face as I read, nodding her head when I tried a word that was bigger than any I had learned at school.

"Keep on," she encouraged me. "You're doing just fine, darlin'."

After I got to the end of a chapter in Deuteronomy she told me it was okay to stop reading. I closed the Bible and made to get up, but she ringed my wrist with her fingers.

"Pearlie, I want to talk to you." She swallowed. "I got something I need to tell you. Then I'll want to rest awhile."

"Yes, ma'am," I said.

"I don't like that hobo that's been coming around." She shook her head, rubbing it against her pillow. "Not at all."

"Eddie?" I whispered.

"That's the one." She let go of my arm and patted my leg. "I know he found Beanie and all, but I don't trust him. There's something wicked in his eyes."

Relief swelled through me. I wasn't alone.

"I told your mama and daddy. I just don't think they can see it," she said. "I want you to steer clear of him. Hear?"

"Yes, ma'am." I pushed a loose piece of hair behind my ear. "He confuses me."

"How's that?"

"He says things that I don't understand. About me not being who I think I am and that I don't belong here," I answered. "He makes me feel upside-down."

"All I can tell you is this," she said, blinking real slow. "Someday you might learn that life isn't what you always thought it was. You'll learn how hard truth can hurt."

She paused and breathed deeply.

"But," she said. "But you've got to promise me you'll remember how this family loves you. Everything we've done is because we love you deep down."

I forced a smile. "I know it, Meemaw."

"There might come a day when it'll be hard to know it, darlin'." She squeezed my hand. "Life has a way of taking what we know and tangling it all in knots. It ain't gonna be easy on you to know. The truth never is. But you're a brave girl. And you're strong in the Lord."

She closed her eyes and opened her mouth in a big yawn.

"I better get some more rest," she said. "Can you please pull this blanket up?"

I covered her shoulders with the sheet and quilt.

"Now give me a kiss, honey, before you go." She smiled.

I leaned down and kissed her cheek.

"Every storm has a beginning and every storm's got an end. They never last forever," she whispered. "God is the one who saves. Don't forget it."

Her door creaked closed behind me, and her snores started as soon as I reached the steps.

## CHAPTER EIGHTEEN

Mama and Daddy stood in the kitchen, talking about his paycheck. I sat at the table, drawing on a tablet of paper with a dull, graphite pencil. It didn't feel right to me, hearing them go on about money. In my memory, I didn't think they discussed so much as the spending of a penny within my hearing.

"It won't be as much as usual," Daddy said. "State's cutting back on everybody's checks now."

"I can't make a grocery list until I know how much you'll get." Mama crossed her arms and leaned back into the counter. "I don't feel right taking credit at Smalley's with him tightening his belt the way he has."

"Might be half of what I usually get."

"About sixty then?"

Daddy nodded. "We've gotta make it last. I'm worried about what January will bring."

"That's okay," she'd said. "We'll make do."

Mama put me to work, writing a list of all she said we needed. Flour. Coffee. Molasses. Yeast. I wrote with a careful hand, practicing my penmanship and hoping Miss Camp would be pleased once school started back up in January.

"I think that's about it," Mama said when she'd told me the last ingredient she needed, which happened to be sugar. "You want to come with me?"

I nodded, happy that Mama wanted me with her.

"Button all the way up," she said, handing me my thick sweater. "It's real cold out."

"Do you want me to drive you?" Daddy asked.

"It's not a long walk." Mama smiled and pushed her hands into the sleeves of her sweater. "Besides, I don't have that much to buy."

Mama and I walked out in the chilly, almost-Christmas air. I tried to remember the last time I held her hand and why I'd stopped. I wondered if she missed it like I did sometimes.

The little grocery store was quiet. Only Mr. Smalley sat behind the counter. He stood as soon as we walked in.

"Ladies," he said, a big smile across his face. "Merry Christmas."

"Merry Christmas, Mr. Smalley," I said.

"Come to get a few things?" He stepped out from behind the counter, leaning a hip into a shelf that used to hold jars full of candies. The jars were all empty.

I tried my very hardest not to be disappointed.

Mama handed him her list and the two of them talked in between finding all her groceries. Soon the stack of items grew on the counter.

"Looks like we might have to make a couple trips," Mama said, smiling.

"I can help you carry." Mr. Smalley pushed up his glasses.

"Don't worry. Johnny can help us, can't he?"

"Well, Bea took the kids." Mr. Smalley turned toward a shelf, reaching for something on a high-up ledge. "They went to New York. She's got family there."

"For Christmas?" Mama picked up a small can of milk and inspected the label. "You should have gone with them."

"Thing is, they ain't coming back. She didn't want to fight the dust no more." He faced us. "She told me not to come there."

"Oh." Mama nodded slowly, lowering the can of milk to the counter. "I'm so sorry."

"She said once she's got enough money, she wants a divorce."

"Pearl, darlin'," Mama said, not turning toward me. "Go on out and sit on the bench a spell. I'll get you when I'm ready to leave."

I obeyed, even though I wanted to hear more from Mr. Smalley. I'd never met somebody who was divorced before, but I'd heard Pastor rail about it many times. I wondered what it felt like to have your family split in half like that. It seemed it would hurt like crazy.

Outside on the bench, I pulled the collar of my sweater over my mouth and nose to keep from getting cold. Leaning close to the door, I tried my best to hear Mama and Mr. Smalley talking through. All I could make out, though, were mumbling voices.

As much as I hated being in class with Johnny, I felt bad that he wasn't going to be around his father anymore. Mr. Smalley was a good man, and Johnny would grow up not knowing it.

I stared across the street at the courthouse. The big doors were closed, but a few of the windows on the second floor were cracked open. I figured Millard was in his bedroom, snoozing the way he liked to on a cool afternoon. I only knew that because Daddy would tease him about it every once in a while. Turning my ear in that direction, I tried to catch the sound of him snoring but couldn't hear much of anything at all.

Then I heard a woman yell. "Stop it! Leave me be!"

There wasn't a single person on the street. Turning this way and that, I tried to see who had yelled. Nobody was in sight.

The woman cried out again, and someone yelled a cuss at her. I realized the sounds were coming from the alley behind Mr. Smalley's store.

Peeking through the window, I made sure Mama wasn't stepping out just then. She stood, facing Mr. Smalley with her hand to her chest. I figured she'd be there awhile.

I walked around the side of the store, in the direction of the voices I heard hissing at one another. Stepping toe-to-heel like I read the Indians did back a long time ago, I snuck, trying not to make any sound at all. Daddy's Indian book had said walking like that helped them sneak up on their prey. That must have only worked for them walking in bare feet because, hard as I tried, the grit under the soles of my shoes kept grinding.

I pushed the shoes off and carried them, my toes gliding across the cool dirt.

Careful that I wouldn't be seen, I spied around the corner with just one eye and looked into the alley.

Eddie and Winnie stood in the alley, face-to-face. Neither of them seemed happy. Her face was set hard like when she faced Pastor. His was the same as when I'd seen him at the rabbit drive. I didn't like that look on him one bit.

He pushed her against the brick wall and kept his hand on her chest, holding her still.

"Be quiet," he grumbled in her face. "You best not say a word to nobody."

"No, I ain't gonna be quiet," she said back. She pushed at his hand and wiggled to get free. "I want you to leave her alone."

"She's got to know." Eddie turned his head the opposite way from me and spit his plug of tobacco out. "Ain't that why I come all the way here? So you'd get her?"

"You just come here to get revenge. That's all." She slapped at his hand again. "You wouldn't never come to help me. I'm not stupid."

He lowered his hand, but didn't step away from her. "I come here to help you."

Winnie said a word that Mama would have called barnyard talk. "You didn't come for nobody but yourself. And I'm gonna tell them about you."

"You ain't gonna do nothing, Winnie. You hear?" Eddie yelled. "You're gonna keep your mouth shut, or I'll shut it for you."

"I ain't scared of you." She snarled at him. "I'm gonna tell them who you are. Just see if I don't."

Eddie put his hands on her, struggling to pin her back to the wall. He punched her right in the mouth, making her head hit the brick behind her. She sputtered and spit blood. He held her arms down so she couldn't touch her lips, check her teeth, wipe the blood. He growled like a wolf, baring his teeth at her.

Winnie had stopped fighting and let him hold her against the wall. She did sob and turn her head to one side. The blood streamed from her mouth.

"I never did know what my brother seen in you. You dirty little whore." He got so close to her face that his nose nearly touched her cheek. "All he did was write about how he got some no-count girl in trouble."

"We were gonna get married," Winnie said, thick and mumbling through the blood and spit and already-swelling lips.

"He wasn't never gonna do that." Eddie laughed at her, pushing her harder against the wall. "He never would've."

"He said he loved me," she whimpered.

"You're stupid." Eddie's voice gave me the chills and made my stomach turn. "My brother never loved nobody."

"He did love me," Winnie cried. It was like she was begging for it to be true.

"Nope. He never did. Even told me so much in one of his letters." Eddie turned and spit again. "He never loved nobody. Not even our mother. He came out wanting to hurt anybody he could. And he done it, too. He hurt everybody."

Eddie shoved her again, moving his arm up across her throat so hard she yelped and gasped for breath.

"I'm just like him. You hear?" Eddie said. "And I'm gonna do just like he done."

"You ain't like him," Winnie said, choking. "It ain't too late for you. Just leave. Go back to Tennessee. Nobody's got hurt yet."

"You think so, huh?" He eased up on her.

"Remember that girl? The one you found? You helped her." She got one of her hands loose and used her sleeve to wipe under her bottom lip. The fabric soaked up the red. "You didn't have to help her. You knew who she is, but you saved her anyhow."

"That ain't the whole story." He turned his head toward me, but kept his eyes on Winnie. "Y'all don't know nothing but what I want y'all to."

"What happened?"

"I ain't telling you." He wrinkled his nose and shook when he breathed in and out. "I can't trust you, can I?"

"You can. I promise."

"But you was gonna tell everybody about me, weren't you?"

"No," she said, shaking her head. "I won't do that. You were right. I'm on your side, Eddie."

"Good. 'Cause if you tell anybody a single thing about me, I will kill you." He grabbed a handful of her hair and pulled it hard, forcing her to look in his face. "I will."

He punched her once more, and she fell to the ground.

I rushed back to the bench and waited for Mama to get done in the store. I shoved my feet into my shoes and tried to imagine I'd not seen anything. When I closed my eyes, though, all I could see was Winnie's bloody face and her falling to the ground.

When Mama opened the door to the shop and called me in, I held my hands together behind my back so she wouldn't see them shaking.

"You okay, Pearl?" Mr. Smalley asked. "You look like you seen a ghost."

"Yes, sir. I'm all right," I answered, pushing a smile on my face and holding it there.

"What's wrong, darlin'?" Mama felt of my forehead. "You aren't getting sick, are you?"

"Nothing's wrong, Mama." I made the smile bigger. "I'm just excited for Christmas."

I lied because Eddie's threat to Winnie was for me, too. That I knew clear as day.

CHAPTER NINETEEN

It was the afternoon before Christmas, and Meemaw was still feeling lousy. She wouldn't hear about Mama calling a doctor, though. When Mama asked, Meemaw just waved her off from where she still lay in her bed.

"All a doctor's going to say is that I'm old and nothing can be done." Meemaw coughed. "He'll tell you I'm dying of old age and then take your five dollars for his troubles."

"Mother, don't be so ornery," Mama said.

"I'm old. That's all I've got left to do."

"Well, you rest. I have faith this will pass," Mama said, closing Meemaw's door.

Beanie and I stood in the doorway of our bedroom. We heard every word between Mama and Meemaw. I could about feel Beanie's heart breaking. She leaned against the frame of the door to brace herself, still weak from the night she got hurt. I looked at her face, still colored yellow and blue and purple and pink from the beating she'd taken.

Tears streamed from her eyes. "I don't want Meemaw to die."

"She didn't mean it," I whispered. "She's not dying. Just sick is all."

Beanie steadied herself against the wall and made it to the steps. I followed her, sure she would tumble down the stairs. Grabbing her arm, I helped her. Between me and the banister, she made it downstairs for the first time since the attack.

Mama stood in the living room, arms crossed and looking out the big front window.

"Mama," Beanie said.

Mama turned and, seeing Beanie's face, rushed toward us, grabbing hold of both of us.

"She's going to be just fine," she said. "I'll ask Daddy to call for a doctor."

"Meemaw don't want one," Beanie cried.

"It doesn't matter. We'll get her one, anyhow." Mama used one hand to push Beanie's wild hair off her face. "She isn't going to die. Not just yet, at least."

"She is," Beanie said, thick spit stretching into strings between her lips. "And she's gonna go take care of Baby Rosie."

Mama pulled Beanie to the davenport and had her sit down. She held her just like she was a little baby and hushed her.

"Darlin', shush. We want Meemaw to get some rest. She needs it," Mama soothed. "She'll be just fine."

I sat beside them, praying that Jesus would come back to snatch us up into the sky like Pastor always said He would. I couldn't imagine a world without Meemaw. And I knew it would tear Beanie up to lose her.

She would be like a tree without roots.

❖

For as long as I could remember, Mama and Meemaw had made big business out of getting our house ready for Christmas. They'd spend days baking cookies and sweet bread. The two of them stayed up late into the night, wrapping presents and filling stockings. We never got a whole lot of presents, but what we did get was more than most the kids in town did.

For days before Christmas, Mama and Meemaw would shoo me and Beanie out of the kitchen so we wouldn't sneak treats.

Christmas was the most magical part of life in the Spence house, even if we never did have snow fall in Red River.

The Christmas of 1934 was different. I could see it in the way Mama moved slower and hear it in her sighs. What with Meemaw in bed and less money in our pockets, it was bound to be a little less magic and more just making it through the day.

I told myself not to be upset about that.

Mama stood, shoulder-sagged, at the kitchen counter, holding the sugar canister.

"I don't think I'll be able to make cookies this year," she said. Then looking at me, "I'm sorry, darlin'."

"That's all right, Mama," I said.

"I'm just about clean out of sugar. Mr. Smalley didn't have any, either." She put the sugar canister on the top shelf of the cupboard. "It'll just be a simple Christmas."

"Can I make paper stars?" I asked, using my happiest voice and making myself smile at her. "We could hang them in the living room."

"I think your daddy's got a crate of old newspapers in the cellar. I'm sure you could use those." Mama touched my cheek, and she looked at me with soft eyes. "I would love to have some stars. Do you think you can get your sister to help? She needs a little distracting."

Beanie and I sat on the living-room floor, sharing Mama's good shears and cutting out stars from the old newspapers. Our fingers smudged the black print.

"Better not get that on your dress," I said to Beanie.

She just kept cutting, her tongue sticking out one side of her mouth.

I flipped through the paper, waiting for my sister to hand me the shears, looking for funny pages. Most of the sheets of newsprint were covered with advertisements for medicines and housewares. I turned to the front page of the paper to see the date. It was from over ten years before. The year I was born.

"Why would Daddy have papers from that long ago?" I asked.

Beanie didn't answer. She clipped the scissors around the pages, cutting strange shapes that didn't look a thing like stars.

I looked through the whole stack and realized all the papers were from the same date. Then I looked at the headline. It was the day the paper ran the story of Daddy shooting Jimmy DuPre. The picture of the rat face sneered from the cover of each newspaper. His eyes glared right through me, as if he knew something about me.

It sucked my breath out. I flipped the whole stack of papers over so I couldn't see his face anymore. Gulping in air, I closed my eyes, trying to erase the rat-faced killer from my mind.

Jimmy DuPre. He was dead, I reminded myself. He couldn't hurt anybody anymore. Daddy had won. The thoughts calmed me.

I opened my eyes and looked back at the newspaper and remembered the day when Ray and I had looked at the paper in the half-sunk-in cabin, a part of it had been missing. I remembered that I'd felt the place where it had been torn out.

Sitting on the floor at home, I touched the whole front page that covered my lap, tracing where it had been ripped out of the other copy. I skimmed over the words with my eyes.

"Baby Found on Church Steps," it read.

I had to read it over a few times to understand.

Touching the words, it seemed I could feel them through my fingertips, bumping up from the surface of the page. I read the story of a newborn baby found abandoned on the church steps. The same church I'd lived next door to all my life. Somebody had found her, and she was all right.

"Mama," I called, getting to my feet.

"Yes?" she answered from the kitchen.

"Did they ever find the baby's mother?"

"What's that, darlin'?" She pulled a pan from a cupboard by her knees. "What baby?"

"Here in this paper." I held it up for her to see. "Did they find out who left the baby?"

She took the paper and didn't even look at it. Swallowing hard, she met my eyes.

"I don't recall," she said. "They must have."

"Who was the baby?"

She shook her head.

"It's sad, don't you think?" I grabbed for the paper. "A baby all alone like that."

"Yes. Very sad. But that was a long time ago." She put her best smile on. "How are the stars coming?"

"All right." I leaned close to her and whispered. "Beanie's aren't looking so much like stars."

"Well, that's just fine, don't you think?"

"You want to see the ones I made?" I led her to the living room to look at my stack. "I've got a whole bunch of them."

"Very nice." She touched my cheek. "You done a good job."

We strung the stars with sewing thread and hung them across the room. Even the ones that looked more like a blob that Beanie had made. They looked about as good as they could have, and Mama said they were lovely.

❉

Daddy admired the newspaper stars and blobs when he got home later that day. He said they were about the prettiest Christmas decorations he had seen in all his life.

Beanie's smile beamed like nothing bad had ever happened to her. That made me glad.

Daddy walked under the garland we'd made, touching each shape with his fingertips, making them flutter.

Smiling, I watched them dance. My smile dropped, though, when I realized that all of Beanie's odd shapes had been cut around the story of the abandoned baby.

CHAPTER TWENTY

On Christmas morning, I lazed in bed with Beanie still snoring next to me. Brewing coffee and something sweet baking smelled so good it made my stomach rumble. I wondered how Mama had gotten enough sugar to make something that smelled so good but decided it didn't matter. I just wanted to eat whatever it was as slow as I could. That way the good flavor would stay in my mouth longer.

Mama stepped into our room with the prettiest of all her smiles. She wore her red dress, the one she saved for special occasions. Most surprising of all, she had her hair down. Brown curls rested on her shoulders, and I thought she looked just like a movie star.

"Merry Christmas, girls," she said. "Now get your lazy bones out of bed and come on downstairs."

Beanie rolled over, turning her backside toward Mama.

"Beanie Jean," Mama laughed. "Nobody wants to see your underthings first thing in the morning."

Beanie grumbled and rolled back the way she'd started.

"Pearl?" Mama reached for me. "You want to come down? See what Santa brought?"

I hadn't believed in Santa for a long time. Ray had told me he was make-believe a few years before. Still, my heart swelled so big it almost hurt. To think that there might be a present for me, even if it was a small one, it was more than I had expected.

"Get up, Beanie," I said, pushing on my sister. "Come on."

She rolled out of bed and stood next to Mama. Allowing Mama to smooth her hair, she slumped, letting her shoulders roll forward.

"Pearl, hand me that ribbon, would you?" Mama asked.

I grabbed it from the dresser and gave it to her. She wrapped it around Beanie's hair and tied it tight.

"There," Mama said to my sister. "Now I can see your beautiful face."

Beanie's beautiful face was still swollen in a few places from where she'd been beaten.

"It hurts to smile," Beanie said. She grinned anyway.

Some moments I looked at my sister and almost believed she was like any other girl. But then she'd do something strange or look at me in an odd way, and I'd remember that her mind would never be like everybody else's.

"Well, let's go." Mama grabbed Beanie's hand and walked with her out the room and down the stairs.

I followed behind them.

Meemaw was up and sitting in her rocking chair, a bright-colored afghan tucked around her legs. She had on her big, wide smile. She didn't have a lot of color in her face, but her sparkling eyes made up for it.

"Merry Christmas," she said. "Well, look at you, Beanie Jean. Just as tall as your mama."

Beanie looked at Mama, and Mama looked back. My sister had the blank expression again. I didn't think she understood why it mattered how tall she was.

"Getting all grown-up," Mama beamed.

"Not too growed-up for a kiss." Meemaw reached her arms for Beanie and then for me so we'd give her pecks on the cheek.

Daddy carried a cup of coffee into the living room. He nodded at the davenport where two bundles lay wrapped in cream-colored cotton.

"One for each of you," he said.

"I didn't think we were getting anything." My eyes moved over the small bundles. "You shouldn't have gotten us anything."

A lump caught in my throat. I remembered Mama and Daddy talking about not having much money. Then I thought about Ray and how his day wouldn't be different than any other. Most the kids in Red River would have sparse Christmases.

Guilt settled in my gut. I didn't see why I deserved any better than the other kids.

"It's okay," Mama said, moving to stand beside Daddy. "Go on, girls."

Beanie walked to the presents, staring at them. I handed her the one with her name on it, and I took mine. We sat on the floor, our hips touching, holding the unopened gifts on our crisscrossed legs. I regretted being so close to her as soon as her sharp elbow jabbed at me.

Mama got down on the floor next to us. Ladies didn't sit on the floor, not in their best dresses. That was what she had taught us. But that morning, Mama did. Christmas magic changed the rules.

I opened my gift as slow as I could, wanting to make the feeling of not knowing last a little longer. It was the only thing I would open that year, maybe even for a few years.

As for Beanie, she worked at the cotton, tugging it and loosening it as fast as she could. I shielded my eyes from her present just in case we got the same thing. I didn't want the surprise ruined.

Pulling back the last of the cotton, I drew in my breath. I lifted green fabric and it fell out of a neat fold. It was a beautiful dress. Green with a thin white ribbon along the neck and at the bottom of the sleeves. I stood, holding it up in front of myself. It wasn't made of a feed sack. It was store-bought fabric. The buttons were shiny, sun-catching, pretty. And they all matched. I recognized them off my old yellow dress, the one that had gotten ruined at the rabbit drive.

"Thank you," I said to Mama.

Beanie stood, too. She held a dress up by the shoulders. It was tan, her favorite. I'd never met anybody before whose favorite color was tan. The color of dust.

"What do you think?" Mama asked, getting up from the floor.

"It's beautiful," I whispered. "Green as grass."

I remembered grass. It could get as green as that dress. I remembered how bright the fields were after the rain. Even before the dust came, it didn't rain all that often, but when it did, we thanked God over and over. Back then, I would pretend that I was a flower standing tall in the downpour. Mama would call me in, but I'd only obey after I'd let the drops fall on my head and in my mouth and run all the way down my body.

Those were days when I never felt thirsty or hungry. Green was the color of enough.

Before I knew it, I was hugging my new dress and crying hard because all the green had dried up and gone, never to come back again. The desert was killing us. All of us. Little by little. Drying us until we were nothing more than sun-bleached bones in a pile of dirt.

If the dust didn't get me, Eddie would. I didn't know which was worse.

"Are you disappointed?" Mama asked, touching her lips. "I know you probably would have liked a toy . . ."

I shook my head. "I love this dress."

"Then what is it?" She wiped at my cheeks with her hanky. "Why are you crying?"

Shrugging, I tried to swallow down my sadness.

"It's just so pretty."

It would have been too much to explain all the rest.

❖

I changed into my new dress, the soft fabric hanging loose on my body. Mama had thought to put ties on the back of it, and I was thankful for that. Cinching it into a bow above my rear, I was glad that I wasn't like to outgrow it too quickly.

When I came downstairs in it, Meemaw had me spin a few times to show how the green swirled out around my shins. Dancing about the room made me feel like a princess. All sad thoughts fell away.

"Oh, honey," Meemaw said, clapping her hands. "Ain't you pretty?"

Out of breath, I stopped, the room kept on twirling, though. We all had a laugh while I staggered toward the davenport. After the dizzy spell ended, I pushed the hair out of my face. Mama hadn't had the chance to braid it yet.

"Mama, can you please put my hair up?" I asked.

She smiled and nodded, her thick curls bouncing and swaying. If I had hair like hers, I never would have pulled it back. But hair as straight as mine just hung in my face and got in the way.

"Come on." Mama took my hand and pulled me into her room. "Sit on my bed there a minute."

I did as she said, rubbing my hands on the firm mattress. She never forgot to make her bed, no matter how much she needed to do or how tired she was. From the grit against my palms on the bedspread, I reckoned it was a good habit. I would have been better about it myself if I hadn't had to share with Beanie. At least that's what I thought.

Mama used her silver-handled brush to smooth my hair. Closing my eyes, I listened as she hummed and brushed. It pulled a little when she twisted my hair into a bun, but I didn't mind. I could have listened to her humming all day long. She used a shiny pin to secure my hair. I reached behind, feeling the pin, knowing it must have sparkled.

"You can keep that," she whispered, holding up a mirror so I could see myself. "I've had it since I was about your age. It looks real nice in the gold of your hair."

"Thank you, Mama," I said, catching a glimpse of both of us in the mirror.

I didn't look a thing like her.

❧

While Mama finished cooking our Christmas dinner, Daddy set Beanie and me down at the table. He pulled a deck of cards out of his pocket. He put a finger to his lips and made a shushing sound, winking at the two of us.

"Mama doesn't let us play cards," I whispered.

"It's Christmas," he answered. "She'll let us just this once."

He shuffled the deck, making the cards fall on top of each other.

"Besides," he said. "Meemaw's snoozing. She's the one who'd take a switch to our behinds for this."

Daddy helped us form our hands around our cards, teaching us to make a fan out of them. "Hold them like this so you can see all of them."

Then he taught us to hold them up. "You don't want nobody seeing what's in your hand."

"What's this game?" Beanie asked, trying to hold her cards right.

"Poker," Daddy whispered.

"Is this good?" Beanie showed him what she had. Three of the aces.

"Yup. About as good as it gets." Daddy smiled and turned to me. "Remind me to never put money on a game against your sister."

Next Daddy tried to teach us how to shuffle. That ended with the whole deck shooting into the air. "Make sure you find all fifty-two cards," Daddy said.

We played a couple hands, and Beanie won about all of them. Whenever she did, her smile would grow even bigger.

"Seems I gotta teach you about having a poker face, darlin'," Daddy laughed. "You never want the fella you're playing with to know how you're feeling, good or bad. Keep the smiles and frowns tucked tight inside your cheek, like this."

Daddy made his face blank as could be. Which made me giggle so hard my stomach hurt.

"You better try it too, Pearlie Lou," Daddy said, keeping his face flat.

We all practiced holding our faces straight and not letting a smile inch up on us. Not one of us could go long without a smile cracking and giggles erupting.

There was laughter in our house. Enough to kill most of my fear.

❈

Mama walked circles around the table, setting the plates and glasses and the like on top of her laciest tablecloth. She'd go between that and stirring something on the stove and checking the chicken and dumplings in the oven. Our house smelled like comfort with the rich smell of gravy and dough baking.

"Can I help?" I asked.

"Oh, darlin', thank you," Mama said, handing me a stack of cotton napkins.

We worked side by side, putting together the nicest Christmas table we could. I remembered to put the napkins to the left of the plate and was proud that I hadn't needed her to remind me. Then I helped her put the silverware out, too.

"You're doing a nice job," she said.

"Mama," I said. "I feel real bad."

"Why's that, darlin'?"

"Well, I didn't get you or Daddy a present." I put the last butter knife down. "I wish I could have gotten you something real nice."

"Don't feel bad. I never expected anything."

"Do you want me to tell you what I'd give you if I had a lot of money?" I asked.

Mama nodded at me to follow her into the kitchen. "That would be sweet."

I told her about the hose I would give her as she sliced the bread. Then I told her that I would buy her a gold-chained necklace with a locket and a brand new dress. New pots and pans and dishes that didn't have any chips along the edges.

"And Mama, I'd buy a camera for myself," I said.

"You would, would you?" She grinned at me.

"Yes, ma'am."

"What would you do with a camera?"

"I'd take pictures of you opening all the presents so I could always remember your smile."

She put down her slicing knife and wiped the crumbs from her hands. Reaching for me, she pulled me tight against her.

"Did you know that I love surprises?" she asked.

"You do?"

"I do." She kissed the top of my head. "Did you know that you were a surprise?"

"No," I said, tilting my head so I could see her face.

"We never expected you, but God brought you to us anyway." She lifted her eyebrows. "All the gifts you want to give me are nice. They sure would be good presents. But not a one of them is as good as having you."

She held me again, and I turned my face, looking at Meemaw and Daddy and Beanie. If I never got another present in my life, I'd be happy just so long as I had them.

❈

Daddy wanted us to hold off eating until Millard came. The old mayor had joined us for our Christmas meal as long as I could remember.

"Good lord, but these dumplings are going to be all dried out by the time we sit down." Mama peeked in the oven. "I do wish Millard would hurry up."

"He'll be here." Daddy checked the clock on the wall. "I suppose it can't hurt none if I go check on him."

He put on his hat and opened the front door.

"I won't be a minute," he said, closing the door behind him.

He wasn't a minute. More like half a second. We heard him and Millard talking on the porch. Their conversation ended with Daddy saying, "Sure, let's go inside."

The door opened.

Mama took a step or two into the living room and smiled.

"Hi," she said. "Come in. Y'all hungry?"

A woman and two girls stood wide-eyed, staring, just inside the door. Daddy walked in behind one of the girls and put his hand on her shoulder. She jumped when he touched her, and he lowered his hand. Millard stood beside Daddy. He winked when he caught me looking at him.

"Don't be shy," Daddy told the visitors in his most gentle voice. "We've got plenty for everybody."

"I have some chicken and dumplings in the oven and a couple loaves of fresh baked sweet bread." Mama talked as she made her way to the kitchen. "More than enough."

"I don't mean to put you out." The woman didn't talk loudly enough for Mama to hear her, so she said it again, louder. Too loud. It came as a shout.

"Oh, you aren't putting me out. Not at all. Y'all make yourselves at home while I put some beans on. I won't be long." Mama moved through the kitchen, her skirt swirling. "Pearl, be a dear and set a few more plates, please."

The woman joined me, not listening to the protests of Mama. Together, we set three more places at the table. Thank goodness Mama had enough dishes. Daddy and Millard carried in the extra chairs. Between us, we had the work done in no time at all.

"Now, here I put you to work and I didn't even introduce myself." Mama gave the pot of beans a quick stir before turning and grabbing the woman's hand, giving it a gentle shake. "I'm Mary Spence. This here's my girl Pearl. Over yonder is my mother-in-law, Mrs. Spence, and my oldest daughter there is Beanie Jean."

"Good to know you." The woman didn't take her eyes off Mama to look at a one of us. "I'm Esther. Them's my daughters Jael and Tamar. We're good Christian folk."

I met eyes with Meemaw. She grinned and nodded. She'd told me once of Tamar who had turned into a loose woman and tricked her father-in-law in a way that Meemaw wouldn't explain, so I figured it had something to do with fornication. All the parts of the Bible she blushed about had to do with fornication. And I'd read on my own about Jael pounding a stake into a man's head, the point of which went all the way into the ground.

I wondered if that Esther woman had any idea how ugly it was to name baby girls after those women in the Bible. I figured she did not.

"Pearl, darlin', would you please show Tamar and Jael where to clean up?" Mama turned back to the beans. "We should be ready to eat in a minute or two."

The girls didn't talk at all in the bathroom. They looked around, eyes as wide as when they walked in the front door. Running tiny fingers along the porcelain tub and touching the shiny faucets, they glanced at each other with meek smiles.

"The water doesn't come out of those anymore," I said. "You've got to get water from this here bucket."

Their shoulders sagged and I could tell they were disappointed. When the water got cut off in Red River, I'd felt the same way.

But when the girls looked up and saw themselves in the mirror, I thought I'd never get them back out to the living room. They stared and stared, making different faces. Jael even stuck her tongue out, which made the two of them giggle just as hard as anything.

"Haven't y'all ever seen yourselves in a mirror before?" I asked.

Both girls lost their smiles and looked down at their hands, scrubbing them with bars of soap. I guessed that they'd forgotten I was there.

"Girls," Mama called. "Come on."

I didn't say another word to Jael and Tamar. The three of us just walked back to the dining room. I had hoped they might become my friends. I felt foolish for even thinking of it.

Keeping my eyes down, I watched the sway of my green hem until I heard all the adult voices in the dining area.

When I lifted my eyes, I about fell over at what I saw. Eddie was in a chair all pulled up to the table, his plate piled high with chicken and dumplings and bread and beans.

"Come on over, girls," Mama said, directing us to the empty seats.

Beanie sat beside Millard, her shoulders slumped and looking about as unhappy as a toad. She made a few of her little noises. I figured the room was too full of strangers for her. That always made her real nervous.

"Hey there, Pearl. You get anything for Christmas?" Eddie smirked and popped a piece of chicken into his mouth.

"Young man, I don't know what kind of upbringing you had," Meemaw scolded. "But in this house we say grace before we eat."

"Mother," Mama gasped. She turned to Eddie. "You'll have to excuse her. She hasn't been feeling herself lately."

"Don't make excuses for me," Meemaw said. "I'm feeling just fine, thank you very much."

"But we don't need to be rude to our guests."

"He ain't my guest. Besides, he's the one who was rude first. Eating before we've blessed the food."

"Mother, shame on you."

"Nah, don't scold her. I should've known better." Eddie winked at me. "Pearl how about you come sit beside me. I don't like nothing better than sitting with a pretty girl at Christmas dinner."

"No. I do believe Pearl will be sitting beside me today." Meemaw reached for me. "Isn't that right, honey?"

I nodded and let Meemaw pull me.

Eddie's smirk turned into a sharp glare.

"Another time, then," he said.

Meemaw kept her hand on my leg and her eye on Eddie all through dinner.

❈

I had never tried to murder someone before. But during that Christmas dinner I worked at killing Eddie with my hate. Meemaw had taught me that to hate someone was just the same as killing them in my heart. She'd told me Jesus was the one who said that. Hoping that it was true, I willed my hatred to be a sharp and swift weapon—I imagined Eddie choking on a forgotten chicken bone or tipping backwards out of his chair and knocking his head on the floor.

So much for the charity and good will of Christmas. I'd become a killer in my own soul, and it surprised me how I didn't feel anything about it.

"Now, Eddie, I'm sure you've got family somewhere that's missing you today," Mama said, scooping a soft bite of dumpling onto her fork. "Wouldn't they have liked to have you home at Christmas?"

"Nah, they don't miss me none." Eddie sopped up the gravy on his plate with a wad of bread. Then he glanced at me. "I don't got much family no more. Most of them's passed on."

"I'm sorry to hear that," Daddy said.

"Not me. My folks would've rather seen me dead than home on Christmas morning."

"Oh, I don't believe that for a minute." Mama smiled at him.

"Some families ain't as sweet as yours, ma'am." He kept his eyes on me, the blue of them chilling me all the way through.

"Some folk don't deserve sweetness," Meemaw said, sounding like a hissing cat.

"Mother," Mama whispered. "What has gotten into you today?"

"Full of piss and vinegar I suppose." Eddie forced a smile. "She's got the right at her age."

He went back to eating, keeping his eyes on me.

Oh, how I wished his heart would just stop beating.

❧

Eddie didn't stick around long after dinner. He didn't bother making an excuse, and that was fine by me. I didn't care where he went or what he did, just so long as he didn't stay a minute longer in our home.

Beanie seemed glad, too. She sat on the floor by Meemaw's rocking chair, her head on our grandmother's knee. I thought for sure she would fall asleep right there with Meemaw playing with her curls.

Daddy and Millard went out on the porch to sip cups of coffee and smoke cigarettes.

Mama and I stayed at the table with Esther and the girls. Jael and Tamar still worked on eating their dumplings. All the rest of us had been done a long time before.

Mama had served coffee to Esther, promising sweet bread whenever the girls were ready for it.

Esther closed her eyes with every swallow of coffee, the slightest upturn at the corners of her mouth. I didn't think she would ever finish that first cup for fear of having no more. I wanted to tell her that Mama would make her as much as she could drink.

But Mama wouldn't have liked for me to say something like that. She would have worried about it making Esther feel ashamed.

"Goodness me," Mama said. "I think I'm going to get me another cup of coffee. Would you like some, Mother?"

Meemaw nodded and hummed her yes from the living room.

"Esther, you go on and drink that up. I'm fixing to put a fresh pot on the stove." Mama smiled. "Christmas comes but once a year."

"So long as you're making more." Esther finished her cup and exhaled, her eyes closed. "I do appreciate it."

Meemaw had told me so many times about the Good Samaritan. Right then, as she perked another pot of coffee, Mama sure looked a lot like a Good Oklahoman to me. And she did it all while humming "Silent Night."

I wished so deep that one day I could be a little like her.

Mama came back to the table to collect the empty plates. When she got to Jael and Tamar's, she leaned close to them.

"You girls still working on that?" she asked.

Wide-eyed still, both the girls nodded. The way they ate, slow and with such little bites, about made me cry.

"They ain't seen that much food in a good while," Esther told Mama. To the girls, she nodded. "Don't you girls make yourselves sick eating."

"Yes, ma'am," Jael mumbled.

"I'm happy to send some along with you folks." Mama put the plates in the sink. They clinked against each other. "I don't know as we can eat all we've got left over."

"Now, I won't take no more from your table," Esther said. "Folks is hard up all over, and I don't got a mind to take from nobody."

"I'd be glad to send food along. Truly," Mama said, her back toward us.

"I seen a man walking down the road." Esther wiped a finger under her nose. "This was near about thirty miles east of here. I seen him with a shovel, scraping up dead animals off the side of the road. He said he was fixing to eat it. It weren't fresh meat, and I told him so much."

Mama held the edge of the counter as if she'd collapse without its support. "How horrible," she said.

"We never been that hard up." Esther shook her head. "God's been providing."

"Please let me send food along with you." Mama turned, her eyes sparkled with tears. "I wouldn't feel right unless I sent you folks with something."

"It sure would be a kindness." Esther stood and collected the used glasses, carrying them to the kitchen. "Let me wash up these dishes for you."

"No."

"I'll wanna work it off. Pay you back for your hospitality."

"I won't hear of it. Today's Christmas." Mama tried her best to smile. "Nobody's doing dishes today. Go on and rest a bit. The coffee should be ready soon."

Esther watched Mama for a minute before sitting back down at the table.

"That man that was here," Esther said. "He's a hobo ain't he?"

"You mean Eddie?" Mama brought over the cups.

"I believe so." Esther looked over at Tamar and touched her shoulder. "I seen him at the camp."

I knew she meant the Hooverville.

"That so?" Mama asked.

"You okay, darlin'?" Esther asked, giving her attention to the girls.

Tamar nodded, but her face wore a frown. "Getting full up."

"Don't force it in." Esther turned her head toward Mama. "Y'all don't mind having him here? That hobo."

"I suppose not. He's done no harm to anybody." Mama checked her sugar bowl, scraping a spoon against the bottom of it. "I don't have but a grain or two of sugar."

"As for me," Meemaw said from her rocking chair. "I don't trust that man."

"You made that clear, didn't you?" Mama asked, taking the coffee off the stove. "I sure am sorry I don't have any sugar for your coffee, Esther."

"That's all right. I take it black." Esther blinked a few times. "I ain't had coffee in so long I wanna be able to taste it."

Mama poured three cups, one for each lady.

"Pearl, will you get the sweet bread off the counter?" she asked. "It's sliced already."

When I carried over the plate, Tamar started crying. A quiet, shake-the-shoulders cry.

"What's wrong with her?" Beanie asked. She'd gotten up from the floor and stood a foot from the table. "Why's she crying?"

"I don't got no more room," Tamar said, still crying.

"Honey, you don't have to eat it all right now." Mama grabbed a fresh hanky from her pocket, handing it to the little girl. "I'll send some with you. I've got a whole other loaf just for you and your sister."

"What if I ain't never hungry again?" Tamar asked.

"You will be. And when you are, you can eat it then."

"Are you okay now?" Beanie asked, leaning forward to look at Tamar. "Can you stop crying now?"

Tamar nodded and dried her face with the hanky. She sipped from her water glass and pushed her lips into a smile.

"That's a girl," Mama said. "You go ahead and keep that hanky, too."

"Thank you, ma'am," the girl whispered.

❀

Jael and Tamar sat on the same chair all through dinner. Even with plenty of chairs empty after most excused themselves, they still shared. Their bodies were so little, they fit just right.

I didn't mean to stare, but I couldn't hardly help myself. They weren't shorter than me, not really. Their legs hung long off the end of the chair. It was just that they had no meat on their bones. I wondered if they ever had.

Their feed-sack dresses hung off them with no shape. No buttons. It was like someone had just cut holes in the bags for their heads and arms.

I ran my finger over the soft green of my own dress. Felt the way it tugged in the back to fit better.

I figured out how to be like Mama and the Good Samaritan.

"May I be excused, please?" I asked, pushing out of my chair. "Just for a minute. I'll be right back."

Mama nodded.

I went straight to my room. There, I grabbed a couple things from my closet and returned to the table.

Jael and Tamar looked at the fabric draped over my arms and their mouths opened as wide as their eyes.

"You can have these if you want them," I said. I handed each of them a dress that I'd grown out of. "If it's all right with your mama."

Before they even looked at the dresses, they turned to Esther and waited for her to nod her head. I was so glad she would let them keep the clothes.

The girls touched the dresses, so gentle, like they worried the cloth would fall apart under their fingers. They met eyes, and I thought they were talking to each other without words.

"That's real nice of you," Esther said, holding her fresh cup of coffee with both hands. She blinked out her tears. "Real nice, darlin'. What do you girls say?"

They both told me "thank you" and put the dresses in their laps.

"Wouldn't you like to try them on?" Mama asked, dabbing at the corner of one eye. "I'll let you go in my bedroom to change, if you'd like."

The girls nodded their heads, making their bobbed hair swing against their cheeks. Mama showed them where her room was and pulled the door to.

"You are good," Beanie said. She looked me right in the eyes for the first time I could remember.

When Jael and Tamar came out from Mama's room, they were even more shy than before. They took small, shuffling steps and kept their heads lowered.

"Look at you girls," Mama said. "How beautiful."

The girls touched the sides of their new dresses. The fabric was from a couple sugar sacks, but they were clean and had flowers printed all over them. Mama had made those dresses just for me, not knowing how pretty a couple other girls would look in them after I'd gotten my use out of them.

Tamar dared a smile, and that made her sister smile, too. Not big smiles. Tiny, shy, just-for-themselves smiles.

❈

Tamar and Jael sat on either side of me while I read to them from my book of fairy tales. They wanted to hear the story of Cinderella. I didn't reckon either of them could read, so I changed the story so the evil stepsisters didn't chop off their toes or get their eyes pecked out by birds.

I would have hated for them to have nightmares on Christmas night.

"How about I scrub the girls' other dresses?" Mama offered. "It won't take me but a minute and a little lye."

"Oh, no." Esther shook her head. "I can't have you doing that. You done so much already."

"It's nothing at all."

"I haven't gotten to wash them dresses in weeks. Not since we left home." Esther used her knuckle to stop a tear in her eye. "I'm so ashamed."

"With all this country in a scrape, you're going to be embarrassed by a couple dirty dresses?" Mama tilted her head. "That doesn't make sense to me."

Esther smiled. Mama brought that out in folks.

She had a way.

❈

I pulled the blankets back from Beanie. She always stole them from me when she rolled over. In her sleep, she grunted but didn't fight me for the covers.

She'd fallen asleep about as soon as her head hit the pillow. Meemaw's soft snores from the other room told me that she was sleeping sound, too.

My thoughts kept me awake. I wished I could slow them down. My body was tired, and I wanted to rest.

All I could think about, though, was Tamar and Jael and their wide-and-wondering eyes. I worried for them. The next morning, they would be hungry and have a little something to eat that Mama sent with them. They would have fresh, clean dresses to wear.

But then they would be hungry again and again until the food ran out. One day they would grow too tall for the dresses. Either that or the fabric would wear thin.

I worried at the pictures in my head of them eating jackrabbits or tire-flattened animals while wearing their filthy, too-small dresses.

What I had to tell myself over and over that night was that they had gone to bed that Christmas with full bellies. I tried to remember that God loved them more than the sparrows He'd fed and the lilies He'd clothed.

I just hoped they would find other Good Oklahomans along the road.

❊

A couple days after Christmas, Mama asked Daddy to go on down to the Hooverville to check on Esther and the girls.

"I don't like them staying down there without a man to watch over them," she said. "It's not safe."

Daddy agreed and made his way out the door.

"Can I go, too?" I asked, already double knotting my shoe.

"I guess that would be all right," Daddy said.

"Take your jacket," Mama called after me.

Daddy and I walked at a nice, easy pace and kept our voices still. What

I liked about Daddy was that I never felt lonely with him, even when we were quiet together.

He helped me up and over the stacked-up sand and into the Hooverville. It still smelled as bad as I remembered it, but the makeshift camps were less zigzag and more even lines.

"They're staying this way," Daddy said, putting his arm around me, guiding me down one of the lines. "Stick close to me, darlin'."

We walked past a man bent over the engine of a truck, a handful of kids huddled together under a flimsy tarp, a group of men squatting low in the dirt. A few of the folks greeted Daddy, and he stopped to ask after them.

Daddy was kind to them. He listened to their troubles and their plans. He wished them luck and left them with slight smiles on their faces.

In the Hooverville, my daddy was famous because he was good.

We reached a spot in a line of camps, and Daddy humphed and scrunched his face to one side.

"That's where they were camped," he said.

The space was empty, but I could see where something had been dragged, leaving a shallow ditch in the dirt.

They were gone. Not even so much as a scrap of paper left behind. My heart ached.

"Hey, fella," Daddy called to a man standing nearby. "You know what happened to the family that was here? A woman and two little girls."

The man removed his hat and rubbed at his forehead with a wrist. He let his eyes follow the drag mark where the camp had been.

"Yeah," he said. "Seems just the other day they got on a truck with a family and rode off. Don't know where at they went to."

"Thanks kindly." Daddy nodded once like men did and took my hand.

We walked out of the camp, Daddy once again helping me over the pile of dirt. When he noticed I was crying, he wiped the tears with his thumb.

"Pearlie, people have got to keep moving," he said. "That's the way of the world. If they sit too long, they'll never get ahead."

I didn't understand but didn't ask him to explain. It didn't matter.

The way of the world never seemed to make folks happy.

CHAPTER TWENTY-ONE

I had waited all the days between Christmas and Sunday to wear my new, green dress. Each morning, I'd peek at it in the closet and hold it up against myself to make sure I hadn't outgrown it, even though I knew that wasn't like to happen so fast.

When I got up for church that Sunday, I pulled the dress off the hanger as careful as I could and stepped into it. The buttons eased into the holes, and I smoothed the collar. I tried doing my hair the way Mama had done it on Christmas. All I did was twist it into a sloppy mess.

The pretty hairpin Mama had given me was in a small cedar box on the top shelf of my closet. I poked around the arrow heads and old pennies before I got to the hairpin and pressed it into the palm of my hand.

I knew that Mama would be happy to put my hair up for me.

Charging down the steps, I realized that I didn't smell oats cooking or coffee perking. And Mama hadn't baked the day before, so we had no biscuits or bread for breakfast. I wondered what we had to eat. A little nagging fear spread through me that we'd run out of food.

I got to the bottom of the steps when I heard Daddy and Mama. They were standing face-to-face in the living room.

"What are we going to do?" Mama asked, her voice sounding far away.

"I don't know," Daddy said. "Only thing we can do is get Hank Eliot." Hank Eliot the mortician.

Gasping air, I held onto the wall. Someone had died.

My mind went to Ray and Mrs. Jones first. I thought maybe the roof of their dugout collapsed, or a rattlesnake got one of them, or the pneumonia that took Baby Rosie.

I wouldn't let myself think about one of them going the way Mr. Jones had. It would have been more than I could take.

"How will we pay?" Mama asked.

Daddy's answer was a long sigh.

My feet had grown too heavy, anchored to the bottom step. Air chopped its way into me, but jolted right back out. My heart thudded so hard it hurt.

"Mother had some money in her mattress." Daddy coughed.

It was true. Meemaw did keep money in her mattress. "Just in case," she had told me. And that money was needed to pay Hank Eliot because someone had died.

Someone.

I needed to know who.

"She wouldn't have wanted that money to go for that," Mama said.

"I don't know what else to do."

My legs became weak, wobbling and threatening to collapse under me. I forced my feet to move from the step and into the living room.

"Tom," Mama said, covering a hand over her mouth. "It's too much. All that's going on. I can't take it all anymore."

"Mama?" I asked. "What happened?"

"Oh, darlin'." Mama rushed to me and pulled me up into her arms.

"Who is it?"

"It's Meemaw," Daddy said, his voice soft as velvet. "She's passed on."

Meemaw had told me once about the wailing women in the Bible. It was their job to cry and carry on when a family lost somebody. They wanted folks in town to know that they were suffering.

The way I wailed, everybody in Red River must have heard. And when Beanie came to us, she added to the carrying on.

Mama decided we weren't going to church that day.

Still, I wore the green dress.

❀

"I want to see Meemaw," I said, sitting by Mama. All my crying had dried out, replaced by a floating, numb feeling.

"You don't have to," Mama said.

Daddy brought both Beanie and me a glass of water. I was glad for it. My mouth had no wet left in it. I took a sip. The cool water soothed my throat and chilled me. Then the sadness burned the cool off and made me cry all over again.

"I miss her already," I managed to say.

"Me too." Mama held me, taking the glass. I heard it tap on the floor.

"I want to see her before they come to take her away."

Mama nodded and used her sleeve to wipe my eyes. "Let's wash your face first. Okay?"

She led me to the kitchen and wet a washcloth with cold water Daddy had just pumped. She pushed it against the skin of my face, dabbing it under my eyes and over my forehead. The fingers of her other hand pulled up on my chin, lifting my face so she could see my eyes.

"Ready?" she whispered.

❀

Mama pushed open Meemaw's bedroom door. Sun touched the floor in beams that shot between the parted curtains. The mirror on the wall had been covered with a black shawl Meemaw had worn every Sunday I could remember.

I looked from it to Mama, an ache forming behind my eyebrows.

"It's something we do," Mama whispered. "It doesn't mean anything, really."

Before that morning, I would have asked Meemaw about a thing like that. She would have told me the truth. I knew she would have.

Taking a deep breath in through my nose, I turned and saw Meemaw in her bed. Her whole body, even her head, was covered by a sheet. The outline of her curves and angles rose and dipped under the fabric. Her nose and the arms crossed over her stomach and her feet formed sharp ridges.

When I stepped closer to the bed, I clasped my hands behind my back in case I would be tempted to touch her.

I didn't want to feel her.

Mama sniffed, and I believed she was crying. She didn't sob, though, so I didn't go to her.

"Would you like me to pull the sheet back a little?" Mama asked. "You could look at her face if you want to."

I just nodded and kept my eyes on the bed.

Mama pinched the top of the sheet between her fingers and thumbs and raised it just enough so it wouldn't drag on the unmoving face. Then she folded it down below Meemaw's chin and used the palm of her hand to smooth the wiry white hairs that had stood up with static on Meemaw's head.

"She looks peaceful, doesn't she?" Mama whispered, sitting on the edge of the bed. "Your daddy said he reckoned she passed in her sleep. We don't think she suffered at all."

I drew in a long breath. Meemaw had been all alone when she died, and that bothered me something awful.

"That's the best for her," Mama said. "Don't you think?"

Tears made it hard for my eyes to stay open. But I forced them not to close all the way. I wanted to see Meemaw just a few more minutes.

She'd been alone during the night. I didn't want to leave her. I didn't want her to leave me.

I studied her face through my vision-blurring tears. If I hadn't known better, I would have just thought Meemaw was sleeping real hard, except that her skin was a color I didn't have a name for. It was like nothing I'd seen before.

"She's gone on to her reward," Mama said.

I knew she meant that Meemaw had gone to heaven, and I was glad for that. I decided that I should stop saying curse words and thinking bad thoughts so that one day I could be in heaven with her.

Then I remembered what Meemaw'd told me, about how I couldn't do a blessed thing to earn heaven. She liked to call it God's free gift. "That's from the Bible," she'd said. I prayed from my heart to be able to someday understand God the way Meemaw did. I wondered if I'd ever figure it out now that she was gone.

"Do you want to touch her?" Mama pushed some hair behind her ear.

I didn't want to and told her so.

"That's all right, Pearlie." She made to pull the sheet back over Meemaw's face.

"Wait," I whispered, holding one hand in front of myself. If memory was a well, I wanted to fill it up all the way. And I wanted to make sure I remembered Meemaw's gap-toothed smiles and kind words, her warm laughs and Bible stories.

Looking at her in that bed, what I remembered best of all was the way she loved me.

I decided that I would never stop missing her.

Not ever.

❖

We never did bury Meemaw's body. Daddy told me that Hank Eliot took her to a place where she was made into ashes, and I told Daddy I didn't want to hear how they had done that. He said it never hurt her.

I told him I still didn't want to hear about it.

Pastor held a service for her, and most the folks in town came to it. I did my best to listen to every word he said about the life of a righteous woman. But him talking about how great a soul Meemaw was made me miss her something terrible.

I wondered how long my heart would feel broken in two.

❖

The nightmares had gotten worse since Meemaw died. All of them were of her. She came to my room in a cloud of dust and ashes to warn me about Eddie and Winnie.

In that dream, which came back most every night, she told me that I'd be with her soon enough.

Each night I woke up shivering and sick to my stomach from the fear, not able to move an inch.

I never did tell Daddy or Mama about those nightmares. It only would have worried them and made them ask too many questions that I didn't have an answer for.

When I dreamed of dying, I saw Meemaw and her ash-dusted skin and unmoving face.

# CHAPTER TWENTY-TWO

When I woke up on the first day of 1935, I expected I would feel different somehow. Instead, I felt the same old tug of hunger in my gut and tear of sadness in my chest.

The hunger was easy to get rid of. All I needed was a couple spoonfuls of oatmeal. The sadness didn't go away so easy.

Meemaw's room was empty. Dust still buried Red River. Eddie kept coming around to smirk at me. And Beanie was folding up into herself more and more each day.

That New Year's morning seemed more like stale leftovers than the fresh start I'd hoped for.

Millard's voice carried all the way from downstairs up to my bedroom. The laughter that had always come along with him was gone, and I missed it something terrible. In the days after Meemaw died, his voice had gotten lower and sounded weaker.

I couldn't hardly look at him with his watery eyes and red nose. It broke my heart. He missed her as much as the rest of us did.

Daddy tried to get him talking about how things were before the dust had come. I liked listening to his stories. They kept me from thinking on the sadness so much.

I got out of bed on that New Year's Day and pulled on one of my sack dresses. I hardly got a comb through my hair before running down the steps.

"Well," Millard said from his seat at the table. "Look who we have here."

He tried at a smile, but I could tell it took a lot of effort.

"Good morning," I said, giving him a grin, hoping it looked easier than his.

"I still don't have any of those candies you like," he said, patting the pocket of his flannel shirt. "I'm real sorry about that."

"It's okay."

"Smalley said he can't put in an order for them no more. Maybe after a little bit." Millard shrugged and put his pipe between his lips. "I sure am sorry."

"Don't be sorry."

Millard lit the pipe, puffing clouds of blue smoke. I breathed in the rich aroma. His hands shook. All of him shook, as a matter of fact. I knew he was old, but he'd never seemed so fragile to me before.

Daddy put a steaming cup of coffee in front of Millard and sat across the table with one of his own.

"Morning, darlin'," Daddy said, sipping from his cup. "You sleep well?"

"I did." It was a lie, but I didn't want him to worry about me.

"Beanie still asleep?"

I told him she was.

"That's fine."

"Go ahead and set the bowls on the table," Mama called to me from the kitchen. "Oatmeal's just about done."

I put the bowls out like Mama asked and the spoons, too. She smiled at me and whispered her thanks.

"You know, I'm an old man," Millard said, spreading his napkin on one knee. "Real old."

"Nonsense." Mama pushed a serving spoon into the pot of oats. "Abraham was old."

I wanted to ask Millard how old he was but knew that Mama would have scolded me. So instead, I asked how old Abraham was. Mama couldn't remember exactly. Meemaw would have known. It sent a pang through my whole body, missing her. I tried to swallow it back down so nobody else would know I was hurting.

"Old as I am, I still remember the first time I seen Red River." Millard took a few last puffs of his pipe before setting it down so he could eat. "Back then, there was still water that flowed through the middle of town. We'd swim in it all summer long. Just splashing around in that cool water."

"Did you fish, too?" I asked.

"That we did." Millard looked at me while he sipped of his coffee. "I never caught much of anything other than a boot and tin can. I've never been all that patient for waiting around until a fish bit."

"Did you ever see buffalo?"

"Some. My pa'd hunt them." He took another drink of coffee and sighed. "Beautiful creatures, them buffalo. A sight to behold. Spitting shame we went and shot them all."

I imagined green fields of tall grasses held down by the weight of a hundred brown beasts.

"Your dad over there ever tell you how the town got its name?" Millard asked, breaking my vision of buffalo. "Why they called it Red River?"

"No, sir," I answered, hoping he was fixing to tell me the story.

"When the old settlers moved out this way to get their piece of the land, they didn't expect that the Injuns were still here. Them red men weren't so welcoming as you might think."

"I don't suppose I would have been, either," Mama said.

"They put up a good fight," Millard went on. "A couple good fights, matter-of-fact. But they weren't no match for the white man's rifles. The bodies of the Injuns piled up, and the river run red with the blood. Some dandy come from back East seen it. He got sick as a dog. Said he had never seen a red river before. Name just stuck, I suppose."

"That's terrible," Mama said, sitting in her chair. She looked at Daddy. "Would you say grace?"

Daddy said a short prayer, and Mama spooned the pasty oatmeal into our bowls.

"My pa always said the Indians that survived the fighting put a curse on this land." Millard rested his spoon on the side of his bowl. "They say they put a curse on all the folks that lived here and those who would later on. Seemed they had them a powerful hex."

"Oh, I don't know if that's true." Mama touched the napkin to her lips. "I don't put much faith in curses."

"Well, I remember when the paint still dripped off'n the buildings." He winked at me. "When I seen the wet paint, I couldn't hardly help but run my finger through it."

I smiled, imagining Millard as a naughty little boy.

"I was born over to West Virginny. My pa had fought for the Confederacy." He puckered his lips. "He was a hard man, my pa. I reckon the war done that to him. After the war, he didn't have nothing left, so he brought my ma and me out here. Seems he got a handbill that advertised cabbage the size of a man and carrots longer than a house. Folks said this place was the next best thing since the Promised Land."

Millard shook with an airy laugh.

"Even had pictures on them handbills of five men riding a watermelon like it was a horse." He scratched the side of his nose. "Such foolishness."

"Was it true?" I asked.

"Nah. It never was. I don't know how they done it, but they made them pictures up," Millard said. "When they got here, all my folks seen was a wild piece of land. Not a tree for a hundred miles, either."

"Was that before the Indians got killed?" I asked, leaning forward on my elbows.

"After. A good many years after, I guess." He steadied his coffee cup as Mama poured him more. "My ma, when she seen the dugout we was to live in, she sat down right there in the dirt and cried her eyes out. She boohooed like the world was coming to an end."

Daddy and Mama smiled and laughed softly along with Millard. I didn't know why it was funny. I imagined a young lady sitting on the ground, spoiling her pretty dress with her tears and the red Oklahoma dirt.

"'Course, we didn't have money to turn around and go back. My pa wouldn't have wanted to, neither. To him, going back East would've meant defeat. So we stayed on here."

"Was your father a farmer?" I asked, scraping the bottom of my bowl.

"Sure was. He got on the wheat wagon straight away." He sighed, and his eyes caught a stream of light from the window. "It was hard going for a spell. Real hard. But the land was good. The soil was rich. Government told all us farmers we oughta go ahead and plow up all the land. Every last bit of it. Said it would bring the rains."

"Did it work?" I asked, even though I knew that it did not.

Millard shook his head. "Never did."

The four of us stayed quiet at the table, finishing our oatmeal.

Millard lit his pipe again.

"The land got its revenge all right. Don't know if it was the Injun curse that did it or what. But the land's sure punishing us now." Millard breathed in a puff of smoke and held it before pushing it back out again. "Dirt ain't good no more. It's dead. Some days I feel ashamed to look at this bare naked land. We raped it and left it bare naked."

"Mill," Daddy whispered.

Millard's eyes focused on us again, like he'd been awakened from sleep. "I'm sorry," he said. "That ain't a way to talk in front of ladies."

Sad as Millard looked, he didn't cry a single tear.

# CHAPTER TWENTY-THREE

Day ran into day with hardly anything to make one different from another, apart from a duster rolling through every once in a while. The roof of the school building had caved in, and Miss Camp had had enough of Red River. Her mother sent money for her to take the train back home to Kentucky or South Carolina or one of those states back East.

Nobody could find a reason to blame her for leaving.

We didn't have school anymore, which was fine by me. I had all the books I could read. Besides, most of the kids in town had left or were fixing to with their families. All of them on their way out West to find work. Sundays were the only days that felt different from the others. Sundays were the days of my green dress and extra food cooking on Mama's stove.

Sundays we had a houseful for dinner.

Mama let Ray and Beanie and me sit on the living-room floor to eat so we wouldn't be so close together at the table. None of us gave a word of complaint. We didn't have to hear the grown-ups talk about Roosevelt or how this year would be better than the last. And we didn't have to hear talk about Germany, whatever was going on there.

The best part, I thought, was that I didn't have to see the cornflower-blue eyes of Eddie on me through the whole meal.

One Sunday, Ray leaned in close to me, like he had a secret to share. I hoped it was about something exciting like a circus coming to town.

Instead, he about broke my heart.

"We're fixing to go to California," he said, biting into a lump of fried dough. "Ma said she seen a handbill. Mr. Smalley read it for her. It said they got jobs in California for fruit pickers. Paying jobs. For women, even."

I thought about the handbill Millard's pa had seen back before they came to Oklahoma. I wondered if the advertisement Mrs. Jones had seen was as full of lies as that one had been.

"You aren't really going," I said. "Your mother has a job here."

"Washing laundry doesn't get her enough." He shrugged. "If you don't believe me, fine. Guess you'll find out for yourself when I'm gone."

"I ain't never leaving," Beanie said, using her spoon to spread around the sauce from her beans. "I ain't never gonna leave Meemaw here."

Neither Ray or me knew what to say to that, so we finished eating without talking.

❀

After dinner, the men all climbed into Daddy's truck. They were going to take a look at the cattle that were still alive.

"We gotta see if any of them are still good," Millard had told me.

Daddy'd invited Ray to go along and even messed up his hair as they walked out the front door. Ray shimmied into the bed of the truck and sat up a little straighter than I'd ever seen him. I waited on the porch for them to ask me to come, but they didn't.

They drove away, and Ray waved at me, a big grin on his face. Not a smirk, but a real, happy smile. I decided I couldn't be mad at him just then.

It was just as well. I wouldn't have wanted to be around Eddie all afternoon, anyhow.

Still, getting left behind stung.

"Read me a story," Beanie demanded as soon as I stepped back into the house.

"Where are your manners, Beanie Jean?" Mama asked, clearing a stack of plates.

Mrs. Jones stared at me, like she was studying me. I couldn't meet eyes with her. I was grateful when she turned and went to the kitchen to help Mama.

"Please," Beanie begged, tugging on my arm.

"Sure, I'll read you a story," I said, going over to the shelf. "Which one?"

"The boy and girl." Beanie grinned for the first time since Meemaw'd passed away. I wondered if she'd forgotten all about her. "The story about the boy and girl dropping crumbs."

"*Hansel and Gretel?*" I pulled the thick fairy-tale book from the shelf.

"How about you take it up to your room to read?" Mama nodded, letting me know that I didn't have a choice.

Beanie and I obeyed and sat on our bedroom floor, the book open in front of us. I read for a few minutes before Beanie got up and climbed into bed.

"Keep reading," she instructed.

Before long, she was fast asleep, her breathing deep and her eyes shut tight.

I got on my tummy, leaning on my elbows, and read to myself. The clinking and sloshing of washing dishes from downstairs ended. Then I heard Mama's voice.

"What exactly are you getting at, Luella?" she asked. "Just be straight with me."

"All I'm saying is you done it before." Mrs. Jones's voice wasn't as clear, still I could make out her words.

"I don't understand."

"I'm asking if you won't take Ray."

Silence from below. I rested my head on the floor, hoping I could hear better through the spaces between the boards.

"Take him?" Mama asked. "Take him where?"

"Keep him here. As your son."

"Luella . . ."

"I can't do it no more, Mary. I don't got any life left in me." Mrs. Jones's voice sounded like she was crying. "I don't trust nobody else with him. I know y'all would take good care of him."

"What are you saying?"

Quiet again.

"Luella, you ain't thinking of—"

"No. No," Mrs. Jones said, interrupting. "I ain't gonna kill myself."

"Good lord, but you're making me nervous the way you're talking."

The scraping sound of a chair being pushed. Then a cough.

"Mary, I've got to leave. And I can't take Ray."

"I don't know why not."

"Because he's better off here."

"That isn't true."

"Well, he ain't getting a good life being with me," Mrs. Jones said. Shoes clomped on the floor.

"We can't take him," Mama said. "Luella, he belongs with you."

"I got nothing to give him."

"You're his mother. He needs you. Especially after all that's happened." Another round of clinking plates. The cupboard door shutting.

"You've took in a kid before." Mrs. Jones's voice was flat.

"Luella, I'll ask you to keep your voice down," Mama scolded. "The girls are upstairs."

"All I'm saying is you done it before."

"I know," Mama said. "But I can't do it again. It's—it's just different now."

"Mary, you're the only hope I got for him."

"No, Luella."

Quiet for longer than I liked. I wondered if Mrs. Jones was about to leave our house. But then she spoke again.

"Mary, I'm begging you. I don't want him ending up like Rosie. And I don't want him turning out like Si."

"The answer is no," Mama said.

# CHAPTER TWENTY-FOUR

Mama sat between Beanie and me in our usual pew, the second from the front on the right-hand side. Even after nearly a month, it still felt wrong to sit there without Meemaw. I didn't reckon that would ever change.

I had never seen the church so full of folks from Red River. Not on Christmas or on Easter. There was no room for any latecomers that day—all the pews had backsides in them. I hadn't realized so many people were still in town. With all the people packed in, nobody talked. The only sound anybody made was a cough here or there and a few crackles of old wood pews.

It wasn't even Sunday, but still I wore my green dress. Town meetings seemed a fitting reason as any to wear it.

Daddy and Millard stood at the front, both of them with their hats in hand and their hair smoothed back. Daddy caught me staring at him and gave me a quick wink.

Millard cleared his throat. It sounded like all the gunk in Oklahoma had got stuck in there. I wondered how he resisted spitting it all out right there in front of everybody.

"Now get yourselves settled," Millard called out.

The folks in the pews stopped shifting to get comfortable. They all sat up straighter and turned their faces right toward Millard. Everybody seemed eager to hear what he'd called them in for.

Pastor and Mad Mabel sat in the front row on the left side. He held his arms crossed tight over his chest and his eyes shut up tight. I didn't know if he was sleeping or praying. She kept her face turned toward the window next to her, watching. For what, I didn't know. But I was just glad she didn't turn her face toward me. She gave me the heebie-jeebies.

I hoped Pastor was spending his time praying for Millard. The way he and Daddy stood in front of the whole town, sweat beading on their foreheads, I figured they both could use a little praying for. Sneaking another quick peek at Pastor, I decided that he was, in fact, sleeping by the slow rise and fall of his chest and his wobbling head. So I offered up a word or two to God on behalf of Millard and Daddy.

Millard pulled a bandana from his overall pocket and wiped his face before he got to talking.

"Well," he said, "might as well get this along."

He cleared his throat one more time, giving the people in the pews another moment to get adjusted.

"Now I called y'all here today to talk on a couple of matters. I bet y'all got questions, and that's fine. But I ain't going to have nobody starting a fight. Pastor don't want no punches swinging here in the church." Millard nodded toward Daddy. "That's what I brought Tom along for. To keep the peace."

A couple men, including Daddy, snickered at that. Millard grinned at his joke before he went on.

I didn't understand what was so funny, but Mama didn't seem to be in an explaining mood.

"Now first off, I hear some of y'all that's been getting the relief checks have been worried," he said, his voice carrying all the way through the sanctuary. "Some folks don't think it's enough."

"It ain't," somebody added.

"I hear you. I wish to God I could put more cash in your pockets. I do."

"I wish you could make it rain." It was the same man.

"Wouldn't that be something." Millard put his hand up as if to still the man from interrupting anymore. "Now, I think we got a solution to help you get a little folding money."

A murmur moved among a few people, and Millard waited for it to pass before he went on.

"I know y'all been hearing talk about President Roosevelt sending his men for our cattle." Here he paused again and let a few of the old ranchers and sharecroppers grumble a bit. "Thing is, we got ourselves a couple of choices to make. One is, are we gonna sell our livestock?"

"Hardly nothin' left to sell," a man said from way back in the sanctuary.

"Now hold on, Harold. Just hold on." Millard put the bandana back in his pocket. "You ask me, I'd say we gotta sell them. We can't feed the cattle. Ain't no use in watching them waste away like they're doing."

"What about when things turn around?" An old man stood, holding for dear life to the pew in front of him. "Things ain't gonna stay bad forever. If we sell all our cattle for a little folding money, then next year when the rains come back and the wheat's thick, we've gotta buy them all back again. I bet that's why Roosevelt's doing this. To get us to give them right back that money they give us. And with interest."

"Now, Orvil, you got an idea there. You do." Millard pulled that bandana back out and wiped his forehead. "Problem is, we don't have a reason to think next year will be any better."

"Millard, you know as well as I do that it's gotta rain sometime."

"I know it. I know it." Millard nodded. "But we've gotta think about right now. We can't get to next year if we all starve this year."

"How's about they pay us in gas so we can get outta town and head west?" I didn't recognize the voice, but a few people must have. And they made loud agreements with what he'd said.

"Well, if that's what you want, then you should go ahead and do it. Nobody's gonna stop ya. And it don't hurt my feelings none. Anyhow, you gotta make the decision for yourself. I know what I'd do. But I ain't you. And I don't own a single head of cattle for myself. All I got is a place to stay in the courthouse. But if I did have a herd, I'd see what I could get for them." He nodded his head. "I would make sure I got a fair shake. And I want the same for you."

"Any idea what we can get for 'em? Seein's I paid a good price, I wanna know that I'm gonna get the right amount."

"Now I don't know for sure. But they're gonna give them a good looking over and see how old they are. See if they're healthy and check their teeth. Let me be God's-honest-truthful here. If them cattle's no good, they're gonna have to destroy them."

"Listen here, I don't like that none."

The men in the meeting got to grumbling. Women chattered to each other. Millard stood in front of them, one hand in his pocket and the other still holding his hat. He looked out the same window Pastor's wife did and waited for them all to get their anger out.

Nothing but Israelites grumbling in the desert, that's what I thought of, listening to them. I wondered if they'd take one of those skin-and-bones cows and paint it gold, horn to hoof. I closed my eyes and imagined the folks dancing around that gold cow and building a big fire like the picture in my Bible.

A crying baby caught my attention. It was a weak cry. A hungry one. Without much breath behind it. I was sure it could feel all the upset in the room. I knew I could.

"Well, if you want, I guess you could watch them waste away." Millard scratched the back of his neck. "Just the other day I went out with Tom here and a few other fellas. We watched the cattle rooting around in the dust, looking for something green to eat. Y'all know it's been that way a couple of years now. I can't explain how they've survived this long. How any of us have, for that matter. They can't live on tumbleweeds no more. And neither can we."

The room went quiet except for the whimpering of the baby. Millard looked right at it and sighed.

"There ain't enough food to go around," he said. "We've gotta feed the kids first. Us next. Then the livestock last. Maybe a bit of money from Washington can help us feed our young with a little for us, too."

A woman cried out, frustrated. I turned to look, but Mama tapped me on the knee and gave me a shake of the head that said I better not stare.

"But what are we gonna do for milk?" a woman asked. I wondered if it was the mother of the whimpering baby. "You get rid of all the cows, and we won't have none for the kids."

"Now if any of you can tell me in truth that you've gotten any good milk outta one of them cows, I'll say you should keep it," Millard said, his face kind even though he spoke sternly. "Far as I know, though, most of y'all ain't got so much as a drop in months. Maybe years. Even when you did, it was nothing but mud. Ain't that right?"

"Now, what I wanna know is how they're fixing to destroy them," a man said. "I know it don't matter, but I gotta know."

"Well, that's the next thing you gotta decide." Millard swallowed. "If they decide the cattle is no good, they're gonna slaughter them."

"But how? I wanna know how," the man said.

"Now, I hear from Boise City that they shot them in the head with a rifle."

"Who done the shooting? And what gun'd they use?"

More grumbling.

"Now, hold on, folks. I'm getting to that." Millard waited for them to quiet. "Eddie, would you come on up here, son?"

My stomach flopped, and I wished I would have stayed home.

It took some nerve for that man to step foot inside a church.

Eddie made his way up the middle aisle to the front of the sanctuary, looking about as out of place as Winnie had at the revival. He slouched and had his hands shoved all the way into his pockets.

I imagined Jesus storming in just at that moment with His cord of a whip or whatever it was He'd had when He cleared out the temple in Jerusalem. It made me smile to think about Jesus using His whip to hit Eddie and hollering that His house was being turned into a den of thieves.

It wasn't a good daydream to have, and I shouldn't have thought it was funny. Mama elbowed me to get me to pay attention again. Boy, had her elbows ever gotten sharp over the years of drought.

"This man here's been appointed to help with the slaughter." Millard put a hand on Eddie's shoulder.

"Now, listen here," a man barked from somewhere to my left. "Ain't no man gonna slaughter my stock but me."

"I hear you." Millard nodded. "I do. Let me finish what I was fixing to say."

The crowd settled a bit.

"You can choose to do the killing yourself if you want," Millard said.

"Doggone right I can."

"Were it me," he went on. "I don't think I'd have the heart to do it myself."

"What if I just go on out to my field now?" the barking man hollered. "Shoot 'em all? Then at least I'd get a little meat off 'em."

"Well, you could do that if you wanted. It's still a free country, far as I know. But you wouldn't get a single red penny for a one of them. And you ain't like to get any meat off them, either." Millard tossed his hat on the floor behind him and stepped forward. "Listen, I understand you gotta take care of your own. You know I do. I just reckon you ought to think about waiting until the government fellas come. See what they've got to say." He shrugged. "Heck, they'll even let you use their gun and bullets, too. Save on yours. But if you can't see to do it yourself, there's this man here to do it for you."

All the murmuring and crying had hushed. Daddy rubbed his forehead and looked over at Mama. It was like he didn't know what to say and didn't want to be standing up there on the stage. He didn't smile or frown or anything.

"I'm trying to have faith that you'll all get a fair shake. I do hope that you'll get some money to buy some food or shoes for your kids." Millard nodded to someone near the middle of the room. "Maybe you'll get enough to hold you over until the rain comes next year."

"We been waiting on next year forever." I knew it was Mrs. Jones's voice by the cool and flat tone. I turned and looked at her, even if Mama did elbow me.

"I ain't got another year in me," she said. "And I don't got no cattle to sell off, neither. What am I gonna do?"

Ray squirmed in the pew next to her and wouldn't look at me. He kept his eyes on the floor.

"Ain't no work, and I ain't got nothing left from the food I put up. I'm doing as much make-work as I can, but we're hungry. My boy's trying to grow, and he's hungry all the time. We can't take it no more."

"Mrs. Jones, I sure am sorry about that." Millard nodded at her, letting her know she could sit back down. She didn't. "Ain't y'all getting the relief food?"

"They don't give us enough of it. Since Rosie and Si's gone, we get even less. I don't need much to eat, but I got me a growing boy here. I can't keep him fed on a couple cans of beans and a little bag of flour. That ain't sticking by him." She stopped and licked her lips. "We ain't had meat in about forever. Growing boys need meat."

"I don't rightly know an answer to give you, Mrs. Jones."

"I've never been outside of Red River except to bury my baby girl. You know that?" Mrs. Jones's voice cracked. "I was born in the dugout I'm still living in. I never aimed to leave. This is my home. My pa and ma's buried right here beside each other. We done all our living and birthing and dying right here. Last thing I want to do is go, but I don't think I got no other choice, do I?"

"I don't know." Millard stepped toward her and took her hands in his. His touch just about broke her. She cried, right out loud, in front of everybody and God. "Mrs. Jones, I do know things is hard on you right now. We're all broke up about Si and the baby."

She nodded and pulled one of her hands loose, resting it on her forehead like she had to hold her head together.

"If you'll kindly let me finish this talk about the cattle, I'll meet up with you and talk about what we can do for you and the boy."

"I ain't looking for a handout," she said. "I don't want no more charity. All I want is a chance to work for what we need. That's all."

"I know. I know. We all got our pride to care for. And ain't nobody here gonna think bad of you if you do need to take a little gift now and again. 'Specially after all y'all been through lately."

Mrs. Jones sat down, her eyes fixed on her hands.

# CHAPTER TWENTY-FIVE

The government men came on a Wednesday at the end of January. They carried their clipboards and briefcases. We watched them get out of their cars and walk around with Millard and Daddy.

"They're wearing overalls," I said.

They weren't new overalls, either. I could tell by looking at them that they were of soft fabric, not stiff like brand-new ones would have been.

"Well, isn't that smart?" Mama asked, standing next to me on the porch.

"Why's that?"

"Men in this town don't trust suits and ties. Men in suits are the ones who took everything they had. Bankers and lawyers wear suits." Mama smiled. "Folks here trust somebody who looks down home. Like those men there."

Mama and I stayed on the porch for a bit, watching. All the sharecroppers and old ranchers and anybody who had even a single milk cow led them all toward Watsons' ranch. I sat on the steps, and Mama joined me.

"It's a hard day for these folks," Mama said. "It's like they're giving up."

They moved the cattle, slow and steady. They couldn't go any faster—the animals were all ribs and hide. All the fat was gone off them. Every once in a while, one of them would stumble or sink into a soft spot in the dust.

"All they have to do is get the cattle to the ranch," Mama said. "Dear Lord, get them all out there."

It took a better part of the morning, but most of the men and cattle made it down the old road to the ranch. I watched as they became nothing more than dots along the tan sand.

Mama went inside to see to the housework. I stayed to keep watching, not knowing what it was that I wanted to see.

The old days of exciting cattle drives were gone. Nobody had any fight left in them.

After a bit, a man came down the road, pulling along the skinniest cow I had seen yet. It seemed that was the only one he had, and it didn't look as if it would make it. They still had a long way to go, and the cow stumbled and heaved. The man slapped its haunches, pulled at the rope around its neck. The man was about as skinny as the cow.

Finally the animal crumbled to the dirt. The man squatted next to it and stayed like that for a long time. He put his ear to the face of the cow.

Eventually, the man stood up and walked back the way he'd come, leaving the cow where it lie.

I wished I'd gone inside when Mama had.

❧

The shooting started about the time I lost sight of the skinny man. One shot at a time that echoed all the way to our house. Thankfully the ranch wasn't within sight of our porch.

With every blast, I imagined Eddie looking down at the cattle with that sneer of his. The sneer he wore when he clubbed the rabbit, and the one he had when he punched Winnie in the mouth.

I couldn't sit on that porch anymore. My eyes kept falling on the cow that had stumbled and died right on the side of the road, knowing that a whole lot more of them would be laying in the field at Watsons' old homestead. I couldn't take the thought of it.

Going inside wouldn't help. Beanie was about an inch away from having a spell over all the noise, and Mama would try to feed us oatmeal that my stomach just couldn't take that morning.

So I started walking. Around to the back of the house and into the field. Past the old windmill that complained with each wind gust that forced it to turn. Out by the road to the sharecroppers' cabins. I turned the other way, toward a field that had once been full of wheat. So much wheat I used to believe the crop went on forever and ever. That was before it all dried up and died.

Had it been warmer that day, I would have kicked off my shoes, rolled off my socks, and let my feet shuffle through the sand. It had been months since I'd walked barefoot. It had been that long since I'd felt free and easy, since my daydreams weren't laced with dark shadows.

The toe of my shoe caught on something. I didn't fall, I barely caught myself. Looking down, I saw a bit of rock peaking out of the dust. Grabbing at it, I pushed the dirt off until I uncovered it. It was about the size of my hand and weighed about the same as one of Mama's good drinking glasses.

Never before had I found the urge to throw something. But I did that morning. I threw the rock, screaming with all the yell I had in me. Just making that sound brought up a whole bucket of tears.

I found where the rock had landed and threw it again. I chucked it as hard as I could for losing Meemaw. Running, I went where it was and threw it again. That time for Baby Rosie. Again. For all the dust that was choking us. The hungry look in Jael's and Tamar's wide eyes. For Ray.

One last time I picked up the rock, tossing it up and down so it would hop against the palm of my hand. It slapped against my skin. I ran the fingers of my other hand over the rock. It was smooth and cool. I figured all the dust from the last few years had rubbed it clean, smoothed over the sharp and jagged parts. Turning it, I let the sun catch the tiny sparkles I never would have known were there unless I pulled it close to my face.

A bit of blue gleamed on the rock. Blue as Eddie's eyes. My hate for him soured my stomach. I hated the way he smirked and winked and how his rotten teeth stunk. I hated the way he talked to me and that Mama and Daddy didn't realize he was bad. Hate for the way he treated Winnie, even if she was a dirty, nasty woman. Hate for how he worked his way into our home.

But most of all, I hated how afraid I was of him.

I pulled that rock back as far as I could, cocking my arm like I imagined a baseball pitcher would. Letting loose my hold of the ball, I threw it as hard as I could, my whole body leaping forward with the effort. A scream pushed up from my gut, through my body, and out into the air.

Then I heard the rock hit. It clattered and banged on something metal. Looking around, I tried to figure out what had made the sound. I quieted myself, fearing that somebody else was in the field. All I could see was tan dust making mounds and valleys of the field.

I heard something move around in the dirt.

"Hello?" I called, my voice thin as paper.

The rustling noise came from where the rock had hit.

I thought my heart would stop and that the air I'd sucked into my lungs would make my chest explode.

Some draw I didn't understand tugged me toward the sound. I asked Jesus in a whispered prayer to keep me from evil. It didn't make me any less afraid to ask that of Him. My heart ached, it drummed so hard.

I took two steps closer, the moving-around sound still drawing my curiosity.

Some kind of metal jutted up through the dust. The closer I got I realized they were cellar doors. They must have been there for near to forever, but I never knew it from the wheat and dust that hid them.

The rustling noises started again, telling me that I was not alone in that field.

Everything in me screamed for me to run, but I didn't obey. I couldn't seem to. My curiosity was stronger than fear.

Hardly able to breathe for the nerves tightening my chest, I stepped nearer to the cellar doors. It was then that the noises stopped.

I'd been spotted.

"Hello?" I said, my voice still not my own, still weak and pinched. "Anybody out there?"

Gasping, almost screaming, I jumped back and pulled my hands up, clenching my face.

Right from next to the cellar doors, a rat hissed at me before darting out. It got past me before I could kick it. If I could have, I would have sent that thing clear to the other side of the county.

"Stupid rat," I muttered, hoping he didn't have any friends hiding nearby, waiting to sprint at me.

I turned toward my house to see if all my screaming and carrying on had gotten Mama's attention. It was then I realized how far I'd wandered from my back porch. Far enough away that nobody would even know where I was.

That was all right. I didn't need Mama or anybody else seeing me sneak into a hidden cellar, which I fully intended to do. I only wished I'd had Ray with me. He had a way of building up my courage. I was sure he was helping out at the cattle drive, though.

It took all my muscle to pull up one of the cellar doors. Dirt slid on the rusty metal before I dropped the door and looked down into the hole in the ground. Without giving myself a chance to turn back, I climbed down the steps to the dirt floor.

Inside it smelled musty like rat droppings and unwashed armpits. I wished I'd had a light of some sort so I could better see what was around me. The wide-open door let in a little light, but not enough to see into the corners. Luckily my eyes adjusted pretty quick to the dark.

Someone was living in that cellar, and whoever it was traveled light, as Millard would have said. All that was kept down in that hole was a bedroll and a plate with a cup sitting dead center on top.

Nothing too interesting, really. I decided I should climb my way back up the steps and out and go back home so Mama wouldn't worry about me. Turning around, though, my eye caught the sight of something pushed all the way up against the wall. A beam of sun touched half of it, making me wonder what ever it could be.

That old curiosity of mine got the better of me again.

Taking a step or two closer, I recognized the object as a box. Mama would have whupped me into next Tuesday for being in that cellar. Oh, but she would have made me real sorry for picking up the box and lifting its hinged lid. Still, I did just that.

At first glance it looked like nothing more than a collection of old newspaper clippings. Meemaw'd had a pile like that of death notices and wedding announcements. I figured that was all that box was full of. Still, something pulled at me to look at it all.

I backed up to the steps and took a seat so as to have better light.

Holding the first paper clipping close to my face I saw it was the article about Jimmy DuPre getting himself shot to death by Daddy. I unfolded the paper to see that the story of the abandoned baby was still attached. Someone had circled the article about the baby and drawn a line up to the picture of Jimmy.

The handwriting was smudged and I couldn't make out what the note next to Jimmy's head said.

Folding the newspaper, I put it to one side. I shuffled through a half-dozen envelopes, not bothering to read what was inside them, figuring they were just somebody's old love letters. Mama liked to read old love stories, but I did not. They bored me to no end.

As I sorted through the pile, a photograph dropped, upside-down, on my lap. It had been torn out of an album, I could tell from the black paper still glued to the back of the picture.

Right away I recognized Mama's handwriting on it.

"Pearl Louise Spence. Ten years old. 1934."

The photo fluttered my hand trembled so. Flipping it over, I saw an image of my face filling most of the space between the border. It was a picture Daddy had pasted in an album that sat on his desk at the courthouse. I couldn't make sense of why that picture would be in a stack of letters in that makeshift cellar home.

Sticking it back into the papers and not wanting to think of what it meant, I hoped it had found its way there on accident.

My whole body shaking, I continued through the box. More and more letters. Then more newspaper clippings. I felt of the last paper. It was stiff, crisp. I feared that if I wasn't very careful, it would crumble in my fingers and I'd be found out for the snoop I was.

The print on the old paper was so faint, I inched up another step or two so the sunlight would make it easier to read.

"Man Kills Wife, Then Self," the headline reported.

I read the story, my already-soured stomach churning.

In some town I had never heard of, police came to an old farmhouse after one of the children was caught stealing food from a market in town. What they found in that house was a woman who'd been strangled to death and a man with a gunshot wound to the head. A small boy was hiding under a bed.

Both children had said that their father had killed their mother and then put a gun to his own head.

"The children, James and Edward DuPre, have been moved to the home of an aunt," the article said.

James DuPre. Jimmy.

The sun glinted on something at the very bottom of the box. At first glance, I thought it was a quarter. When I looked closer, I saw that it was a dog tag.

"Edward P. DuPre. U.S.A." The letters had been stamped into the metal disc. They were just like the ones Ray showed me that had belonged to his father. On the backside somebody had etched "Eddie."

I found it difficult to breathe, and not because of the dust or the musty smell. Panic reached its hands around my neck and squeezed, strangling me sure as the woman in the old newspaper article.

Pushing all the letters back into the box, I lowered the lid and settled the whole thing back against the wall.

I ran away from the cellar, knowing that Eddie DuPre had come to Red River for one reason. He'd come for revenge.

He'd come for Daddy.

It wasn't until I got to the back porch of my house that I realized I still clutched the old, crisp newspaper in my hand. I decided I needed to show it to Daddy.

But then Eddie's voice came to me, "I'll kill you. I will."

I crumpled the paper and shoved it into my pocket.

❧

Mama stood at the stove, frying lumps of dough. Using a spoon, she turned them in the pan, filling the house with the rich smell. She jumped with another gun blast.

"How many of them are they going to shoot?" she asked, more to herself than me, I thought. "I swear, there must be no cows worth keeping."

"Mama?" I said, still standing by the door, my hand on the knob.

"Yes, Pearl?"

She looked over her shoulder at me. Her eyes were red like she had been crying all morning. I didn't doubt she had been. When Mama cried, her hazel eyes looked more green than brown.

Sticking a hand into my pocket, I fingered the balled-up newspaper. I couldn't help but picture the scene of a man choking his wife and then shooting himself. The ugly pictures in my head made me dizzy. I wondered if Eddie was the little boy who'd gone out to steal food or if he'd been hiding under the bed.

Hiding in a room with his dead parents.

I wouldn't allow myself to feel sorry for Eddie DuPre. I just plain refused.

"Did you want to ask me something?" Mama asked.

"Would you like me to set the table?" I took my hand off the doorknob.

"Wash up first, please." She went back to turning the dough. "Just four places. Daddy won't be home until later."

She stopped and sighed.

"Sorry," she said. "Only three plates. I forgot."

She'd forgotten that Meemaw was gone. Sorrow had a way of piling up on my heart.

❀

By the time Daddy got home that evening, we had all gotten so used to the shooting that we didn't even notice that it had stopped.

Daddy went straight to the kitchen sink and washed all the way up to his elbows. Then he splashed water on his face. Mama stood behind him with a fresh hand towel ready.

"Thank you," he said, drying his face before kissing her lips. "What a day."

"Are you hungry?" Mama asked, reaching for him and pulling him to her by the shoulder.

"You don't want to get too close, darlin'." He tossed the rumpled towel on the counter. "I'm a mess. And pretty ripe."

"I don't mind." But she let go of his arm. "I fixed a plate for you. I could heat it up."

"I don't believe I could eat right now even if I was starving to death." Daddy got busy unbuttoning his denim shirt, showing his sweated-through undershirt. "I'm dead tired."

"How about you go sit down a spell?" Mama moved the towel from the counter to the sink, rinsing it.

"I want to get cleaned up."

"We heard the shooting all day," Mama said. "It about wore out my nerves."

"Most all the cattle had to be slaughtered. They dug a ditch and drove the cattle in before shooting them. The men from the government said they were surprised the animals lasted this long." He rubbed his forehead. "They were all in bad shape."

"How did the men take it?" Mama asked.

"Okay, I guess. Millard did a good job preparing them for what would happen. Still, they were broke up. One or two cried right there in front of everyone." Daddy moved his head from side to side, making his neck crack. "Somebody thought we ought to cut up a couple. He said we might as well get the meat off them before they shoved the dirt over them. The government men said that was fine. When they started butchering one of them all that came out of it was a bunch of dust. All out of its stomach and lungs and heart. It was all full of dirt."

Mama curled her lip and shook her head. "The idea of it makes me sick to my stomach."

"Makes me wonder how much dust is inside us." He sighed. "I don't want to talk about it anymore, if that's okay with y'all. I'd like to forget this whole day if I can."

"Fine by me." Mama smiled. "I'll go draw you a bath."

"That sounds like heaven."

Mama went about getting Daddy's bath ready, and he sat on the floor, untying his laces. Once his feet were out of the boots and socks, he stretched out his legs.

"That feels good," he said. Then he looked at me. "What's wrong, Pearlie girl?"

"Nothing," I answered, looking back down at my book but not reading the words.

"You look all out of sorts."

"I just feel bad about the cattle," I lied and reached in my pocket to be sure the old newspaper was still there.

"Me too, honey." He closed his eyes. "Me too."

# CHAPTER TWENTY-SIX

I never fell asleep that night. My body jolted at every hint of a sound. Whenever I got close to sleep, I was sure I heard the banging of a gun or the moaning of a cow. My heart wouldn't slow down its heavy beating, and my head wouldn't stop twirling.

It was just as well. All sleep would have done for me was give me horrible dreams.

At some point in the darkness, I heard somebody moving around downstairs. When I smelled cigarette smoke, I knew it was Daddy.

Getting up, I pulled my wooly sweater off its hanger and onto my body. The rest of the house was quiet, just not Daddy. He never was one to move about the kitchen in a quiet way. I could tell he was warming up food in Mama's cast-iron skillet by the way it clanged against the top of the stove.

When I got to the bottom of the steps, I stood and watched him. He moved a wooden spoon around, stirring his food. The smoke rising from the skillet and his cigarette mixed to create a rich aroma that smelled like a campfire.

"Daddy," I said. "I can't sleep."

"You have a bad dream?" he asked, turning toward me.

"No. I just can't stop thinking." I sat in the dining-room chair Meemaw used to occupy.

Daddy put a towel under the skillet and set it on the table. He stuck a fork into the food and stirred it around, scooping up a piping hot bite of potatoes. He hardly blew on it before putting it in his mouth.

"You want a plate?" I asked.

"I didn't want to dirty one." He took another bite. "Don't tell your mama."

"I won't." Usually sharing a secret with Daddy would have lifted my spirits. That night, though, it seemed nothing would.

"You hungry?" He pushed the skillet between us and got up for another fork.

He took big, heaping bites. I only poked around at a couple potatoes, taking nibbles here and there. He'd been working all day, I hated to eat up his food. It didn't take long for him to finish it all off.

Daddy leaned back in his chair, lighting another cigarette. He smiled, but it wasn't his usual happy smile.

"What did you do today?" he asked.

"Nothing much," I answered, unsure how I'd tell him that I'd poked around in some hidden cellar and found proof that Eddie was bad, after all.

"Guess there isn't a whole lot of trouble a girl can get into around these parts."

I felt a glint of guilt. Sheriff's daughters should know better than to go digging into a man's personal things. And should know better than being in a man's space without permission, even if he was evil. I wanted to tell Daddy that there was plenty of trouble for me to get into. I'd already gotten into enough as it was.

I wished I hadn't taken the few bites I had. They roiled in my tummy.

"How you doing, darlin'?" He leaned forward, resting his elbows on the table. "A lot's happened lately. You okay?"

I shrugged, not saying anything at all. The truth was scary, just the way Meemaw said it would be.

The clock on the wall ticked, and a low, growling wind stirred outside.

"Hope we don't have a duster coming." Daddy stood and watched out the window. "Don't know how many more we could take."

"Daddy?"

"Yes." He didn't leave the window but looked over his shoulder at me.

"Can I tell you something?"

"I guess you can." He smiled.

"Meemaw never liked Eddie."

"No, I don't suppose she did." He poked around in his shirt pocket until he found a toothpick. He stuck it in his mouth. "She never did trust a man who tramped around like Eddie does."

"Is he ever going to leave?"

"I don't know. Probably. Once things around here get dull, he'll move on." Daddy took a few steps and relaxed back into his chair. "Fellas like him don't stick around a place too long."

"He's a bad man," I said, my voice shaking. "I think he's fixing to do bad things."

The way Daddy looked at me, I couldn't tell if he was thinking about what to say next or if he was angry with me. He stood up again and moved around to my side of the table, sitting in the chair where Beanie usually did.

"Pearl, you can't go around saying things like that."

"I've seen him. He does bad things."

"Your mama told me you've had a couple nightmares about him."

"No, Daddy. Not just dreams." I took a deep breath. "I've seen him hurt someone. In real life."

"Darlin', sometimes bad dreams feel real." His forehead creased all the way up to his hair. "They trick us into believing they're real. But they aren't. It's just a way our minds work ideas."

"He beat up Winnie." The truth spurted out from me. "He hit her so hard."

"When?" he asked. "Why didn't you tell me?"

"Before Christmas." I whispered because I was so afraid that Eddie could hear me somehow, that he'd know I was talking about him. "They were in the alley talking about something, and he hit her so hard. Her mouth was bleeding, Daddy."

"Pearl, you can't feel sorry for That Woman. She's all bound up in nasty stuff."

"I know that. I know what a cat house is now," I said. "Eddie told me she's going to stop doing that."

"When did Eddie talk to you?"

"Late one night. After Beanie got hurt. He came here. I tried to tell Mama, but she wouldn't believe me." I tried to swallow, but my whole body had gone dry. It was like I was pushing sandpaper down my throat. "He scared me, Daddy."

"Did he do anything to you? Did he . . . hit you?" Daddy asked, his eyes moving all over my face. "What else did he say?"

"I don't know. No. He didn't hurt me, really."

"Okay."

"Daddy, there's something I need to show you." Reaching into my sweater pocket, I pulled out the crumpled-up article about the DuPre family killings.

Daddy took the paper and smoothed it against the tabletop. About halfway through, he rubbed hard against his forehead. Before he spoke or even looked up at me, he lit another cigarette, smoking it all the way to a stub.

"Where did you find this?" he asked, smashing the cigarette next to the other ones in the skillet.

I told him about the box and all the letters, even about the dog tags I'd found. As I spoke, his eyes wandered, and I didn't know if he was listening or not, he seemed so distracted.

"Daddy?"

"Hm?" He glanced back at me for half a second.

"Is it the same Eddie?" I asked.

"I don't know for sure."

"He's going to try to hurt you."

"I don't know about that." Daddy shook his head. "But I'm not going to wait to find out, darlin'. He isn't going to hurt anybody."

He lit another cigarette and smoked as he rubbed his free hand through his hair. I knew he was thinking and I shouldn't ask any questions just then.

Daddy stood up, his chair teetering before banging against the floor, sounding so much like the shooting of cattle that it startled me. He dropped the still burning cigarette into the skillet and paced next to the table.

"Beanie ever talk to you about the night she got hurt?" he asked.

I shook my head.

"I can't believe I never thought of him before." He grabbed hold of a tuft of hair and stopped walking. "You seen Eddie hitting Winnie?"

I nodded.

"I'm scared of him," I whimpered. "He's going to hurt us, isn't he?"

"No," Daddy said, his voice stern. "He will not hurt you girls. I won't let him get near you."

He knelt next to me and held my shoulders. I still couldn't stop shaking.

"Are you sure about all this?" he asked. "About the box and Winnie and all of it? It's real?"

"Yes, sir." I wished I could have said it was all just a bad dream and had it all fade like my nightmares always did.

"I need to ask Beanie a couple questions." He jammed his eyes shut so his face wrinkled. "Why didn't I ask her about Eddie? It should have been obvious."

"You think he hurt her?"

He didn't answer my question, he didn't have to.

"I'm going to have to wake her up," he said.

"You think she understands what happened?"

"I don't know." He drew me closer and wrapped his arms around me. "I will never let him near you again. You hear? I won't."

Daddy left, climbing the stairs, leaving me sitting at the table.

I still had so many questions.

❧

Daddy woke Beanie and got her wrapped in a warm blanket. Mama came from their room, tying the robe tight around her waist.

"Why in heaven's name is everybody up?" Mama asked, yawning and sitting at the table with us. "It's the middle of the night."

Daddy didn't answer. He sat with eyes closed, wringing his hands.

"Tom, what is going on?" Mama reached across the table to touch him. "What's got you so bothered? And why did you wake us all up?"

"It's just . . ." He stopped, licked his lips, and turned to Beanie. "Darlin', I'm sorry."

Beanie glared at him. She never did like being woken, especially before the sun was up.

"What are you sorry about?" Mama asked, gathering the neck of her robe in one hand. "You better tell me what's going on."

"Beanie, I've got to ask you about what happened that night." Daddy swallowed hard. "The night you got hurt."

Beanie shook her head like a wild woman, her eyes shut tight. She grunted and moaned.

"Beanie. Violet Jean," Daddy said, looking at her with soft eyes. "Open your eyes. Talk to me."

After a few more shakes of the head, she stopped and focused her eyes on his chin.

"I know it was a bad night. That night you got hurt is a bad memory." He leaned toward her. "But I've got to ask you a couple questions."

"Tom, why now?" Mama asked, checking the clock on the wall. "We should all be sleeping."

"Beanie?" Daddy said.

"Don't wanna." Beanie clenched her teeth. "Never wanna think of him."

"Think of who?" Daddy breathed in deep. "Do you remember who hurt you? Did you see his face?"

She nodded. "But I lied before, and I don't wanna make you mad about it."

"I won't be mad. Sometimes we tell fibs when we're trying to protect ourselves."

Mama's eyes shifted between Beanie and Daddy. She leaned forward and set her jaw hard. "I'd like to know what is going on."

"He told me I couldn't never tell nobody." Beanie pouted. "He said if I tell anybody he's gonna hurt us."

"Who is going to hurt us?" Mama's voice raised with an edge to it. "Why isn't anybody answering my questions?"

"It's okay," I said to Beanie. "You can tell Daddy. He won't let anybody hurt you."

"He already done the hurting, that man," Beanie said through her tight-together teeth. "He hurt me real bad."

"Who hurt you?" Daddy asked.

"The man with the blue eyes. The man who shot the cows." My sister looked at me. "Eddie the hobo."

"I don't understand," Mama said, her eyes on Beanie's face. "Tom, what is she saying?"

"Eddie the hobo hurt me. He hit me and made me bleed." She pointed at her eye and her mouth and stomach. "He squeezed my neck and called me bad names. It was Eddie."

"No, darlin'," Mama said. "You're confused. Eddie's the one who helped you. Tom, she's confused. You shouldn't be asking all these questions so late at night. She needs her sleep."

"I know it's true," Beanie said. "I'm dumb, but I know this."

Mama slumped her shoulders and crossed her arms. "I don't understand."

Beanie shut her eyes and told us all that Eddie had done to her, how he'd told her he would kill her if she told. It was as if she was reading a script, it all came out so smooth, like she'd memorized every word. Truly, I wasn't sure she understood all she said. I didn't think it mattered, though.

"He squeezed and squeezed so hard I couldn't breathe," she said, touching her throat. "Then he let go and told me I best not tell. That's when he helped me up."

When she finished, she opened her eyes, and her face was dry. That surprised me. I would have thought that the memory would have made her cry. But it didn't.

"Why didn't you tell us?" Mama asked, dabbing under her own eyes with the sleeve of her robe. "We could have done something."

"I can't tell." Beanie let her eyes meet mine for a moment. "He'll hurt Pearl if I tell."

"But he's been in our home," Mama said, flashing anger in her eyes. "He's taken meals with us."

"I've got to find him." Daddy got to his feet. "I'd bet he's drinking up the money he made today."

"Tom," Mama said. "What can we do?"

"I'm going to find him and shove his sorry behind in jail." Daddy's voice was low and slow and grumbling. I could tell he was holding back a roar. "Lord, help me not to kill him where he stands."

"Thomas Spence." Mama covered her mouth.

"Do you know who his brother is, Mary?" he asked. "Jimmy DuPre."

"He's come for you, hasn't he?" Mama sobbed. "You can't go after him."

"I'm going to get Millard first. He'll know what to do."

Daddy moved around the house, dressing and strapping on his gun. He kissed both of us girls on the forehead and then Mama on the lips.

"Be careful," she told him, her face still close to his. "You come home soon, all right?"

"I will." Daddy pressed his lips against hers again. "Millard and I'll get together a posse. We'll try and end this peaceful as we can."

Daddy locked the back door and jammed a chair under the doorknob. Then he went to the front.

"You lock this behind me, hear?" he said. "And get that shotgun out of our room. It's under my side of the bed. It's loaded. There are extra shells in my drawer."

Mama met him at the door. "I hope I won't need it."

"Me too. But if you do need to, shoot to kill."

Daddy walked out the door.

Mama clicked the lock into place.

# CHAPTER TWENTY-SEVEN

M ama sat in the rocking chair. She'd positioned it so she could see between the front and back doors. Daddy's shotgun rested across her thighs, and she gripped it for dear life. If she blinked more than a couple times, I didn't see it.

She hummed, soft and gentle and soothing as a lullaby. As tired as her humming made me, I tried not to fall asleep. If I fell asleep, I might dream. If I dreamed, the dreams were sure to terrify me. And if I didn't stay awake, I would never be able to stop whatever bad was surely coming. I pinched my arm in that tender spot near the armpit to keep myself awake. It seemed to work, but I just knew I'd have a mighty sore bruise the next day.

Beanie lay curled up on the davenport, her mouth wide and face relaxed. If she ever had a nightmare, she didn't tell any of us about it. I didn't think she ever pinched herself to stay awake. When things got to be too much for her, she always dropped right off to sleep. Part of me envied that.

"Poor thing," Mama said, taking her eyes off the doors for a second to glance at my sister. "She's wore out."

"It's been a bad night," I said, watching Mama.

"Sure has. For all of us."

"Are you scared?" I asked.

"I don't know." She pulled the shotgun closer to her middle. "Guess so."

"Me too."

"When I was little, my mother used to tell me there was nothing to fear in this world." Mama blinked about twenty times all in a row. "I don't think she had ever been afraid in her life."

"I'm scared all the time."

"I know, baby," Mama said. "There's a lot to be afraid of. A whole lot. It's a scary world full of scary people. Can't hardly tell sometimes who's safe and who isn't."

"Mama?"

"Hm?"

"Do you think Daddy's stronger than Eddie?"

"I reckon." She flicked her eyes between the two doors. "I hope he is."

"That's good."

"But a man with a grudge can be mighty dangerous, you know. It doesn't matter how strong or weak a man is." She sighed. "Revenge can make a man do terrible things."

"Eddie's holding a grudge against Daddy, right? For shooting his brother?"

"Indeed, I do believe he is." She swallowed. "I'm praying really hard, though, that God won't let his hatred win over your daddy."

Quietly, without making a noise or moving my lips, I prayed that exact same prayer. And I added on a quick request that God wouldn't let Eddie hurt any of us. With all the "pleases" I said, I hoped the Good Lord would answer my prayer. And quick.

"Mama," I said. "Eddie really was here that night."

"I should have believed you."

Mama rocked in the chair.

"Have you gotten any sleep?" she asked.

"No. I'm not tired," I answered. "I want to stay awake."

"Why don't you try and get a little rest, at least." She took one hand off the gun and rubbed at her earlobe.

"Mama . . ."

"It won't hurt your daddy any if you sleep a little. He's going to be just fine. God's watching after him." She smiled. "Now, go on up. You can sleep in the bed by yourself."

As much as I wanted to stay with her, I didn't think she needed a fight from me. Besides, my bed would be more comfortable than the floor. I got up and kissed Mama's cheek, leaning over the gun in her lap.

"Good night, darlin'," she said.

"Good night."

"I do love you." She touched my face and looked deep into my eyes. "You know that, don't you?"

"Yes, Mama. And I love you, too."

"I'm sorry. For not believing you."

I nodded, not knowing what to say to her.

"Sleep well, Pearl."

I went up the steps and climbed in bed, not even bothering to take off my wooly sweater or socks.

Within a handful of seconds I drifted off to a floating, numbing sleep.

❖

Meemaw visited in my dream. Instead of the black dress and shawl she had worn in life, she had on green from her bonnet to her shoes. Her dress was just like the one I'd gotten at Christmas. She smiled, her eyes wrinkling in the corners.

I reached for her and called her name, hoping she'd come and hold me. Instead, she put up one finger and wagged it at me.

"No," she said. "I gotta stay right here, darlin'."

"Can I come to you?" I asked.

She wagged the finger again. It wasn't crooked like it had always been before.

"He's the God who saves, you know." Her voice came from far away, and I wished I could have felt her near. "He is. No matter who you are or what you've done, He's the one who saves. Do you believe He is?"

"Yes," my dream-self whispered. "I do believe that."

"He will save you."

"From what?" I tried to take a step toward her but couldn't. Something held me back. "What's He going to save me from?"

"He will save you."

"But . . ."

"I want you to say it," she said. "'He will save me.' Say that."

"He will save me."

"Again."

"He will save me."

"That's fine, darlin'."

Then she opened her mouth and screamed. She screamed like evil itself had grabbed her by the neck and pulled her down.

She was gone.

The screaming got louder and louder.

❖

Sitting up straight in bed, I woke with fast and shallow breaths. Dizzy and cold, I pulled the blanket up to my shoulders.

Then I realized that Meemaw's screaming hadn't stopped. Pinching my arm, I checked to be sure I really was awake. It wasn't Meemaw's voice.

It was Mama's.

And Beanie's.

They screamed, and Mama yelled for someone to get out of the house and that she had a gun. That she wasn't afraid to shoot his head clean off. Then yelling. A man's voice shouting the foulest, dirtiest of all words. Furniture clattered and crashed against the wall and floor.

The blast of the shotgun stole my breath.

I was sure she'd shot him, and I hoped that his head or chest was blown to bits. Not taking in breath, I tried to hear what was going on.

Two thuds, that was all I heard. That and my thumping heartbeat.

"Where are you?" the man yelled. "Pearl!"

Eddie DuPre was in my house. He was calling my name.

He had come to hurt all of us.

"I know you're in here, girl."

His voice drew nearer. The third step from the top, the one that had creaked all my life, sounded out a warning.

"Don't you hide from me." Closer and closer. "I will find you."

I couldn't get myself to move except to tremble.

"I don't want to hurt you, but I will if I've got to."

His voice came from the other side of my bedroom door, so close. Too close.

"I've gotta talk to you. Gotta tell you a couple things that's important."

He passed my door, going toward Meemaw's old bedroom.

Daddy. I had to get to Daddy.

I rolled off my bed, praying that the springs wouldn't betray me. They did not. Tiptoeing, I made my way to the window and pushed it up. It stuck, and I shoved it, feeling the fear-sweat beading on my skin.

"He's going to save me," I thought, trying not to make any noise.

One last shove and the window went up, thudding. I looked down at the soft dust mound under my window. I could jump and not get hurt. Then I just had to run like the dickens to find Daddy or Millard or anybody else. I sucked in breath before climbing out.

My bedroom door swung open, banging against the wall. Screaming, I turned, putting my back against the open window.

"Well, there you are," Eddie said, eyes wild. "Where do you think you're going?"

I didn't answer, just stared at him.

"It ain't warm enough to keep a window open." He took a step toward me. "Shut it."

We glared at each other. Time went slow, our eyes locked like that. Without giving it any thought, I ducked my head through the window and was half out, ready to dive to the ground below.

But Eddie grabbed my ankles and pulled me back in, making my face scrape and bump against the windowsill. He shoved me on the floor and leaned over me, holding me down by the neck.

"I told you I didn't wanna hurt you," he growled in my face, a line of spit hanging from his lips. "You done give me no other choice."

The back of his hand connected with my cheek, and I tasted blood inside my mouth.

"Try and get away again, and I'll do worse than that."

Pulling me up by the arms, he hefted me over his shoulder and carried me out of the room and down the stairs.

"Mama," I screamed.

Eddie laughed at me.

"She can't hear nothing," he said, stepping around the table and into the living room.

That was when I saw what made me more afraid than anything before in my life.

Mama lay on the floor, her head bleeding and her body not moving. Beanie was next to her, eyes closed.

"You killed them," I screamed.

I kicked my feet against his legs and stomach and pounded my fists against his back. If he was going to kill me, too, I would holler and carry on so the whole town would hear me first.

"Shut up," he snarled, grabbing for me and slapping at my legs. "Stop it."

I didn't obey. In fact, I got louder.

He dumped me on the living-room floor like a sack of potatoes. My head thudded twice against the hard wood.

"I said to shut up."

"Are you going to kill me?" I shrieked.

"Not yet." He looked down at me, his hands on his hips. "But you keep screaming and see if I don't."

I looked right at his face and let loose all the noise I could.

He kicked me in my ribs, making me curl my body and gasp for air. I watched him grab the shotgun from the floor between Mama and Beanie.

"You done?" he asked.

Even though it felt like it would break me in half, I drew in a deep breath and screamed like a wild animal one last time.

He laughed and shook his head.

"You ain't gonna make this easy, are you?"

He pulled his fist up.

Jarring, sharp pain in my cheek.

All was black.

# CHAPTER TWENTY-EIGHT

Opening my eyes proved a struggle. A thick crust glued the lashes together. Rubbing my eyes knocked most of the sticky mess away, but even then, they only opened a slit. I couldn't see a thing. Wherever I was had no light to speak of. It was like drowning in dark.

Lifting my head sent throbbing, thundering pain shooting through my neck that traveled all the way down my spine. Still, I sat myself up and leaned against what I thought must have been a wall behind me. I tried not to think that there might be centipedes skittering near my head.

I decided to collect all of what I knew to be true to keep what I didn't know from terrifying me. I was away from my home. True. Every part of my body hurt. True. It was dark and dry and hard to breathe where I was. True.

The fear, though, of not knowing where I was or if I'd ever get back home jolted me with a sick feeling all over.

Even though I tried to be quiet, a groan released from deep inside me.

"Well, sounds like you finally decided to wake up." It was Eddie's voice, and it was so close I could smell his foul breath before his face came into focus. "Good morning, sunshine."

"Eddie?" I whispered. "Where are we?"

I could see him just enough to know that he smirked at me.

Fast as I could, I tried to push myself away from him. Digging my heels into the dust floor under me, I pushed against the wall, sliding to my right until I got stopped up in a corner. Then I pushed again, wishing I could break through and get as far away from Eddie as I could.

*He's going to save you.* I heard Meemaw's voice in my head. *God's going to save you.*

"I ain't gonna hurt you," Eddie said, grabbing for me. I didn't have any strength left to push his hands away. "Not unless you give me cause to."

"Let me go," I said, wishing I had even a little scream left in me.

"You gonna be a good girl?" he asked. "I don't wanna hurt you."

"You already did," I said back.

He let go of me, and I sat still, so afraid of his fist I didn't want to move at all.

"Couldn't hardly help it, could I?" He struck a match, holding it in front of his face, letting it burn toward his fingers. "You didn't give me no choice but to knock you out. I couldn't have you screaming for the whole town to hear. You would've spoiled my plans."

The flame licked down the matchstick until it got near enough to singe his fingers. He dropped it into the dust, and the flame died immediately. Lighting another, he touched the fire to the inside of a lantern, filling the space around us with a dim glow. Still, I couldn't tell where we were.

"Trying to figure her out, ain't ya? You don't got a idea where we are, do ya?" He held up a canteen. "Thirsty?"

"Aren't you going to tell me?" I asked.

"Tell you what?"

"Where we are."

"Don't you worry about that." He poured a little water from the canteen into a tin cup. "You gotta drink a little."

"I'm not thirsty."

"Drink it anyway."

He put the cup in my hand. I sipped it. The water tasted like dirt and gritted between my teeth. I forced it in anyhow and handed the cup back for more.

Blinking against the muggy air, I realized I'd been in that place before. The lantern lit the room enough for me to see a bedroll and the steps leading up to a couple cellar doors. Up against the wall opposite me was a box. The box that had all the articles and pictures and Eddie's dog tags.

He'd brought me to the cellar in the middle of the dust field. If only I could get out of there, I could get home. Thoughts of home reminded me of Mama and Beanie, bleeding on the living-room floor.

"Did you kill my mama and sister?" I asked, trying to keep from crying, my voice shaking anyhow. "I saw them. Are they dead?"

"No. At least I didn't aim to kill them. I just hit them to keep them quiet." He smirked. "It worked, didn't it?"

Clenching my teeth, I tried to keep him from seeing my relief.

"What are you going to do with me?" I asked.

He didn't answer.

"Are you going to kill me?"

Again, he didn't answer.

"You don't know what you're going to do." I put on a hard-edged voice like I learned from Mama. "It's not such a smart thing to steal a girl if you don't know what you're going to do with her."

"It ain't so smart to sass a man like me, girl. You best mind your manners, little missy." He stood and spun the cap back on his canteen. "Don't think I won't hit you again."

He walked to the other side of the room, dropping the canteen in the dirt. From where I sat, I could get to the steps in a matter of seconds. The only problem was Eddie stood in the way.

"You got any food?" I asked, hoping he'd move out of my way.

"Nah," Eddie answered, climbing up the steps and opening the door above him, peeking out.

I tried to listen for the sounds from outside. I couldn't hear a thing. No creaking windmill. No chugging train. No sounds of people laughing or hollering. I decided to save my scream for when I thought somebody out there could hear me.

"Why did you take me?" I asked.

"I can't tell you that yet." He lowered the door and took a seat on the bottom step. Taking Daddy's gun, he looked in the barrel. He cussed and threw it to the side. "Ain't no more shells."

"Are you going to try and get back at my daddy? I know Jimmy DuPre was your brother."

His smirk was joined with a loud snort. "You figured out that much, didn't you?"

"What are you going to do to him?"

"Well, I ain't gonna just knock him over the head, I can tell you that."

"Then what?"

"I'm going to kill him."

I hadn't wanted Eddie to see me cry. Weakness seemed to put him in a hurtful mood, and I didn't want to get hit anymore. I couldn't help it, though, the sobs wouldn't stay in me. When I wiped my face with the collar of my sweater, I felt how tender my nose was. I wondered if Eddie had hit me there.

"I don't know why you care so much about him," Eddie said. "The man's nothing but a liar."

"He's my daddy." I snarled at him, hoping the anger would take the place of my fear. "He loves me."

Eddie laughed like he was fixing to go crazy. He kicked dirt my way. "That's funny right there, did you know that?" he said.

"What's so funny about it?"

"You know, Pearl, I've been meaning to talk to you." He made his way over to me and plopped down on the floor. "There's something I've gotta tell you that's gonna change a whole lot for you."

I didn't turn my face toward him but watched him out of the corner of my eye.

"Thing is," he said. "This secret I've got's been kept for a long time. Too long, you ask me."

He tapped his foot against the dirt. His boots were about all the way worn through. The laces had been tied in a bunch of places where they must have snapped from years of use. They were frayed and worn thin.

"Lots of people don't want you to know this secret." He knocked his shoulder into mine, getting my attention back to his face. "But I do. Oh, but do I ever want you to know."

"I don't want to know," I said. "I don't care what you've got to say."

"Well, ain't it a good thing it ain't up to you?" He groaned. "It ain't something I can tell you all at once. Least that's not how I want to do it. I been keeping it so long, I really wanna enjoy telling it. I can't wait to see the look on your face."

I thought of Daddy teaching Beanie and me poker on Christmas Day.

"You don't want to show anything on your face, good or bad," Daddy had said. "You've got to keep your face blank. Never break your poker face. Tuck your feelings in your cheek."

I made my face blank as I could, refusing to look Eddie full in the eyes. I pretended that I'd turn to stone if I did meet his gaze.

"The secret's about you, Pearl." Eddie inched his face even closer to me. "It's about who you really are."

"I don't care."

I'd spoken true. The secret he had was last on my mind. First was how to get away from him. I wondered if he would catch me if I made a run for it. I could throw a handful of dirt in his eyes, scratch my fingernails down his face, and scramble up the steps. I counted them. There were ten steps. I could make it up, push the doors open and scream for all I was worth. Somebody was sure to hear me.

"If I were you, I'd care. I'd care a whole lot," he said. "You ain't who everybody's been letting on you are."

Ten steps. I could make that in just a few seconds.

"See, you've been going on for, what, ten years as Pearl Spence." Eddie's mouth went on even though I wasn't paying him much mind. "You've been living in that house and eating meals around that table with folks you called your family. They've been raising you as their own."

He paused, and I glanced at him. He smiled the first real smile I'd ever seen on his face. It was a smile that would have made me trust him if I hadn't known any better.

"I've been fixing to tell you this a long time."

"Tell me what?" I put my focus back toward the steps and my freedom.
"Thing is, them folks ain't your family."

Slow and quiet and numb, that was how I felt. The world seemed to have grown thick. Just like the day when Daddy took the gun from Mr. Jones.

I turned back to Eddie. "What are you talking about?"

"Tom and Mary Spence ain't your parents." He smirked, and it made me feel sick how he enjoyed that moment. "They found you on the church steps when you was nothing but a baby. Your real ma didn't want you. She threw you away like you was nothing."

"The baby in the paper?" One of Beanie's newspaper Christmas blobs was folded and sitting in my cedar box with my special things. I hadn't known why I wanted to keep it. "That baby is me?"

As soon as I said the words, I knew it was true. I was nothing but an orphaned child.

"Well, look who's finally caught on." Eddie's laugh spooked me all the way down to the heels of my feet.

Eddie's words made it seem like my whole body was bobbing at the surface of a wide ocean, unanchored. I didn't like the way that felt one bit.

Eddie grabbed my wrist, his calloused hand on my skin anchoring me to what I knew was true. Maybe the only truth he'd ever said. I tore my arm away from him, the rough spot of his palm scratching against my wrist. It stung, and I wanted to scrub it clean.

"You're lying," I whispered, wishing I could make his words untrue. I cradled my hand against my stomach more for comfort than because it was hurt. "I hate you."

"You shouldn't hate me," he said. "I ain't been the one lying to you your whole life. I'm the only one telling you the truth."

"You made it all up." I leaned away from him, wishing I had the nerve to run. "That baby could have been anybody. But it wasn't me. Mama would have told me."

"Would she have? I don't know that you know her so well as you think."

Eddie got right up to my face and smirked at me. I hated him more and more with each second.

Before I knew what I was doing, I spit right in his face. He flinched, and then, figuring out what I'd done, he hit me right in the eye.

I saw the starbursts behind my eyelids before I felt the pain. Tears spilled and added sting to the hurt. My eye would swell and turn all kinds of purple and blue and black, just like Mrs. Jones's.

But I could run with just one eye if I needed to.

Eddie used a bandana to wipe my spit off his face. He wasn't smirking just then, and I decided that it was worth getting punched to see him without that stupid grin. I stared straight at him and forced myself to stop crying.

"If you ever pull something like that again . . ." He didn't finish. He didn't have to.

I knew from the way he glared all the way through me that he would kill me.

❖

Eddie sat on the steps under the cellar doors, staring at me and smoking cigarettes. He smoked one after another, filling the air around us with more choking thickness. The light from above streamed through the gap between the doors, shining on just the left-hand side of his body. Only one of his eyes glowed blue.

We'd gone without talking about that secret of his for hours, at least I guessed it was that long. In fact, neither of us had said so much as a word. I figured he was real sore at me, and I didn't care one bit if he was. He finished what had to have been his seventh cigarette and tossed it in the dirt, where it burned down to nothing.

"You love them?" he asked, gruff voiced. "Tom and Mary Spence?"

I nodded. The movement, small as it was, made my whole head ache. I would have done about anything for another sip of water but wasn't going to ask him for any favors.

"Even though they ain't your family?" He shook his head. "You still love them."

"Even if they weren't." I still fought against believing him. I didn't want him to be right.

"Why?" He wrinkled his forehead like he really cared about the answer.

"They're my family."

"But they ain't."

"So you say."

"Well, let's just say they are your family. It still don't mean nothing." He spit and it landed just a couple inches from my foot. "I never loved no one in my family."

"Why not?"

"Because we were just plain awful to each other."

"I heard about your folks," I said. "Is it true?"

"What'd you hear?"

"About when you were little."

"That? About how my old man killed my ma?" He rolled his eyes. "Yeah, that's true. How'd you hear about that?"

"I just know about it," I said, deciding not to tell him how I'd found the paper in his box. "Were you sad about it?"

"It ain't sad. I ain't sad about it."

"But your father killed himself, too." I hoped the barb would stick.

"That's where you got it wrong." He scratched at his scalp. "That's the story we told the deputy, but it ain't what really happened."

Just like I did when Daddy told a story, I waited for Eddie to go on. His eyes were far away, like he was thinking on something. I thought that maybe if he kept on talking, he'd forget all about me and I could make a run for it. All I needed was to make it up the ten steps.

"Don't you wanna know what really happened?" he asked. "Ain't you a little bit curious?"

"I guess so."

"Well, my pa killed my mom. She said something to him. Can't remember what it was. Whatever she said set him off. He jumped on top of her and beat her bloody. Then he strangled the life out of her." He pulled another cigarette from his pocket. His hands shook when he brought it to his lips. "I don't suppose you ever seen a man strangle somebody, have ya?"

I shook my head no.

"Awful thing to watch. It took her a terrible long time to die. And the sounds she made." He closed his eyes and smoked in quiet. "I'd crawled under the bed. I was scared he'd come get me next. Never was so scared. Jimmy wasn't scared, though. No, sir. Jimmy never was afraid of nothing. Something in him snapped, seeing our pa do that. After our pa got off Ma, he was wore out. It's hard work, squeezing the life outta somebody. He fell back on the ground. Just then, Jimmy grabbed our pa's pistol and pushed it right against my father's head."

Eddie made his finger look like a gun and put it up to the side of his own head.

"Pa lifted his hands like he was going to make for Jimmy's throat. That's when Jim shot him." Eddie made a noise like a gun blast. "Just like that. Never have seen nothing like that since. What a mess."

I rested my head against the wall behind me. It was cool, and I hoped it would soothe the pain that swelled in my skull. Shoving down the pity for him, I remembered the hand marks that were on Beanie's neck for weeks. Marks Eddie'd made when he hurt her.

I wondered what had made him stop squeezing.

"When you tell me how you love them folks who pretend to be your family, it don't mean nothing to me." He looked at the dirt. "I never loved no one in my life. Family or otherwise. I don't even know what it would be like."

The world was full of awful people who did terrible and ugly things. Most of them were only awful because of the scars on their hearts.

I thought on Meemaw's dream words.

*God is the one who saves.*

I really wanted to believe that was true.

# CHAPTER TWENTY-NINE

I must have slept for hours, the way my neck ached and my legs tingled. I couldn't tell if it was daytime or night. The strong stream of light that had come from the doors was dusky and dim. Eddie's lantern had gone dark.

A blanket of dust covered all of me. When I opened my mouth to take in a deep breath, all I got was dirt.

"You slept through a duster," Eddie said through the darkness.

Spitting the grit from my mouth, I felt a clenching in my chest. All a dust storm could do was bury us in that cellar, hiding us from Daddy until we ran out of air.

My eye throbbed, and I felt of it with my fingertips. My skin stretched tight over the swollen part. Was it ever tender. I wondered if it would feel better if a little of the fluid behind the skin could drain. What I wouldn't have done for a cold washcloth just then.

On the other side of the cellar, a light flickered at the end of a match, then grew to a flame. The brightness of it stabbed clear through to the back of my head.

Eddie carried his old lantern to me, an unlit cigarette hanging from his lips. He poured me a cup of the dirty water.

"Drink this," he said.

"Can I go home?" I asked, sipping the water. "I promise I'll never tell."

"I don't believe you'll be going home." He took the cup from me, tilting the canteen. "More?"

I shook my head. It took all my strength not to panic. The only thing I wanted to do was go home and be back in my bed. My head pounding and stomach churning, I nearly let loose all my fear with a scream.

But Eddie DuPre wouldn't see that part of me. I wouldn't allow it. So I faked calm. Made believe. Played the part of the brave Indian princess.

God would save me. Meemaw promised. It built up my imagined courage.

"I'll go home. You can't stop me," I said.

"And just how are you gonna do that?"

"I'm going to go home." I turned my eyes away from him, watching the lantern light flicker on the old wood wall.

"Who you gonna go home to?" He gulped straight from the canteen, emptying it. "Tom and Mary ain't your folks. Or did I knock your brain silly when I hit you."

I refused to talk back to him. He pushed my shoulder with his fingers.

"Hey, I was talking to you," he said. "Who you gonna go home to? Your pretend family?"

"Why's it any of your business who my family is?" I turned to him and narrowed my eyes when I spoke to him. "Why do you care?"

"I'm warming up to that." He shoved me again with those fingers of his. "I got my reasons. Believe you me, I've got a pretty good reason for caring."

"I'm going home to the Spence family," I said. "And they'll be glad to see me. They'll grab hold of me and hug me and kiss me all over my face."

"Why would they do that?"

"Because they love me," I said, more to silence any doubt that had stabbed its way into my mind. "They want me."

"They don't love you." Eddie rolled his eyes. "They feel sorry for you."

"That's a lie."

"No, it's true. They found you when you was a little baby, left by a mother who never loved you enough to even feed you." He smirked. "The sheriff and his little wife never would have told you the truth. They felt sorry for you then, and they feel sorry for you now."

"Why does that matter?"

"Pity ain't love."

❊

Eddie paced across the cellar. Watching him made me realize how stiff my legs were from sitting on the dirt floor for so long. I pulled my knees up, bending them so I could hug my arms around my shins.

I wondered if he'd let me leave the cellar if I told him I had to use the restroom. I hadn't had enough water to make me have to go, but it might be worth the try.

"I've got to go," I said.

"There's a jar in the corner," he said, stopping in the middle of the floor and looking at me. "You'll use that."

"But you'll see me."

"I won't look." He shoved his hands in his pockets. "I'll turn my back."

"Never mind."

He climbed up the steps and peeked out between the doors. Light filled the room for just a moment, and I had to blink to keep it from hurting my head.

"Where is she?" he murmured, turning and sitting on the steps. He held his head in his hands.

If he fell asleep, I could get out. But not if he drifted off on those steps. I'd need to get him to move. He needed to keep talking long enough for me to draw him off those steps.

All I had to do was stay awake longer than he did.

"You ever kill anybody?" I asked.

"What?" He lifted his head.

"Have you ever killed anybody?"

"Why do you wanna know a thing like that?" he asked.

"Just wondering." I shrugged.

"Well have you ever killed anybody, Pearl?"

"Not yet."

Setting my face hard, I stared him down. I never could have killed him, not even as mad as I was at him. But he didn't have to know about that.

"It ain't something a man brags about." He put his head back down. "Killing ain't something to have pride in."

"Jimmy DuPre killed lots of people."

"So what?"

"My daddy said he bragged about them plenty. I bet he killed more men that you ever could."

"I killed plenty," he mumbled. "And he never killed more than me. He wasn't so tough as everybody thought. Just a lucky shot is all. It's not like he was in the war or nothing."

The thought of his brother got him off the steps and pacing again. Just what I wanted.

"I shot down plenty of Krauts in the war." He snarled. "Never meant nothing to me to shoot them. They come rushing at me. All I could do was keep shooting."

"Did it make you feel bad?"

"They didn't look like people." He scratched his cheek. "They were more animal than human. It was them or me. That's all war is. Them or me."

He grabbed the canteen and shook it. Just a few drops rattled against the tin sides. He spiked it back to the ground.

"A couple of the guys would mess themselves in the fox holes, they was so scared. They'd cry for their mamas." He curled his lip. "Not me. I never did have a mama to call out to, anyhow."

"You weren't scared?"

"Nah. I never was. I wasn't never afraid to die. Didn't make much difference to me," he said. "Living is more a risk than dying, anyhow."

"You tried to kill my sister."

Turning toward me, he shoved his hands in his pockets. "What makes you say that?"

"You choked her."

Closing his eyes, he tipped his head back. "I couldn't finish her like that. It was too much . . ."

Too much like how his mother died.

"I don't wanna talk about it no more," he said, climbing up the steps again, checking for something out the door.

"What are you looking for?"

He didn't hear me or at least pretended not to.

"It won't be nothing to kill the sheriff. It won't bother me one bit," Eddie said. "That girl didn't do nothing wrong. The sheriff, that's another thing."

I clenched the sides of my nightgown with my hands, so hard it hurt my knuckles.

"You don't have to kill him," I said, trying to keep my voice steady. "There's got to be some way else to get revenge. He could get you money."

"I don't want no money."

"What do you want?"

"I got me a score to settle," he said. "Lord, I did hate Jimmy. He was hardly a human, all the bad stuff he done. He beat me more times than I can count. But a man's got to get revenge sometimes."

"Jimmy hurt people."

"You think I don't know that?" Eddie shook his head. "He was a bad son-of-a-gun. I'm sure he had it coming to him. Still I've got to do my duty by him."

"That doesn't make any sense."

"War never does."

❖

Eddie checked the cellar doors every minute or two, never leaving the steps. He blocked my only way to freedom, and I was out of ideas of how to get him to make way for me.

"Why ain't she here yet?" he'd mutter about every time he looked.

"Who are you waiting on?" I asked.

He roared his frustration, storming down the steps and toward me, his face sharp and terrifying. I thought he was going to kill me right then.

Drawing back his fist, he threw punches, one after another. His hand slammed against the wall over my head, sending dust falling all over me. I crawled away from him, thinking I might be able to make it to the steps. My numb legs dragged on the dirt floor, slowing me down. Needles of pain jabbed through the bottoms of my feet. I forced myself to keep moving even though every part of me hurt so bad.

My only hope was that he would break his hand. I prayed for just that to happen.

"Where do you think you're going?" he hollered at me.

I shook my head and sunk close to the floor, trying to make myself a smaller target.

But he didn't hit me. It seemed he hardly saw me.

He walked around me to the bottom step and plopped down. Turning his hand, he checked the damage to his knuckles. Blood covered them, but he bent his fingers anyhow. They weren't broken.

"What are you looking at?" he growled.

"Nothing." I went back to my spot and leaned my back against the wall.

Quiet pushed its way into the cellar once more. After a bit, Eddie looked out the doors again.

My stomach rumbled. Eddie turned toward me and rolled his eyes.

"I'm hungry," I said.

"Tough." He wrapped a bandana around his knuckles.

❈

Time came and went without anything to mark it but the dim light that came through the doors. I tried to imagine the tic-tocking of Mama's clock. Counting the seconds, I passed the time. It didn't help me figure out how long I'd been in there, though.

*Tic-tock.* I tried to figure out how to get out of that cellar.

*Tic-tock.* If I could get to the steps, I'd be free.

*Tic-tock.* Every second I stayed made it harder and harder to get out.

I tried to ask Eddie questions about when he was a child, or what the war was like, or where he had lived before coming to Red River. He acted like he didn't even know I was down there with him anymore. He didn't answer a single one of my questions.

So I decided to ask myself. I answered silently, just inside my head.

When I was a child, I was happy. I had a family that loved me and took good care of me. I'd never lived anywhere other than Red River, Oklahoma. I never wanted to live any place else, either. I knew nothing of war, and I was glad for it.

Except for the war Eddie fixed to wage.

Closing my eyes, I tried to think of a way to beat Eddie at his own battle.

So wrapped up was I in my plans, I almost didn't hear the squeaking of the cellar door or notice the downpour of sunlight that bathed us.

All I could see was that someone was walking down the steps. More of a shadow than anything, really. And I could see that she had on a skirt. That was all.

"I've been waiting for you." Eddie stood from his seat on the stairs.

"I got the message you sent." She stepped on the dirt floor and turned toward Eddie.

"Anybody follow you?"

"No."

"You sure?"

"Eddie, what is going on?"

"Winnie, I gotta show you something."

That Woman. I wondered what she was doing there. I hoped that she was going to get me out.

"Why are you down here?" She looked at her feet. "Are you living down here?"

"I got something for you." Eddie climbed up the steps and pulled the cellar door down with a slam.

"Are you hiding down here?" She stepped away from him when he took the final stair to the floor. "Folks in town are looking for you, you know that, right?"

"I figured they would."

She lowered her voice. "What've you done?"

"You're so stupid." He put his hands on his hips. "That's why I'm down here. Because you're stupid."

"Don't call me stupid."

"I'll call you whatever I wanna." He took her by the elbow and turned her. "I got a surprise for you."

She pushed his hand off her and faced him again. "Eddie, I thought we agreed that you was skipping town. I gave you money."

The way Eddie pulled at her, she moved into the stream of light. It glowed on her hair, making it look like gold.

"I had a little business of my own to take care of first."

She sighed and stepped out of the beam.

"Don't you got a light or something? I can't hardly see nothing."

Eddie stooped and picked up the lantern, carrying it over to me. Winnie turned and saw me for the first time.

"Oh, Eddie," she gasped. "What have you done? Did you do that to her face?"

She touched the fingertips of both hands to her mouth, and her eyes grew round.

Eddie squatted next to me.

"Pearl and me have had us a little talk." He knocked into me with his elbow. "Ain't that right, Pearl."

I kept my eyes on Winnie.

"We've been talking about how Tom and Mary ain't her real folks." He frowned. "Problem is she don't believe me."

Winnie lowered her hands to her sides. Her purse fell to her wrist, swinging against her hip.

"Pearl, you see Winnie there?" he asked.

I didn't answer him.

"She's the proof that what I'm saying is true."

"I don't understand," I said.

"Pearl, I want you to meet your ma. Your real ma." Eddie laughed. "Come on, Winnie. Don't you got a kiss for your baby girl?"

Winnie didn't move, and I didn't either. Her blond hair and mine. Her small nose that sloped just so and mine. The way her eyebrows curved the same way mine did.

I realized that Eddie might have been telling the truth for the first time in his life.

"I said come on and give her a kiss," Eddie growled.

Winnie obeyed, rushing toward me, but she didn't kiss me. I was glad she didn't.

"Why are you doing this?" she asked, stopping just a few inches from me.

"She's got to know." He stood. "Don't you think it's best? The truth will set us all free. Ain't that what the Good Book says?"

Her standing in front of me with a tear rolling down her cheek, I wondered why I hadn't ever realized it before. Probably because I wasn't looking then.

"It don't make no difference if I'm her ma or not," she said. "I never done a single useful thing for her."

"You told me you wanted her." Eddie stepped forward, puffing his chest out. "Ain't that why you wrote me that letter? You even sent me her picture. Or did you forget about writing me?"

"No. I never forgot."

"You wanted me to come here to help you get her."

"I changed my mind." She lowered to my level. "I'm sorry. I done everything wrong."

"So you don't want her no more." Eddie crossed his arms and turned to me. "How's that feel?"

"It's true?" I asked, using the wall behind me to rise to my feet. "Are you really my . . ."

"Yes. Only because I gave birth to you." She shook her head. "But I never was your ma like Mary's been. She's been good to you."

Winnie didn't reach for me the way Mama would have. She didn't wonder about my swollen eye or cracked lips. The way she looked at me was the way somebody would look at a wounded cat she was too afraid to touch.

It was just as well. I didn't want her hands on me, anyway.

If it was true, that she'd left me when I was too little to do anything for myself, then I'd been unwanted from the beginning.

She hadn't wanted me.

She was nothing but a stranger to me. I couldn't figure out why that made my heart ache so deep.

# CHAPTER THIRTY

E ddie had finally fallen asleep, sitting upright against the wall across the room from Winnie and me. He'd put a padlock on the doors, and the key was tightly held in his hand. In his other hand, he had a pistol loaded and cocked. His head tilted back, and his mouth hung open.

I hoped a whole cup of dust would fall past his lips and that he'd choke on it.

The lantern sat on the floor between Winnie and me. The flickering light played on her soft skin. I couldn't make a guess at how old she was. In that gentle light, she seemed younger than I would have thought before.

She'd promised to look after me while Eddie slept. He told her to make sure I didn't do anything stupid. When he'd said that, I thought of about half-a-dozen things to sass at him, but decided to keep my mouth shut instead.

"I'm hungry," I said after Eddie'd been asleep for a bit. "He didn't bring any food."

The way she looked at me, her eyebrows lowering, I figured she didn't know I was asking for something to eat. Mama would have understood. Mama would have found something for me to eat. I asked Winnie if she had anything in her purse. Rummaging through her handbag, she found a few pieces of chewing gum.

"Sorry I don't got no food," she said, watching me chew on the gum. "I wish I'd have put a couple crackers in my purse."

"This is fine." I had to keep swallowing, but the spit cut the edge off my thirst.

"I'm sorry for a lot of things." She nodded and turned her eyes to her fingers. "I am."

Her nails were chewed and ragged. Mama'd told me that ladies didn't bite their nails, and I wondered what she would have said to know that Winnie did. When she realized I was looking at them, she curled her fingers into her palms.

"Why didn't anybody tell me? About you?" I asked.

"It wasn't all that easy, Pearl."

She reached into her purse again and pulled out a small picture. It had the same black paper scraps glued to the backside as the one I'd found in Eddie's box.

"Tom—your father—he gave this to me." She held it in the palm of her hand. "He took a couple out of an album in his office. Said he felt bad that I didn't have any photos of you."

She handed it to me. It was of me sitting on our front steps, smiling as wide as I could, a big hair bow on the top of my head. I remembered that day. I'd lost my tooth during Sunday dinner. The sight of my own blood had frightened me. I feared that the flow wouldn't stop. But it had and quick.

"Did you ever get them birthday cards?" she asked. "I got you one every year."

I nodded, thinking about them all sitting in the pages of my fairy-tale book. "You never signed them," I said.

"Your father didn't think I oughta."

"Did you and my daddy . . ." I left off, not knowing how to ask how a man and woman would be together to make a baby.

Winnie leaned closer to me. "What are you asking?"

"Did you fornicate with him?"

"I never was with Tom like that. He never would've did that." She took the picture from me and put it back in her purse. "He's a real good man. He'd never stray from Mary."

"Who is my father?" I asked, glancing at Eddie sleeping with his mouth so wide and his teeth all rotting. I prayed it wasn't him.

"You got Tom Spence. He's good to you," she said.

"But who's my real father?"

"I don't think you got to know that." She lifted one of her hands to her mouth and worked at chewing a nail. "I hate myself for letting the man be anything to you."

"Was it . . ." I stopped myself, needed to swallow. "Was it Eddie?"

"No." She shook her head. "No. I never knew him back then."

"I'm glad it's not him," I whispered.

Her eyelids only lifted halfway up when she looked right at me. "I'm afraid it's worse than that."

My heart sunk. "Who?"

"You gotta understand. I was young when I met him. He was good to me. He'd pick flowers for me and took me out to dinner every once in a while." She blinked fast. "He wasn't bad to me then. Nobody'd ever been so nice to me."

"Who was it?" I asked. "Who is my father?"

"Jimmy DuPre." She squinted at me. "I hate that it was him, but it's the truth."

The whole world might as well have dropped out from under me. I would have been happy to sink into nothing and never feel another thing again.

The sweet gum in my mouth turned to tasting like poison. The blood that moved through my body was from a bad and evil man. A person who would have killed the man I had called "Daddy" since I could babble words.

Rat-faced Jimmy DuPre was part of me, and I was part of him.

I got sick all over the front of my nightie.

❦

Winnie didn't help me clean myself up. What she did do was pull back, disgusted by me. Mama would have moved heaven and earth to get me into a fresh dress and feeling better.

Real mothers were the ones who cleaned up the sick and pushed away the tears and hugged a child tight around the neck. Blood or no, that was what they did.

Winnie watched me push the mess off myself and into the dirt.

"I never was meant to be a mother." She frowned at me when I spit. "I wasn't planning on keeping you. Back then there was a doctor who'd take care of girls in trouble."

"How'd he do that?" I asked, wiping my mouth against the sleeve of my sweater.

"If a girl got in a, well, family way before she was married, this one doctor would kill the baby for her."

The idea about tore me in two. If I'd had anything left in my stomach, I would have gotten sick again.

"Jimmy told me not to get rid of it," she said. "He said we'd get married. He said he wanted to keep the baby. Said he'd always wanted to be a daddy."

"Did my daddy know Jimmy was my . . ."

"No. I never told him," Winnie said. "Didn't tell your mama, either. Only Eddie and me knows."

My body ached, but not near as bad as my heart did. I wanted to give up, quit the fight to stay awake. My eyes closed, and for a minute or so, I kept them shut tight. It eased the pain in my head a bit.

"Was Jimmy bad as they say?" I asked, forcing my eyes open again.

She shook her head. "Not all the time."

I swallowed down another wave of bile, remembering Eddie's story of Jimmy shooting his father in the head. How somebody who did a thing like that wasn't bad all the way through, I didn't know.

"Jimmy'd get into these moods," she said. "They was real dark. Real scary. He'd be mean and look at me like I wasn't there. Like I was see-through."

Turning my head, I rested my cheek against the wall.

"When I told him I was going to have you, he was real happy at first." She smiled at the memory. "He told me he'd never wanted nothing so much as to be a father. He told me his bad days were behind him. He was gonna do better. He wasn't gonna drink no more, and he wasn't gonna break the law no more, either. I thought things was fixing to change for us. But then he got in the dark mood again."

"What did he do?"

"So many bad things." She closed her eyes. "Some days I just wished he'd kill me and get it over with."

"Why didn't you get away from him?" I wanted so bad to touch her hand, but I didn't do it. I thought she'd just pull away from me. "If he was mean, why did you stay?"

"I loved him." A few tears caught on her top lip and she licked them away. "It's stupid."

"It's not." I thought of Mrs. Jones never getting away from Mr. Jones.

"I reckon I'm the only one in the world who ever loved Jimmy, you know."

I didn't disagree with her.

"He got all bothered one night. Said he didn't believe the baby was his child. He said all kinds of things about me tramping around on him. Back then I wasn't working in the cat house. Still, he didn't believe it was his baby." She put both hands on her stomach. "He beat me. He hit me in the stomach, trying to make the baby die."

"He tried to kill me." I closed my eyes so I couldn't see the world spinning anymore.

"I bled so much I thought the baby was dead." She cleared her throat. "I was so scared. That baby was the only thing I had to make Jimmy stick around. All I could think to do was go to Mary Spence . . ."

"You did?" I looked at her.

"Yes." She lit a cigarette, narrowing her eyes when she pulled air through it. "She said she could still feel the baby moving in there. She said it was going to be okay."

Winnie was beautiful when she smiled.

"I was so happy, I cried for three days," she said. "I'd feel the baby— you—bubble around inside me, and I'd tell you that I loved you."

"You did?"

"Yes."

"You loved me?"

"I know it don't seem like I did. I sure never acted like it." She sighed. "What kind of mother leaves the baby she loves?"

*A terrible one*, I thought. I didn't say it, though. To speak of it would have been to really believe it.

"I never could have been a mother to you, Pearl. I knew that. I couldn't have kept you clean or fed or in a safe place." She finished her cigarette and put it out in the dirt. "A baby can't have a good life if it's raised by a woman like me. It was either give you up or let Jimmy be your pa."

She rubbed both hands on her stomach again. Flat as it was, I could imagine it being big and round with me inside.

"I couldn't let your life turn out like mine."

"Maybe it wouldn't have been," I said.

She swallowed, going on as if she hadn't heard me.

"When you was born, I was all alone. I didn't know how it was supposed to be. I was sure I was dying it hurt so bad." She stared off into nothing. "But then you was there, crying stronger than I ever heard a baby cry. I hadn't heard anything so pretty in all my life."

She put out her hand and touched my cheek, just enough so I could feel it. Then she pulled it back.

"I washed you up as best I could and wrapped you in a bed sheet. I held you as long as I could stand it." She shook her head. "I knew if I held you a minute longer I would never be able to let you go. Oh lord, but you felt good in my arms. You felt the way life should be."

She grabbed around herself, hugging tight. I was glad she wasn't reaching for me again.

"Why didn't you just try to live a different life?" I asked. "You could have at least tried to change."

"It was too late for me." Winnie's eyebrows moved together. "So I took you to the church steps. I knew Mary would hear you, as strong as you cried."

"Then you left me there."

"No." She pushed at a tear with her hand. "I stood across the street and waited. When I seen the sheriff coming, I knew you was going to be all right."

And I was all right. My life had been about as good a fairy tale as Red River could afford.

"I went back to where I was staying and found out that Jimmy was dead." Winnie's makeup smudged when she rubbed at her eyes. "It was too late for me to go back and get you, so I bought myself a ticket out of Red River, and I was never going to look back."

"But you didn't leave."

"No. I couldn't do it."

"Why not?"

"I wanted to watch you grow." Her voice faltered. "I wanted to see that you were okay. And you are. You're more than okay."

Face-to-face with her was like looking into a mirror.

"Winnie?"

"Yeah?"

"Do you think I'll end up just like him?" I asked. "Like Jimmy?"

Her face hardened. She looked stern. "No. You're nothing like him."

I didn't flinch when she touched my knee. "I'm not?"

"You ain't even like me."

I exhaled, relieved.

"You know who you're like?"

"Who?"

"Tom and Mary. Your mama and daddy." She tried at a smile that ended up being more of a frown. "You're a Spence through and through, and you always will be. I wouldn't never want you to be anything else."

Rustling and groaning came from where Eddie slept. We turned, both of us did. The lantern light caught a glimmer in his open hand.

In the palm of that hand, Eddie held my freedom from the cellar.

The key.

# CHAPTER THIRTY-ONE

Winnie moved slow and on tiptoe to where Eddie slept. He never stirred, not even when she plucked the tiny key from the palm of his hand.

I obeyed when she motioned for me to come near.

"We're getting out of here," she whispered. "Once I get this door open, I want you to run. Don't even think about me. Just run. Hear?"

"I don't know if I can get home," I said, voice shaking.

"When you get out, run to the left." She pointed. "And keep going. Don't stop. Crawl if you gotta."

I nodded, hoping my trembling and weak legs would get me up the ten steps and across the field.

Winnie went up ahead of me. I stood on the fifth step, waiting, praying, begging God to save us.

The key scraped into the lock, turning with a gritty, crunching sound. It clicked open, and she eased the lock off and pushed the door up.

Strong wind whipped around, grabbing the door from her hand and slamming it open with a loud bang against the hard ground.

"What do you think you're doing?" Eddie yelled. He aimed the gun at Winnie. "You get back down here."

Winnie dropped the lock and put her open hands up next to her ears. She stepped down, pushing against me so I would move, too.

"Just let her go, Eddie," she said. "Please."

"I can't do that, can I?" He nodded his head toward the back of the cellar. "Get."

We did as he said. I feared that any fast move would make him shoot one or the other of us. I kept my mouth shut.

"Let Pearl go home," Winnie said. "You can keep me. Do whatever you want to me. If you need money, I can get some for you."

"Why would I need money?" he asked.

"You could get out of town. Go to California. Get a good job. You could start all over." She licked her lips. "Just let her go, would ya?"

"Now you wanna be like a mother to her?" He glared at her.

"She ain't done nothing to harm you. She's the only one innocent in this whole mess."

"I need her, don't you see? Without her, I got no revenge against Tom Spence. Long as I got her, he's gonna come right to me." His face pinched up and turned bright red. "I got to get him back for what he done to Jimmy."

"Eddie . . ."

"I would've thought you wanted that, too, Winnie. Weren't you the one blubbering over how much you loved Jimmy?"

"I just want this all to be over with. I been living under the weight of Jimmy too long."

"The sheriff's gonna come for her." He pointed the gun at me. "And when he does, I'm gonna make him pay for what he done to my brother."

"If you do that, you won't be any better than Jimmy," Winnie said, her voice soft. "And I do believe you're still good somewhere in there."

"It's too late."

"Eddie, please."

Winnie took a step toward Eddie with hands reaching for him. The gunshot tore through the air, making me fall to the floor. Then I couldn't move. Not an inch.

All I could do was scream.

# CHAPTER THIRTY-TWO

Winnie's body had fallen on top of me, and I couldn't hardly breathe. Pushing at her, I tried to get her to sit up and let me go. But she wouldn't move.

"Winnie?" I screamed. "Get off me."

Then the blood gushed from her body. It pooled around her. Around us. Spilling all over me, making me warm.

Her eyes had turned toward me, but they weren't bright like before. They were dry and dull looking. Like marbles.

She couldn't see me. Couldn't hear me, either. Still, I screamed, not realizing I had the strength and not knowing how long my voice would keep on. But I didn't quit.

"Oh God," Eddie screamed, falling on his knees beside us. "What have I done?"

He threw his hands over the wound on Winnie's chest, making his fingers turn red with her. He pushed down, tried to gather the blood to put back inside her. He only made the spurting worse.

"Don't you touch her," I screamed, pushing Eddie away as hard as I could. "You killed her. Don't you touch her!"

Eddie didn't move away, so I used my nails and scratched him across the face. His skin shoved up under my fingernails. He put one of his blood-stained hands on his cheek, his blood and Winnie's blood touching.

He lifted the gun that was still in his other hand. I drew in a final breath and clenched my eyes shut, just knowing that I was next.

Instead of shooting me, he got up and made his way to the steps. He sat down and lit a cigarette, gulping down the smoke. After he'd gone through all he had left, he dug in Winnie's purse for more.

Using the last of my strength, I worked my way out from under Winnie. Her body flopped, and panic grabbed hold of me all over again, sending me into screaming cries.

"Shut up," Eddie hollered at me. "Shut up!"

"Why did you shoot her?" I screamed.

"I never meant to." Spit flew from between his lips when he yelled. The way he grabbed a handful of his hair and pulled, I thought he'd rip it all out. "I never wanted her to get hurt."

Pushing myself up, I slipped and fell into the blood on the floor.

Getting back to my feet, I stumbled, all feeling gone from my legs. The only thing I could hear was my own breathing. Everything else seemed far away, like I was watching it at the movie theater.

"Are you going to shoot me?" I asked.

"I don't know," Eddie answered, then looked at Winnie. "What have I done?"

He was sobbing. Using the backs of his hands, he wiped against the tears running down his face.

"Please don't," I said. "Please."

"I have to. It's too late."

"Please."

Then I heard my name. Quiet at first, but then louder and louder. Eddie had heard it, too. He stood and backed away from the steps.

Daddy's voice from up above, yelling for me.

"Just let me go," I said, not caring to cover up the begging in my voice. "I won't tell anybody what you did. You can get away. Nobody'll miss her but me."

"I can't do that," Eddie said, setting his face hard. "It's too late."

Daddy called my name again. "Pearl?"

Looking Eddie full in the face, I screamed.

"Stay away, Daddy!"

"Over there," someone from the surface yelled.

"Don't come down here," I screamed. "He's going to kill you."

"It won't make a difference," Eddie said. "He'll come for you no matter what you say."

I knew Eddie was right.

# CHAPTER THIRTY-THREE

A shuffle of feet drew near to the cellar doors. Deep, hushed words moved about, too.

"Tom Spence," Eddie yelled. "You out there?"

The outside noises all stopped.

"I am," Daddy answered. "You got my daughter down there?"

"Far as I know, she ain't really your daughter, now is she?" Eddie drew in a long breath through his nose. "You still want her back?"

"More than anything."

"Come and get her then." Eddie didn't smirk. Instead he did something I'd never seen him do before. He shuddered. "Come on down."

"Daddy, don't!" I cried.

"Oh, would you shut up?" Eddie snarled. But he didn't dare touch me, not with Daddy so near. "I ain't gonna shoot him 'till we're face-to-face."

"I'm handing my gun off," Daddy said. "I'm coming down unarmed, Eddie."

"Suit yourself."

"I'm going to keep my hands where you can see them. I'd appreciate the same from you."

"Don't mean it's gonna happen, Tom."

Daddy's boots were the first thing I saw. The scuffed-up leather on the toes and the dust that powdered them. I remembered evenings after supper when we'd sit on the porch, my bare feet on the step next to those boots.

Then his legs appeared. The lap I'd sat on when I had a nightmare or when he'd tell me a story. His hips. Stomach. His chest that I'd rested my head against to hear his heart. His shoulders, neck. Then his face.

The smile I'd loved all my life wasn't there. His mouth was a thin, straight line with wrinkles of worry deep on his forehead.

Eddie had his gun pointed right at Daddy's handsome face.

But Daddy had his eyes on me. He didn't even pay Eddie any mind.

"Are you hurt?" he asked.

"Not too bad." Then I blubbered, knowing I didn't need to be strong anymore. "But Winnie . . ."

"It's all going to be over soon, darlin'." Daddy glanced at Winnie's still body, then back at Eddie. "You've got me now. Let my girl go."

"Daddy?" I asked.

He turned his eyes back to me. "Darlin', when Eddie says so, you've got to go up those steps. You understand?"

"Yes, sir."

"That's a good girl." His voice soothed me. "Then you have to give Millard a big hug. He's been so worried about you. You know that?"

I nodded.

"He'll see that you get home to Mama."

"She's okay?"

"She will be once she sees you."

His smile flashed up and down, but his eyes never sparkled.

"Daddy, won't you come with me?" I asked.

He shook his head. "Not this time, darlin'."

"Eddie's going to kill you, isn't he?"

That was when I panicked. I screamed, feeling the room spinning again.

"Darlin'," Daddy said. "Darlin', I need you to breathe, please."

"I won't leave you," I cried.

"Pearl, darlin'," he said, keeping his voice steady. "I'm coming over there. And I'm going to take slow steps so I don't scare Eddie. He's going to be a gentleman and let me come talk to you. Ain't that right, Mr. DuPre?"

Eddie didn't answer, but he kept his gun aimed at Daddy.

It seemed a whole hour passed before Daddy got to me. When he did, I fell into his chest. His rich scent wrapped around me. He held me so tight and let me cry. He didn't hush me or try to make me stop. He just kept saying over and over again that he loved me. He loved me.

He loved me.

When I was finally able to stop, he moved me so he could see into my face.

"I know about the baby on the steps." My lips pulled down at the sides. "It was me."

He nodded. "I'm sorry that I never told you."

"I'm not your daughter."

Daddy kissed both my cheeks. "You are. You always will be."

Eddie grunted.

Daddy turned toward him. "Just a few minutes more. Please."

Eddie didn't lower his gun, but he nodded.

"That night, the night I found you, I was so scared." He swallowed hard. "Something bad had happened, and I was walking home."

I nodded because I knew it was after he'd shot Jimmy DuPre.

"I heard your crying. At first I thought it was coming from a house. But then I saw you. You were all bundled up. And so small. You were tiny. I was afraid to pick you up."

"But you did anyhow."

"I did. That's right. And, honey, you just cried louder. I figured you were hungry." He breathed in. "But as soon as I started talking to you, you calmed right down."

He kissed my cheek again.

"Pearl, I took one look at you that night, and you were so pretty I cried."

"Why did you cry?"

"Because right then I couldn't do nothing else." He cleared his throat. "Pearlie, I picked you up off those church steps because it was what I had to do. I never could have left you there. From the very moment I saw you, you were mine. I knew it then, and I'll never un-know it. I carried you into our home and to your mama."

"Am I like him?" I asked. "Am I like Jimmy DuPre?"

"Nah. Not even a little. Because you're mine."

He left his lips on my cheek for a long time. Then he held me close again.

"Tell Mama and Beanie that I love them," he said, his voice still smooth. "Will you do that?"

"Daddy . . ."

"And tell yourself, too. Tell yourself how much I love you every day." He kissed my forehead. "Be brave."

I cried so hard that I tripped on the first step. Then I stumbled on the second.

"Just wait until she's gone, okay?" Daddy asked.

"I can't," Eddie answered.

The gun blasted.

# CHAPTER THIRTY-FOUR

H is eyes didn't close. Still open, they stared at me, not blinking. His head was on the floor, his body slumped over. The gun he'd held to his own head still in his busted-up hand.

I glared back at him, looking right into those cornflower-blue eyes.

"Shut your eyes," Daddy said, pulling my face into his stomach. "You don't need to see that."

He lifted me, holding my head so my eyes couldn't see Eddie's body. Daddy's boots clomped on the steps up and out of the cellar.

"Take her," he said. "Pearlie, you're going to go with Millard, just for a minute."

He passed me off, and Millard's arms were gentle and so warm. Daddy slammed the cellar doors and stood, staring at them.

"It sure is good to see you," Millard said touching my chin to get me to look at him. "You cold, darlin'?"

His words didn't make sense to me. Nothing did, really. Not the fading sunlight or the breeze on my face. It felt as if I was on a different planet altogether. I couldn't even figure out who I really was.

Millard lowered me to the ground. Knocking together, my knees struggled to keep hold under the weight of my body. He unbuttoned his flannel shirt, showing the white cotton of his undershirt. It was warm as a hug when he draped it over my shoulders.

"Better?" he asked.

"I gotta get her home." Daddy rubbed his forehead, leaving a smudge of dirt on his skin.

289

"What about him?" Millard asked, concentrating on buttoning me into his shirt.

"We don't have to worry about him going anywhere." Daddy reached for me. "Let's get her home."

❀

Daddy carried me, walking across the old field. When he stumbled a few times, Millard steadied both of us, putting a hand on my back.

From the middle of the field, I could see the sharecropper cabins. The few folks that still made their homes there stepped onto porches, watching us pass. Not a one said a word or moved toward us. All they did was stand and stare.

I was glad nobody asked what had happened. I didn't know myself.

Leaning my head against Daddy's shoulder, I wished I could sleep for as long as it would take to forget all that had happened. Already, I was numb. It would have been a mercy to sleep the memory away.

Mrs. Jones and Ray stood on the porch of their dugout, a lantern between them. The glow of it shone all the way to me. Ray took off running toward us. Daddy stopped, and Ray stood beside us, his chin shaking.

"You okay?" he asked.

There wasn't a good answer to give him, so I didn't say anything at all. The way he nodded told me he understood.

"Come on, Ray," Daddy said. "Let's get her back to her mama."

Mama. I'd never wanted her more than right then.

Daddy held me close. Millard kept a hand on my back. Ray held my hand.

Eddie DuPre still held my fear.

❀

Mama had to cut the nightie off me, the blood had made it stiff and the buttons dried to the fabric. She had me in the warm water of our tub in no time. I sat in it, letting her scrub my skin clean, until the water turned cold.

I only knew it had cooled because she told me.

Mama hummed as she dabbed me dry with a towel and helped me into a fresh nightgown. Holding me by the arm, she led me to my room and helped me into bed.

"Go on and rest a bit," she whispered. "I'll fix you something to eat when you wake up."

Cool sheet under me and one above chilled my still damp skin. Goose pimples bumped on my arms and legs and my body shivered. Mama piled another blanket on top of me and another folded up and across my legs.

I fell asleep, her hand in mine.

❋

The bullet tore through Winnie, dropping her in a slow fall. Her body spun to one side as she fell, her arms hanging in the air above her. Just like a ballerina, she spun so graceful. Her crushing weight landed on my legs, pushing them deeper and deeper into the dust floor below me, making me sink into a grave beneath her.

When I woke, I was screaming and kicking at the blankets, tearing at the sheets.

"I'm here," Daddy called to me, his voice coming from next to my bed. He sat up and reached for me, holding me until I calmed. "It's okay."

"Winnie . . ."

"I know."

The whole night was full of fitful sleep and bloody dreams and Eddie's voice saying, "You'll never get away from me."

The next night was more of the same.

It got where I fought sleep with all my might.

Daddy slept on the floor next to my bed every night. Beanie was set up in Meemaw's old room. As for Mama, she went between all three of us, checking to be sure we were all okay. I swore she didn't sleep for weeks.

Nights when I'd scream my way out of a nightmare, Daddy would hold me.

"It's over now," he'd whisper. "He can't hurt us anymore."

He was wrong. Eddie went on hurting me over and over again, whenever I shut my eyes.

Dreams were where Eddie's ghost lived.

# CHAPTER THIRTY-FIVE

Life went on after the cellar and Eddie killing Winnie and himself. Dusters rolled through, blanketing us in filth. Pastor went on preaching sermons to the faithful few in the pews. Mr. Smalley packed up and went off to find his family in the East. Millard still ate dinner at our table each night.

What didn't go on was me.

When Mama brought me a cup of bouillon, I'd thank her, not knowing what to call her. Nights when I woke in terror, I didn't call out for Daddy by name. The house in which I slept and ate and stared at the walls wasn't truly mine. It was just a place I stayed.

I'd never asked Winnie what she would have named me if she had kept me. Whatever it was, I wouldn't have wanted to change from being Pearl.

No matter what, I wouldn't take the name DuPre. Not ever. I hoped I'd be allowed to keep the Spence name.

If everything else was taken from me, I wanted to keep that.

❧

It had been three weeks since I came home from the cellar. Mama had started helping me get down the stairs to sit in the living room during the days. She wouldn't hear of me lifting a finger around the house.

"Not for another week or two," she had said. "After you're all healed up."

She didn't understand that the part of me that would heal had already done it. The rest of me, my mind and heart, would never mend by sitting around.

Nobody talked to me about Eddie or Winnie or what had happened in the cellar. I wouldn't have said a word to them if they had, anyhow.

In that house of people I'd always believed were my family, I felt more alone than I had in the cellar.

It was a Sunday. The only reason I knew was because we'd gone to church that morning. If I'd got worn out listening to Pastor hoot and holler before, it was worse that day. He preached on the wages of sin. He never made it to the gift-of-God part. That man was just too excited about damnation to think about eternal life.

After church, we sat around the table, and Mama served us her last can of beans and a few biscuits she had left over from her baking the day before. With Mr. Smalley's store closed, she couldn't pick up and get our few needs so easy anymore. The closest store was a good hour's drive away.

"I don't know that we've got enough flour to get us through the week," she said. She hadn't taken a biscuit for herself, and her puddle of beans was so small it wouldn't fill the belly of a mouse.

"I'll have to take a trip up to Boise City." Daddy tilted his head, eyes on Mama's plate. "Mary . . ."

"I'm not hungry."

Daddy blessed the food, asking for God to provide for us and all of Red River. He said his "amen" and scooped up a forkful of beans.

Beanie fidgeted with her napkin and wiggled in her seat. Her lips pushed together and stuck out from her face.

"Beanie Jean," Mama said. "Eat your food before it gets cold."

My sister noticed her beans and biscuit like it was the first time she'd ever seen such things. Lifting her fork, she held it over the plate, then lowered it again, clattering it against the side.

"Something wrong?" Daddy asked.

Beanie nodded but kept her eyes on the plate.

"What is it, darlin'?"

"I don't want her to go away," Beanie said, moving her eyes from her plate to mine.

"Who's going away?" Mama reached for Beanie's hand.

"Pearl."

"She's not going anywhere."

"But she ain't my real sister no more." Beanie let Mama rub her thumb against the back of her hand. "In the stories, the not-real sisters always go away."

"Beanie," Daddy said, getting up and kneeling beside my sister. "Do you remember when we brought Pearlie home?"

She closed her eyes and nodded. "She cried a lot."

"That's right."

"It made me scared," she said. "I thought Mama was hurting her. She wasn't never hurting her though."

"I'm glad you remember that." Daddy smiled. "Do you remember what you said when we let you hold her?"

Beanie shook her head and opened her eyes.

"Well, we couldn't let you hold her right away for fear you'd drop her. You were just six, and your arms weren't very strong." Daddy cleared his throat. "You'd cry and fuss that we wouldn't let you, so we got you set up on the davenport over there and put her in your arms."

"Did I drop her?"

"No, ma'am. You did good holding her."

"Did I hurt her?"

"You did not."

"I was good?"

"You were, Beanie Jean. You were," Daddy said. "And you know what you said? You said, 'She's my sister.' Nothing's changed, darlin'."

Beanie glanced at me, and our eyes caught for just a moment. As soon as my eyes filled up with tears, she looked away.

"Is she mine?" she asked.

"She sure is," Daddy said. "She's ours."

Beanie grabbed her biscuit and put it on my plate.

# CHAPTER THIRTY-SIX

I t was the day for the relief truck to come to Red River. For the first time, they made a stop at our house. Mama took in the bundle of beans and flour and odds and ends. Without saying a word, she put them away in the kitchen and started mixing dough for a loaf of bread.

"Can I help?" I asked, standing behind her.

"How about you go rest a spell? I need to do this myself," she answered.

When Mama made bread, she didn't have to measure. She just knew the right amount of everything that needed to be put together.

"Will you teach me some day?"

"Not today, Pearl."

Mama turned to grab for something, but I was in the way. Shutting her eyes, she sighed.

"Why don't you go read or something?" she said.

Slumping, I walked out of the kitchen and grabbed my book of fairy tales.

I hadn't so much as touched that book since the cellar. Cinderella, Hansel and Gretel, Snow White. All with parents who gave them up. It was enough to make my head spin.

Sitting on the floor, I opened the book and pretended to read the stories.

My make-believe world had passed. The only daydreams I allowed anymore were ones where I was Mama and Daddy's real daughter. Pretending to be anything else seemed like a waste to me.

"You aren't really reading, are you?" Mama asked. She stood over me, her arms crossed.

"No, ma'am," I answered. "I don't much feel like it."

"How about you come in the kitchen with me." She put her hand out to me and helped me up. "Seems I can use your help, after all. I'll teach you how to bake bread the way Meemaw liked to."

Mama hummed as we worked the dough with our hands.

"Am I doing it right?" I asked.

"You're doing just fine, darlin'."

❧

Millard had made a habit of coming over every afternoon with his checkers set. We'd sit at the table and tap our round pieces against the board, moving them from one black square to the next. He let me win almost every time.

"You're just better than me," he'd say and pretend to be upset about the loss.

Each day he apologized for not having any candy to give me.

His visits were sweet enough, anyhow.

On one of his visits, he peeked his head in the door and smiled at me. I was already at the table, waiting on him to come.

"Darlin'," he said, not taking a step in the door. "I'm real sorry. But I'm not fixing to play checkers with you today."

I about cried for disappointment.

"That's okay," I said, trying to make myself believe it was.

"Somebody else said he wanted to play with you." Millard stepped back and talked to someone outside. "Go on. Take the board."

Ray ducked his head when he walked into the house, as if he was too tall for the door frame. He did look taller, but not so tall he wouldn't fit inside my house.

"Hi," I said, surprised at the way my cheeks warmed at the sight of him.

He gave me one of his closed-lip smiles. "Wanna play?" he asked, the board in his hands.

"Yeah."

We set up our game on the table. Ray used the black pieces, and I had the red ones. We'd played two games without so much as saying a word to each other. It was just nice to have him with me. I had missed my friend.

Ray won both games. It didn't hurt my feelings at all.

Setting up for a third game, Ray cleared his throat.

"You doing okay?" he asked.

"Guess so." I lined up my red pieces.

"I'm glad."

I watched Ray place each of the black pieces on his side of the board. He wasn't careful to make sure they were right in the middle like I had.

"Are you all right?" I asked him.

"Most of the time."

"That's good." I sniffed. "You go first."

He moved one of his pieces, and I took a turn, too. Keeping his eyes on the game, he smiled, looking more like a little boy than he had in almost a full year.

"That duster we had the other day?" he said.

"Yeah?"

"I seen a bird flying right through it."

"You did not."

"Sure I did. He was flying backwards."

"Birds can't fly backwards." I jumped over one of his pieces.

"They can so." He moved one spot. "Well, this bird was flying backwards, at least."

"Fine. Whatever you say."

We each took a few turns. Try as I might, I couldn't seem to get as many of his pieces as he got of mine.

"Wanna know why?" he asked.

"Why what?"

"Why that bird was flying backwards?"

"I guess." I rested my chin on my hand.

"So it wouldn't get dust in his eyes."

Ray jumped over my last piece on the board. I didn't care because I was giggling.

Goodness, but did that feel good.

# CHAPTER THIRTY-SEVEN

March brought us endless days of dust. Storm after storm after storm buried us, blinded us. Our old enemy attacked with no mercy. The only word I could find for it was *evil*.

It held me down so I could hardly move.

I tried not to give a thought to how much the weight of the dust reminded me of Winnie's body, bleeding on top of me.

Mama kept the four of us holed up in the living room, damp sheets hung over the windows and doors. We all wore masks the relief truck had brought with the latest load of food.

For as much as she rushed around, battling the dust, it still got in. It found a way. It always did.

It wasn't the dust or the house-shaking wind that got my nerves rattling. It was the dark. The blocked-out sun. The dim, closed-in living room. How it felt like I was underground, trapped.

Days blustered into one another, rolling away with the dust clouds so I couldn't tell how long the darkness pressed down on us. Mama kept track as best she could, marking each day with an *X* on the calendar.

As soon as the dirt started to settle from one duster, another storm followed, hitting harder than the last.

We didn't have a break to catch our breath.

Mama had served us lumps of fried dough she'd made a few days before. I didn't feel much like eating but knew she would worry if I didn't. I forced down a few bites.

"I'm sorry," she said. "I wish I had more to give you."

"This is just fine," Daddy answered back.

"We can't hardly live on what that truck brings."

"There isn't much else we can do."

We finished eating our small meal in quiet. I was grateful that Mama didn't try to get me to eat anything else.

❈

A storm rolled through while we were sleeping. Whether it was morning or night or the middle of the day, none of us could tell.

Daddy pulled Beanie and me close to him, us all hunching on the floor in front of the davenport. The wind roared something awful. The house shook like it was scared.

Something outside cracked sharp and crashed against the house. A window upstairs smashed in.

I breathed in and out and kept my eyes shut tight against the dust that stippled on my skin. More banging and crashing from outside. Then a blasting sound.

Just like a gun shot.

The weight of all things crushed down on my chest and my heart about thudded its way free from my body. My lungs wouldn't take in any air, not because of the dust, but because of the fear.

Moaning and groaning, it sounded like the wind called out to me. It spoke my name.

Daddy's arm wrapped tighter around me, squeezing me hard.

"Let go!" I screamed. "Don't touch me."

Gulping as much air as I could manage, I pushed away from him, scuttling across the floor to get to the other side of the room. Blind, I felt my way, pushing against the rocking chair and feeling the side table that held the radio.

"Pearl?"

I couldn't tell if it was Daddy or the wind or Eddie DuPre calling after me.

"No," I said back. "Leave me alone."

Breath couldn't come fast enough. I tore the mask from my face and sucked in. Grit filled my mouth, covered my tongue. I bit down on it, crunching it. When I breathed in, it scrubbed against my lungs. Try as I might, I couldn't spit it out.

Head spinning, I struggled to get the mask back on my face. It covered my nose and mouth and I gulped in chopped and jagged breaths. Every one hurt like little knives in and out.

"Pearl?" Mama and her gentle, mask-muffled voice settled close by me. "Darlin'."

Her sweet voice soothed and I tried my very hardest to put my mind only on her words. She felt of me, kind fingers touching lightly. She found my shoulders and drew me into herself.

"It's just me," she cooed. "You're going to be just fine, darlin'."

The wind sobbed again. All of my muscles tensed, and I tried not to make a sound.

"What is it?" Mama asked. "What's wrong?"

"It's Eddie," I mumbled. "He's come to get me."

"Oh, honey," she said. "He won't never hurt you again."

"He's here."

"No, darlin'." Mama rubbed circles on my back with her hand. "Eddie's dead, honey. He's gone."

Still, I could have sworn he was riding on the wind, calling my name.

# CHAPTER THIRTY-EIGHT

April came, elbowing out March and its endless days of dust. Mama rushed around the house for hours on end, working to evict all the memory of the bad month with her broom and washrag. She had a list as long as my arm of things Daddy would need to fix. Windows had to be replaced, part of the roof needed mending, a shutter hung crooked.

Looking at that list of Mama's, Daddy whistled and shook his head.

"You know what, Mary," he said. "I better go check on things around town. Make sure nobody's buried."

"This list is just going to be here waiting for you." Mama raised an eyebrow at him.

"I'm sure there's somebody looking for a little make-work."

"Thomas Spence," she scolded, then grinned at him. "I guess you'd better go."

"It's my duty."

"Best wear your mask." Mama grabbed it from the kitchen counter. "Don't take it off. I don't care what Millard says about it."

"Yes, ma'am." He pulled it over his face, adjusting the strap on the back of his head. "Girls, you wanna come along?"

"Tom, I don't think—"

"Mary, they need to get outside. Both of them." He picked up two of the masks and handed them to Beanie and me. "I promise we'll come back right soon to help you around the house."

Stepping out on the porch, I tilted my head toward the sky. It wasn't crystal-clear blue, but it wasn't muddy-brown, either. Gray was a fine enough color for me.

"You gotta keep the masks on," Daddy said. "At least until we get out of your mama's sight."

I thought to ask about taking off my shoes, too, but didn't want to press my luck. The air on my arms and face and legs felt good enough. I settled for that.

Beanie and I followed behind Daddy, walking side by side. I could hear her grunting sounds even through her mask. She stopped more than once to feel of the dirt with her fingers as she passed it by.

Daddy led us down the main strip. Old wood had been nailed over the windows and door of Mr. Smalley's shop. It looked like all the rest of the stores and diners and businesses that stood empty.

"You know when I was a kid, that right there," Daddy said, pointing at one of the buildings, "that was a place for men to get suits and overalls. My pa got me my first tie there."

I tried to picture Daddy with a tie around his neck. He would have been handsome.

"And right next to that was a butcher. Meemaw didn't trust him, though." Daddy laughed. "Said he'd put his thumb on the scale so he could charge more."

Daddy stopped walking, and Beanie and I stood on either side of him. He turned his head both ways, looking up and down the street.

"And over there was the diner." He nodded at the crunched building across from the empty market. "Fella that ran that place sure made a good cup of coffee. And the best pie I ever ate."

"What about Mama's pie?" I asked.

"Well, hers is good, too, I guess." He winked at me. "Don't tell her I said that. I'm fixing to have her make a whole house full of pies once we get a little money."

"Okay, Daddy."

"This street used to be full of folks walking places and shopping, going to watch a movie. Folks didn't hurt for work then. They had all of it they wanted in the fields." Crossing his arms, he let his shoulders slump. "Red River's about a regular old ghost town nowadays."

The three of us stood on that corner, Daddy remembering what the town had been and me trying to picture it all. Beanie had her own thoughts, I was sure of it. Thoughts that ran different than mine.

"Hey, y'all gonna stand there staring all day?"

Daddy turned his head toward the courthouse and slapped both hands on his thighs. He let out a laugh that could make the sun want to shine through the gray.

Millard stood just outside the doors of the courthouse. Dust had piled all the way up to the porch, sloping down to the street.

"You stuck?" Daddy hollered, taking a step into the street.

Beanie and I followed him, not having to look both ways first. No cars were like to drive through any time soon.

"I think we need us some shovels," Millard said as we got closer. "I do wish this was snow instead of dirt."

"We could build ourselves a giant of a snowman if it was." Daddy walked back and forth along the sidewalk, inspecting the dust mound. "Well, if ever I wanted to take over Red River, now would be the time, you stuck in the courthouse and all."

"You wanna run this place?" Millard put both hands up in surrender. "You've got it."

"No, sir. I don't believe I'd be any good at it."

"I think you'd surprise yourself." Millard grinned at both Beanie and me. "How you girls holding up? Doing all right?"

"Yes, sir," I answered.

"And your mama?"

"She's to home cleaning."

"That's fine." He nodded. "I expect most everybody's doing that today."

"We're headed out to the cabins." Daddy nodded at the dust-covered steps. "If we can break you out of there, you wanna go along?"

"Sure would."

Daddy used a shovel, and Beanie and I had brooms. In about no time

we had it so Millard could get out. He went down the stairs with shaky
steps, holding tight to the railing.

He cupped his hand against my cheek and smiled.

"Glad to see y'all," he said.

❖

Not much of the sharecroppers' cabins survived the month of March.
The ones that had stayed in one piece were so blocked by dust, a body
wouldn't have been able to get in or out without a whole lot of digging.

Mrs. Jones stood next to where their dugout had been. Dirt and dust
and parts of other cabins piled up on what had been their roof. It was
caved in, but completely. Next to her, Ray held his hands over his face, his
whole body looking like it would collapse on itself any minute.

"Lord have mercy," Millard said under his breath. "Ain't they been
through enough?"

Mrs. Jones saw us coming. At first, she made to walk away but gave up.
There was nowhere for her to go, anyway.

"Y'all okay?" Daddy asked.

Mrs. Jones didn't turn to him and didn't answer him. She just kept her
eyes fixed on the pile of her house.

"Where you been staying, Mrs. Jones?" Millard asked, putting a hand
on her shoulder.

"Over to that one there." She moved her head in the direction of a cabin
a few yards away. "Nobody's been there a long time. We didn't think it
would do no harm."

"That's fine. Glad you done it."

Ray lowered his hands but didn't raise his face. It was better that way.
He would have been embarrassed if he'd known I noticed the streaks of
wet under each eye.

"Y'all can stay at our house," Daddy said. "We got plenty room."

"We can't do that," Mrs. Jones said. "We'd hate to put you out."

"Mary wouldn't forgive me if I took no for an answer, Luella."

Loose skin hung from the bones in Mrs. Jones's arms. Her body had gotten so skinny, it looked like she'd stopped eating weeks ago. She pushed her hair back. Hair that had become brittle and thin. Her cheeks blazed red.

"I don't mean to shame you," Daddy said. "But you've got to have a place to sleep."

"We're just fine over in that cabin."

"Ma," Ray said. "Please."

Shaking her head, Mrs. Jones pushed her lips together. Her jaw clenched, and she crossed her arms.

"You go on," she said. "Raymond, you just go on and stay with them. I ain't gonna."

"Ma . . ."

"I ain't hearing nothing outta you." Her eyes were closed, and she bit at her top lip. "You go on and stay at the sheriff's. And you do your best to help out."

"I want you to come."

"You mind your manners, too, boy. I don't wanna hear nothing about you being rude or mean."

"Luella," Daddy said. "There's no shame . . ."

Lifting her lids, I saw the ghost eyes and the red rims where her eyelashes should have been.

"Sheriff Spence, shame's all I got left to my name." She touched Ray's shoulder. "I'll come check on you later. Be good."

"Come on, son," Daddy said, reaching an arm around Ray.

We all turned to leave. All except Beanie, who stood watching Mrs. Jones.

"Beanie," I said. "Let's go."

Mrs. Jones turned away from all of us, but Beanie walked around to be in front of her.

"Darlin'," Daddy called. "We best get home."

My sister acted like she hadn't heard him at all.

"We'll take care of him," Beanie said. "He'll be a good boy."

Mrs. Jones turned to look at a field full of ruin.

"You're a good mama." Beanie blinked real fast and rubbed at her nose. "You'd be better if you came to our house."

Reaching for Beanie, I grabbed her hand. She followed me all the way home, her hand in mine.

❖

Millard came over to the house with us. Mama set two extra plates at the dinner table for him and Ray. She'd pulled together a good meal for us. The beans may have been a little runnier than normal, but they were steamy hot and tasted better than stale fried dough, so none of us complained.

"Welp, the town didn't fair too well the last month," Daddy said once he'd chewed and swallowed the last of his food. "There's lots to do."

"I don't hardly have the will to do nothing no more," Millard said. "I'm wore out."

"There are plenty of men left. We'll get her done."

"I wanna work," Ray said. "I'm strong."

"I know you are, son," Daddy said. "And I'll be glad for your help."

"Tom, I meant what I said earlier. I'd like you to take over for me." Millard crossed his arms and leaned back into the chair. "I wanna ask you to act as mayor until the folks can get together an election."

"Well, why would I do that?" Daddy asked.

"This town's in need of somebody younger. Somebody who can rebuild it." Millard shook his head. "I ain't got it left in me. The fire's all burnt out."

"I don't know, Mill." Daddy turned his eyes toward Mama's. "I'll have to talk to Mary about it."

"There ain't a pay raise." Millard laughed. "And you'll still need to wear that sheriff badge."

"You trying to talk me out of it?"

"Maybe I am. I ain't making it too attractive, am I?"

Daddy took in a deep breath and puffed it back out. "I'll have to let you know about that one, Mill."

"I know it. Take your time." Millard smiled. "There's nobody else in this county I'd trust, son."

Daddy didn't say a whole lot for the rest of the afternoon.

I imagined it was a heavy weight on him, the thought of rebuilding a town that was just about dead.

❖

Mama wore a bandana tied around her head while she cleaned. She said it was to keep the dust out of her hair, but I thought she looked real pretty in it. Like Cinderella in my fairy-tale book.

It surprised me that the thought of one of my old stories didn't make my head spin or stomach upset. I guessed that meant I was healing up a little bit in my soul.

Daddy had taken Ray out back with him to clean up the old windmill. It had broken right in half during the month of dusters. When he'd asked Ray to go with him, that boy smiled as big as he could.

Beanie was in our room. Mama had asked her to take the dirty sheets off our mattress. The soft snoring I heard through the vents told me that she'd not gotten her task done.

I swept the dust out of every corner and from under the furniture, just like Mama had asked. It felt good to move, to be of use. It passed the time and kept me from thinking about the scary memories that hid in the corners my mind. I made believe that I was sweeping those out along with the piles of dirt.

Daddy came in through the back door. "Mary, do we have any bread or biscuits or anything?" he asked.

"I can get you a couple slices," Mama answered, lowering herself from the chair she was standing on. "I don't have butter."

"Ray and I don't care. We're starving."

"I'll bet you are." Mama smiled at him.

310 A CUP of DUST

"Mary . . ." Daddy took a step closer to her. "You are beautiful."

She touched the bandana on her head and turned her eyes to the floor. "I'm all grimy."

"That doesn't matter. Not to me." Daddy touched her hip. "Dance with me."

"Tom," she said, touching his shoulder but looking out the window. "The neighbors."

"What neighbors?" Daddy laughed. "They're all gone."

He took her hand in his, the other hand reached to her back.

"We don't have any music," she said, letting him lead her in a swaying back and forth.

"Sing something."

They spun, and Mama's feedbag dress swung around her knees. She laughed, catching the bandana as it slipped off her head. Daddy pulled her closer and their cheeks touched. He hummed a tune, one I'd heard on the radio but didn't know the name of. Mama joined along with him. She reached her arm all the way around his neck.

They were all the fairy tale I needed.

# CHAPTER THIRTY-NINE

The morning sun forced its way through my bedroom window, warming my face. Beanie had moved back into the bed with me, making space for Ray in Meemaw's old room. He'd been with us less than a week, but it felt nice to have him around so much. I'd swear he'd put on five pounds from eating Mama's cooking.

Beanie snored beside me, not taking any notice of the bright light beaming on her face. The way she lay, with one arm bent and resting over her head and her face turned toward me, just so, she looked pretty. I'd never thought of her that way before. Most of the time she grimaced or scowled or wore confusion between her eyebrows. But sleeping, her face relaxed, she looked the way I thought God must have seen her. Beautiful.

"Rise and shine," Mama said, rushing into our room, insistent as the sun. "I declare, this is not a day to be lazing around in bed."

Pushing the curtains to either side of the window, she let in the full brightness of the morning. It soaked my room and filled my heart with warmth I thought had left forever.

"It's Palm Sunday," she sang. "Not a cloud in the sky, and it's as blue as you could imagine."

Beanie grunted at her, rolling over and smashing her face into the pillow.

Mama laughed. Her bright smile was prettier than all the sunshine that had ever shone on any day in all of history. I wanted so bad to tell her that but couldn't find a way.

"Is Daddy coming to church with us?" I asked, climbing over Beanie to get out of bed.

"Well, he's cleaning up." That smile was still on her face. "And he's letting Ray borrow one of his nice shirts."

I imagined Ray would look mighty handsome dressed so nice, even if the shirt was too big for him.

Reaching for my green dress, I imagined us all walking into the sanctuary. I would hold Daddy's hand, and Beanie had Mama's. Ray didn't need to hold anyone because he was strong and didn't like touching all that much.

"What a beautiful family," someone would say.

We'd save seats for Millard and Mrs. Jones. Of course, she'd agree to come stay with us after seeing how happy Ray was.

I stepped into my dress, feeling the fine fabric against my skin.

For the first time in months, I felt that life would end up being just fine.

❋

During church, those of us who had come sang loud *hosannas* with all the strength we had. We did believe that morning that God was the one who saves. The One who would raise us up from the tomb of dust.

Pastor had even declared that the hard times were done. He said the rains would come along on the coattails of that sunny day.

I'd never heard so many *amen*s in all my life.

The rest of his sermon I didn't take in. Instead, I allowed a daydream to ease up from inside me. It felt like going home.

In my daydream, all of Red River was as it had been. Wheat grew thick and tall, and the pastures were full of fat cattle, maybe even a buffalo or two. The old butcher charged too much for meat, and the diner served up the best pie in all of Cimarron County.

My dream made me never know about Eddie or Jimmy or even Winnie. The cellar didn't exist. Mama and Daddy were really mine, blood and all. And Beanie's brain worked the way it should.

Model Ts chugged up and down the main street, coughing smoke that rose slowly into the sky. Relief trucks never came to us because we had plenty, and we all stood proud for that.

Every table had more than it could hold. A roast or a chicken steaming with creamy mashed potatoes and thick slices of bread. No beans or fried dough.

We were all smiling and healthy and safe.

And we didn't have so much as a cup of dust.

# DISCUSSION QUESTIONS

1. Before reading *A Cup of Dust*, what did you know about the Dust Bowl? The Great Depression?

2. The 1930s were a time of rich storytelling. Daddy and Millard told tales that were sometimes believable and sometimes fantastical. What are some stories shared by your family that are close to mythological? What are some stories that are more plausible?

3. A popular teaching during the Dust Bowl was that the disaster was caused by the sin of the people. Many preachers taught that it was the punishment of God, much like Pastor Ezra Anderson did. What is your reaction to such theology? How does Pastor's teaching contrast with the teachings of Meemaw?

4. How does the theme of fairy tales run through *A Cup of Dust*? Why does Pearl rely less and less on them as the story unfolds?

5. The author used historically accurate language for the description of African American and Native American people. How did those words sit with you? Do you believe that we've made progress in relations between people groups?

6. One tagline for this novel is, "Where you come from isn't who you are." What does that mean when reflecting on Pearl's story? What does it mean for you?

7. In the cellar, Eddie told Pearl "pity ain't love." What do you think about that within the context of the story? How about in your life?

8. What did you think of the scene in which Daddy comes into the cellar? Did it end the way you expected? What did it tell you about Daddy's character?

9. Palm Sunday in 1935 started as a beautiful, sunny day. That's where *A Cup of Dust* ends. What do you think is next for the Spence family?

A F T E R W O R D

A t the age of sixteen I read John Steinbeck's *The Grapes of Wrath* for the first time. As soon as I closed the book I knew I wanted to read it again. Reading Steinbeck led me to the photography of Dorothea Lange. Steinbeck's novel told me the story, and Lange's photographs showed me the people.

The more I thought about the folks who survived this time, the more I felt compelled to learn as much as I could about the Dust Bowl—why it happened and how the people survived.

I found it curious that such an ecological disaster hadn't warranted more than a short paragraph in my US history textbook, and that so many families displaced by dust would be all but forgotten in the enormous narrative of the Great Depression.

For nineteen years I found out all I could about this period in history. I wrote plays and short stories and poems about it. When given the opportunity, I led discussions on Steinbeck's work and the history behind it at my alma matter, Great Lakes Christian College.

When asked how a Michigan city girl ended up being interested in the Dust Bowl, particularly with Cimarron County, I placed the blame on my Steinbeck obsession.

At the age of thirty-five I announced to my husband that I was going to write my Dust Bowl novel. He said, "It's about time." He knows me so well. To demonstrate his support, he bought me books of photography from the 1930s: one of Dorothea Lange's work and one of Arthur Rothstein's.

Each of these photographers worked for the federal government to document the everyday life of those living in the hard times of the Depression. Many of my characters were born as I studied the faces in the photos.

In all my years of studying the Dust Bowl, I've gleaned the most from the work of two men: Ken Burns and Timothy Egan. Both men have connected with scholars to learn the why and wherefore of the "Dirty Thirties" and spent time with those who lived it to learn their experience. Burns's documentary *The Dust Bowl* (PBS) and Egan's book *The Worst Hard Time* tell the stories of courageous folks who did what it took to survive.

After writing *A Cup of Dust* I find that my admiration for the Dust Bowl survivors has grown. They were courageous, faithful, optimistic, and generous with what little they had. After all, who knew what the next year might bring. It very well might bring rain and mercy from the Lord Himself.